THE MANO

T M

Previously published under the Title Captive

ISBN 978-1-910236-36-9 Paperback

978-1-910236-37-6 Kindle

The Manor and Murder

First paperback edition printed in 2021 in the United Kingdom

A catalogue record for this book is available from the British Library

ISBN
Paperback 978-1-915742-05-6
Kindle 978-1-915742-04-9

Published by The Creative Peak(TCP)

Book Design: T M Goble
Cover Image: Copyright Shutterstock

T M Goble's Website

www.tmgoble.com

Action Thrillers
Detective Murder Mysteries
Standalone Murder Mysteries
Historical Fiction
Contemporary Fiction
History of Peak District Literature
Seasonal Recipes

I occasionally send newsletters with details on new releases, special offers and other bits of news relating to my books.

01

The chill, damp fog hung low between the trees of the Rivelin Valley, smothering detail, eradicating colour and leaving a monotonous grey. The unrelenting rain soaked all in its path. People with raincoats tightened and umbrellas lowered over their heads waited in silence. The grey rain pounded, the drops landed on a makeshift shelter of tarpaulins then cascaded off, forming puddles on the sodden earth. A constant drip produced a regular heartbeat on to a scaffolding pole where a microphone hung. The barely audible resonance of the pulsing drops filled the misty landscape.

The priest stared at the brass plaque. Inaudible to the congregation, he recited the words, 'Luke Kennedy, Luke Kennedy, it shouldn't have happened.' His stare didn't waver. As Luke's mother threw in a handful of earth, he formed the sign of the cross. The diminutive woman stepped back. Motionless, the priest waited for the two elder brothers. Each left their mother's side, glared down with furrowed brows and released a fistful of soil which splattered across the coffin. The priest's gaze remained unflinching as he tightened his eyes in anger.

Matthew wouldn't see the burial of his twin. The priest prayed, his eyes half closed, his lips moved, but no sound emanated. Two hundred mourners with drab clothes and unsmiling faces swarmed silently around the deep hole and took time to pay their last respects. The priest never deviated his stare, his solemn face etched with sadness.

'Father, may I?' Ma Kennedy's voice broke the silence, brittle but clear. He didn't look up but nodded. She unfurled a green flag with a golden harp at its centre and let it float downwards to drape the coffin.

When it had rested, the priest raised his head. The bright lights suspended from the angular frame of the television cherry-picker dazzled him. Disgust crossed his face, he muttered, 'Intrusive. Do they have no respect?' The noise level rose as the mourners left the cemetery spooking the eight black horses which had pulled the hearse. The priest scowled as his eyes scanned the swarming crowds and the hordes of press waiting in the road.

'Bless you, Father.' Ma Kennedy, a short wiry woman ignored the beating rain, her silvery eyes peered from under the wide-brimmed black hat to glare at the priest. 'People here will judge Luke and condemn him for his lawless behaviour.'

'My good woman, only the Lord may judge, go with peace in your heart,' he intoned as he caught her bony hands. 'I have known Luke for many years. A headstrong young man but I perceived the goodness in him. Loyalty always came first.' Ma Kennedy nodded. 'His soul is with the Lord and he is at peace.' The priest's solemn and unsmiling face stared across at the two tall men at their mother's side.

'I shall find the man…'

The priest raised his palm towards the man's face. 'Shush, John, no vengeance in the presence of the Lord.' John's wild and bewildered eyes fixed on the Priest's face. 'Your task is to support your good mother in this time of grief. I wish you and Mark to go home, and with your Ma, read from the Book of Romans. The passage is "Vengeance is mine saith the Lord". Listen while your mother reads for the spirit of Luke?'

The priest withdrew from their path as the sons took their mother's arms. They picked their way across the sodden grass as the rain teemed, bouncing in the puddles, but they took no notice.

As they passed into the drizzle, a man emerged from the gloom to stand beside the priest, who continued to peer at the fading figures. 'I didn't notice you at the service, Wayne.' The Priest didn't turn his head to the man.

'No, Father. Churches give me the creeps.'

'Then you should be fearful for your soul.' The priest's words were heavy and deliberate. His lips quivered as he looked at the fluorescent yellow jacket and the green Wellington boots, 'I presume you have come for your money for the singers you supplied for the service. As their agent I suppose you collect the fees.'

'Did you find them uplifting?'

A slight quiver twisted across the priest's lips. 'I have to admit the blend of Gregorian chants and pop music may have appealed to Luke, but I found the songs flighty.'

'As I know the Kennedy family well and do business

with them, I wouldn't dream of a financial reward on this sad occasion.'

A crash of thunder rolled through the churchyard. Both men looked up at the clouds. The vaguest of smiles crossed the Priest's face, then disappeared.

'On behalf of the family I thank you. They have been generous in their donation to the church restoration fund. The money I put aside for the singers I shall add to the fund.'

They stood side by side in silence as the black horses pulled the empty hearse from of the churchyard. Wayne gave the smallest flicker of a smile, 'I haven't told you before, but I took on a popular international singer last year and she has the same surname as you, Manning.'

The priest glowered and his eyes narrowed, 'Charlotte, I presume.' An edge of irritation sounded in his clipped voice. 'Margaret, my sister, and I disapprove of Charlotte's chosen career, so I would appreciate it if my relationship with her did not become widespread.' With an expression of displeasure etched across his face, he strode away.

02

Her nose brushed the soft velvet drape which smelled old and damp. A growling sound emanated from her churning stomach. She pulled herself tall and straight. An insistent voice inside her head commanded. Wait. Wait. She had no alternative. Making no noise she didn't move a muscle but released a slow controlled breath.

A bead of perspiration rolled down her forehead. Her long blue fingernail flicked at it but missed. The droplet seemed immense. She closed her eyes and felt it trickle down her eyelid. Her eye opened to the salty sting. Smoothing a hand down her long blonde hair she stared into the black space which surrounded her.

The excited jabbering voices on the other side of the velvet drape became louder. Even if she concentrated, she couldn't distinguish words, only a jumble of voices. Her heart thudded. The wait would end soon as the first strains of the music commenced. The volume of voices decreased as the music soared. Luigi's favourite. *The Ride of the Valkyries.* The pounding music saturated the air.

She clasped her fists. Anytime now. The music diminished. A voice resounded through the speakers, 'Ladies and Gentlemen, the Luigi collection, led by the world's top supermodel, Andrea Cain.'

The curtains flew wide, but she remained still. The lights scorched her eyes so she could see nothing. With an expansive smile fixed on her face, she counted silently in her head, 'One, two, three, four, five,' holding the pose and remaining motionless. Then in three flowing strides she reached the middle of the dais. The edge of the stage appeared among the glaring lights.

The continuous flash of cameras and the deafening music hit her like a wall. Keeping the dazzling smile fixed in place, the voice inside her head shouted, 'Glide, glide, glide!' Her shimmer along the catwalk brought the crowd to their feet. The quivering blue silk dress became an instant winner. The count of ten steps led her to the end of the catwalk. She stretched the blue faux ostrich boa across her shoulders allowing it to drape around her arms. As she paused with one foot in front of the other, she let one arm fall to her side. The other she reached up into a high-five. More applause.

Shouts came from behind the cameras to hold it. Motionless with her chin lifted and the smile fixed, the bulbs flashed. Then she twirled on the ball of her foot. The sparkling stiletto shoe dug into her toe, she gasped and started the count of the catwalk. At the end it would hurt again, but she pushed the pain aside and concentrated on her movements. Ten steps and she spun. The smile stayed on her face as the cameras continued to flash. She gave them another ten second pose. Luigi would want her to hold it until the applause ended.

Another flourish of the boa and she stepped through into the backstage. Darkness engulfed her and she couldn't see. Someone grabbed her and kissed her on the cheek. 'Magnifico! Magnifico!'

Still smiling she hugged him back. 'The audience loved it, Luigi, they loved it. Beautiful clothes created by the master.'

He released her and scrambled to peek through to the stage. The music indicated the second model on the catwalk. Speed became essential. Focusing on the task in hand, she blocked out the excited voices and loud music, and strode into the room where her dressers waited. They reached up, unclipped the dress and let it drop, then they towelled her body, legs and arms.

03

'Where's my bloody dresses? Don't stand there, fetch my clothes,' yelled a nearby woman who flung her arms wide in a dramatic gesture.

Andrea ignored the outburst and focused her return to the catwalk. Time was short and she didn't need any distractions. A dresser held the evening gown, she stepped into it. It fitted her slim figure. Checking her cleavage in the mirror, the cut of the dress looked good as it stretched across her breasts, the black sequined gown contrasting with her pale skin.

The woman began shouting again, 'Stop crying.' She wagged her finger towards a wailing woman knelt on the floor with her head in her hands. 'Find my dresses, don't you understand?' Her voice rose with an edge of hysteria.

Irritation coursed through Andrea. 'No, she doesn't, she only speaks Italian.' A dresser held black velvet shoes for her, so she kicked off the ones that hurt and slipped into the new ones. They still hurt. 'Can you help? Do you speak Italian?'

Andrea bit back the caustic comments which leapt into her mind. Didn't the woman realise she was busy?

Instead, she took a calming breath. 'Go to reception, they will help.' She stared at the pretty face framed with curly, shoulder length dark hair. Not a model, too small. Probably part of the entertainment.

'Three minutes, Andrea,' called a distant voice.

'Yes. Almost complete.' She focused in the mirror and adjusted her hair. Andrea left the dressing room, heading once again for the wait behind the curtain and the promenade along the catwalk.

As she returned towards the dressing room, the loud wailing sound reached her before she opened the door. The entertainer stood in the middle of the dressing room howling. Everyone ignored her. The Italian woman, recipient of the earlier invective, huddled on a chair weeping. Andrea glanced at the woman. 'Stop that dreadful noise!' she shouted above the wails. Tears of frustration streamed down the sobbing woman's cheeks. 'We're in Italy; people speak Italian, not English.'

The woman scowled, but the tears and the noise stopped. 'Will you help me please?' she stuttered in a whimpering voice.

'Provided you stop shouting and wailing.' Her face seemed familiar from the newspapers. Andrea slipped out of her dress. 'I'm Andrea Cain.'

'Charlotte Manning.'

'The singer?'

'Yes.'

The recognition pleased her. Andrea spoke to the huddled woman on the chair, 'Dove è vestiti di questa signora?'

'You speak Italian,' marvelled Charlotte.

'Too clever by half if you ask me.'

Andrea turned to greet her friend, 'Patsy, great to see you.'

'And you darling,' Patsy stared at the singer, 'Listen to Andrea she always helps.'

'How's life?' Andrea directed her remark to Patsy but sensed that Charlotte had become agitated again.

'Envious.' Andrea gave her another hug. 'Envious of you receiving the headlines for the right reasons and me having them for the wrong ones. Must go, I'm due on the catwalk.' Patsy left the room with a swagger.

Charlotte repeated, 'You speak Italian.'

'No need to sound surprised.' Her dresser adjusted the shimmering turquoise evening gown and changed her jewellery, 'Italy is the country of fashion; it helps to be part of it if you speak the language.'

'Fermato al confine,' muttered Charlotte's dresser.

'That's the answer then. They are caught in customs.'

Charlotte whimpered, 'It'll be a disaster.'

'Luigi, come here please. Stop crying. Luigi can't stand women who cry.'

The little bald, fat man scurried over, 'This is Charlotte Manning, your singer. The dresses for her performance are stuck in customs.'

'Why do you tell me,' he shrugged and waved his arms in the air, 'I am a designer not a customs expert, ask reception.'

'Think of it, Luigi. The first singer in the fashion world to wear your creations.' He hesitated, Andrea continued, 'Not today's premiere collection, they are wonderful, but the specials you keep back.'

Luigi's lips sunk at the corners, but he transformed

them to smile at Andrea, 'Pablo,' called Luigi. They whispered in Italian. 'I shall do as you say.'

Andrea kissed him on the head and Charlotte hugged him.

'Two minutes, Andrea.'

'On schedule.' She turned to Charlotte. 'Remember today is not about you and me. It's about Luigi. Make sure you show Luigi's lovely dresses.' This brought a twirl from the smiling Charlotte.

Andrea laughed, 'Pablo, teach her to do it properly.'

'One minute, Andrea.'

'Coming.'

04

The Lord Lieutenant spoke into the microphone in the Painted Hall at Chatsworth, 'This ceremony is to award the George Medal for gallantry. Among the many medals on Colonel Manning's chest is the George Cross awarded for extreme gallantry as a serving officer in our local regiment. It makes me proud to be in the distinguished company of these two brave men. If I may ask Colonel Manning to read the citation.'

Gerald strode forward to the edge of the stage and declined a microphone. His loud resonant voice permeated the air, 'He displayed the most conspicuous gallantry and extreme devotion to duty in the presence of a suicide bomber. With the full knowledge there had been three similar explosions in other towns he walked to the man and sat with him on the steps of the shopping centre, his action allowing other members of the police service to evacuate the town centre. He persuaded the man not to pursue his intention.'

A tremor passed through Andrea as she listened to the words. On the outside a smile still adorned her face while inside her stomach churned with anxiety, as the outcome could have been so different.

'Thank you, Colonel.' The Lord Lieutenant paused, and his eyes swept around the hall. He turned to Chief Superintendent Martin Cain. 'By the powers invested in me by Her Majesty Queen Elizabeth II, I award you the George Medal for Gallantry.'

Andrea gasped with pride and smiled with happiness as the Lord Lieutenant pinned the medal to her husband's jacket. The audience applauded, led by an enthusiastic Gerald Manning, who strode forward, hand outstretched in a gesture of congratulation. Two photographers arranged the four men for the press shots.

As they moved into position the Chief Constable turned towards Andrea, 'How remiss of me. Mrs Cain, your husband has asked that you join us on the stage.'

Andrea stepped onto the stage and allowed herself to be arranged for the photograph. Martin and Andrea Cain formed the pinnacle of the picture with the three smaller men on the flanks. Andrea swelled with pride as she posed next to her brave husband.

Gerald approached Andrea as the photo session ended, 'You have a brave husband.'

'Thank you. Your daughter mentioned you would be here today,'

'Margaret?'

'No, Charlotte. You must be proud of her outstanding singing career.'

With a grim expression on his face, he caught Andrea's elbow taking her to one side, 'I do not support the route she has chosen in her life and cannot condone her performing on stage in the outfits she displays.' His displeasure not only obvious from his choice of words but also by the cold and contemptuous tone of his voice.

Andrea shook off the hand gripping her elbow, her eyes flashed with annoyance and challenge, 'Does your criticism of the entertainment industry include my job?'

'I wouldn't be so disrespectful to offer judgment regarding your chosen line of work.'

By disapproving of Charlotte's career, he must also hold hers in contempt. Did he expect everyone to enlist in the army? Irritation coursed through her.

'Charlotte is my daughter, I have expressed my sentiments to her, but she has preferred not to listen.'

05

A two-tone alarm blared. 'Stand clear! Coming through!' Andrea skipped to one side as she stepped from the lift. A nurse and a doctor rushed past pushing an equipment trolley. The huge red letters on the side read, 'Cardiac Arrest Equipment. Emergency Use Only.'

A police constable stood to one side allowing the trolley to enter a room. I hope it's not Calum, so she stepped towards the policeman who had his back to her. 'Excuse me, officer.'

The officer reacted, 'Sorry madam, only approved…' but as he turned, 'Sorry Mrs Cain, we weren't expecting you.'

'Which room is Calum's?'

'Not that one, I'm pleased to say. Inspector Brodie is in C-24.' He pointed to the next door along the corridor.

'Are you guarding him?'

'Inspector Brodie? No, I'm keeping an eye on this one, although he's not capable of escaping,' he indicated the room with shouts of 'Stand clear'.

Andrea knocked on the door of C-24. 'Come in,' came the bold reply.

Before opening the door, she plastered a smile

across her face and straightened her shoulders. 'Hello, Calum, I mentioned to Martin I would visit you. I'm Andrea Cain.' She offered her hand.

He gave it a brief shake. 'Yes, I know who you are,' his staring eyes impaled her with an unblinking glower. 'At least you had the good sense not to bring any fruit or flowers. Can't take any more.' Calum sat in bed and opened his hand at the expanse of the room filled with bouquets in elaborate vases and baskets of fruit. A broad forehead and deep-set eyes gave him a desperate appearance, not improved by dishevelled brown hair and several days of stubble on his face.

'I believe you have been seriously hurt.'

'Shot twice, once through the shoulder and the other through the leg, I lost half my blood and spent three hours on the operating table. So, if you count that as seriously hurt, then yes.'

His abruptness took Andrea by surprise. She perched on the bedside chair and regarded him with a quizzical expression. 'I worried when I saw the equipment in the corridor that something had happened to you.'

'No, that's for our friend next door,' the corner of his mouth kicked up into a sneer, 'where the copper is outside, he must have practically had it, judging by the activity of the medical staff.'

'When do you hope to leave hospital?'

He ignored the question, 'I suppose you are more attractive than the Chief Constable's wife.'

'I'll take that as a compliment.'

'Sorry, I'm sore and irritable.'

'I can leave if you wish. But with your injuries you're entitled to be frustrated and irritated.'

A hint of a smile crossed his face, 'Your husband came half an hour ago.'

'I didn't realise as I'm back from London earlier than planned, so came to visit.' Andrea, not certain on how to proceed with the conversation, crossed to the window to gather her thoughts. She wasn't used to men being grumpy and uncommunicative towards her, so it had become a new experience and she didn't know how to handle it.

Calum's gruff voice interrupted her thoughts, 'It's a lousy view even though we're on the seventh floor.'

She nodded her agreement as people walked across the tarmacked car park. One man comparable to Martin, the same tall stature and way of moving, strode towards the gate, but as the rain continued to pelt down from the leaden sky, he wore his overcoat collar up and a tight-fitting flat cap. A woman in a multicoloured anorak ran up to him. Andrea couldn't see her face because of the hood. She flung her arms around him and they kissed. They hugged but then separated and glanced around. 'You're right. Nothing to see except two lovers enjoying themselves.'

'Everyone else does, except me.' He had contempt in his voice. Andrea brought herself back to the difficult conversation with him.

A nurse entered the room and interrupted her thoughts, 'I didn't know you had a visitor, the policeman shouldn't have allowed you in, as he requires rest not a continuous stream of people. Keep the visit brief, please.'

The nurse examined the drip, she would want rest for her patients. 'I'll go. Can I come and visit you again?'

'I bet you don't.'

As she passed the nurse, she read the name badge, Margaret Manning. It would be an unsuitable time to explain her friendship with Charlotte in case it engendered the same reaction as her father.

Calum's mouth twisted into a dark frown, 'Don't bother going in next door.'

Andrea stopped and turned confused by his angry remark, 'I wouldn't, he's very unwell.'

'That's because your husband shot him.'

06

A loud scream filled the air. Andrea peered from the window of the Strines Manor House. A woman in a nurse's uniform raised her palm and slapped Charlotte across the face. A Priest stood nearby and wagged his finger at Charlotte. The nurse raised her hand again. Despite the distance, she heard Charlotte Manning squeal as her arms rose to shield herself. They stood on a small path near the tree-lined drive that led from the narrow country lane to the house. The dense trees and bushes which bordered the drive obscured them from anyone at ground level, but Andrea stood in the window of a turret, that constituted the corner of the house, and had a clear view of the aggressive scenario.

The Priest continued to wag his finger then he and the nurse jumped into their car and drove away. Andrea bubbled with anger at the way they had treated her friend.

Charlotte, now alone, glanced around and up to the house but didn't move. Andrea stepped behind a shutter so she couldn't be seen. The violence she had witnessed upset her. Why be so aggressive to Charlotte? What had she done to upset them?

Five minutes later Charlotte walked into the car

park at the front of the house.

'Hi, darling.' Andrea moved to meet her. They hugged.

'Wonderful to see you, Andrea. You always have a delightful smile for me.' She gave her an extra hug and studied Charlotte's face as their cheeks brushed. The newly applied make-up with deep eye shadow and red blusher hid the marks from the slap on her face.

'Was that your sister in the drive?'

'What did you see?' Her hand flew to her face.

'See? Your father told me your sister is a nurse. I saw her at the hospital a few weeks ago but I didn't introduce myself as she had a patient to treat.'

'Yes, it was my sister, shall we go in?' Charlotte moved from one foot to the other.

'Are you okay? Has anything happened? You seem agitated.'

'Sorry, I'm apprehensive about tomorrow.'

'Why? It will be a limited audience.'

'I'm used to large crowds who I don't know, they're faces, but tomorrow's audience are prominent people. The audience has so many star names. I'm nervous.' She paused and took a deep breath. 'I didn't mean to snap at you, I'm sorry Andrea as I would hate to lose your friendship. We've only known each other a brief period, but we have gelled and by coincidence we both live near Sheffield.'

'Please don't worry. The fashion show and your singing created a successful event in Florence that drew rave reviews. Luigi likes the idea. He wants to launch new clothes, plus his favourite designs, at diverse venues and with selected audiences.'

'Launching new fashion in a medieval house is different, especially away from London and in the heart of the moors.'

'That's better, you're smiling.' Andrea put her arm around her as they entered the house, disappointed that she didn't want to confide. What had the dispute been about? Why had her sister slapped her? Too many questions, but no answers.

'Luigi has a new outfit for me.'

'I guessed he would find you a special design.'

'Hi, darling.' The voice came from behind.

'Hello, Martin.' A sweep of worry flashed across his face but then the smile returned. Andrea glanced over her shoulder to discover what had provoked his apprehension. What had he seen? Only Charlotte stood behind her. 'You know Charlotte don't you, Martin?' Neither of them spoke. Charlotte studied the carpet. A quizzical expression came to Martin's face. 'Didn't you say you interviewed her over threats from the audience?'

'Good grief, what a memory, I'd forgotten.' He walked up to Charlotte, shook hands, 'Are you singing at this event?'

'Yes, but I didn't realise you were Andrea's husband.' Her blue eyes flashed between Andrea and Martin. 'If you'll excuse me, I need to see Luigi.'

Andrea kissed him again on the cheek, 'Are you okay, darling, you seem worried?'

'I'm under pressure with the armed robbery as we're not making headway. I didn't bring Calum…'

'I'm glad, I find him the most awkward man I've ever met.'

'That's not nice, but I won't take offence.' Calum

stood in the doorway behind her. Andrea blushed.

'Andrea! He's a friend and colleague.'

'I'm sorry to be rude.' Andrea looked at the carpet in embarrassment.

'Calum didn't come with me as he drove himself. He wants to see behind the scenes at a fashion show. Will you show him how it operates?'

'Yes. That won't be a problem.'

'I'll leave him in your care. Be gentle, he hasn't been up and walking for long.' Martin kissed Andrea goodbye.

How to deal with him? She needed to make an effort after being rude. He has no interest in fashion and appeared bored as he stared at the tapestries hanging on the wall. So why did he want to come here?

'Mind your backs please!' The shout came from the main entrance. Two men pushed a large trolley stacked with clothes trunks. Calum and Andrea stood to one side under the stag's head against the wall. She caught the eye of one of the men pushing the trolley, but he glanced away and focused on the floor. Men stared at her all the time and tried to catch her eye; they rarely broke the contact.

07

'Take notice of the roadies when they return.'

The bored expression dropped away, and sharpness came to Calum's eyes. The men trundled the trolley back towards them. 'Four hundred years old,' Calum read the plaque on the wall. The men bundled an empty costume basket through the entrance hall and left the house by the front door. 'I don't know the fat bastard, but the tall man has dodgy connections,' Calum announced as their retreating forms moved across the car park.

'Who is he?'

Calum raised himself to his full height and stared Andrea in the eye, 'Why should I tell you?'

'Because I asked.'

'Only if you tell me what's wrong with them.'

Andrea straightened into her full height, and at 6ft 3in peered down on the broad-shouldered man, 'Calum Brodie, are you always so awkward?'

'Only with you.'

Focusing on his face, he had no twinkle and no smile to break into the joke. Walk away? Why did Martin rave about him? 'You're a pain, I know the... the fat bastard. You go first.'

'Thank Christ you're not a copper.' Andrea kept a deadpan face and gave no response to his comment. 'His name is Wayne Smith and claims to be a showbiz agent in Sheffield.'

'And?'

'No and,' Calum responded with a frown.

'I don't believe you.'

'Martin wouldn't want me to tell you.'

Silence fell. 'I'm waiting,' she folded her arms and tapped her foot with impatience.

'Two were shot in the bank robbery. One of them is in hospital, next door when you came a few weeks ago. The other died on the operating table.'

Andrea shivered and fought back the emotion to speak.

'What about sympathy, they shot me as well.'

Andrea's colour faded as it could have been Martin, she suppressed the fears that spun through her. As a policeman he faced dangers. She worried about his job, but he never revealed information. 'I am sorry you were shot,' Andrea gave a soothing smile.

'The robbers came from the Kennedy family, who run a car hire company. Stretch limos. All that crap.' Calum puffed out his cheeks. 'Because of his show business connections, Wayne Smith is their main client. The police would have talked to him about his relationship with the family.'

'So…' Andrea demanded.

'No more.' He winced and rubbed his thigh as he moved away to examine an extensive portrait of Elizabeth I dressed in her finery. Silence filled the air between them. Andrea strutted around the medieval hallway in an agitated manner glancing at portraits with a dismissive air. The paintings didn't interest her enough to stand and study them. Her heeled shoes clicked on the stone floor as she moved restlessly.

'Now your side of our arrangement,' he turned his gaze away from the portrait with a smug expression on his face.

'His name is Fitzwilliam, he's a gutter journalist.'

'Ah.'

'What's "ah" mean?' She glared at him. 'Come on tell me,' Andrea pouted. Such an irritating man why didn't he respond to her? She shook her head to clear her thoughts as Calum decided to answer.

'Fitzwilliam did an article in a Sunday tabloid on gangland protection rackets and his main story featured the Kennedy family.'

'So why are they roadies?' Andrea questioned with an impatient shake of her head.

'We have a point of agreement in that question,' his low voice growled, and he dumped himself on an ornate carved wooden chair with a small groan and stretched his legs out in front of him. He rubbed his injured leg and winced with discomfort.

'I thought you were off duty?'

'And I thought you were a model? But they are suspicious,' Calum replied with irritation in his voice.

'I'll keep an eye on them,' Andrea exhaled with exaggerated patience.

'Wouldn't Fitzwilliam expect you to recognise him?'

'I have arrived a day earlier than the published schedule.'

Calum had lost interest. How do I get rid of him?

She gave him a long assessing stare as she didn't want to show him around. Such an irritating man. Shall I tackle him on what he wants to see and why? Calum heaved himself out of the chair and crossed to the window. He pointed, 'Why are they doing the jobs of roadies? They're sweating up as they're not used to it.'

Andrea joined him at the window. The two men struggled to lift a large box. Her mind raced, Fitzwilliam will be after a story, but who? The frown on Calum's face intensified, but he didn't speak.

I can't be stuck with him for hours. We've nothing in common. I don't like him, and he doesn't like me. Why are we going through this charade? What to do? She rolled her eyes skyward and battled with annoyance. Martin won't be pleased if I get rid of him.

'Hi, Andrea.'

Andrea recognised the strong Italian accent, 'Hello, Maria. Are you my dresser for tomorrow?'

'Yes, and Angelina.'

'I'm pleased, I hoped it would be you.' Andrea smiled at the pretty dark-haired woman. Calum had left the window and joined them. For the first time since arriving he gave a genuine smile but not towards Andrea as his eyes never left Maria.

Maria gave a small wave of her hand to acknowledge the compliment from Andrea. 'Your show clothes are ironed and hung, is there anything else you want me to do?' Maria noticed Calum's attention and smiled back, 'Hello.'

'Yes, Maria, Calum is interested in fashion shows and wants to look around. Could you show him what happens behind the scenes?' The smile gave Andrea the answer she needed. 'Is that okay with you Calum, I need to check my running order for tomorrow?'

Maria talked and waved her arms Italian style as Calum limped along beside her. Andrea had offloaded him, so she fetched the running schedule from the changing area and found a quiet room. She yawned, rubbed her eyes and dropped into a huge wing-backed chair. The sun beamed in through the French Doors. In a few minutes she had fallen asleep.

08

'For Christ's sake stop trying to run my life and stop calling me a whore. No, you take notice, you're past it, old and out-of-date. I don't give a damn for your opinion.'

The shouting woke Andrea, but she didn't move. 'Please be reasonable.' Charlotte's voice. How long had she slept? The wing-backed chair hid Andrea from Charlotte's view. She'll think I've been eavesdropping if she spots me. Andrea stayed still. 'No, no, you can't come over.' The gulps of her crying echoed, making Andrea cringe. 'Next time I'm on stage I shall strip naked to see how that embarrasses you.' The sobs continued but broke off as the door slammed.

Andrea left the room through the French Doors and stepped onto the lawn as dusk fell. She assumed the phone call had been with Charlotte's father, Colonel Manning. Poor Charlotte, such an odious man. Why couldn't he appreciate her success? He held antiquated views which he tried to thrust on poor Charlotte.

The lawns stretched before her, bordered by flowerbeds and a large ornamental fountain in its centre. The green sward ended at a small coppice on the edge of the property. Sudden glinting light in the bushes made her step behind a large statue. She recognised the shape of the man, Fitzwilliam, with another person who must be a photographer if they were hiding. What would his story line be? Fitzwilliam isn't here to report the fashion show, so he's spying on someone. Who?

Andrea knew the devious tricks of the gutter press. He would ferret for information trying to find a fragment of gossip that would lead to a front-page revelation. Who would be the unlucky recipient of his attention? Better to stay out of his way, so she tiptoed along the outside of the house behind the statues, passed several windows and entered a dark room through the French Doors.

09

The silhouette of two figures stopped her attempt to nip through the room to the passageway. They broke apart. 'Just giving Charlotte a hug as she's apprehensive about tomorrow.' Luigi's voice had a nervous edge. Andrea flicked on the adjacent table lamp. They blinked.

'Luigi has been a tower of strength helping me relax.' Andrea glanced into a mirror on the wall. Charlotte had turned away to re-button her blouse.

'Have you finished with Charlotte?'

'Yes, I leave now.' Luigi's broken English faltered. He pecked Charlotte on the cheek, gave Andrea a quick hug and brushed cheeks, 'See you tomorrow.'

'Luigi, have you seen the roadies?'

'No, they've left. It's only you, Charlotte and me.' With a flamboyant wave of his hand, 'Chou', he disappeared through the French doors.

Silence fell between them as they stared at the doors listening to the retreating sound of his footsteps on the gravel.

'Charlotte?'

'Harmless fun.'

'Remember that he's a dear friend of mine.' Andrea

paused as another issue came to her mind. 'Who is your agent? I wish to change mine and I assume yours is local.'

'Wayne Smith.'

'Has he been here today?'

'Not that I know.' Charlotte came up to Andrea and hugged her. 'Thanks for being so wonderful since I've known you, but I must go, darling.'

'See you tomorrow,' Andrea stood by the window as she walked to the car. The gravel crunched under the wheel spin of the Porsche as she departed with a throaty roar down the tree-lined drive.

Silence fell. The oak panelling creaked. Andrea shivered at the eerie house. Time to go. On the way to fetch her bag she stopped. Footsteps? Silence. No, a slow rhythmic squeak. Did the house have a ghost? She shook her head. Don't be so absurd. An old house will always creak, she shivered again, this time because she'd become chilly. It had been a sunny and warm day, so she hadn't brought a jacket. The last vestiges of twilight had brought the cool air rolling down from the moors.

The squeaking stopped. It made her uneasy, so she moved from the long gallery into the hall. A single small bulb threw large shadows of the weapons onto the wall. The pike and the claymore appeared huge and their blades seemed ominous in the deserted hall. The squeaking started anew, louder and more rapid.

10

Nerves gripped her so Andrea decided to run for the car. Squaring her shoulders, she took hesitant steps along the hall towards the large door. Her heels echoed on the flagstones and sounded loud in the house. The squeaking stopped. Andrea held her breath and listened, her heart thudded, and a ball of anxiety formed in her stomach. Someone else is here. Her muscles tensed and she shivered again. A voice inside her head screamed run!

Bending over and with fumbling fingers she took off her shoes but listened. Coldness enveloped her. She stared at the door but her means of escape would be along the length of the hall. Once outside she could run across the gravel to her car.

The creaking started again, a more distinctive rhythm of footsteps. Slow and heavy. Which direction? Her ears strained and her mind twirled with frightening images. Somewhere in front of her. Would he intercept her? Her thoughts swirled. Relief swept over her as she remembered and grasped at her thought. 'Fitzwilliam, is that you? You've frightened the living daylights out of me.' Her voice echoed through the large hall disappearing into the shadowy recesses. 'Where are you?' Her voice trembled. No reply.

The squeaking stopped. Once again, she held her breath as she listened. The silence hovered in the air. A chill traced through her body. 'Fitzwilliam,' her voice trailed off. A door slammed, she jumped. A chilly breeze blew along the hall. Dropping her shoes, she sprinted for the door. 'Damn! Damn!' It had been locked and bolted. Had she become trapped?

Grabbing at the top bolt, her hands trembled as she pulled at the huge bar. The old and heavy metal didn't budge. She struggled and pushed her shoulder against the door and wiggled the unyielding bolt, she had to escape.

'Let me help,' a deep voice sliced through the air. A large hand appeared from nowhere.

'Ahhhh!' She spun around and cannoned into him. 'Get off! get off!' A piercing scream of panic flew from her open mouth, her eyes widened. The man stepped back. 'Who are you? What do you want with me? Go away.'

The shabby security uniform hung off his shoulders, the huge boots creaked as he shifted from foot to foot. The gaunt grey face broke into half a smile as he stared at her. His deep voice broke through her thoughts like a roll of thunder far away, 'Sorry, I didn't mean to frighten you, I came to investigate the noise of footsteps. After all, I am security.' Eyes of palest watery blue stared at her, his thin gaunt face and untidy hair gave him a creepy appearance in the shadowy light. He grinned, exposing yellow uneven teeth, and then the noise of his laughter echoed in the hall.

Andrea clenched her fists, 'Do you want me to help you with the door?' He moved towards her, so she leapt out of the way. 'It's old and heavy.'

Despite his thin body he shot back the bolts and turned the key. Andrea eased round him. His stubble and decaying teeth reflected in the dim light. Grimacing at the smell of his sour breath as he turned towards her, she lowered her head and attempted to slip through the small gap as he held the door. 'Before you go,' He stepped in her way. 'You called out a name, Fitzwilliam, wasn't it?'

'Yes,' but her words trembled.

'Is he still here? I don't want to shut someone else in. People say I frighten them when I lope up behind them.' His cackling laugh filled the hall again.

'I saw him in the woods, I didn't know whether he had entered the house.'

'Ah,' he gave another flash of rotten teeth. 'Is he the photographer or the fat one? I've been watching them.'

'The fat one, he's a reporter searching for a story and he might still be around.'

'Not for long.'

'How do you know?'

'As soon as you go, I shall let the dogs out of the van. They'll find them and are partial to a chew on a reporter.' He appeared pleased as Andrea smiled at him. 'Goodbye,' he moved from the door. 'I'm sorry I frightened you.'

'No harm done,' but she relaxed as she stepped through the door. Shoes! She turned, but one glance at his face in the gap of the door made it an easy choice, she would pick them up tomorrow. The door closed and with it the light disappeared from the porch.

11

Blackness surrounded her. The harsh, chilly wind blew through her thin clothes. She took a few painful steps across the gravel and reached the sleek Jaguar sports car. Comfort came as the engine started and the lights lit the gravel drive. A wisp of moorland mist swept across the car and swirled in the headlights; the ghostly appearance made her shiver. Her trembling hands gripped the steering wheel and her heart thumped.

With her arms and legs stiff with the cold, she longed for the heater to work. Warmth, she wanted warmth. 'You're acting like a scared schoolgirl,' she muttered out loud as she pulled away, left the drive and turned right towards the Strines. In fifteen minutes, she would be home and warm, she pictured herself curled up on the sofa in front of a log fire sipping a hot cup of tea. Perfect. She smiled hoping that Martin would be there. She relaxed as the early hint of warmth flowed up her legs.

The moon reflected on the water in the reservoir and the village lights of Bradfield twinkled in the distance. The cloud covered the moon. She accelerated then held a consistent speed over the undulating road. A tricky road to drive in broad daylight but the darkness made the treacherous bends more problematic. The road wound its way through several minor valleys and narrowed across small stone bridges, where she would have to apply full concentration. It began to rain. She misjudged the first bend and had to brake hard, so she slowed. Now a straight section along the deserted road through the black conifers. The car lights shimmered off the trees.

She gripped the steering wheel to handle the jerky movements as the car bounced along the uneven road surface. The metal of the exhaust grated on the road which made her gasp, so she slowed. 'Steady, steady.' Remain calm, a voice inside her head demanded. She had been driving erratically as her desire to get home increased. Checking her rear-view mirror, it showed nothing but blackness. She inhaled deeply to calm herself. More warmth came through. Next, a right-hand bend then a steep descent to a hairpin bend with a bridge across the river.

She accelerated and the powerful engine roared away from the bridge. The car swayed from side to side as the tyre grip on the wet slick surface failed. Andrea fought to regain control. It finished up at an angle as she brought it to a halt. The car stalled. Inky blackness and silence wrapped around her. She thumped the steering wheel in frustration wanting to shout out loud. She panted. Taking large gasping breaths of air, she tried to calm herself.

She shouldn't have lost control. The evening had become black and sinister, she had to move. Why had she become so agitated? The security guard had unnerved her, and the dark spookiness of her surroundings didn't help. Taking a long slow breath, she restarted the engine and pulled away up the slope. The warmth covered her as she drove onto the open lane across the moors. The rain pelted harder making the windscreen wipers swish in a hypnotic rhythm backwards and forwards. Concentrate. Concentrate. Tiredness seeped into her. No other thoughts, she told herself. Keep focused. She willed her eyes to open wider and stared at the headlights as they sliced through the blackness, yielding a ghostly appearance through the rain and mist. Concentrate on the driving.

The headlights picked up a large mound in the road. Grey and shadowy like a huge limestone boulder, she braked as it would be too big to drive over, but she had enough space to drive around providing she didn't panic. She slowed as she approached but then relaxed and gave a small smile as the lights picked up the obstruction. A sheep using the warmth of the road for its bed. Passing around it with ease gave her a hint of reassurance that her driving had become more controlled. The panic from earlier had subsided. She concentrated on the road ahead.

Only one more hairpin bend, then the Strines pub and across the open moor to the main Sheffield to Manchester road. Only ten minutes from home. A smile of anticipation crossed her face. Warmth, comfort and security awaited her. This would be the deepest valley, so she'd take it slowly. Moving through the gears she reduced the speed.

Darkness surrounded her with none of the fading light penetrating the dense tree canopy. The rain teamed. Huge raindrops splattered on the windscreen. The wipers moved wildly over the deluge and struggled to cope. Creeping along the winding road, the bridge approached. Narrow and awkward. Her view of the road became complicated by the excess water. The wipers couldn't match the downpour. She drove through water as it gushed across the road from the pounding rain.

12

'Aargh!' Thrown sideways, her head cracked on the side window. She jammed on the brakes and clung to the steering wheel. The thumping noise of the braking system terrified her as the car skidded. A loud resonating thud stopped the car and thrust her forward. With wide eyes the windscreen came towards her face. The scream hadn't started when her vision went grey. The airbag had stopped her crashing into the windscreen, throwing her backwards and sideways it then deflated.

What had she hit? Weakness came over her. The world began to spin. 'I can't pass out!' she screamed into the silent darkness. A cloud enveloped the car and a burning smell hit her nostrils. Panic seized her. The car must be on fire. She grabbed the door handle and stumbled out on to the road and scrambled away. A voice inside her head screamed petrol explodes. Her bare feet slipped and slithered on the tarmac as she scrabbled across the wet ground to distance herself from the car. Everything became a blur as she sprawled and sobbed in the pouring rain.

'Help me, help, you've crashed into me. Help me!' she screamed, but her voice disappeared into the darkness.

She hoped to hear someone coming to her rescue, but she heard no one. The only sound came from the rain pounding around her. As she turned towards her car, its lights went out. Think. Think. Without the car lights darkness engulfed her. Her thin saturated clothes hung like limp rags and her wet hair clung to her face. What to do?

Dread filled her mind like an icy tendril strangling her thoughts. The unyielding ground hard and cold stabbed at her trembling body. She flicked the rain away from her face and forced herself another glance at the car. Steam, not smoke. Most had dispersed. She remained slumped on the floor expecting help, but no one appeared from the inky blackness. Her eyes focused back on her car. It had hit the parapet of the bridge. She couldn't see another car. Why had she hit the bridge? The empty road stared back at her. She shouted, 'Help, help!'

But heard no movement or reply. Cold, wet and frightened, her whole body trembled, and it wouldn't stop. The realisation of what had happened hit her. Fear paralysed her. Had she been hurt? Or disfigured? Her head swam and blood covered her hands.

What would Martin do? Thinking of him calmed her. She moved her arm, it hurt, but had only been grazed. Struggling to her feet, weakness came over her as she teetered to the parapet and leaned on it. Her limbs didn't belong to her and moving them felt as though shifting concrete. What had happened? The question repeated itself over and over in her mind, but she didn't have an answer. Although her bruised body ached and trembled, she hadn't been injured. Shocked, she craved to curl up in a ball and wait for rescue.

The solid stone of the bridge gave her support as she breathed slowly trying to placate her racing mind. The initial signs of relief came to her as she became cognizant of her surroundings. She had hit the bridge. The long scratch of blue indicated where the car had struck the stonework and a block from the bridge had been dislodged. The impact had thrown the car into the skid, but she didn't understand why it had happened as she had been driving with care. She had slowed and put the car in a lower gear as she had approached. Those actions were distinct in her mind.

The total darkness terrified her. Soaking wet and frightened she continued to lean against the bridge. The wind and driving rain blew into a squall and the black trees moved and creaked with menace. The roar of the river plunging over the rock beneath the bridge filled the air during a lull in the wind. She must act. She must do something. But what?

What would Martin do? Phone. Get help. Her eyes peered through the inky blackness back to the car. No, the pub is nearby, that's a better idea. If it's closed, she resolved to wake them as they would look after her while she waited for someone to rescue her. She stared at the road in front of her as it climbed the hill out of the valley. The overhanging trees formed a complete canopy of black. A long tunnel of darkness stretched before her and her courage ebbed away. The darkness engulfed her, and her body screamed to leave the nightmare. Her imagination ran wild as a groan escaped her lips.

'I can't go that way,' she shook her head in despair. Her phone would be in the car so with heavy legs she forced herself to move away from the bridge. Her bare feet, cold and numb ached like the rest of her as she stumbled towards the car. The shaking of her body became worse. The car creaked. She stopped. Fear engulfed her with each second and seemed to last a lifetime. Should she approach it? Might it explode? The endless possibilities of this nightmare made her shake more.

Martin why aren't you here? She sobbed to herself while her tears intermingled with the rain that beat across her face, but she had no alternative, it had to be the car. With slow precision she put one foot in front of the other while her eyes never left the blue Jaguar. After each step she paused as she waited for changes or indications that the car might explode. The steam had gone, only creaking remained. Andrea opened the door as though moving in slow motion. Nothing materialised. She let out a long sighing breath as she snatched her bag from the passenger seat and staggered back to the parapet clutching it.

From the dark recesses of her bag she extracted her phone. The phone slipped and slid in her cold and shaking fingers as though alive and not an inanimate object. The small screen gave a bright and welcoming light in the darkness. Her heart plummeted. No signal, not even a single bar so she switched it off and back on again, she moved it around holding it this way and that, but still no signal.

A large heaving sob escaped her body, perhaps the car will go? She wrenched the door opened climbed in and turned the key. The starter motor turned and the engine spluttered. 'Please. Please!' she whimpered. A screeching grind of metal followed by creaking, but the engine refused to start. Andrea fell over the steering wheel as exhaustion overwhelmed her.

Her mind raced. What next? She fell out of the car and staggered again only keeping her balance by leaning on the car bonnet. Stones dug into her feet. Andrea stared at the black tunnel that led towards the pub. Dark and terrifying, she turned her attention in the opposite direction. The night sky was visible at the top of the hill from where she'd come, relief from the total blackness of the other direction. It's high ground so could have a signal, she staggered and swayed up the lane as though drunk and disorderly.

The shivering blurred her vision. The trees blew in a squall of rain. Her feet were covered in mud and dirt. The blood from the cuts on her feet merged with the mud. The trees ended as she emerged onto the moor then the wind whipped at her sodden hair and clothes. Would this nightmare ever end? She staggered and dropped on to a large rock. Her shaking hands clutched the phone, and she pleaded with it to work.

A signal. A sliver of hope crashed through her. 'Thank God.'

She pressed Martin's number, 'Hiya,' came the quick reply.

'Martin! Martin! I've crashed the car,' she screamed and gabbled.

'Where are you, tell me, I'll come?' The sound of his voice came as a relief, he would rescue her.

'Strines, just...' Beep, beep, beep.

'Martin! Martin!' She checked her phone. Battery - No charge. The screen shone into her face then died.

Gasping and panting she half collapsed onto the rock and with her head in her hands, tears streamed down her face. She wanted to be still, but her body shook. She'd spoken to him. Relief spread through her and she breathed more slowly as she'd heard Martin's voice. He knew. She hoped he'd heard enough, but it wouldn't matter, he knows. Even if he didn't hear "Strines", he'll search.

What would Martin say? Be somewhere visible. I must go back to the car. She pushed herself up from the rock, the shaking had eased, and she could walk straighter. Coldness seeped into every pore of her body. The rain had stopped. The moon came out from behind a cloud, but it didn't change the haunting darkness of the trees. She walked along the middle of the lane, stopped and peered at her watch. Midnight. Had she passed out?

She hadn't been injured, her feet hurt, but nothing serious. Martin came into her mind again. Protect yourself. Be wary. Be alert. If someone comes, hide until you're sure. That made sense.

With a jerky walk Andrea followed the middle of the lane in the feeble moonlight as it emerged from behind the rain clouds. The shadowy frame of her car had wedged into the bridge. Something scuttled across the road making her jump. The light glinted on the fur of the fox as it scampered away and disappeared into the bushes.

Her eyes sought a place to shelter. How long would help be? Partial strength had come back and while cold, the shaking lessened as she neared the bridge. The bushes and fence on the lane had been smashed. Andrea hadn't hit them, but something had as fresh splinters of wood covered the road, so she placed her feet on the verge and peered down to the river through the broken bushes.

13

'My God!' Andrea shuddered at the shape of a car, wedged into the base of a tree. It had gone through the bushes and ended twisted at a dangerous angle about twenty metres down the steep bank. A tree had blocked the car halfway to the river. The river pounded on the rocks, in full flow, and roared down the narrow valley. The steep bank would be treacherous to climb down. 'Anyone there?'

Had she hit the car forcing it down the bank. What had happened at the accident? Andrea racked her brains to get the sequence of events and closed her eyes to think. The recollection came back, she'd struck something, lost control and the second hit came when the car crashed into the bridge. A tremor ran through her, she hadn't seen the car. Andrea held on to a damaged piece of fence and took a step down the bank. Stones hurt her bare feet as she slipped and slid on the greasy grass and mud.

Holding on tight, 'Anyone there?' she shrieked in her strongest voice. 'Try to make a noise.' The flickering light of the moon played on the windows preventing her from looking inside the narrow rear window. The letters on the back of the car P...O ... R. Porsche. Andrea's gut twisted as Charlotte drove a Porsche.

Charlotte wouldn't have been coming the other way unless she had been returning to the Manor for a reason. Often forgetful, she could have chosen to return. I must go down. Her arm throbbed from holding the fence, her foot slipped, a stone dug in the heel. 'Ahhhh!' As she slid, she grabbed the fence, her momentum wrenched her shoulder, but she hung on.

Which route down the steep bank? She wouldn't be able to grip the rough grass. There might be a route near to bushes and trees that would allow her to reach the car. She sat, gripped the bushes and slid towards the car. Sharp leaves and twigs dug into her hands, but she couldn't let go until she had the next grip. The registration plate came into view, 'CM1'. Panic knotted her stomach.

'Charlotte, Charlotte!' she screamed. No reply, merely the deafening roar of the river at the bottom of the bank. The steep angled bank ended in the water. She tried to move further down, but had become stuck, caught on a bush. Wriggling her legs didn't help, so she released her grip on the bush to free herself. A ripping sound came as her dress tore but no longer caught, she grabbed at the bush but missed and slid.

Grabbing at the grass, it slipped through her hands. Bracing her legs, she hit the rear of the car which creaked but didn't move. The driver's door remained closed covered by a thick bush. The river twisted and swirled with a great roaring sound. Andrea worried she might slip further. She would have no hope if she fell into the river; it would be too deep and powerful to survive. She held on to the car and eased herself towards the passenger's door. Holding onto a bush she freed the door which swung back. Kneeling on the ground she dragged herself far enough into the car to see.

Oh, my God, it's Charlotte. She had slumped on the steering wheel. 'Oh, Charlotte! Charlotte!' Andrea reached as far as she could but still couldn't touch her motionless friend. She would have to clamber into the car to help her. Andrea braced her legs against two grass tufts and pushed. The effort allowed her to spread across the front seat. She grabbed Charlotte's wrist and tried to find her pulse, but her cold hands shook, and her numbed fingers couldn't feel.

The metal groaned and Andrea froze as the car lurched. Would her shaking from the cold and tension dislodge the car, but she couldn't control the shivers that racked her body? Andrea gripped Charlotte's hair and lifted her head. Blood covered her face. Staring eyes penetrated the blood and the matted hair. She squealed at the broken face. The bleak face of death. The car lurched again. 'There's nothing further I can do for you now my darling. Rest in peace.'

How could she leave the car without it moving? She rested Charlotte's head back down and wiped her wet hands down her dress. Be careful. Slow and steady. With small movements she eased out of the car and wedged her foot on the grass again, but it had become numb from the cold and wet. The last push with her other foot gave enough momentum to slither to a bush which she grasped for all her worth.

Another large metallic grinding groan came as the Porsche slid sideways. Heaving on the bush she yanked herself from the path of the tail of the car as it twisted past. It built up speed bouncing and screeching down the slope. Flattening two bushes it wedged into a large rock crevasse with the bonnet in the rushing water of the turbulent river which seemed to grow in ferocity. The river would sweep it away.

She tried to pull herself up, but exhaustion filled her arms and legs. Do nothing foolish. Putting in her last effort she strained her muscle sinews but collapsed back against the bush, her strength had gone. The shivering from the cold amplified by the startling death of her friend rendered her powerless. Her hands were numb, and her grip failed so she lay back and wedged her foot on the base of a bush.

'I can't move.' But her words were lost in the thunder of the river. She closed her eyes with the expectation energy would be restored to the muscles and she could grope her way up to the road. Charlotte's dead face appeared out of the dark. Andrea screamed and opened her eyes, 'I've killed Charlotte, I've killed her,' she sobbed.

14

What's that? A car, yes, it's a car. Please let it be the police as I'm defenceless. Andrea struggled to listen above the river's noise and in a lull heard the car engine die, it had stopped. Two car doors banged. This is it. Who are they? Twisting her neck to peer up through the bushes and long grass showed no movement. Lie still and hope.

'Mrs Cain… Mrs Cain!'

The cry reached her through the darkness loud enough to overcome the river's roar. 'Down here,' she yelled but her voice didn't carry. She had to make more effort, as he hadn't heard, but relief spread over her.

'Mrs Cain!'

She took a large lungful of air, 'Down here!' It took all her effort, but she shouted again, 'Down here!'

'I can hear you, Mrs Cain. Over here, Mike. Keep talking, we'll find you.'

'Down here near the stream. Down here. Please help me.'

'We're coming.' The sudden brightness dazzled her eyes. 'There she is, we're coming.'

'There's no radio signal.'

Andrea heard the twigs snapping and the leaves

rustling above her. 'Mobile signal, top of the hill,' she shouted.

'I'm coming down.'

'Be careful, it's steep.'

'Don't bother about me, stay there and don't move.' The light bounced over her and the nearby bushes. 'Nearly there.'

Andrea had never been so pleased to see a pair of policeman's boots as they slid down the slope towards her.

'My legs are numb, I'm wedged against the bush, but I will slip.'

A huge arm came across her. 'Lean against me, I will not move.' He wriggled around and she leaned towards him, a big fluorescent jacket covered her.

'My friend is in the car down there, she's dead. I didn't, I didn't!'

'Don't worry about her. We'll take you to safety. Help is on the way. The team will reach the car.'

The jacket kept the wind off, but the cold and shaking didn't stop although she was safe. The policeman tucked the jacket in around her. 'I don't know what happened.'

'We'll work it out, your husband is on the way, he didn't hear your location, so we've been searching. Jim will tell them at the Control Centre, and we'll have help here soon. The paramedics are on the way. We'll stay here until the others arrive and they'll take us up. Are you hurt?'

'No, I don't think so. I could walk after the crash. I'm shivering but not hurt. When I saw my friend's car down here, I had to try to reach her.'

'You're a brave lady, attempting to help on this steep

slope.' Andrea heard cars. 'Here comes the cavalry.' His voice remained calm and pacifying. The darkness filled with blue flashing lights and shouting voices. 'Down here.' The policeman flashed his torch towards the road.

Andrea heard a strange rattling of metal, but she couldn't see anyone.

'Ladder in place and secured,' shouted a voice below her on the slope. Two firemen had secured a ladder flat on the ground fixed to the trees, one of them waved.

A paramedic appeared at her side and lifted the coat, 'Move your arms and legs, please.'

'They're numb.'

'They are moving.' He wrapped her in metal foil, tucking it underneath with the help of the policeman.

'Floodlights coming on!' The area lit up. The policeman rolled aside from her.

Martin slid down next to her. He hugged her. 'Oh God! Andrea.'

The paramedic put the jacket back over her, 'She's okay. That's not her blood. There are no major abrasions to cause that amount.'

'It must be Charlotte's, she's dead. In the car that's down there. I killed Charlotte in the accident.'

'Andrea,' he hugged her, 'the others will get to her. We need you out of here. I'll see you at the top, I will leave it to the professionals, they will carry you to an ambulance,' he kissed her on the cheek, then moved away.

Three firemen and another paramedic slid to her side after Martin disappeared.

'Mrs Cain, are you in pain, do you need gas to move?'

'No.'

'Then relax, we will attach straps and then lift you on to a stretcher and take you up. Just lay back.' They eased her into a solid padded hood so she couldn't move her head and neck. They lifted her and set her down again. A firefighter tightened straps across her.

She expected to be dragged but a chain of people lifted and passed her stretcher between them. Each face smiled. She could only move her eyes as her head wouldn't turn because of the padded hood. Andrea appraised the uniforms, she expected police and paramedics. The first few were firemen and the label on the next said, 'Senior Fire Officer', her face so pretty with a gorgeous smile. The labels on the remainder of the chain read, 'Mountain Rescue'. As soon as she reached the top of the bank four of the team carried her to an ambulance where another two paramedics greeted her.

'Let's check you out.' She removed the foil and connected Andrea to apparatus.

'I'm warming up.'

The paramedic pulled the doors of the ambulance closed, 'We'll clean you up.'

In a few minutes they had removed Andrea's wet clothes and she wore a thick tracksuit. The warmth enveloped her, but the image of Charlotte's dead face wouldn't leave her. She was safe but Charlotte was dead. Had she hit her car? Was she responsible for her death?

With support she climbed to her feet, 'I'm okay. Let me get my balance. My legs feel weak, but I will not collapse.'

Martin opened the back door and slipped into the ambulance. He hugged her then they stepped from the vehicle with him supporting her. Wrapping his arm around her they walked away from the bridge. The rain had stopped, but the night remained dark.

'What happened? I've become confused and have lost all track of time.' She shivered at the memories and took a deep breath, 'I need to know, did I kill Charlotte?' a whimper escaped her lips and tears filled her eyes.

'Are you sure you want to know?' Martin kept his arm around her. Warmth from the thick tracksuit spread through her aching limbs. The horror of finding Charlotte wouldn't go away. The image of her bloodied face had been imprinted on her mind. She turned pleading eyes towards him. 'Please Martin. I'm shaky, but warm and only have a few cuts and bruises.'

Martin waved and a police officer came across to join them. 'The Porsche went through the fence and the offside clipped this parapet which dislodged and fell into the road. The car then slid down the hill and wedged into the tree. In a second movement it slipped into the river. Mrs Cain hit the section of parapet that had fallen into the road, then skidded across the road to strike the other side of the bridge.'

'Does that mean I didn't hit Charlotte?'

'The two accidents were separate, and both cars were travelling in the same direction.'

'She left about fifteen minutes before me but why did Charlotte go through the fence?'

'We're checking for an injured animal or any other reason, but we'll know more when we recover the car. It could have been mechanical.'

'Come on darling, that's enough, let's go home, we'll leave it to Mike and the traffic division.'

‘Thank you all,’ called out Andrea. Those nearby waved.

‘Sir, sir.’ A policeman scrambled back onto the road from the direction of the Porsche. The policeman stood in front of them, but he didn’t speak.

‘What is it?’ The policeman glanced at Andrea. ‘She knows Charlotte’s dead.’

‘The crash didn’t kill her, sir. She’s been shot.’

15

That hurts. Andrea peered at her back in the mirror after stepping from the shower. It had been a horrendous night, but she hadn't been injured, only grazes and bruises which could be covered with make-up for Luigi's show. Poking at the marks on her legs she could only find a small graze here and there, she'd been fortunate. The show should be dedicated to Charlotte. Poor Charlotte.

Weakness flooded through her, so she sat on the edge of the bath. The sleep had helped, but the nightmares had been vivid and terrifying. After Martin had brought her home last night she had wanted to sleep and hadn't wanted to talk about the ordeal. Tiredness had swamped her. On waking this morning, thoughts of Charlotte had filled her mind the minute she opened her eyes. The shower revitalised her though her legs were stiff and shaky. A few minutes sitting on the edge of the bath helped, so she shuffled back to the bedroom towelling as she moved and put her face close to the mirror.

The white and languid face staring back didn't look like her. She ran the tip of her finger around her red-rimmed eyes. Puffy, and as she pushed the skin, it had no bounce. The make-up girls would sort it out later. Flopping on the bed she rested her weary head on the comfortable pillow but resisted the urge to pull the covers over her as the nightmares would return. Her whole body ached from the stresses and strains of scrambling on the slope and she shuddered as the roar of the deadly river echoed in her head. The thought of the energy needed for a show weakened her and she closed her eyes.

Charlotte's dead face appeared making her shiver again, the memory had become sharper and more powerful than the reality. The warped image of Charlotte's face came every time her eyes closed. Tears trickled down her cheek, but the mind's picture wouldn't leave. The pain she suffered, the show and fashion were negligible compared to Charlotte's life. Perhaps the show should be cancelled, but she preferred to leave the decision to Luigi. The summer morning's warm air floated into the bedroom. Under normal circumstances she would have revelled in the start of a promising day, but she dreaded the agony the next few hours would bring. As she lay on the bed her listless body remained motionless, but her mind raced in overdrive.

You can't be shot by accident. Once they'd formed, the words hit her with power. She gasped. The words held no consolation, but emanated fear. Why would anyone want to kill Charlotte? The words spun in her head, her death hadn't been an accident, she had been murdered. The realisation sent a shiver through Andrea.

Martin wouldn't explain the details as he kept undesirable aspects of police work away from her. A murder would be added to the investigation of the armed robbery making his workload unbearable. She had become involved because Charlotte had been her friend and she had found the body, but her involvement in a case would make him uncomfortable.

A noise from outside made her jump. Grabbing a dressing gown, she sprang up from the bed and stole towards the window as it had been a noise she didn't recognise. Someone in the garden? She hid behind the curtains as her legs weakened and a shiver coursed through her body. Peering between the curtain and the window frame, the noise came again, 'You daft bitch.' She laughed out loud at her paranoia. A sheep scratched itself on the outside of the garden fence.

Using the mirror to start her make-up, the stairs creaked. Andrea froze. What should she do? The bedroom door opened; her strength drained.

16

'Darling,' Martin crept through the opened door. 'I expected you to be in bed, but you're up.'

Andrea hugged him, 'I must speak with Luigi about the show this evening.'

'I don't expect there will be a show. A murderer is on the loose, so I want you safe and sound,' he kissed her on the forehead as she smoothed his hair.

'The show has been booked for months.'

Ignoring her words, 'We've not worked out who's involved, but everyone at the house yesterday will be giving statements. And that includes you.'

'Yes, I expected that, but that won't take long will it?' Andrea perched on the bed, watching Martin with anxious eyes.

'Murder enquiries take a lengthy time; you'll be questioned about Charlotte and how long you've known her. But that's only the start. Yesterday's events will be examined.'

'Whatever's needed, darling, I'll help,' she smiled encouragement at his stern face. 'The show is raising money for charity; I'd like it to be dedicated to Charlotte.'

'Rearrange it!' His mouth turned down in irritation.

Andrea bit back a comment as she wanted to help Martin, not to argue with him, but he wandered around the room like a visitor at an art gallery, examining each picture as though seeing them for the first time.

'Rest is what you need, you shouldn't have left your bed.'

'I'm shocked, but not hurt. Every time my eyes close, her face appears, so I need activity not lying in bed.'

'Stay home today as I want a clearer picture of the events to consider whether they might strike again.'

'Martin?'

'No, Andrea, I said no,' he pressed his lips together in a tight grim line, 'don't you understand, it's horrible to be involved in the world of murder, death and maiming, it's touched you but I intend it gets no closer.'

'Tell me what happened,' she leaned back against the pillow and hugged her knees to her chest.

'No, as it could prejudice your statement.' Andrea didn't reply. He sat on the edge of the bed leaned towards her and stroked her arm, 'I want to protect you darling, please listen.'

'Yes, I will, but you can't wrap me in cotton wool, so I'll be careful, I promise.' She stretched across and kissed him on the cheek, 'You're under pressure with the robbery and now this murder which will mean you working horrendous hours.'

A glazed expression flickered on his face as though distant thoughts had entered his head. In an instant it disappeared to be replaced by an angry scowl, 'No! I forbid you to go out.' His hands gripped her shoulders.

'Don't speak that way. Murder is gruesome, I saw

it for myself, you're so brave to deal with those types of people.' He didn't respond but dropped his hands from her shoulders though his gaze remained fixed on her face.

'Have there been death threats against me?'

His eyes widened, 'No, but we need to catch the killer.'

'Darling, if there is nothing specific then I'll be mindful.'

'I've the power to cancel the show.'

'You have, but that's not related to me leaving the house.'

Andrea stood up, picked up her bag and searched in it, 'I planned to meet Luigi early this morning, I need to ring him, but I must have lost my mobile last night.' She crossed to the bedside table, 'Where's the phone, it's not in the cradle.'

He turned away, 'I've taken both as I forbid you contacting or seeing people involved in the case.'

'This is absurd. I've a life to lead, and a show to do tonight.'

'I can cancel it.'

'Even if you show your supposed power, I will meet the show people to discuss the next steps.'

'No, I don't want you to go.' In a flash he moved across the room and grabbed her wrist.

'Let go, that hurts.' Annoyed at his overprotective attitude she tugged and yanked her wrist free. The dark glowering expression on Martin's face made her gasp. 'Whatever's the matter. Your eyes. Is there something wrong?' The pupils had dilated and turned black. The green irises, a favourite feature for Andrea, had gone.

17

The black pools stared, unblinking and expressionless. With his hands clenched by his side, he remained motionless and seemed like a stranger. What had happened to her handsome, fun loving husband? Irritation bubbled to the surface. 'I've had enough of this, return the phones,' her voice rose with indignation, 'I expect to be treated like any other witness, nothing special, nothing unusual, but I will meet my friends. Cancelling the show is your decision but we will have to determine when to put on the event.'

'I forbid you to go out,' he spat the words out with ferocity.

'The phones!' Ignoring his hostility, she held out her hand, palm upwards. The black pools fixed her, but he took one from each pocket and flung them on the bed. Without another word he stormed from the bedroom. Heavy thumping steps on the stairs ended by the slamming of the front door. The wheel-spin on the drive gravel indicated his angry departure which then cleared to silence.

What had caused the hostility? She moved to the dressing table to complete her make-up. The routine of applying and blending each piece became therapeutic. With the added assistance of some deep breathing her body and mind calmed. Poor Martin, she shouldn't have argued with him. With a long slow breath, her shoulders relaxed. Why did she defy him? This world of killers and gunmen is the one he knows, she had to listen to his advice.

The phone with a cheery tune shattered the silence of the bedroom. Should she answer? Luigi's name popped up on the screen, so she pressed accept. 'Hi, Luigi.' She forced her voice to sound cheerful although the exact opposite of her mood.

'How are you, darling? Such a drama for you! You poor, poor, woman,' but his strong accent became difficult to follow, but hardly pausing for breath, 'What can I do for you?'

'Luigi, Luigi, listen.'

But he wouldn't listen and before she could speak his anxious voice echoed down the line, 'I'm so worried about you. Are you okay, Andrea? I'd perish if anything happened to you.'

'Luigi, listen, please.' He ran out of words. 'I'm okay.' He didn't acknowledge her comment but continued with his train of thought as though she hadn't spoken.

'The police tell me the show might be cancelled.'

Andrea could hear the tension in his voice, 'They have to make the decision, they know best.' She sat at the dressing table with her phone clamped to her ear while prodding the puffy skin around her eyes. 'Luigi, we must help them with the death of Charlotte.'

'But the show can go on and we'll dedicate it to Charlotte,' his voice rose as he sounded near to tears.

'That won't impress the police.' Silence came down the line, so she waited.

'But could you talk to him. Martin, your husband is in charge.'

'I've tried, but he is determined to cancel the show,' she sighed as Martin's earlier attitude returned to her.

'Cannot he accept it's dedicated to Charlotte.' Luigi huffed in resentment.

Andrea listened as he rambled on, but she moved from the mirror and wandered the room to ease her aching muscles. She couldn't influence Martin, but the show should go on.

Andrea closed her eyes as she stopped and leaned against the wall for support. Charlotte's grey face and the gawking eyes of death came to her. She shook her head. That's not right for Charlotte, wrong image! I won't remember her fractured, bloodied face with staring eyes.

The notion of a young pretty woman dressed in one of Luigi's gowns, ready to perform to an audience, had to be forced into her mind. Andrea's thoughts jumped around as she returned her focus to Luigi. He didn't need any words but wanted to talk so her mind jumped again to Martin with his black eyes. Charlotte, the staring eyes of death. The rescue queue with compassionate and caring eyes. Brave men and women forming a human chain to lift her away from danger. She moved across the room only half listening to Luigi's ramblings.

Martin had slid down the bank to be by her side which despite the dangerous circumstances had brought a smile to her lips. But his face this morning caused the smile to slip away. Those black pools, dark and deep. She shivered. Charlotte singing, her face alive and vibrant.

Charlotte dead, her eyes wide open and still. The images flashed as Luigi jabbered on.

Charlotte and Luigi had been together last night. More than good friends but when had the affair started? 'Luigi.'

He took no notice of the interruption and his voice continued to flow. 'Charlotte such a wonderful singer and a lovely person.' The strong accent hadn't left him.

Andrea changed her tone, making it authoritative and urgent, 'Luigi!' Silence emanated from the other end as he stopped talking.

'Yes, Andrea?' The chatter had gone, but would he listen?

'Charlotte and you?' He went to speak, but Andrea continued, 'Luigi. This is serious. Questo è grave è omicidio. The police will ask you about Charlotte, they will probe. Do not lie, Luigi, do not lie,' her voice rose as she uttered the words.

'The English police are good, but it has no relevance to them.'

'Luigi!' her voice became shrill as she slumped on the dressing table seat. A pale face unlike her normal complexion stared back with no smile. 'Tell the truth, the police discover everything.' Silence fell. Tears formed as the trauma of last night evoked haunting memories, but she brushed them aside to focus on Luigi. 'Were you having an affair with Charlotte?' Andrea waited.

An audible sigh reached her, 'Yes, you know as you saw us together last night. It started in Florence, she liked me.' The last three words were full of emotion. The sadness in his voice made Andrea gasp. She went quiet. Martin would cancel the show. Luigi had been the lover of the person murdered. Reports always claimed the murderer would be close to the victim. No, Luigi is not a murderer. Such a lovely man. Martin sometimes showed his thought processes outside of work and their coldness frightened her.

'Luigi, please tell them everything. If you lie, they will arrest you, so please do as I say.'

'Will they suspect me?' his voice, slow and quivering showed his fright.

Andrea grasped the phone tighter, 'They will ask questions and draw conclusions. Suspicion falls on those that lie and the ones closest to her.'

'We were lovers.'

Andrea wandered towards the window and stared through unseeing eyes at her favourite view across the field to the distant hills. 'Did she plan to meet you?'

'Yes, I expected her to come to my hotel, but she had another meeting first.'

'What about? Where? Who with?'

'She didn't say,' Luigi gasped, his sorrow evident.

Andrea sighed, 'Do you want to do the show?'

'Yes, it must go ahead, I shall tell the police.' She could hear his footsteps as he paced backwards and forwards, she supposed him to be in the large entrance hall with its stone slabbed floor. 'When are you coming over?'

She didn't reply as Martin's words resonated. She didn't know better than him. 'The police investigation will take time today.'

'But not during the show, come let's talk.'

Andrea's stomach turned as a mixture of emotions engulfed her. She would have to decide.

'I need you Andrea as you are my friend and understood poor Charlotte. You are the star of my show,' his voice pleaded full of sadness, 'it's a tribute to her.'

She hesitated, 'I can't come now but I'll be over soon.'

Luigi sighed, 'Arrivederci.' He ended the call.

Andrea held the phone in her trembling hand and stared at it. Had she made the right decision? Weakness wracked her body. She closed her eyes and struggled to make sense of the murder. Charlotte's dead face sprang at her, but Martin's eyes as deep as black pools replaced it. 'Don't close your eyes,' she muttered out loud.

The mobile phone ringing once again brought her senses back. The call hadn't come from her address book but she recognised a local number. She went to press the busy button, but instinct made her answer, gripping the phone for comfort as her hand shook. As the voice came through, she moved the phone to her ear fearing the worse.

18

A man's voice, 'Mrs Cain?'

'Yes,' she'd guessed the caller. The clipped, precise tone of his voice singled him out.

'This is Gerald Manning.'

'Colonel Manning, please accept my condolences.' But her mind jumped back to the call she'd overheard between Charlotte and her father during which he'd called her a whore. A temper outburst or did he think so lowly of her? Did he regret those words now? Would it have been his last call with her? Whatever their differences, the last contact would eat away at him. Andrea hoped they'd reconciled their differences later but sensed a further conversation would have been unlikely. Would he keep rerunning that last phone call through a never-ending loop? No matter how many times he replayed it his aggression would always be paramount. A never-ending trauma for the man.

'Mrs Cain, I will be brief,' his cool authoritative voice seemed to vibrate, 'you will be shocked at the terrible event.'

'Yes, Colonel Manning, it's difficult to comprehend.'

'I want you to help my family.'

Every nerve in her body shuddered at his words. Andrea didn't want to go near the Colonel as his aggression towards Charlotte unnerved her. Why ask for her help? He didn't approve of her role as a fashion model as it was too close to Charlotte's world.

Andrea had been Charlotte's friend, she remembered the slap across the face from her sister and the look of disdain from her brother, the Priest. Andrea assumed priests would be kind and forgiving but it hadn't been evident during the meeting between them. Charlotte had been on her own as her family had disapproved of her chosen career. Her father must have given her a constant barrage about her success. He'd disapproved and wanted to control her life. Poor Charlotte. No, she didn't want to help them.

'Mrs Cain?' his voice broke through her thoughts, 'are you still there?'

'How did you get this number?' she blurted out.

'I rang Mr Luigi and explained, so he obliged.'

Luigi should have consulted her first, but the damage had been done and couldn't be reversed.

'What help do you want?' Her voice sounded strained and her body turned rigid with tension.

'We wish you to advise us.' His formal tone irritated Andrea. Why be so calm?

'Advise?'

'Dealing with the press and the police. As you are from Charlotte's world, you will be familiar with reporters.'

'I cannot help in that respect. While I am in the media spotlight, others handle the press and I know nothing of police methods as my husband must maintain confidentiality.' Delivering her words in a flat and condescending tone she sighed loudly to highlight her unwillingness. Slumping on the edge of the bed, her whole body ached, and her head throbbed, why can't he leave me alone? 'So, I can't help.'

'You sound reluctant to even hear our views and difficulties.'

'Colonel Manning, you expressed your dissatisfaction with Charlotte's lifestyle and indirectly criticised me. Charlotte confided in me that she had a poor and unsupported relationship with her brother and sister, you and your family took every opportunity to criticise her.'

Gerald fell silent. Had she said too much? She considered herself a caring and friendly woman. That description did not fit with her current attitude. What had changed? Closing her eyes in frustration, Charlotte's face appeared, her dead face, but she wanted to remember the vibrant, alive person. With a shake of her head, she forced the image away. What would Charlotte expect? Charlotte, tell me! Please, please, she screamed silently in her mind.

Gerald stuttered. Andrea waited. 'Mrs Cain, I'm a proud man, you would use the words pompous and high-handed. That aside, I am conscious of my failings as a father.' The stuttering came again. Andrea grimaced as the poor man sought to control his emotions.

'Forgive me,' Andrea muttered as she shouldn't have been so brusque.

A period of silence ensued, 'If I may continue, my daughter has been murdered and I wish to lay her to rest with the knowledge that justice has been done. That is the priority. Second, I must address what a bad father I've been. I suspect that will never be laid to rest and will torment me for the rest of my life.'

Colonel Manning's words sliced through her and a single tear escaped and trickled across her cheek, 'I am so sorry.' Her negative thoughts about this man appeared callous as he did care. It's such a pity Charlotte never realised. Why had they never managed to communicate? Charlotte's fault or the Colonel's?

'Mrs Cain, if you think helping me would compromise the case then please refuse me.' Martin's words and eyes loomed at her and he would be angry. 'You risked serious personal injury in descending the slope to the car and I want to thank you for attempting to save my daughter's life. You may fear for yourself and I will not add to that burden.' Andrea gulped. 'I am a failed father who is trying to make amends in death.' She gripped the phone as tears slid unchecked down her cheeks. 'I can only hope the Lord has mercy on me. I am desperate, so may I beg for your help?'

Andrea sucked in a deep breath, 'Where do you live?'

19

Gerald Manning's ashen face, as he opened his front door, made Andrea gasp. Her eyes concentrated on his crooked tie. He had been suffering, but he didn't speak and turned his back to walk through the hallway, his shoulders slumped. The upright and precise man she'd met before had disappeared. Even though she didn't like him, as she could not forgive his bullying attitude towards Charlotte, she sympathised with him.

Andrea stepped into the oak-panelled entrance hall of the spacious house in Ashford-in-the-Water, her heels making no noise on the deep pile cream carpet. The grandfather clock chimed the quarter hour as she followed Gerald. The house silent apart from its rhythmic ticking. Pausing at the wide oak door at the end of the hall, his shoulders rose and with a deep sighing breath, 'Come into the lounge.'

The sight of her had caused his emotion to well up but he would never admit to it.

Walking to the centre of the room, he turned, pursed his lips as though to speak but remained silent and looked at his feet. Traditional battle pictures on the walls took pride of place in the room, with its neutral colours of brown and cream. It appeared an antique gallery rather than a home, stiff and formal. Large dark furniture was adorned with a selection of military related ornaments and paraphernalia. On the bookcase war stories and armed forces' biographies dominated.

Every object in the room occupied its designated space, precisely in its right position. A television in the corner and newspapers in a magazine rack gave the only manifestation of a home. A rapid movement took her by surprise as a man in the wing-backed chair stood up and offered his hand, giving her a feeble, damp handshake, 'Edward Stonehouse.'

'Andrea Cain.'

Gerald looked up at Andrea, 'I'm sure Charlotte mentioned Edward.'

Glancing between their faces, he expected 'yes'. Edward smiled at her but not one she appreciated as he leered at her through narrowed eyes making her skin crawl. Andrea chose the easy option, 'Of course, Edward.' The lie slipped out as easy as putting one foot in front of the other. Edward nodded and a thin edged smile appeared on his lips. 'Please accept my condolences.'

A tinge of colour spread across his face, then he broke eye contact and stared at the carpet. With a soft audible sigh, he lowered himself back into the armchair. He's nervous, is it grief or is he hiding something? She pushed the negative thoughts aside, I shouldn't judge, I've unnerved him.

Gerald gave an anxious cough as if preparing to make an announcement, 'We had pencilled in Edward and Charlotte's marriage next year.'

Andrea's head screamed, What! She couldn't believe

what she'd heard. To cover her astonishment, she delayed her reply by opening her bag and putting a tissue to her eyes. 'So tragic.' Her words sounded inappropriate and meaningless but neither Gerald nor Edward took notice.

Charlotte had never mentioned Edward or marriage next year, so she studied the man hunched in the chair, his long pale face, receding brown hair and shadowed sunken eyes didn't combine to make him a handsome man. Had Charlotte found him attractive? Had she loved him? She wanted them to talk, to explain the details of the relationship, 'How long had you known Charlotte?'

'About a year.' Edward lifted his head and stared. 'We bumped into each other in Sheffield, I nearly knocked her over. I bought her a cup of coffee and fell in love at first sight.'

Andrea didn't want the focus to return to her as she wanted Edward to talk. Nothing seemed authentic. When you're in love, you can't keep quiet about it even if you wanted to. Charlotte always talked about men. 'We saw different sides of Charlotte.' Even to her own ears her words sounded bland and evasive. Gerald didn't react and stared through the French Doors down the garden. 'If it's not too distressing, tell me about her.'

Without being asked, she perched herself on the armchair opposite as it gave her time to weigh up Edward. Unlike Gerald, Edward showed no signs of emotion, his composed face gave no hint of suffering.

'We were deeply in love.' Wiping his hands on the side of his trousers, he glanced at Gerald's back, 'Charlotte had a great devotion to her singing career. I felt torn as I didn't want her to be on the stage in front of everyone but performing made her happy.' He wrung his hands and sweated despite the coolness of the room. 'I suggested a compromise, she should finish this round of success, and then we would marry and have a family. Many singing stars have done similar things.'

'What did she say?'

Gerald turned from his gaze of the garden and joined the conversation. 'Edward has been excellent with Charlotte, he made progress with her by encouraging her to consider a peaceful life and I hoped they would marry, it would have stopped her being on the stage and singing.'

Why were they so against Charlotte's success? She enjoyed entertaining and buzzed before and after being on stage. A glaze came over Gerald's eyes as he stared down at the brown patterned carpet.

Edward stood up and stared with hypnotic intensity at Andrea's breasts. Men looked away when she faced them. Edward didn't, she shivered at his presence. Although she'd only just met this man, she resented him as he made her skin crawl. Unable to take the leering, she slipped out of the armchair and joined Gerald who faced the garden with closed eyes. She wouldn't close hers because of the images that would erupt into her mind.

Gerald turned and grabbed the top of her arm, his strong fingers squeezed hard and it hurt. His abrupt movement had taken her by surprise, 'Please help me,' his wide pleading eyes bored into her and his face much too close for comfort.

'Colonel, that hurts.' She flinched and tried to move away.

'Call me Gerald. Can I call you Andrea?' He had a vice-like grip on the top of her arm with the pressure increasing.

'Yes,' she gasped as pain shot down her arm, 'but your hand is hurting me.' She struggled to pull away, but the movement caused his fingers to dig further into her flesh. The agony spread across her face. She would have a bruise which would need disguising with makeup as her show dresses were sleeveless. Finally, he dropped his hand, but a puzzled expression crossed his face with his eyes fixed and brow creased. He blinked and refocused, 'I am sorry, I've creased your blouse.'

Before Andrea could speak, he stroked his hands over the creases and his fingers ran down the side of her breast. She turned away as she hadn't expected him to put his hand there, he deserves to have his face slapped. Edward stood behind her and she had to step to one side to avoid him. Both men gave her the creeps, she shivered with distaste and wanted to leave them behind. Before she could will herself to leave Gerald's house, Charlotte's image forced itself into her mind.

Andrea stood in the middle of the room struggling to regain her composure, losing her temper would not help. Taking steadying breaths, she moved to examine one of the battle scenes on the wall, *The Charge of the Light Brigade*. It held no interest for her but gave her time to calm herself to deal with the two obnoxious men.

20

Gerald's voice broke into her thoughts, 'Come with me,' he ordered as he strode across the room. 'Stay here, Edward,' he barked out the command and didn't wait for a reply. Edward nodded his agreement to Gerald's departing back.

Her muscles tensed as she followed several paces behind Gerald who marched along the hall and turned with military precision up the stairs. Without looking back, he stomped up the steps, his back ramrod straight and shoulders back. Andrea gulped, she hesitated as her foot hovered over the first step. What awaited her at the top of the stairs?

She longed to return to the safety of her home. Why had she come? Grabbing the handrail for support she forced herself upwards, but she shivered, and her legs weakened. By the time she reached the landing Gerald had his hand poised on a bedroom door. He stood motionless, silent and waiting.

With a pounding heart she walked with small reluctant steps towards him. He hadn't opened the door, she joined him, but received no recognition, although he must have been aware of her presence. Staring at the white panelled door, it held no clues. What would happen in the room? Unease clogged her throat and her breath stilled. Every nerve in her body tensed as though on high alert. Before today nothing would have happened, but does a distraught Gerald know what he's doing? People behave out of character following a sudden bereavement. The creaking of the handle forced her to focus on Gerald's back, he trembled as the door opened with a slow precise movement.

As the door swung back, a young girl's pink bedroom came into view. Gerald left the door wide open as he strode in. His shoulders slumped. A large pink fluffy elephant, complete with a white spotted bow tie, dominated the bed. Andrea hesitated. Trepidation swirled through her. Had he come here for something specific? Who did this room belong to?

Andrea couldn't remember whether Charlotte had nieces. A few items could belong to a teenager but the contents favoured a seven or eight-year-old girl. 'Charlotte's room,' his voice flat, he stood in the middle of the pink carpet as though rooted to the spot.

'Charlotte's?' Andrea's voice came out as a high-pitched squeak and she shivered. This is morbid. Why had Charlotte's room remained unchanged? It can't have been touched for twenty years apart from cleaning. As her eyes moved around the room in a whirl of confusion, she tried to organise the chaos of her thoughts. Everything is so pink. The pink bedspread, the dolls with pink dresses even the teddy bear sported a bright pink ribbon. Why has he brought me here? What is he doing? What's happening?

'Charlotte's mother would have been proud.' Gerald

waved his arm on a sweep and then dropped on to the bed with a sigh and stroked the pink elephant. Andrea wanted to leave as she doubted Gerald's sanity. Why had he kept the room unchanged? I can't cope, this house is too confusing and frightening. Martin tried to protect me from the sad world of murder, and I didn't listen to him.

'Charlotte never mentioned her mother.' Andrea frowned with confusion. A jigsaw puzzle with pieces missing. 'Olivia died in childbirth with Charlotte. We looked forward to our new daughter. Complications set in and the doctors couldn't save her.' His eyes closed and his faced contorted to stop his emotions.

Andrea turned her back on him and looked at the dressing table as she had to give the poor man a chance to regain his dignity. He would be appalled to break down in front of her, 'I loved Olivia so much, but she died bringing Charlotte into the world.' Andrea shuddered; he needs professional help. 'I tried to over compensate with Charlotte and to make her be everything her mother would have wanted.'

'I'm sure your wife would have been proud of Charlotte, such a lovely person and a wonderful friend.' How would he react?

'I've struggled to see past her stage life in recent times.'

'When did she leave home?'

'For many years I was a strong, military man and used to working with tough soldiers, not an adolescent girl.'

'Did her sister Margaret help?'

'Not after she left home.' He stopped stroking the

elephant and stood up. 'The Army asked me to work abroad. Charlotte had become a teenager and Gloria, my sister, volunteered to have Charlotte at her home.' His face turned white, he stretched out and caught Andrea's hand, but the harsh grip of earlier had gone. 'Andrea I must tell you the truth, if I am ever to reconcile myself with Charlotte, I must confide in you.'

Not knowing what to expect she took in a deep breath but remained silent.

'I failed her,' he looked at the floor and a long silence developed before he spoke again. 'The story, I have told you, is the one that my sister and I agreed. I have repeated it so many times I have believed it to be the truth, but it's lies.'

'Do you need to tell me?' She didn't want to hear the answer. What revelation would there be? She wanted to put her hands over her ears to block out the sound of his words. The pain etched across his face distorting his features, while she waited wide eyed.

'I lost my temper one evening with Charlotte and came near to hitting her. Although I stopped, the incident frightened her.' He stood up close to Andrea. Too close for comfort. His eyes looked distant as he recalled the memory and he cupped Andrea's hand. 'The next time I would have hit her,' his sigh resigned and weary, 'so I told my sister. She is a pragmatic woman who knows me well and suggested the solution. The army would always use me, so when I volunteered for overseas duties, they accepted. Charlotte went to a boarding school and then stayed at my sister's during the holidays. I didn't see her often; it became the best compromise.'

Gulping, his eyes filled with tears. After a deliberate

effort to control his emotions, he continued, 'I failed her then, as I have failed her since she has been an adult. Distressingly, I couldn't change.' His dark lashes brimmed with tears which then rolled unchecked down his cheeks. Andrea caught his other hand, realising his torment in the past would be something he could not change. 'I can't make amends for the past but I'm so desperate to do her right in death.' His sunken and pale eyes scanned her face, 'I need help in a world I don't understand. Edward is a respectable man who adored Charlotte, but he is not worldly wise, my son and daughter wouldn't understand.'

The weight of his despair pressed down on her shoulders and squeezed the air from her lungs. Tears rolled down both their cheeks as she held his hands.

Gerald looked at her through the tears, 'When she was thirteen, I didn't understand. I blustered and bullied. When she became a singer, I didn't understand and so I continued to bluster and bully.' His hands tensed, 'I don't understand now so I need help.' He drew a deep breath, 'You asked me why I have requested your help?' Pausing and closing his eyes, 'Outside the family I only know the army which is a different life. The routines and the daily predictable pattern suited me. So organised but distant from family life. I immersed myself in the military and blotted out my problems and failures. Edward, Margaret and Alexander, who is a priest, are kind and supportive but they don't understand either. You are the only friend Charlotte had. There's no one else. Please help me to help Charlotte.' His ashen face stared as he opened his eyes again, 'There is one judgement I can make about you.'

'What's that?'

'My tears and emotion will not be regarded as a sign of weakness.'

Andrea looked into his eyes, 'A sign of strength not weakness.' The doorbell rang but Andrea did not release her grip, 'I shall do my best to help you and Charlotte to become closer.'

21

She dropped his hands. 'And now, Colonel Manning, you have visitors.'

'Thank you, Andrea, it means so much to me.'

Andrea looked at him, 'Your tie, Colonel.'

He looked in the mirror and adjusted his tie. Andrea heard his steps as he strode along the landing and down the stairs. What have I let myself into? Perhaps Charlotte told me about Edward? But she shook her head. No, his name had never been mentioned. Why did I agree to come here? I don't like Gerald. Did he blame Charlotte for the death of his wife? Is that why he resented her? Taking one last look around the pink bedroom she closed the door and followed Gerald down the stairs.

As she descended a priest and a nurse stepped into the hall, Charlotte's brother and sister. No smiles of greeting and no words of comfort were exchanged. Margaret didn't kiss her father. None of them displayed emotion, no anger, no sorrow, no compassion. It was hard to believe a family could come together so soon after a tragedy and show no reaction.

'Margaret, Alexander, this is Andrea Cain,' he waved his arm in Andrea's direction, 'Charlotte's best friend.'

The blank emotionless faces of Charlotte's brother and sister stared at her. 'Please accept my sincere condolences on your loss.' Andrea's words sounded empty and formal, but she'd become too confused to have clarity of mind. Margaret nodded.

Alexander raised his hand, but no smile appeared, 'Bless you.' As they followed Gerald into the lounge, Andrea trailed behind them and yearned to go home. Gerald had his son and daughter with him plus Edward. Would her presence be intrusive? Before she had a chance to make an excuse to leave, Gerald ushered her into an armchair. Four pairs of eyes watched her every movement. Andrea had become used to being the centre of attention but for once she hankered to disappear from view.

Gerald waited for them to be seated. 'It is time for a family council,' he announced with military precision. He studied Margaret and Alexander who remained motionless perched side by side on the large sofa. Both sat up straight with their hands resting in their laps, their faces remained blank and emotionless. 'Edward, I think we agree, is part of the family.' They acknowledged Edward with a small nod of their heads, he smiled back uneasily.

'I've asked Andrea to help us in these difficult times.' She studied Margaret and Alexander. They listened to their father with intense concentration, their faces still expressionless. 'I believe her undoubted personal skills will be of great comfort to us.' The words surprised Andrea. What comfort did he expect her to offer? She'd expected the mention of similar lifestyles. 'May she join this family council?'

Andrea waited for the argument against her. Would she receive a subtle put-down or a downright dismissal? Margaret nodded towards her father, 'We accept your judgement without reservation. You make the correct decisions.' She turned her gaze, 'Welcome Andrea. Any help will be gratefully received.'

With no smile, Margaret's words didn't sound welcoming but more akin to a rehearsed speech. Alexander smiled but his eyes were empty. His dour face transformed as he nodded acceptance and he gave a gentle squeeze on his sister's hand to show agreement.

Gerald stood up and moved to a large sideboard. In a military easy pose, hands behind his back, feet shoulder width apart, his eyes scanned the room, 'I believe we have much to discuss so shall we start.'

'Shall I begin with a prayer?'

'Alexander, I am so far from God's grace at present I must redeem myself before I enter his presence and ask for forgiveness.'

Alexander pursed his lips, 'We tried in different ways to dissuade Charlotte from her chosen way of life and we prayed and hoped. To you, Edward, Margaret and myself she became the prodigal who we hoped would return. God will judge her.'

Andrea could not accept Alexander's words as pious statements as they held no ring of truth. The meeting with Charlotte that she'd witnessed remained fresh in her mind. Their aggression had been so obvious ending with the slap from Margaret. How could a priest condone such behaviour? A two-faced liar. Andrea's eyes fixed on the priest who continued, 'We believed Edward's love for Charlotte would return her to the family. Through Edward's good persuasion, Charlotte had indicated good intentions and therefore God will return her to the bosom of her family.'

'Thank you, Alexander.' Gerald nodded.

How can such exchanges in the family be lacking emotion? No one here regrets the loss of Charlotte. Not only dead but murdered. Edward could become part of the family because he showed no emotion either. He acted as though a son and brother. He fitted in, but Andrea had seen the other side of Gerald.

Either they didn't care which Andrea didn't believe, or it had become a family where emotions were not tolerated. Perhaps during their formative years, the show of emotions had been stamped out. They bottled it up. Brave or foolish? Andrea struggled to comprehend how to help them. She allowed her gaze to wander between the three men and the woman. What did they expect of her?

Apart from Gerald, did they want her to be involved with the family and its affairs? She had undertaken a task where she would be out of her depth. A worried knot formed in the pit of her stomach. Without warning the images of finding Charlotte's dead body in the car surfaced causing a shiver to rake through her body. She breathed deeply trying to calm herself and obliterate the distorted picture, she gripped the arms of the chair and hoped nobody noticed.

'There are many matters to discuss, first, we must consider the funeral.'

He glanced at Alexander, who nodded, 'I will deliver Charlotte's soul to the Lord.'

'Thank you.'

Andrea shifted in her seat, her mind focused on the problems ahead, 'Colonel?'

'Yes, Andrea.' She sensed a general appreciation she had referred to Gerald by his rank. 'May I make a suggestion?'

'Yes.'

'There are immediate matters that demand resolution before the arrangements for the funeral.' Confusion reigned on their faces, she could sense no animosity, only uncertainty. 'Charlotte had become a popular singer, fame and fortune came to her.' They needed to face facts whether they liked them or not, 'Perhaps you do not realise how much her career had developed.'

Margaret went to speak but Andrea raised her hand. 'Margaret, I'm not promoting her or trying to defend her singing career against your wishes.'

An uneasy tension filled the room. Margaret glanced at Gerald who said, 'You're leading to something Andrea. I suspect it is important.'

'She became an international star particularly popular in Italy. The Italian press will be here. You've heard of the paparazzi; it is an Italian word for a good reason. When they arrive, they will invade your privacy as they will congregate outside your house. They will have their cameras focused on every window and door.'

Gerald shuddered and his face paled, 'What do we do?'

'You might considerate it inappropriate.'

'I will listen to your advice.' Gerald moved away from the sideboard and perched himself on the edge of a chair.

'Issue family statements through your solicitor.'

'If you consider that is necessary, I will make the arrangement.'

Andrea searched their faces for a reaction, but their expressions hadn't changed. 'If financial considerations are not a problem, then I would recommend you employ a security firm to protect this wonderful house and its grounds.'

Gerald's eyebrows rose with surprise, 'Do you suspect they will try to break in?'

'No, they are too wary of the British police. But I can see your garden, and they will hop over the fence in the dark and lie under the bushes, so that when you open the curtains in the morning, they will take your picture.'

'Ghastly,' mumbled Margaret.

'There could be twenty in the garden trying to snap the picture,' Andrea emphasised, 'the picture.' They looked stunned. Silence hung in the air.

Edward recovered first. He gave her a skeptical and questioning look, 'Why is that so important?'

'The right photo associated with the death of an international celebrity can raise tens of thousands from syndicated news agencies. It's rumoured that some paparazzi can earn over £100,000 for the right shot.' The scenario she explained would be a world away from their normal lives. But it would be likely to happen and they needed to be aware.

'Right shot?' queried Gerald.

'That's the problem no one knows until they take it. It could be sadness and sorrow, but an innocent smile when you see a robin in the garden as it will give them a headline and picture.'

Margaret shivered, 'That sounds awful.'

'I understand and will arrange for private security.' Gerald moved from the chair and positioned himself in front of the door. Andrea suspected that he would have stood near the French Doors overlooking the garden, but he now peered at them from the other side of the room with a perplexed expression on his face.

'But won't the police arrest them?' asked Alexander with a frown.

'Only when they show aggression.'

'I will find any presence of the paparazzi vexing.' A flash of annoyance crossed his face. Andrea studied the priest. Why did he use Biblical language in his everyday speech? His arrogant manner infuriated her.

She took a deep breath to control her irritation before responding, 'Please ask your solicitor to arrange for a daily statement.' She searched in her large handbag, found a card, stretched across and handed it to Gerald, 'You can contact my solicitors, who will advise you on the correct procedures.' The earlier tension had been replaced with an uncertainty of what lay ahead and how they would cope.

'One last word of advice,' Andrea straightened and looked at Gerald, 'If you meet the press, convey a positive message about Charlotte but never try to answer their questions. They will bombard you, waiting for a story. One small slip on your part could have devastating results. They won't rest until they have delved into every aspect of your life and spread it across the front pages of their newspapers.' A heavy silence followed this remark. Andrea hoped they were good actors and would not reveal their true feelings about Charlotte and her career.

'Thank you, Andrea. Your advice is valued,' Gerald's voice held a note of sincerity. Andrea couldn't believe they were so naïve. Gerald clapped his hands together to refocus everyone's attention, 'I suggest we take Andrea's advice so I shall make the arrangements at once.' Gerald left to make the calls.

Edward and Alexander talked about the weather and their predictions for the week ahead. Margaret crossed the room and stared down the garden. Andrea joined her, but both became lost in their own thoughts. Margaret spoke in a whisper, 'You came to the hospital, didn't you visit the police inspector?'

'Yes, my husband is Calum's Superintendent.'

22

'Ah, the celebrity couple.' Margaret's emotionless face showed no animosity with the remark and it appeared to be a throwaway comment.

'Have you been a nurse for long?'

'Twenty years. Time flies.' She gave a satisfied smile which slipped away to be replaced by her usual bland expression.

Andrea persevered, 'I admire you for being dedicated to such a worthwhile job.'

'It's a good job, but the money is poor, so I ask father and he helps me.' Margaret shrugged, pursed her lips and wandered away from her and out of the room. Why hadn't she wanted to chat? Is this the stress of her sister's death or is she not at ease in social situations? Or perhaps she doesn't like me.

Gerald returned and joined Andrea at the window. 'Thank you for that advice, a problem I hadn't anticipated but the arrangements are in place.' She nodded her approval but remained silent, her thoughts still trying to unravel Margaret's attitude. How to cope with such unresponsive people? In the fashion world everyone wanted to talk, to air their views and be noticed.

Gerald's clipped tones broke through her thoughts, 'I believe you talked to Margaret.'

'I told her how much I admire people who are dedicated to nursing. Frequently, they are the unsung heroes.'

'Yes, I'm proud of Margaret, it is not a well-paid job, but she's never asked me for money. Somehow, she manages. Margaret and Alexander have dedicated their lives to the service of others and they make me a proud father.' His mobile phone rang, so he moved away to answer it.

Andrea's thoughts jumped back to the last two conversations. Which one is lying? Did she or didn't she ask Gerald for extra money? Did he give her extra cash but didn't choose to admit it? Why would someone lie in such a trivial conversation? Andrea returned to her chair.

Having settled herself, she rummaged in her bag for her mobile phone as she needed to check for any missed calls as it had been in silent mode since her arrival.

Only Alexander remained, his frown didn't break as Andrea sat. Having checked her phone, she leaned back in the chair. Once again, she started a conversation hoping for more success. She settled for a topic she hoped he would wish to discuss. 'Were you ordained in Sheffield?'

Alexander's eyebrows shot up in surprise as he hadn't expected her to speak. 'No, I had my ordination in Ireland.'

As he didn't elaborate, so she asked another question, 'Did you spend time there?'

'Many years.'

Another succinct answer. This would be another difficult conversation as he appeared content with silence. She would not be beaten, so she'd keep trying.

'Didn't you ever want to follow your father into the army?'

'I did.'

Andrea waited. The silence lengthened. She focused on him, as he wanted to look away and drop the conversation. He fidgeted. A muscle twitched at the corner of one of his eyes and his mouth formed a harsh grimace making it obvious he didn't want to chat. Tough. She wouldn't give up.

'I joined as a young trooper, but father accepted it when I wished to leave.' He looked away, his eyes darted around the room as though searching for a means of escape.

The shrill doorbell pierced the silence. Its tinny sound reverberated through the house. Muffled voices reached her with the sound of movement in the hall as people approached. If they had visitors, it would be a suitable opportunity to leave as she intended visiting Luigi at the Manor.

23

Gerald entered the room with a brisk walk and held open the door for the visitors. Andrea anticipated friends of the family. He announced, 'The Chief Constable.'

The Chief Constable, a short bald man, in a lounge suit, strode into the room. 'And Chief Superintendent Cain.'

She gasped and drew in a deep breath, her eyes met Martin's, a surprised expression flashed across his face followed by a dour frown. His eyes narrowed, rigid and hard. A piercing stare replaced the usual warmth in his face.

The Chief Constable shook hands with Alexander, accompanied by a whispered word, 'Father,' and then with Margaret and Edward. The three appeared at ease. Meeting dignitaries didn't worry them. Ordinary people did.

The Chief Constable smiled, 'Mrs Cain, it's good to meet you but in sad circumstances.'

She gave him a brief nod of acknowledgement and then glanced at Martin whose eyes locked on to hers. He controlled his voice, 'I'm surprised you are out, darling. You had an unpleasant experience last night, I expected you needed to rest.' A subtle reprimand for not adhering to his advice.

'A brave woman,' added the Chief Constable. 'The reports from the officers at the scene indicate you undertook great personal risk to help your friend. It is sad that it ended in tragedy. My condolences to your family, Colonel.' He received a military nod of acceptance.

'Chief Constable,' said Martin, but the strain on Martin's face showed. He had no smile and a rigid posture. Andrea wanted to see if the dark pools remained, but the room lighting prevented a clear view. She slumped back into the armchair. Weakness grabbed her legs turning them to jelly. Martin's disapproved of her presence and he would be angry.

The Chief Constable raised his eyebrows, 'You have reservations about this case because of your wife's involvement.'

'Yes, sir, but it complicates the case further if she is here.'

The Chief Constable's eyes flicked between Martin and Andrea, but he turned his full attention to Gerald, 'Colonel, I wish to ask for your help and advice. Chief Superintendent Cain is my senior detective officer and he would expect to lead the enquiry into the death of your daughter. However, his wife is a material witness in the case, and therefore he has advised me he will withdraw from any involvement.'

Martin would want to run this murder enquiry, but he would always follow regulations. She tried a small hesitant smile but received no response from her husband as he occupied the world of the policeman. It had never touched her before. But she had seen his expressions when he answered the phone. A changed person when he worked and focused on his job.

The Chief Constable looked at Andrea, 'Before we proceed further, may I ask Mrs Cain why she is here?'

'I am in the best position to answer,' Gerald stood in his usual stand easy pose by the window. 'I rang Mrs Cain and begged her to advise us. She had concerns given the trauma she suffered last night, but I am grateful she has put her own well-being to one side to assist myself and my family.'

'On what matter?' said Martin.

The Chief Constable's eyes flashed in resentment at the interruption.

'My daughter Charlotte and Mrs Cain are international celebrities. My family and I are unfamiliar with the world of fashion and music. Mrs Cain is experienced at being in the limelight and I felt sure that her expertise would be of valuable assistance to us. The "paparazzi" will pursue us, so I've asked Mrs Cain's advice how best to cope.'

'Very sensible,' said the Chief Constable and the glance at Martin told him to accept the explanation and remain silent. 'I would like your agreement to Superintendent Cain being the senior investigating officer on the case even though his wife is a witness.'

'Will it affect any chance of conviction?' Gerald stared with intense concentration. Martin went to speak but the Chief Constable raised his hand.

'That is a good question. It is my belief it will not. However, there appears only one area where a scheming barrister could compromise this plan. It concerns Mrs Cain's statement and the follow up of issues it may raise.

There is always the potential accusation that a junior officer might accept a less than thorough statement because of the status of the witness.'

'Your proposal, Chief Constable?'

'I will take Mrs Cain's statement and investigate any subsequent issues.' The surprise registered on Martin's face but no one else appeared to notice.

'Chief Constable, I'm happy to give my agreement to your request.'

'Over to you, Chief Superintendent.'

Andrea expected him to pay his condolences. His frown relaxed. Perhaps he felt better now he had everyone's support.

'Colonel,' he began with no pleasantries, 'I believe you have a gun collection?'

Alexander sat up straight and his dark eyebrows drew together in a scowl, 'Is this necessary?'

Andrea shot a frown of consternation at Martin but received no reaction.

'Yes, Mr Manning. Every avenue must be explored in a murder inquiry,' his voice blunt and abrasive.

Alexander's lip quivered with indignation as the title used to address him sank in, he shook his head and his hand rose to the crucifix around his neck.

'Calm yourself, Alexander. They are bound to ask such questions. It's not a secret. I have a gun collection, as President of the National Rifle Society, what would you expect?' He seemed to visibly grow taller as he explained his exalted position. 'Do you wish to see the licences or the guns?'

'I want to take them with me.'

'Martin!' but he ignored Andrea's interruption. His

self-importance and brusqueness embarrassed her. It revealed an aspect of his character that she had never experienced before and didn't like.

'Superintendent, I have several rifles in a secure store,' Gerald's tone remained calm and unhurried. 'Some of them are valuable, so can I request your officers transport them in their cases. It will stop any damage.'

'Of course,' said the Chief Constable as he moved to a hard chair at the side of the room, 'that's not a problem, is it Martin.'

'We'll remove them before we leave. Don't go near them or touch them,' he spat the words out through gritted teeth. Andrea felt embarrassed, but it soon changed to anger. Is this how he performed his job? Unfeeling and arrogant sprung to mind. Upsetting good families instead of finding the killer.

'Can I ask why you want them?' Margaret queried. The tension in her voice became obvious.

'Now, Margaret,' the Colonel moved his hand, in a placatory manner, 'it is a tense time, let's remain calm. Let us support the police in whatever they wish to do. They are the professionals.'

'Father?' said Martin.

'Yes, Superintendent.'

'I believe you ministered at the funeral of Luke Kennedy.'

The priest's lips quivered, he grasped his hands together as though in prayer, 'Yes, I sent the soul of Luke to the Lord.'

Once again he used an arcane method of speaking. Did he do it for effect?

'What relevance is it to this inquiry?'

Martin ignored his comment, 'How long have you known the Kennedy family?'

'A long time.'

In a smooth professional voice, he asked 'And how well do you know a Mr Wayne Smith?' Martin had Andrea's full attention, because of his superficial roadie job at the show venue. She hadn't resolved that mystery.

'He is a passing acquaintance, not a Catholic,' he pursed his lips and gazed at his clasped hands. The dismissive words and his clipped tones suggested finality.

Martin shifted his attention. 'Margaret.' Her deadpan expression never flickered. Her bony face, grey eyes and the thin mouth did not make her an attractive woman. The complete opposite to Charlotte's prettiness and vivacity.

'I've seen you on the hospital corridor where Matthew Kennedy is being treated.' Silence fell, Martin waited. Gerald shifted in his seat.

'The same corridor that treated your Inspector.'

Martin ignored the implied criticism, 'In an exemplary manner I might say.' The quick and smooth response had a ring of falseness. Andrea had never been present before when Martin interviewed. He became unnerving, like a stranger. Margaret hadn't expected a compliment, she turned red as a flush of embarrassment flared across her cheeks. She gripped the arms of the chair with long delicate fingers and her tight-lipped expression suggested that she spoiled for an argument. Martin turned from Margaret leaving her with a darkening frown on her face which suggested a dissatisfaction with the conversation.

'Mr Stonehouse?' Edward shifted in his chair; his

pale forehead beaded with sweat. 'Are you a member of the family?'

'No, Chief Superintendent.' Edward didn't mention his engagement to Charlotte and Andrea wondered about this omission. He had withheld evidence. A strange approach. Didn't he want them to find the person who murdered Charlotte. Had he loved her? His manner gave no affirmation. No one offered the information about a marriage.

Martin consulted his notes, 'Can you confirm you work at the bank where the bullion hijack took place?'

A gape of disorientated surprise appeared on Edward's face followed by a brief second of stunned silence. 'I had no connection with the raid,' Edward's tremulous voice stumbled over the words.

'Please answer the question,' came the curt response.

The colour drained from his face, his eyes wide and his jaw clenched. He struggled to recover his composure. 'Yes, I do. But Superintendent please...' Martin raised his hand, disinterest flooded across his unsmiling face.

'Chief Constable?' Gerald moved towards Edward and patted him on the shoulder.

'How is the bank raid linked to the death of Charlotte?'

'Colonel let me explain. It is not normal procedures to explain our line of questioning but with the Superintendent's agreement I will do so in this case.' Martin nodded and sat on a small chair near the door. He kept his grim face focused on the Chief Constable and didn't glance at Andrea.

Anxiety gripped Andrea as she stared at the thunderous expression which suffused his face. Where had her fun-loving husband disappeared to? She anticipated he would have harsh words with her later. The fact that she had disobeyed his instructions and then he had found her here with Colonel Manning would have repercussions.

'Gun crime in our constabulary area is low, so when there are two crimes within a month, we look for links. We often find innocent connections with no involvement in the crime, but it would be remiss if we did not check them out and confirm them to be irrelevant.'

Gerald nodded, 'Thank you, Chief Constable.'

Silence fell on the group. The Chief Constable's eyes roamed around their faces, 'Can any of you think of a grudge against the family or you, Mr Stonehouse?' With no delay they shook their heads. No one spoke but they shuffled in their seats, with eyes downcast towards their laps or the carpet. 'Please think, if a past event causes concern please let us know. It doesn't matter how small or how long ago, we can then investigate and remove it from our lines of enquiry.'

The Colonel addressed the Chief Constable, 'Can I ask you if you have any leads? And whether you are confident of catching Charlotte's killer?' Andrea heard the anguish in his voice as he mentioned Charlotte's name. Martin looked disinterested as he remained seated but stared ahead with a seriousness that she found unnerving.

'It's early days in the investigation,' the Chief Constable's voice smooth giving the impression he must be well practiced in dealing with delicate situations. 'We suspect it will be someone who knew her.'

'Could it be a maniac who has seen her on stage?'

Margaret suggested. Andrea shivered at the thought.

'Please don't speculate, it will not ease your grief. Be assured that Chief Superintendent Cain is an excellent investigating officer and will find the person who committed this heinous crime.' The last few sentences revealed the horror of the situation. They looked worried. No, Andrea corrected herself, they look frightened. Their bodies tense, they sat hunched, eyes downcast with an unnatural stillness.

'Any further matters to raise?' asked the Chief Constable, as he surveyed the people in the room.

'Sir.'

'Yes, Superintendent.'

'Colonel, I require your help concerning my wife.' Andrea smiled at him. This might be tricky, her stomach tensed in anticipation. What would he say? 'I'd requested that Andrea stayed at home, but I suspected she would not take my advice, so I have arranged for her to have protection.' Andrea glared at him from across the room, unable to shake the growing irritation that bubbled inside her.

'Superintendent?' said the Chief Constable.

'Nothing official, sir. Calum is at home and bored so he's agreed to accompany Andrea when she deems it essential to leave the safety of our house.'

'That isn't necessary,' Andrea blurted out, but Martin ignored the outburst and directed his remark to the Colonel, 'Calum is the Inspector treated by Miss Manning. The hospital has discharged him, but he's not fit to return to duty.'

The Colonel nodded, 'It seems sensible and he will be welcome in this house with Andrea.'

‘Yes, good thinking, Superintendent,’ said the Chief Constable, ‘Inspector Brodie is a first-rate officer.’

Andrea stared at Martin in disbelief.

24

'Outside!' Martin mouthed to Andrea, who trailed after him. As soon as they were outside, he swung round towards her, his face suffused with anger. 'What the hell are you doing?'

'Martin! Don't talk like that.' They stood in the open porch within the extensive front garden. In ordinary circumstances Andrea would have preferred to wander and explore.

'What do you expect when you go against me?' he spat out the words with ferocity.

She gulped at the stranger who stood before her. Trembling she shifted away from the cold fury of his dark eyes realising she'd been rash in visiting Charlotte's family. He wanted to protect her and she'd been awkward.

'Andrea, look at me.'

She wouldn't turn towards him and faced the bushes examining dew drops on a single rose and shivered at the shame of her bloody-mindedness. Why had she been so stubborn and ignored his advice, murder was his world not hers? The thought of the black pools returned, so she continued to study the beauty of the simple rosebud keeping her face averted. Anxiety overwhelmed her.

Wait until he calms. She craved the sparkling green eyes she loved.

'This isn't a bloody game you know,' he grabbed her arm spinning her around.

Andrea brought her other arm across and crashed it onto him. 'Let go!' The black pools deepened. An incredulous expression crossed his face. 'That hurt!' She leaned forward to kiss him on the cheek, but he stepped away. It took a second for Andrea to realise his rejection as it had never happened before. Martin's face, rigid with tension, distorted before her eyes. It had aged ten years since this morning. Whatever is happening? It must be her fault, so she needed to apologise and make amends.

With a calmness she didn't feel, 'I shouldn't have come, but he pleaded with me. After seeing Luigi, I'll go home,' she gave a naughty girl smile which always brought forgiveness. It didn't come out as expected and she received no reciprocating smile as sweat glistened on his brow. A shiver travelled down her spine. The pools didn't change.

'I told you to stay home so why come here?' His words stung, and he hadn't listened. Martin with a deep red face shook with fury.

Andrea trembled, 'Martin, for goodness' sake, calm down, I'm helping my friend's father, so I'll see Luigi and then travel home, I'll be sensible and careful.' She hoped her placid approach would begin the tentative reconciliation.

'What the hell are you doing here?' Andrea backed away from his piercing black stare. Nothing about this confrontation made sense, his anger had spiralled out of proportion.

She needed to appear calm even though tension gripped her stomach and her legs threatened to buckle. 'Martin, stop repeating yourself, I'm sorry about the interviews but I'll keep out of the way.'

'I told you!' he wagged a single finger in front of her face.

'Martin! Charlotte had become a good friend; I want to help her family.'

'One of them is probably the killer.' A cruel sneer formed on his smooth face as he leaned forward. His words terrified her, but she wouldn't give ground. Did he want a reaction, or did he honestly think a member of the family had killed her?

'Don't be so ridiculous!' she attempted with a small light-hearted laugh, 'a planned murder of the daughter, fiancée or sister from this family who are pillars of society.'

The dark pools sparkled, standing motionless, his eyes narrowed, 'Was Edward her fiancée?' His voice had lost its ferocity and sounded calmer.

'Yes, they planned to marry next year.' Did she believe it? Charlotte had never mentioned a fiancé. Had she said it with conviction? Martin digested the information. 'Why do you ask? Didn't you know?' she hoped the conversation could return to normal.

He ignored the question caught hold of her arm, but it didn't hurt, 'A police traffic car will take you home.'

'I want to see Luigi, and then I'll go home but I don't need a police car.'

'Andrea,' his grip tightened and his strong fingers dug into her flesh. 'Don't you realise the danger?' He released her arm and put both hands on her shoulders.

'Someone killed your friend,' his words slow and deliberate as though emphasising their importance, 'it's not a bloody made up fact and it's likely to be someone she knew. There's a good chance you will know the murderer.'

The words shocked her, she wanted to ignore the violent world of crime and murder. 'But Martin, I will be sensible.'

Tutting his disapproval, 'You don't know what that means.'

'Martin!'

'It's not a case of checking whether someone is creeping up behind you. That only happens in amateurish crime novels. In the real world, killers are devious.' She'd been stupid and looked at him in bewilderment, hands outstretched palms facing upwards.

'What should I do?'

'Go home, traffic can take you. They will check the house.'

'Our house? What's that to do with Charlotte?'

'The marks…' He didn't finish the sentence and snapped his mouth shut in irritation with the realisation he shouldn't have let it slip.

Marksman. She hadn't realised. The shooting had terrified her, but assumed Charlotte met the person Luigi mentioned. The murderer had been welcomed into her car then shot her before pushing the Porsche down the bank. Her mind swarmed with unanswered questions. But a marksman, her heart thumped and a paralysing fear coursed through her body and she understood why Martin had become worried. With an effort she recovered her composure, 'I'll ring Luigi and arrange to meet somewhere different. No one will know.'

Martin gave a loud and dramatic sigh. Andrea moved towards him as though to kiss him, but he backed away again. Gulping back the tears which threatened she stared at his anguished expression. He's suffering and I'm adding to his agony.

Andrea took a deep shuddering breath, 'I'll go with the traffic car if I can see Luigi for a short time.'

'They're not a bloody taxi service,' his voice low and harsh as he stepped towards her. The menacing look made her flinch.

'Martin, what's happened to you?'

Ignoring her, 'You are persisting in being bloody stupid that's why I'll put someone decent with you, not the traffic police.'

'I don't like Calum,' she pouted, 'and more importantly he doesn't like me.'

'I'm not interested in who likes who, you'll have bloody protection, it's Calum.'

'I don't need protection!' she took a deep breath to control her urge to scream and shout at him, why wouldn't he listen? 'After the meeting with Luigi, I will go home,' she stamped her foot in frustration. Then the realisation hit her like a blast of loud music screaming through her head, he thinks Luigi might be the murderer. No, a voice inside her head shrieked. 'I trust my instinct Martin; Luigi is not the murderer.'

Ignoring her words, he carried on as though she hadn't spoken. 'Calum will be with you wherever you go. Do whatever he says, don't argue.' She didn't want to be ordered around but her protest had to end. I must help him, so I'll agree. Calum will soon become tired of nursemaiding me. Martin intended continuing his tirade, but the Chief Constable emerged from the front door.

'Good work Andrea, you should be proud of her, Martin, a brave woman who has impressed the Colonel which is not an easy task.' Andrea gave a weak smile. Martin added a grunt of acknowledgement. The Chief Constable continued, 'I don't think there will be any danger Andrea, but it's sensible that Martin has arranged for Calum. Anything out of the ordinary, let me know, and we'll make the protection official.' The Chief Constable's face developed a frown as though remembering something that didn't please him. 'Martin, I want a quick word concerning the interviews before we go back.'

'Yes, sir.'

The Chief Constable noted the press milling around the front gate, he barked at the policeman standing nearby, 'Get the reporters away from the house.' The constable looked confused. 'Get back-up, both ends cordoned off.'

'Yes, sir,' but the constable looked alarmed at receiving direct orders from the Chief Constable.

Martin stepped forward and kissed Andrea on the cheek before following the Chief Constable along the road. The kiss stopped Andrea from walking to the gate. Strangely foreign. What had been different about it? She couldn't tell, but it didn't seem right. Like the kiss of a stranger, she shivered at her fanciful imagination.

The policeman did his best to move the reporters away, but they ignored him as Andrea approached the gate.

'Andrea, give us a statement! What's happened in

the house? Why are you here?'

Normally, she revelled in press conferences absorbing their praise and enjoying the limelight. This would be different and tedious.

'Come on Andrea,' they cajoled, 'give us your view? Why are you here?'

A plan formed in her mind and she could help the solitary policeman. 'Hi Guys. Let's walk along the street, you want to help the police do their job don't you?' The reporters didn't want to leave their spot, but she would speak to them. 'Come on,' she waved her arm in encouragement, 'let's do the interview at the end of the street.' They followed her in a straggling group lugging their cameras and recording equipment.

'Thank you, ma'am,' said the policeman.

Andrea scanned the group as she stood on a patch of grass at the end of the road but didn't recognise any faces. Why isn't Fitzwilliam here? What story had he been searching when he pretended to be a roadie? Something unpleasant, his usual style. Andrea took a deep breath and faced the reporters, 'Charlotte, not only a wonderful person, but a close friend. I've come to pay my respects to her father and family. Such a tragic loss after her amazing success in Italy. 'Era una persona meravigliosa che era una grande cantante ed è una tragica perdita di una vita di talento. One journalist said, 'What did she say?'

Another asked, 'Did you find the body?'

'No questions concerning the police case, I'll talk about Charlotte but not the police.'

25

An old battered Fiesta with a honking horn drove at the journalists and they scattered, swearing and cursing. The car screeched to a halt in front of Andrea. Calum stepped out. 'Piss off. All of you.' They sneered at him, but he flashed his warrant card, 'Now disappear before I nick you for obstructing the Queen's highway.' The press went mumbling along the street.

Andrea looked with disgust, his brown hair dishevelled, he needed a shave, such a vile man, who rubbed her up the wrong way. Arrogant and abrupt to the point of rudeness. 'We meet again. Did Maria give you a good tour of the fashion backstage?' She raised her eyebrow.

Calum gave a short grin, but it disappeared in a flash, 'Yeah, okay.' They strode towards Gerald's house. Calum winced as he walked.

'If your leg still hurts, should you be here?' Andrea's words lacked concern, but she didn't want to spend time in his company.

'I'll make do,' came the grunted reply.

'Why have you come, you are on sick leave?'

'To look after you.'

'But I don't need looking after.'

'That's not what I've heard.'

'Well, you have been misled, as I don't need your time, I've promised Martin I'll be careful.'

Calum stopped walking and Andrea expected him to complain about his injured leg. 'I guessed you'd be awkward, you don't like me, do you?' He gave her a searching gaze from his deep-set eyes.

'That's nothing to do with it.' Andrea squirmed with embarrassment, had she been that obvious?

'So, you admit you don't like me?'

'Don't be so ridiculous, I hardly know you and I've ignored the fact you have been rude ever since we met.' Standing in the middle of the road he eyed her with disdain. Did he resent her? Perhaps he didn't like successful people so had said nothing complimentary. Men she met would offer praise, but not Calum, 'I hope your convalescence is progressing well so you will be able to return to work. Thanks for the offer of help but I will see Luigi and then I'm going home.'

'No.'

'What do you mean, no?' she stopped and faced him again.

'Martin asked me to help you.'

'I don't need help.'

'You are a stubborn and pompous cow.'

'I'm not pompous.'

Calum gave the briefest of smirks, but it broke the tone of the conversation.

'Andrea, someone has murdered your friend. There's a killer of a successful, good-looking woman who acts like a normal member of society, and you want to carry on ignoring the murder.' Andrea stayed silent; his words caused a frisson of fear to race through her body. 'I'm looking forward to a period off work, hobbling around and getting drunk so I don't want to get involved in a marital crisis especially between my boss and his wife.'

'There, you need not stay, you've convinced yourself.'

His face changed from his standard growl to a genuine look of concern. 'But there is a more important issue.'

'What's that?'

'The next call I receive in the middle of the night.'

'What does that mean?'

'When I am called out to a dead body, my boss can't investigate the case because they have killed his wife.' He delivered the sentence with the dead pan monotony of a policeman speaking in court. Andrea shivered. 'That's why I'm not giving up until we understand the motivation for the killing. So here I am.'

Andrea wouldn't be intimidated. With her car parked nearby, could she jump in and roar away leaving Calum behind? Martin beckoned Calum who limped away without another word. Andrea looked towards the house, Gerald stood in the window and stared out to the front garden. The burden of his last call with Charlotte would lay heavy. A conversation he would regret for the rest of his life with no respite. The memory would dim with time, but it would keep eating away at him. Andrea's mind drifted to Charlotte. Did Charlotte have a dark side? It could be possible. What could it be?

Sex? No, Charlotte liked men and enjoyed sex, but no dark side. Not sex. Drugs? The downfall of many of the famous. But Charlotte had been bubbly. She'd seen many models and designers on drugs, but there had been no hint with Charlotte. Perhaps she didn't have a bad side. Andrea shivered.

All these thoughts and unanswered questions kept bringing Charlotte's death much closer. The realisation that she must listen to Martin and Calum hit her as they wanted to protect her, but it would mean restrictions. Gerald still hadn't moved from the window. His grief apparent in the slumped and still posture. I will help him. Her eyes flashed around the nearby groups. The journalists had withdrawn behind a cordon. In the opposite direction, the Chief Constable, Martin and Calum, stood in deep conversation. She looked at the house of the Manning family and her eyes changed to a bright sparkle. What if she could help these groups? I know the world of Charlotte and I can assist them and in the process get back my husband.

Andrea repeated the words in a quiet whisper, 'and get back my husband.' Martin had become a stranger, unpredictable and intense also full of anger and not the man she loved. The repetition of the words, 'I must get my husband back,' gave no comfort. No one watched her as they were embroiled with their own problems. Her mind whirled and possibilities came to the fore, she needed a way to help that didn't appear obvious, otherwise Martin and Calum would stop her. No one in the fashion world would talk to them, but they would to Andrea. A plan formed in her mind, whether they wanted it or not, she would help.

Watching Martin increased her anxiety as his body language wasn't right, he's agitated. Normally he's still, steady as a rock, but he's shifting from foot to foot.

What's he thinking? We've a brilliant marriage, I love him and he loves me. Time to forget about herself, now it's for Martin. With a roll of her shoulders she straightened herself to her full height. An acute sense of purpose drove the negative thoughts from her mind. She took out a tissue and wiped the unshed tears from her eyes.

The constable who she'd helped earlier, came up to her, 'Are you all right, ma'am? Shall I get the Superintendent?'

'I'm fine, thank you officer, dust in my eye, please don't disturb him.' The policeman wandered away. The group broke up and the Chief Constable strode towards his car. Andrea had a glance at the journalists and an idea sprung to her mind.

'Could you give us a statement, Chief Constable?' they shouted from behind the cordon. He glanced at them but approached his car without responding.

'Chief Constable?'

'Yes, Andrea.'

'The BBC have arrived, it's Sebastien Ferriday, their lead on crime.'

'Central will issue a statement later.'

'Do you want an early appeal for witnesses as it would catch the midday news, even in Italy where Charlotte had become famous. Could her murder be linked to her Italian success?'

He frowned at her as he thought. This will not work as he'll think I'm interfering. 'I could help if you wanted me to ask as a friend of Charlotte.'

He hesitated, but approached her, 'Good thinking, it's what we need. Shall we go?'

They walked side by side towards the journalists. Most looked surprised, Sebastien Ferriday looked astounded as he would get a scoop which would be worldwide within the hour and it had been laid on a plate. It only took a few minutes. The journalists were more than happy as Andrea and the Chief Constable stood side by side appealing over the death of an international star. Calum stood behind them as they finished.

The Chief Constable said, 'Thanks Andrea, very professional.' He returned to his car, Martin waved, but perfunctorily.

'Good,' said Calum. A compliment that Andrea hadn't expected, but his normal frown returned. 'Martin is adamant. But you know that.'

'What about you?' Andrea waited for a reaction.

'I'll do my best to make sure you're not the next midnight call.'

'I'm convinced it's unnecessary.'

'Let's not go through that again, I'm here and staying.'

'You know I'm helping Charlotte's family, at Gerald's request.'

'He's the Colonel, isn't he?'

'Yes.'

'I don't think it's a good idea to get involved with them.'

'The Chief Constable thinks differently.'

Calum grunted. 'Chief Constables say things like that.'

'But you disagree.'

'Yes, I do.'

'Why?' Calum hesitated. 'Martin has suggested it

could be someone from the family.'

'Yes, that's the main reason. But you should reduce your contacts until we move further into the inquiry, not increase them.'

'So, are you going to stop me seeing the family?' She'd made her words confrontational as she did not intend to be bossed around.

Calum moved uneasily, 'That's not what I said,' he growled.

She didn't want to lose the initiative but Martin and Calum would solve the case, it wouldn't be the Chief Constable or her. She wanted Martin to hug her, feel his arms wrapped around her and to be loved and protected. A shiver crept down her spine as the loneliness surrounded her, not the physical distance but the emotional distance from Martin. Andrea glanced at Calum's face. He found bullying easy, but with the Chief Constable involved, he would bite his tongue. Fixing Calum with a sharp look, 'You wanted to speak?'

'Why are you such a bloody pain in the arse?'

Andrea smiled, 'Calum Brodie, I will take no notice of your rudeness and abuse. No notice.' He scowled. 'We will visit Luigi.'

'I wouldn't advise it.'

'Your abuse I shall ignore. I shall listen to your safety advice and there will be no objection to you being nearby.'

'Now, look here I'm not…'

'There are rules about coming with me.' Aware of the need to rally herself and organise her thoughts she intended being confident. Her words would rile Calum, but she wouldn't be dominated.

'And what are they and why…'

'I don't know what they are yet,' she gave a flippant wave of her hand. 'I'll make them up as I go along.'

'You can't…' The surprise registered on his face. Andrea used the opportunity to throw him the keys to Martin's Jaguar. 'You drive.'

'What about my car?'

'Do you want to keep up with a 3.0 litre Jaguar in your clapped out Fiesta?'

'You drive,' he snapped, trying to give her back the keys.

'It's automatic so it won't hurt your leg, refusing to take her keys back. Andrea slipped into the passenger seat. 'You can tell me about the case as we travel.'

'Absolutely nothing,' he said buckling the seat belt.

'Do you know the way?'

She received a grunted, 'Yes.'

Andrea reclined the seat. 'The Manning family are the bastions of society; they have a hero for a father plus a priest and a nurse.'

'Bastions fall.'

They drove past Monsal Head. Andrea peered at the viaduct. 'Tell me about the armed robbery.'

'No.'

'Not the police case, the press information will do.'

'No.'

'I'd prefer your version.' Guilt hit her. 'Sorry.'

He glanced but had to brake hard because of a sheep in the road. 'Why are you sorry?'

'You were shot in the robbery so it might be too painful for you to discuss.'

'It's not that.'

'Are you sure?'

'Yes I am.'

'Well what is it then?'

'I'm not talking to you about any of the cases.'

'I'd prefer your version.'

'So, you keep saying. The answer's no.'

'Are you going to tell me?'

'No.'

26

'Hi Tracey, it's Andrea. Please put me through to a friendly press office?' she switched her phone to the ear away from Calum and gazed at the rolling green fields and dry-stone walls of the undulating countryside as they crossed Tideswell Moor in the warm light from a cloudy sky.

Calum glared. Andrea waited for someone to answer the phone. 'Hi, Damien, Andrea Cain.' She listened. 'Yes, I'll give a quote.' The scowl increased on Calum's face. 'Yes, I'm persuaded to help you with a story about Charlotte.'

'Not a good idea.'

Andrea frowned at Calum but didn't comment and continued with her phone conversation. 'But I need a big favour first.' The car stopped at the traffic lights in the narrow high street of Bradwell. 'An armed robbery took place in Sheffield followed by a shooting.' A short reply from the other end. 'Good, you know about it. Can you send the relevant cuttings to my mobile? Brilliant, you're a star and we'll speak later about Charlotte.' Andrea ended the phone conversation with an assured smile.

Calum muttered, 'You can't believe everything you

read in the press.'

'Don't you think I know that? I'm a model, fact and fiction in the press get mixed up which is why I asked for your version.' The telling beeps of the mobile phone echoed in the car as the press cuttings arrived.

He grimaced and without enthusiasm said, 'Only a brief version.'

'That will work out fine; I'll turn off my phone.'

'Four raiders held up bank staff with guns, an armed unit had been nearby and they trapped the robbers. Martin and I arrived and drew arms from a second police car. The Kennedy twins were shot, one died and the other was badly injured. The main suspects for the other two robbers were the older Kennedy brothers, but they escaped.'

What would drive four brothers to commit armed robbery? Would money be the real motive? 'The Kennedy family have a car hire business, don't they?' Calum didn't answer but succumbed as Andrea with a theatrical flourish picked up her phone.

'Yes, in Malin Bridge on the outskirts of Sheffield.'

'Is it a successful business?'

'The cars gleam and the company is busy.'

'What about the Kennedy family?'

'That's the last question,' and he fell silent.

'Can I have the last answer then?'

'There is no father, just a mother and four sons.'

Her head ached, so she leaned against the headrest and closed her eyes. Charlotte's distorted face appeared again. A cold chill passed through her body forcing her eyes open. The countryside rolled by as they wound their way through the twisting roads of Hope Valley. Calum lapsed into silence and continued to frown as he didn't indulge in idle chit chat. As he slowed for a sharp bend Andrea broke the silence. 'Why hasn't Martin been taken off this case?'

'The Chief Constable doesn't have many options for a high-profile investigation and would struggle to get a replacement from another force.'

'Is the reason that simple?'

'Yes,' Calum nodded but kept his gaze fixed on the road ahead, 'A murder enquiry requires early momentum. The Chief Constable will lead but he'll want Martin as he's the best detective in the division.'

Andrea tried to keep the conversation alive. 'Are you keen to return to work?'

'No, I'd be in charge of the monotonous incident room.' Unusually Calum spoke in a conversational voice. 'Were you with Charlotte yesterday after I left the Strines Manor?' asked Calum.

'Yes, we chatted several times.'

'Did you see anything suspicious?'

'Only the same as you, Wayne Smith and Fitzwilliam acting as roadies.'

'It needs following up but doesn't appear important,' came the bland reply. 'Anything else?'

Andrea thought about Charlotte's phone call to her father and Fitzwilliam sneaking around in the trees. He had a poor reputation even among the gutter press, but she kept both snippets of information to herself.

'No, just a normal day.' But would it be different when the Chief Constable interviewed her? Would she tell him? Andrea hadn't decided. They crossed Strines Moor and approached the Strines pub. She braced herself as a rolling sensation hit the pit of her stomach. Last night in the next valley she'd found Charlotte.

Calum swung the car around the bend and into the valley. The sun shone lighting the various hues of the green trees. A complete contrast to the previous night's blackness. Her stomach churned. Attempting to keep the fear under control she focused on the beauty of the wooded valley. A tranquil summer valley, with a river bubbling away, which had moderated from the overnight torrents. Crossing the bridge with the damaged parapet and passing the hole in the fence did not reveal the drama of last night.

Despite the attempt at distraction Andrea's mind went into overdrive as the frightening images replayed themselves with clarity, her stomach twisted and she expected a few words of reassurance from Calum but nothing came. He's heartless. Using her hair as a shield she gazed downward hoping he wouldn't notice the tears that spilled from her eyes.

The car lurched as he accelerated up the hill and he grabbed his painful leg but ignored it and drove over the moors until he pulled into the car park at the front of the Manor.

Andrea jumped out as soon as the car came to a halt. 'I'm not leaving, but I need space.' Calum ignored her comments and followed, staying with her as she passed through the hall. She had a flashback to the security guard and his guttural laughter. 'Have you interviewed the security guard? He watched everyone last night.'

'I expect so,' but something registered with him, 'I'll check. What firm?'

'I didn't notice, but a grey uniform with gold edging.

A tall gaunt man about six foot six with decaying teeth and ghastly breath.'

A ghost of a smile appeared, 'He should stand out.' Calum showed no signs of leaving her side.

She opened the door of the same room where she'd met Charlotte and Luigi together and sadness enveloped her. 'Look there's no one in here.' He peered into the room. 'I must make a phone call in private.'

27

She closed the door and sat at a small table near the bookshelves and rang Martin's mobile, but the call went to voice mail. 'Hi darling, I'm worried, I promise to stay out of the case, as it puts you in a difficult position. I'm a stubborn cow but I'm getting on well with Calum who is being helpful and I'll ring the Chief Constable to let him know I will be available for an interview whenever and for as long as he wants.'

Andrea took a big breath, 'I had a big shock finding Charlotte's body in the car, it's thrown me, but I'm thinking rationally.' She let a few seconds of silence pass. 'Darling, we're not close and I'm losing you, so come home whenever you can, as I want to hug you. Please ring me. I love you.' With a long sigh she pressed the red button to cut the call.

She resolved to follow Calum's instructions, so he would give Martin a positive report. Life could return to normal if someone solved Charlotte's case and if Martin apprehended the other armed robbers. Excitement entered her thoughts as she could take him on the holiday of his lifetime. Martin's such a practical man, but he would love to see exotic places. What did he have on his preferred list? Inca temples, the Taj Mahal. There is another one? The statues of Easter Island. He'll say he can't get away for that long, but I'll ask the Chief Constable if he can have a secondment. Andrea eased out of her chair with an air of satisfaction at the plan.

'Life is traveling downhill for the world's super-couple.' Andrea froze. A figure rose from the wing-back chair that faced the French Doors.

'Fitzwilliam, how dare you spy on me. How long have you been there?' Crossing the room towards her, he put his finger to his lips.

'We don't want your pet policeman to find out I'm here do we, come over to the window.' Andrea hesitated. Should she call Calum as he would love to arrest Fitzwilliam? She stared at the fat man as he shuffled across to the French Doors, 'I've my story, so you'd better cooperate.'

She followed. 'What story?' Although without doubt she knew the answer. The telephone message would be enough for him to write a double page spread.

'How much did you hear?'

'Enough.' She quaked as Martin would blame her which wouldn't help to heal the rift. Calling Calum could make the matter worse as he'd hassle Fitzwilliam and might arrest him. Any action Calum took would infuriate Fitzwilliam leading to a terrible and damaging story.

'What do you want?'

'A little cooperation?'

'But you will still print the story.'

'Andrea, I like you.' She hated his sickly grin and wheedling voice. The man had no morals. 'I'll give you a favourable write up, but it will be world-wide news so think what that would mean to your future income.'

'What's the catch?' her voice edged with sharpness, but she needed to think. How could she solve this mess?

'No catch, I need background facts.'

'Such as…' She stared. His fat hand and thick fingers reached out and caught her hand. His hand felt slimy with sweat, she suppressed a shudder of revulsion. With an extreme effort of self-control, she didn't pull away.

He stood close, 'I looked at the site of the murder this morning. Rumour has it you found Charlotte's body in the Porsche which means you must have gone down the bank.' Keeping his voice low he studied her face, 'That makes you a brave lady.' His breath stank of stale cigarettes, his small eyes and heavily-jowled face grinned up at her.

'How much would it cost me to persuade you to ignore the conversation?'

He squeezed her hand and his face became twisted with a knowing smile, she found it hard but didn't pull her hand back. 'Let's not talk that way as we can both win,' his voice oozed smoothness but his eyes were as hard as flint, 'You go out to the world press as a hero who tried to save her friend and you know what that means on the publicity front.'

Fitzwilliam hadn't fooled her, 'The twist in the story?'

'I would think, something like trying to save her friend despite the personal problems of her marriage being on the rocks.'

'That's not true,' she yanked her hand away from

his sweaty grasp, how dare he suggest that. They had a minor problem that would soon be resolved.

'Keep your voice down, I've a plan,' he whispered conspiratorially.

'What?' she snapped hating every second of the conversation with this odious and devious man. 'In a month's time I'll run another story of how your husband solved the murder and you're back together again. That sounds fair.'

'No.'

He had taken control of the conversation and Andrea felt cornered, 'That's the deal, take it or leave it.'

'Otherwise…?' she tried to keep the question light while she shook with tension.

'I'll write what I choose. Perhaps I'll start with the news that the super couple are falling apart, and the reason is your involvement in the case. I'll leave it to our readers' imagination whether Martin will arrest you on suspicion of murdering Charlotte. Jealousy is a strong motive.'

Andrea couldn't believe the words and had a growing sense of events spiralling out of control, 'Why would I be jealous of her.'

'You can't sing.'

'No, I can't but…'

'You are successful but underneath you are greedy and resent your friend, who had not only good looks but an excellent singing voice.'

'Shut up, shut up,' her frustration and temper rose as he had an answer for every eventuality. Shouting at him would solve nothing and only create more antagonism.

'So, it's cooperating then.'

'Doesn't appear I've a choice,' she snarled, 'but I can't talk now.'

'That's okay but find time to chat with me. I'll be around but I want your version by the end of the day,' he gave a gratified smirk and Andrea shuddered. She remained silent while her mind came up with nasty scenarios she hoped would happen to such a low life.

'Now go back to your pet.'

28

The handle rattled, then the door flew back as Calum kicked at it. 'How long is this bloody phone call?' Calum limped across the room. Andrea glanced behind, but despite his size, Fitzwilliam had skipped out of the French Doors. Calum hadn't seen him.

'I've calls to make so you must wait,' but she trembled from the encounter with Fitzwilliam as she needed to make sure Calum didn't find out, plus she wanted to keep the upper hand with him if possible. Irritating men annoyed her.

'We'll see!'

'I'm taking no notice of your bullying, so you can be close by, but you're not listening to my conversations.'

'Come on, let's go outside,' Calum left the room and walked with a pronounced limp along the hall. Andrea thought about her commitment to Martin, but he hadn't rung back. A quick text would have done. Waiting to hear from him would be difficult. Andrea followed as Calum walked through the large hall and outside to the car park. Luigi was engaged in a deep conversation with his assistant, Pablo. Wayne Smith wearing a suit, stood in the middle of the car park talking in a loud voice, he had a different hairstyle from yesterday when he'd been acting as a roadie. Why had he and Fitzwilliam tried to disguise themselves? There had to be a reason.

A police car drew into the car park and two officers emerged, they spotted Calum and pointed in his direction. Andrea, recognised one of them as he had reached her and stopped her from sliding down the bank. Calum stared at them as they walked towards him and gave a slight shake of the head, they checked their stride then approached Andrea. Calum shrugged and walked away. Andrea tried to decide Calum's approach to the people and events taking place. His eyes had focused on Fitzwilliam who had appeared on the edge of the woods. Why creep through the woods again? Surely everyone knew Calum to be a policeman. Fitzwilliam did.

'Excuse us, ma'am, we've a message for Inspector Brodie.'

'Good to see you're well, ma'am.'

'Thanks for your efforts last night, Jeff, you were brave to come down the bank to rescue me.'

He looked pleased she had recognised his action and remembered his name. 'Thank you, ma'am.'

'Calum is tracking someone who might not know he's a policeman.' The policemen were not bothered if he didn't want to talk to them. Andrea guessed Calum would have been rude to them. 'If you need to get on with your tasks, I will give the message to Calum.'

'Thank you. Can he contact your husband?'

'I'll tell him. Did you come from Sheffield to pass on the message?'

'No, ma'am.' He went silent.

'It's okay we can tell her, she's the Super's wife,

the Chief Constable said she would be here. We need to check nothing is unusual.' Andrea glanced past them to the edge of the wood where Calum and Fitzwilliam argued. 'We need to contact Mr Luigi with a search warrant for the manor, its grounds and contents.'

'Have you a warrant?'

'Not with us but we have heard on the police radio it's been granted by the Magistrates.'

'Are you looking for anything in particular?'

'Anything that looks suspicious.' Andrea guessed Martin wanted to make sure everyone knew he had the deciding power over whether to cancel the show, it seemed in keeping with his attitude earlier.

'Come on, let's go over to Luigi,' she pointed across the car park, 'it won't be a problem.' Fright covered his face. By the time they had reached him he'd turned white and sweated. 'His English isn't good. I need to make it clear to him.' They nodded.

'Luigi, questo poliziotto vuole dare un'occhiata in giro. Offri il tuo aiuto.'

Luigi looked at Andrea, then the policemen, he shrugged and in a heavy accent said, 'Yes, if you need help please ask me.' They were relieved it had been easy. Luigi shouted, 'Pablo, Pablo, show them anywhere! Everything!' He waved his arms around in a frantic gesture, 'Whatever they want!'

Pablo led them towards the manor.

Calum came across the car park and flicked his head indicating Andrea should join him.

In an exaggerated loud voice, 'Excuse me, Luigi.' She walked to Calum, 'As rude as ever.' But he took no notice.

'What do they want?

'They asked you to ring Martin.'

'Okay.' But he didn't react. 'What else?'

'They've got a warrant to search the house and grounds.'

He ignored her. 'Fat arse knows I'm a policeman.'

'Does he?' Andrea waited for anything that would indicate he knew she'd been speaking to Fitzwilliam but nothing materialised.

'They are going to the side of the house.' Andrea pointed to the policemen.

Calum sneered, 'Don't they know that anything of interest will be in the house not the bloody garden?' He set off in their direction.

'Sorry, Jeff,' but she wanted to get rid of Calum so she could talk to Luigi, who scurried over to her as soon as Calum walked away.

'I must speak to you, I must!' His arms waved dramatically.

'Let's go over there.' Andrea indicated the large open grass lawn where no one could sneak up on them to overhear their conversation. 'You must speak to the police, Luigi.'

'I can't, I can't tell them. My wife will find out.' His agitation continued with his flapping arms and the pallor of his face. Andrea had no sympathy for him as he should have considered the consequences before indulging in an affair. 'I will go back to Italy,' his voice rose as panic gripped him.

'I'm warning you, Luigi, they will arrest you.' He stared at the grass deep in thought his forehead furrowed with concentration. 'Even if you get on the plane, they will ask the Italian police to arrest you. Then your wife will find out.'

'I will not tell the police; they do not need to know.' This wouldn't be easy as she must persuade Luigi. He could be a key part of solving the murder. Could there be an advantage in delving into the details of his affair with Charlotte?

'Luigi, look at me.' He looked into her eyes. 'How many times did you have sex with Charlotte?'

'Andrea! Andrea! What are you saying? I didn't, I didn't.' Andrea stared at him, he stopped talking.

'That's what the police will say to you and then, if you lie, they will arrest you.'

'Help me.'

'I can't help you unless you tell me the truth.'

The whiteness had returned to his face, 'She was a beautiful woman.'

'Luigi!'

'After her performance in Florence, we had a drink and it led to ...' His voice trailed away.

'How many times have you met her since then?'

He shrugged, 'It's about six, but nobody knows. We were secretive and went to hotels away from everyone.'

Andrea remembered his comments early that morning during the phone call. 'Who did she arrange to meet before coming to you last night?'

'I don't know, I don't know.' He paced backwards and forwards, his face full of misery and anguish.

'Luigi! The truth.'

'She said a name, but I didn't know it.' He gave a melodramatic sigh, 'It didn't matter.'

'Think, Luigi. Think.'

'I don't know.'

'It could be her murderer?'

Luigi gasped and crossed himself, 'Please forgive me, God.'

Andrea stared at him. She grabbed his hands to stop them flapping. She searched his face.

'An English name.'

'Good, which name?' Andrea could see he tried to remember.

'I know, Eduardo.'

'Edward.'

'Yes.'

'If the police ask tell them what you have told me. Do not forget the name Edward.'

'Do you think they will arrest me?'

'Not if you tell them what you have told me. Now let's organise the show.'

He perked up. 'Dedicated to Charlotte?'

'Yes, Luigi, dedicated to Charlotte.' She let him move towards the house on his own.

Should she tell Calum? Or ring Martin? What to do? She stood in the middle of the lawn looking at the house trying to decide. Both will think she's interfering. She would keep it to herself. Edward? He's a strange man who made Andrea feel uncomfortable, not only the leering but his peculiar manner. Did he find out about Luigi? And if he did, why shoot Charlotte, Luigi would be a more obvious target? Could there be another explanation? Perhaps Charlotte told both her father and Edward that she would run off with Luigi? That would make Edward a prime suspect. But that could bring in Gerald. And he's a marksman. Andrea shuddered at the thought of filicide.

No, this speculating had become too fanciful and guessing didn't help. Work out a reasonable explanation. After the row with her father, Charlotte rang Edward as the peace maker, a role he had performed before. Ashamed of her outburst at her father she arranges a meeting to persuade him to mediate. That's more likely. A simple explanation is the best one. Andrea still stood in the middle of the lawn and looked back towards the car park.

The two policemen peered into various lorries that were delivering lights and props for the show. Even from a distance she could hear a buzz of friendly talk between the roadies and the policemen. Andrea wanted to speak with the roadies. It was the same lorry as yesterday. Fitzwilliam and Wayne must have replaced them with a bribe. No explanation for their behavior as fill-in roadies leapt to mind. Calum walked out of the house and went towards the lorry.

She would extract more information from them than him. Andrea stayed watching from a distance. Calum flashed his warrant card. The jovial banter disappeared. The men looked serious and shook their heads. Calum hadn't received the information he wanted and had been rude to them, she could tell by their expressions. But Calum's attention became distracted by a limo with darkened windows as it drifted into the car park.

Everyone waited for the new arrival to emerge.

29

Patsy stepped from the limousine. 'Oh, no, she's the last person we need here.' Andrea trotted across the grass towards Patsy as Calum closed in on her. Patsy wore a low cut, short dress that emphasised her long legs, she flicked at her wavy blonde hair as she glanced around. Her attractive face wore a huge smile. Andrea couldn't tell whether Calum approached her because of lust or he expected her to be associated with the case.

Andrea closed on Luigi as she skipped across the gravel, 'You didn't say Patsy would be coming.'

Luigi looked offended, 'She's a supermodel, like you,' but with a grin he added, 'but not as good.'

Andrea wished she knew Patsy would arrive because she could have stopped her. Calum and Patsy, not a harmonious combination.

'Hi, Patsy darling,' Andrea cried out with an exaggerated wave of her arm, but Calum had reached her first. On hearing Andrea's voice Patsy turned towards her ignoring Calum. Andrea hugged her, 'Excuse me, Calum, I must talk to Patsy about the show.' He didn't look pleased but wandered away. 'Patsy, darling, this way,' Andrea led her into the house with a firm grip on her arm. Patsy rambled. Getting her away from Calum became her first priority. She walked straight but only because of her model training.

'Where are we going?' Andrea detected the slurs in the American accent.

'To the bathroom.'

'But…' Andrea led her upstairs and along several passages. 'Where are we going, honey?' Patsy struggled to prevent being guided.

'Have a heavy night?'

'Brill, but I've a headache this morning. I need a pick-me-up and then I'll be okay.'

Andrea feared the result and led Patsy into a quiet bathroom away from the noise and commotion of the show preparations. 'Look at me, Patsy babe.'

'You're my best friend, Andrea.'

'Yes, Patsy I am at this moment.' She looked into her eyes. The dilated pupils and the glazed look revealed what she feared. It had been lucky Calum hadn't spoken to her. 'Give me your handbag, babe.' Patsy staggered towards the mirrors and deposited her bag on the surface. She caught sight of herself and tweaked her hair, an instinctive reaction of a model when a mirror appeared. The foil glistened at the bottom of Patsy's bag. Andrea flushed it down the loo.

'Patsy, I need to explain, you must listen.'

'Darling, allow me a hug first, I haven't seen you for so long.' At least she hadn't realised Andrea had disposed of the foil. Andrea hugged her. Patsy rambled. How could she get Patsy away from the Manor without generating suspicion? She wouldn't choose to leave. Patsy would put in a superb performance for Luigi and it didn't matter whether she was as high as a kite or not.

'What a mess we're in babe, we've been on shows together for ten years and this will be the most crucial.'

'But we stun them, don't we?' Patsy returned to the mirror adjusting her hair once again and scrutinising her face. Old half buried memories stirred as Andrea remembered back to a New York fashion show. The world's press had anticipated a stunning performance. A tremendous argument had taken place between the designers and backstage staff who walked out. The situation had spiralled out of control as the designers followed to persuade them to return, but the other models wouldn't perform without backstage support, so they disappeared.

The launch of the show arrived with only Patsy and Andrea there. They worked it out between them by alternating different routines which they made up as they went along, giving time for the other to change. It revolutionised fashion shows and it hit the front- page news.

'Come on, darling, it's time for me to help you out of the mess you don't realise you're in.' Andrea put the toilet seat down and sat. This would be problematic. She didn't want to speculate how much Patsy had previously taken. A shiver passed over her. What if they arrest her with me and Martin finds out? This is too much. If she called Calum, he will arrest Patsy, but she didn't want that to happen.

Patsy had completed her make-up. She'd moved to the window and yanked up the blinds so she could peer over the frosted bottom panels. 'That bastard Fitzwilliam is here. I loathe him.' Andrea joined her at the window.

Patsy rambled, 'Well, I presume he's Fitzwilliam today.' Andrea ignored her ramblings as Calum walked across the car park. His movements became agitated and he challenged people. Luigi waved his hands towards the house. Calum moved quickly despite his limp.

Andrea picked up her phone and dialled Calum's number.

'Where the goddamn hell are you?'

'I'm with Patsy, I thought I'd let you know.'

'I demand to meet you now.'

'I won't be threatened and I'm completely safe. There's nothing to concern you.' She hung up but she had annoyed Calum which would get back to Martin.

'Patsy, there's been a murder.'

'Anyone I know?'

'Yes, Charlotte Manning.' Patsy tried to concentrate, but she shook her head. 'She was the singer from Florence.'

'Oh, yes, the one who kept howling in the changing room?' Patsy thought for a moment. Andrea didn't expect much looking at her glazed eyes, 'I didn't know her. Sorry. Will they cancel the show? I could do with the money.'

Andrea went to offer Patsy money but thought back to her words. 'Pats, concentrate.'

'Yes, darling?'

'What did you mean when you talked about Fitzwilliam, why did you say you presume he's Fitzwilliam today?'

Patsy stared, but the eyes told Andrea her idea would fail. 'I had a great night in London, we were…' Her eyes glazed and she stopped talking.

‘Patsy… concentrate. What about Fitzwilliam?’

‘Two other models and me.’

‘What happened?’ Andrea could tell she had weakened. She searched her bag as she wanted a fix. Andrea grasped her bag closed.

Patsy looked up at her, ‘We had a brilliant night with plenty of clubs and bars.’ Calum wouldn’t be long before he discovered them. ‘At the end of the evening…’ She let out a dramatic groan, ‘I don’t feel well.’

Andrea opened her bag. ‘Nothing there, Pats, you forgot to buy.’

‘Shit.’ Patsy swayed. No information from Patsy, and she would be arrested, but at least she’s not carrying. ‘We sneaked out the back exit. Fitzwilliam hid in the shadows outside the back door, we swayed and he smirked, I’ve got my story. The others recognised him, but I didn’t. Then, one of the other models, Janice, stepped forward and claimed, You don’t recognise me do you.’

Andrea could hear footsteps in the passage. There wouldn’t be adequate time. ‘What happened?’ urging her to reveal the crucial information.

‘Janice sneered, You’re Fitzwilliam, the intrepid journalist, aren’t you?

Yes and I’ve got myself a nice little article. Three models leaving the back door of a club and you can’t stand up. Too much booze and pills.

Janice went right into his face, “Your name was John Stephens when you composed a rave review of me in the local paper in Lancashire, but it cost me.’ Patsy stopped.

‘Go on, go on.’ Andrea hoped Patsy would finish before Calum arrived.

'Janice grabbed him by the balls and said, and then shagged the life out of me when I was fifteen.'

Noise and shouting came from the passage and above the increasing hubbub, Calum's voice.

'I need... I need...' Patsy pulled an old mobile phone from her bag. Andrea struggled to think how to explain to Calum. 'I will puke unless I take something quick.' She removed the back of the mobile phone.

'I'm in here with Patsy,' shouted Andrea, 'we're okay.' Patsy had taken the back off the phone to reveal a foil package.

'Not good enough, I'll give you ten and we're coming in.' Pablo's voice protested.

'You're not having that,' Andrea snatched the foil package and in one movement threw it down the toilet and pulled the flush. Calum shouted out the countdown in the passage. She glimpsed at the lock, but it hadn't been turned.

Patsy looked around because she thought she'd dropped the foil. 'Oh shit, what a mess,' said Andrea.

'I feel sick, there!' She looked down the loo, the foil package floated on the water as it hadn't flushed away so Andrea flicked the lever to flush again but it didn't respond. The realisation hit Andrea, Patsy knew something about Fitzwilliam.

'I'm coming in,' shouted Calum. Andrea glanced at Patsy who glared down the toilet at the foil package. The handle of the bathroom door rattled.

Andrea placed her hand behind Patsy's head, 'You like the foil packages don't you babe.'

Patsy bent lower over the toilet.

30

'I'm coming in.' Calum's voice reverberated in the corridor.

'Sorry, Patsy, you'll forgive me one day.' Andrea forced her head lower and with the other hand stuffed two fingers into her mouth and down her throat. The door burst open. Calum led the policemen and the local security guard into the bathroom where they were met by the resonating noise of Patsy retching into the toilet. The men halted and watched.

'Getting a proper view?' Andrea snarled at Calum. Patsy's backside had greeted them and her short dress had been drawn up to her hips as she forced her head down the toilet. A loud retch from Patsy followed. Andrea shouted, 'Is she wearing knickers today or are you generally looking.' It had stunned them into silence including Calum. 'Don't just stand there, fetch someone to help. Get out.'

'This isn't nice.' Patsy retched again.

'Trust me, it is.' Andrea stroked Patsy's head as she retched. Andrea flushed the loo. At least it would be challenging to prove now as the clear water reappeared. Outside the noise had quietened, Patsy had sunk to the floor and leaned against the toilet.

'What could Andrea do now?' There would be no simple answer. A first aider would arrive. Perhaps she could fob him off with the excuse of food poisoning and send Patsy to her hotel. Pacifying Calum would be next, so he wouldn't complain to Martin. After that she would find Fitzwilliam as they needed to have a chat before he proceeded further with the story. None of the activities would be pleasant, but she had no alternative.

'Leave it to me,' said a deep voice outside the door, accompanied by a knock.

'Come in.' Andrea's spirit plummeted as the same paramedic who had checked her out last night pushed the door behind him.

'Hello, Mrs Cain. Is this the lady with the problem?' He advanced towards Patsy.

'Can I say something before you examine her?'

'Yes,' came the hesitant response, 'do you know what's made her sick?'

'Patsy's a friend of mine. There's nothing wrong with her, she was sick because I stuck my fingers down her throat.'

'Why would you do that?'

'Please don't.' The smile faded from his face.

'Hi ya,' said Patsy, as he knelt on the floor beside her. He caught hold of her wrist, 'You're nice.' Andrea slumped against the wall as he placed a stethoscope on Patsy then held her face and peered into her eyes. What a mess! He stood up and crossed to Andrea who expected him to go to Calum. His movement took her by surprise as he caught her wrist and peered into her eyes. She went to push him back but realised his purpose as he placed the stethoscope against her chest. He kept a deadpan face as he concentrated on Patsy.

'Cocaine? I would guess,' he whispered.

What would Martin say? She shuddered at the prospect. Patsy had slumped into a glazed silence propped up against the wall. Martin had feared drugs and didn't want her to associate with users.

The paramedic looked at Andrea, 'Has she taken some?'

'No, I took it off her and flushed it away.'

'Any more in her bag?'

'No, I threw it away.' He stared at her, 'I understand you have a duty to perform.' He stooped down again and examined Patsy once more and he gave her a drink of water. Andrea stayed silent.

'You were a brave lady last night on the river bank.' Standing up he pointed back to Patsy, 'You don't need friends like her, you are struggling to help but she requires a rehab clinic to dry out.' Andrea gave the thinnest of smiles. The image of Martin's face loomed large as it flashed into her mind. The paramedic crossed to the door. Andrea helped Patsy to her feet and they followed him. Only Calum waited.

The paramedic crossed towards him, 'She's been sick.'

'And?' said Calum.

'There's no "and", she's been sick, but you realised that.' Calum waited for something else. 'Doesn't require a paramedic, she'll be better soon,' he walked past Calum. 'Goodbye.' Andrea breathed a huge sigh of relief and inside her head she said a big thank you to the paramedic.

Andrea spotted Pablo at the end of the passage.

Calum stared at Patsy who had turned a ghostly white. Andrea grabbed her arm and escorted her to Pablo, she gestured to Calum, 'I won't be a minute. Pablo will take her to the hotel.' She passed Patsy across to him with a quick explanation which he had already understood. Andrea drew a deep breath and returned to Calum who hadn't dropped his furious expression.

How to cope with Fitzwilliam? Should she tell Calum? It might appease him, 'I've news about Fitzwilliam.'

'Don't bloody disappear again, you're a nightmare to protect.'

'Only giving a friend privacy to be sick.'

He ignored the jibe, 'Tell me what you've discovered about Fitzwilliam.'

'Not unless you tell me about the Kennedy family article.'

'I'm not making deals.'

'Okay, I'll wait until I meet the Chief Constable then I'll ask him.'

Calum weighed up his options. 'Has she told you something?' He watched Pablo leading Patsy down the stairs.

'No, we were gossiping about former times and friends we know and I recalled an incident from several years ago. But it's only a rumour.'

'Tell me, no exchange,' he growled. Stalling for time Andrea walked along the long passage towards the stairs knowing Calum would follow as he wouldn't be prepared to lose her again.

'I do not want to burden the Chief Constable with an absurd rumour, so I've rung Martin, but he hasn't returned my call.' They descended the broad sweeping staircase to the hall. Mentioning Martin gave her a lump in her throat and she clasped the handrail for support. Calum didn't notice her trepidation but would want information to pass on to Martin and the Chief Constable.

She wouldn't win but needed to pacify Calum. He crossed in front of her, 'What about Fitzwilliam?'

Not wishing to stand face to face with him, Andrea moved to a window seat that lined the hall, so she didn't have to look at him. 'Fitzwilliam writes under various names.'

'All bloody journalists do,' he huffed in annoyance, 'that's not news!'

'After you'd left yesterday Charlotte told me her agent, Wayne Smith and Fitzwilliam are buddies.'

'Wayne Smith is a complete toe rag,' mumbled Calum as he wandered around the hall. He paused before a full suit of armour and lifted the visor, peered inside and then released it allowing it to close with a resonating clang.

'Wayne has developed a good reputation in the industry, he's fair, he doesn't take liberties and is always on hand so I might join him.'

Calum paused as though absorbing this information, 'What's wrong with the one you've got?' he raised his eyebrows, 'A posh one in London I would expect.'

'The leading one in the business,' she gave a mirthless laugh, 'but he's never available and charges a fortune. He's so full of his own importance he hasn't time for me, so I'm obliged to deal with his front office staff which is not a proper service. Wayne has a much smaller business and would deal with me personally.'

'That's for you to decide,' he moved back to the suit of armour for another look. What was he hoping to find? Did he think there was a dead body inside? His movement annoyed her. Despite the suspense of waiting for Martin to come back to her message and working out how to handle Calum she smiled to herself. He had lost enthusiasm in the conversation.

'I don't wish to join him if he's dodgy in his dealings.'

'Aren't all agents?' Calum continued to pace around the hall, he appeared unsettled and bored by the conversation.

'Wayne knew the Kennedys well, he could have introduced them to Fitzwilliam. I think a straightforward explanation is the best,' said Andrea.

'Yes,' he said absentmindedly as he thought through the implications. He sat on a large carved chair and rubbed his injured leg.

'If it's a simple explanation that links them together, I will join his agency.'

'What about yesterday? Wouldn't that put you off? They were underhand.'

'Fitzwilliam…'

'Fat bastard,' grunted Calum.

'He'll do anything to find a story but didn't anticipate Charlotte and me being a day early, he would be after background scandal from tittle tattle around changing room doors. The dressers gossip before the models appear.'

'I wouldn't join him, but I don't understand your world.' He didn't look at Andrea as he flexed his leg.

'What is it about Fitzwilliam? You would know

journalists write under different names why bother bringing it up.'

Andrea gave in. 'He writes under various names for local papers. In Lancashire he adopted the name John Stephens.'

'So?'

'He picks out young girl singers and gives them good reviews. Sex with him is part of the deal, they are probably under age.' Andrea hesitated, 'But it's just a rumour.'

'I don't see the relevance to the current cases,' he rubbed his chin and allowed his eyes to wander around the hall.

'What if he picked up Charlotte as a young singer and bribed her into sex and she recognised him yesterday? It suggests a perfect fit.'

'No.'

'It makes him a prime suspect, doesn't it?'

'Don't be so ridiculous, we don't know whether he had the opportunity and capability for the murder.'

'You mean is he a marksman?'

'No further talk of the case.' He faced her and stared. He had realised the ramifications of what Andrea had said. 'Who told you about a marksman?'

She needed a quick answer, so she didn't implicate Martin. 'I found Charlotte and as my father used to shoot game, I recognised a rifle wound.' The dead image of Charlotte appeared, she stood up and strode along the corridor not waiting for an answer. Her story sounded convincing. She hadn't said Martin had revealed the vital information. Andrea listened as she walked along the corridor.

Calum would call her back if he had any suspicion, but he limped along behind her.

31

'Can we talk?'

Andrea had met Wayne in the front garden and he looked surprised at her request, 'Yes.'

'Let's walk to the border garden.' Calum had followed her from the house but paused when she approached Wayne. 'After several complications, I'm considering moving to a new agent.'

'That's marvellous news,' he beamed, 'you don't have to search any further.'

'But I need to be assured you could deal with my business. You realise who I'm with now.'

'Yes, large, famous, expensive and ineffective,' he chuckled at his succinct analysis of her current agent. Andrea had ceased walking. 'That's the rumour in the industry,' added Wayne, who wore a loud pin-striped suit with an intense yellow shirt and a green tie. Andrea studied him and concluded it wasn't about whether she liked him. Will he believe that I would never consider joining him especially as his cooperation with Fitzwilliam makes me wonder if he's into something underhand? She hoped he couldn't read her mind, so she plastered on a smile.

'So what have you to offer? Charlotte praised your performance as her agent.'

'Personal and efficient service, fast response,' his marketing spiel rattled off his tongue, 'I'd be strong in representing you for new contracts as I'm used to negotiating high profile ones.'

'Such a tragedy about Charlotte probably your best earner.' Andrea sat on a nearby bench and Wayne joined her but frowned. Ignoring his confusion, she gazed out across the immaculate gardens, cross with herself as she'd produced a feeble start with the incorrect words. 'Still, I expect you had her insured?'

'I'm not prepared to answer,' and his thin-lipped mouth turned into a sneer as an expression of displeasure passed over his face.

Carrying on regardless she became determined to squeeze information from him, 'You know the family don't you?'

'What family?'

'The one that did the armed robbery.'

'Why have you mentioned them?'

'You use them for car hire, don't you?'

'Yes, because they are the best hire business in Sheffield.' He flapped his hand in a dismissive gesture, 'I didn't know they would carry out a robbery.'

'Do you still employ them?'

'Yes, as it hasn't been proved beyond a reasonable doubt.'

'The police have charged the one in hospital.'

'But he hasn't been found guilty,' he shot her a venomous glance, 'so I'll keep an open mind.' The conversation paused. Andrea's mind whirled as she hadn't thought through her next question. So far, no useful information, she required a different approach but couldn't think of one.

Wayne's voice broke through her thoughts, 'Do you want to talk terms,' said Wayne, his voice flat and professional.

'I want to investigate you first, to make sure you're legitimate.'

'What does that mean? Of course, I am,' his face flushed and his eyes sparked with anger, 'I can demonstrate it as I've been in the business for a long time.'

'You know Fitzwilliam, don't you?'

'So?'

'Don't you want me to join you?'

'Yes, but let's have a rational conversation, not ridiculous comments!'

She wouldn't give up, 'Fitzwilliam.'

'Yes, I have met him as he's a well-known journalist, but you must know him as well?'

Andrea ignored his question, 'He did an article about the Kennedy family.' Wayne went red in the face struggling to control his impatience. Andrea hoped he would let something slip.

His phone rang, so he gave an abrupt, 'Excuse me,' stood up and wandered away.

A voice close by made her jump, 'I've been listening and you're hopeless.'

'I don't know what you're talking about,' she prevaricated.

'Oh, yes you do.' His words hovered in the air as Calum stood beside the bench looking down on her. She struggled to work out how he had listened, but realised he had stepped out of the large nearby window with a low sill.

'You are interfering in the case, perhaps Martin and the Chief Constable will wish to know you're trying to question people.'

'No, I'm not.'

'And to make it even worse, you're lousy at it, even one of the dimmest recruits could do better.' He snorted with impatience, Andrea had been trapped and continuing to deny it wouldn't help.

How should she react to his accusations? 'I wasn't that bad,' she laughed to brighten the mood but whether she could get around Calum and stop him talking to Martin would be a different matter.

'Aggressive random questioning is terrible, he wanted to talk, but you forced him to clam up.'

'Okay, so I made a few mistakes,' she gave a dismissive wave of her hand. 'Could you do better?' She guessed Calum liked challenges and it might encourage him to lighten his attitude towards her. He eased down onto the bench with a small groan and stretched his injured leg. Although in discomfort she couldn't engender much sympathy as hopefully if the pain increased he'd give up and go home.

Having established himself into a comfortable position, 'At least I would have done research first.' He leaned back with a smug expression of satisfaction on his face.

'I don't have the resources the police have.'

'Neither did I this morning, so I researched his agency on the web.'

Her interest was roused, 'What did it say?'

'As a young man he became a mediocre rally driver.'

'You're winding me up, how can that be relevant,' she flashed back at him with indignation.

Calum ignored her, 'They haven't caught the driver of the car at the armed holdup. According to eye witnesses the driver handled the fast car well.' Her irritation disappeared; she gave a satisfied smile as Calum had talked about the case.

'Could it be him?'

'I don't jump to conclusions but if he wanted to talk, I'd ask him about rally driving.'

'What else?'

'Did you recognise his clothes?'

'Poor combination.'

'Not for me to comment I glanced at the labels and then I looked them up on the web. They are expensive.'

'I could have told you that.'

'Yes, that's the point, you recognise them as you probably know the designer.'

'I haven't spoken to him for a long time.'

'That's irrelevant,' snapped Calum, 'you could admire his clothes, put him at ease.' Andrea stood up and paced backwards and forwards on the terrace thinking through the implications. Why hadn't she checked him out? So obvious but it annoyed her that Calum had made her feel insignificant.

'Will you tell Martin?' Even saying his name caused her stomach to clench with anxiety.

'I might.'

She stopped, clenched her fists and glared at the mean-spirited man relaxing on the garden bench, 'That's spiteful.'

32

'You don't wish to cooperate with me and were awkward with your friend Patsy. So why should I help you?' Calum stood up smiled and wandered off along the terrace. He walked past Wayne, acknowledged him, and departed around the corner of the house.

He despises me because I'm successful. Dismissing the irritating man from her thoughts, she glanced up and smiled at Wayne, moved along the bench and patted the space next to her. With a huge smile, 'I'm sorry Wayne, I'm jittery about Charlotte, you're correct, my agent is inefficient and expensive and has let me down on a big contract. I could have done better myself.'

Wayne smiled, 'Let's start again, shall we?' Andrea remembered Calum. Had he returned to his listening point inside the window? She suggested a stroll on the terrace so they descended the steps and sauntered towards a spacious dome shaped rose arbour.

'Good suit. Love the style and the colour,' she lied, 'I haven't seen Pierre for a long time,' Andrea stopped and smoothed her hand across the lapel, 'Mmm, the fabric has such a delicate surface.'

'You know Pierre Michel?' he grinned, 'Silly

question, of course you would, my suits are handmade to my choosing. I like to be different, no off the peg rubbish for me.'

She took a step back to give the impression she admired his taste. 'Pierre doesn't come cheap.'

'I'm not bragging when I say I'm a decent agent, I take a fair slice for which I strive hard. With a good number of successes my clients are satisfied.' They continued their walk towards the rose arbour with Andrea's mind whirling. Think, think! Calum's advice. What to do next?

As a distraction she sniffed at the roses inhaling the subtle perfume and willed herself to appear relaxed while her thoughts were in overdrive. It annoyed her to take Calum's advice, but she settled herself on the bench and turned her attention back to Wayne. 'I'm sure your clients are pleased with your work; poor Charlotte spoke highly of you.'

Then an idea sprung to mind, 'I'm ashamed about how I handled our earlier conversation.' Wayne smiled which showed him to be in a magnanimous mood. So far so good, think before you speak, she willed herself. 'For once I checked deductions by my agent,' and raised her eyebrows in an extravagant manner.

'Large?'

'Limo from Heathrow to home, how much?'

'With me, £300.'

'Not bad,' said Andrea, 'I'd be £500 richer.'

'£800, that's preposterous. What a rip off!'

'I came to the same conclusion.'

'Sorry about mentioning the Kennedy family, but the transport problem has troubled me as it's such an essential part of my life when I'm working.'

'No problem, they are reliable, polite and flexible. Everything you could wish. For example, I've rung them at two o'clock in the morning to pick up Charlotte at seven o'clock from Heathrow where they arrive on time, and don't charge me extra.'

'Sounds perfect.' She smiled at him but the allusion to Charlotte had disrupted her thoughts. Poor Charlotte. What an awful way to die.

Wayne hadn't noticed her discomfort and carried on the conversation after a slight pause. 'The involvement of the family in the robbery stunned me.'

'But what about Fitzwilliam's article on the Kennedy gang forcing others out of business?'

'Not one of his best as he invented the story. Ma Kennedy had several rivals at the time so worked with low margins. Fitzwilliam's article followed a few chats he had with Ma as they hit it off right away. Once the competitors read the article,' he chuckled, 'they moved out of town. You asked me about Fitzwilliam earlier.'

'I guessed you must know him well.'

'No, I've only spoken to him a few times, Ma Kennedy told me about the story.'

Something didn't seem right, but she smiled at Wayne hoping for more information. What to ask next? What would Calum do? Andrea searched her mind for approaches but had to be vigilant as she didn't want to upset Wayne again. If she did, then Calum would torment her. She willed herself to concentrate, Calum would be some place nearby eavesdropping.

'One service that my current agency supplies is help with snoopers,' Andrea gave a light theatrical sigh and allowed her smile to fade.

'I don't see what you mean.'

Andrea continued her deception using a concerned tone of voice, 'Well, yesterday when Fitzwilliam pretended to be a roadie, I would have rung and they would have sent someone to check.' He gulped although he fixed his face to show no reaction.

He flicked an imaginary speck of dust from his jacket, 'Have you asked Fitzwilliam?'

'No, I haven't but he's up to no good and I don't want to finish up on the wrong end of one of his articles as they are always nasty. Normally, as soon as I suspect something I ring and ask for help.'

'You didn't this time.' Did she detect a strain in his voice?

'No, I know Fitzwilliam,' she paused for effect, 'but became worried as to why he had come to Sheffield. Martin is nearby so on this occasion I do not need the agency to protect me. Do you know Martin, my husband?' With satisfaction she noted he squirmed with embarrassment.

'Only by reputation,' he gulped and his face paled with wide-open eyes, 'Now is not the time to talk. Let's have a relaxed conversation in a couple of days,' he sprang to his feet and offered his hand, 'To a good partnership.'

Andrea stood and shook hands, 'I'll listen to what you have to say.'

'I must go,' he said checking his watch as though emphasising the point.

Sudden inspiration hit Andrea, 'Are you off to the police for your interview?'

He stopped. No alarm came on his face this time,

'They won't want to interview me as yesterday I spent the day in Manchester.' Without a backward glance he scurried across the terrace. Why did he lie about being here? He'd spent the day pretending to be a roadie.

Calum reappeared at her shoulder but she expected it this time. A large yew hedge next to the rose arbour had been a perfect place for a spot of snooping. 'Suspicious, do you think he's a suspect?' Calum laughed. 'What's so funny?'

'Because someone lies it doesn't make them a murderer. Everyone lies in their lives but not everyone commits murder.'

'It wasn't a little lie but a huge great big one,' she pouted. 'He must realise that he won't get away with it.'

'It's not your case,' his gravelly voice was like the ominous roll of distant thunder.

'And it's not yours.'

'No, you're right it's not. It's Martin's,' Calum's cold gaze locked on her face. Martin's name made her draw in her breath as he hadn't rung so her anguish returned. Fitzwilliam jumped back into her mind, she had to sort him out, but how could she get rid of Calum?

'I'll do you a deal,' said Calum.

'What deal?'

'You stop trying to run this case. Co-operate. Try on dresses or whatever you do.'

'And what if I agree?'

'I won't tell Martin and the Chief Constable of your attempts to interview Wayne.' Andrea frowned, but Calum smiled, 'And I won't fetch Patsy from the hotel and interview her as I'm sure I'd find something interesting.'

So, he'd guessed, but she couldn't risk him picking up Patsy.

33

'Okay, deal done. I agree.'

Calum hadn't anticipated her response, Andrea could see that in his face, he must have been bluffing.

'I'm astounded,' said Andrea.

'What about?'

'That you call them dresses, men always say frocks,' she swished past him and marched across the terrace.

'Don't leave the house.'

'Would I?' she called over her shoulder as she headed towards the front door.

She needed to prioritise. Martin hadn't cancelled the show, but he could still make that decision. Fitzwilliam had become top of her list. What else needed her attention? Making sure Patsy didn't become involved and reminding Luigi that he must tell the truth.

Martin, Martin, why won't you ring, I need to talk to you my darling. Luigi stood at the end of the long gallery shouting at Pablo and other staff giving them orders. She needed peace and quiet so strolled out to the walled garden with distant views to the slope of the hillsides. The road swept past the house and disappeared into the valley. Her eyes were drawn towards the dip in the landscape and despite the warmth she shivered as it had been the valley, where she'd found Charlotte.

She would try Martin again, but would be wary of being overheard, so she searched around but no one else had left the house. Martin's words about a marksman sprang to her. She stood tall at the edge of the garden on a slight rise in the ground and could be seen from the distant woods. Grateful for peace and quiet she wandered along a nearby path which passed through bushes and small trees. The bushes and trees would shelter her.

A noise reached her, the sound of a footstep muffled by the soft ground. She froze rooted to the spot and held her breath and listened. Silence, apart from bird song and the mournful sound of sheep bleating in the distance. Her eyes flicked this way and that. Definitely a person, her stomach tightened. A bird fluttered away then the slightest rustling in the undergrowth.

'Who's there?' No noise. The oppressive silence closed in on her. 'Show yourself,' her voice cracked with nervousness. No movement. A car engine revved in the distance and a raucous cawing of a colony of jackdaws filled the air but no sound nearby. She'd hoped it would be a couple of the crew fooling around but they would have moved or spoken. Should she run or scream, she drew in her breath and prepared to run.

A black glove came over her mouth and her running legs went nowhere. The ultimate nightmare. In those few moments she had become powerless. It made the limited strength she had left, drain from her. Fear made her weak. Reality returned as her feet touched the ground.

She had been lifted in the air. A huge man wearing black sprang into her eyeline. She wouldn't be able to fight him, but his accomplice still held her in a rock-solid grip. Time passed slowly. She tried again to scream but the black glove had a firm grasp on her mouth. The man in front had powerful muscles, black clothes and a blackened smudged face. The fierce face smiled.

Andrea shuddered. An evil visage. She struggled, but the grip from behind remained unyielding. It lifted her off the ground again so she couldn't put any power into her legs. Would she be kidnapped? Martin's pain at the news flashed through her mind. Andrea couldn't deal with her emotions. She shivered and screamed but no cry came. The grip remained unrelenting. The smile hadn't changed. Time stretched. The man reached behind him; she anticipated a knife. He flicked a baseball cap on his head.

Andrea melted with relief. That wonderful word 'POLICE'. He brought from nowhere his warrant card and held it in front of her face, she'd never been so relieved. The grip from behind set her on the ground and the glove came from her mouth.

'Sorry ma'am, we couldn't let you set off an alarm.' The powerful officer in front of her then spoke into his radio, 'Woman, tall, blonde intercepted…' His voice trailed off as he recognised Andrea.

She shook her head, 'Don't say.'

'Escorting her to safety.'

'Thanks.'

'Ma'am you shouldn't be out here. Please go back in.' His colleague looked confused. 'This is Mrs Cain, she is Superintendent Cain's wife.' He looked horrified.

A bright young constable, he'd manhandled the Chief Superintendent's wife, 'I hope I didn't hurt you, ma'am.'

'No, you startled me, but you're doing your job. There are no complaints, it's brilliant you are here to protect me and the others.'

'You shouldn't be out here, ma'am,'

'I want to find a quiet spot to ring Martin.'

The young officer said, 'I could get him on the radio.'

She smiled and the other officer shook his head, 'No thanks. I wanted a private conversation.'

'Yes, ma'am,' and he stood to attention.

The older one smiled, 'Isn't Inspector Calum looking after you?'

'Yes, but he has lost me again.' Both tried their best to hide the smiles. Stories about Calum at the station would be welcomed.

'No need to break your cover as I don't think you've been seen.'

'Thanks, ma'am.'

'Are there the two of you?'

'Yes, we came with Jeff, who you met last night.'

'I spoke to him when he arrived today.'

'He dropped us up the road so we could take up positions without being seen.'

A car in the valley glinted in the sun, she recognised it. The policemen had noticed her distraction and they followed her look. The young policeman said, 'Mark II Jaguar. That's an excellent car and it looks in perfect condition.'

'Your eyesight is good from this distance, have you any binoculars?' The young man nipped behind the bush and reappeared with a pair. Andrea focused on the car as she wanted to see the driver. Gerald driving and Edward in the passenger seat. What are they doing?

'Someone you recognise ma'am?' But she didn't answer as the car disappeared into the valley. She waited.

'It has not reappeared.'

'Perhaps it stopped by the bridge.' What are they doing at the spot where Charlotte died? The officers watched her.

'I'll go back into the house and I'll tell Martin and the Chief Constable what an excellent job you're doing.'

'Thank you, ma'am. Do you prefer an escort?'

'No, you won't need to break cover then, you're better off here in case you are required.' She skipped up the path and turned towards the house. Gerald and Edward? Were they the guilty ones returning to the scene of the crime? She shook her head as the straightforward explanation would be the strongest. Gerald had come to mourn. Edward would accompany him. That sounded more plausible.

I need to talk to them. Did Edward speak to Charlotte last night? How did Charlotte's liaison with Luigi come into the plans? Had Edward found out? Too many unanswered questions buzzed through her mind as she approached the house. Calum would be looking for her so she'd needed to find him. He'd be annoyed if he discovered she'd been wandering around the grounds.

As she entered the house, Calum checked each room on the corridor so she hid behind the grandfather clock. His phone rang and he sat in a nearby chair to answer his call. Andrea's luck held as he faced away from her. With no one else in the corridor, she slipped off her shoes and nipped into the next room which he would search after finishing his phone call. She made herself comfortable in a chair and opened a newspaper from the coffee table.

'There you are.'

'Yes, reading the newspaper and I'm keeping my part of the deal.' Calum grunted and left the room.

Why had Charlotte arranged to meet Edward?

34

'Where's your car, Pablo? Give me the keys.'

He had been relaxing on the window seat in the long gallery.

'Hi, Andrea. Losing your policeman again?'

'What type?'

'A Mini on the lane'

'That's brill?'

'Andrea, you are expected to remain here.'

'I won't be long, I promise.' Pablo handed over the keys with a shake of his head, 'Thanks, I owe you.'

'You always do,' he grinned.

'Pablo, Pablo, Dove sei? Dove sei?' They recognised Luigi's voice.

'Coming, Luigi. Please be careful Andrea.'

Andrea sneaked behind the bushes to the lane and within a few minutes she drove into the valley. The missing part of the parapet had been shoved off the road. She turned into an insignificant clearing in the woods and parked next to Gerald's Jaguar. She'd expected them to be in the road or near the bridge but couldn't find them. Where had they gone? What might have interested them? She shivered. Andrea had concluded he hadn't murdered his daughter but peering up the slope of the tree-covered hill, they must be searching for the place where the marksman stood.

Her high heels were not suitable for scrambling around a wooded hillside, but she wanted to find Gerald and Edward, so she passed through a gate, and with no visible path, scrambled up between the trees.

Andrea had to be careful and quiet as she preferred to sneak up on them if possible as their conversation could be interesting.

Slippery undergrowth, soaked by the previous night's rain, made progress difficult. She heard voices, which she recognised, but couldn't see them. As she clambered over a streamlet and dragged herself up higher, she could see Edward. The talking had stopped. She pulled herself around the next bush and tree. A brief glance back towards the road told her that this could have been the gunman's location.

Edward said, 'What are you doing here? You shouldn't be here.' He sweated, his tall thin frame leapt forward and snatched her wrist with a cold clammy hand which sent a shiver through her. He gave her the same piercing stare from his shadowed eyes as when she had been at Gerald's house. Twisting her arm with a jerk he let go.

'Are you following us?' A harsh voice from behind vibrated with power and command. Gerald then caught her arm and it hurt, she spun round but the firm grip held tight.

'Gerald, let go, that hurts,' his pale cold eyes were narrowed, his expression bleak, he ignored her and tightened the grip on her arm.

Edward repeated, 'What are you doing here?'

Andrea put her face close to Gerald, 'Release my arm!' He loosened his grip and she snatched her arm away from him. 'I thought you were a gentleman,' she snarled, 'what would Charlotte think of you attempting to intimidate me. Will you step back and give me space? Or will you grab me again? Make up your mind!' Both stepped back. 'That's better, let's have a sensible conversation.'

Gerald muttered, 'We're sorry.'

'Do the police know you're rooting around up here?' snarled Andrea as she glanced back through the trees towards the road.

Gerald heaved a loud sigh, 'No they don't and please don't tell them.'

'Give me a good reason. What do you expect to find?'

'Nothing,' growled Edward.

'You don't climb half way up a wooded valley slope for nothing.' He looked defiant as he took a small step towards her. 'You were searching for the gunman's position.' Andrea stood her ground refusing to be intimidated and searched their faces.

'Yes,' Gerald nodded with closed eyes; he had calmed. 'The Chief Constable told me what had happened.'

'Is it here?' Andrea looked at the narrow patch of flat ground with the remains of an old tree.

'Not on this patch, either standing on the tree stump or on the slope.' She studied the two places Gerald had pointed out. 'The sniper wouldn't want to leave footprints so would step on branches and undergrowth, so it's difficult to detect ingress and egress.' She supposed his army training would come to the fore in deriving the location. Gerald stared in silence to the road.

Andrea shivered, he can see it in his mind's eye. Edward peered at her again, but she didn't make eye contact and shook her head. Why had Charlotte liked him? It made no sense. Charlotte liked men, but the smooth talkers and good-looking ones, not Edward's type. Far too shifty and not handsome enough. Old and staid before his time.

Gerald walked away from them to the fallen tree and peered towards the road, his face a pale grey mask. Then a loud sigh emanated from him, 'I'm sorry Andrea, you want to help us and when you arrive, we are aggressive towards you. It took us by surprise when you appeared as we'd anticipated being on our own. A foolish decision but I wanted to visualize how it had happened as I thought it would help with my grief, but it doesn't.'

Have they something to hide as they seem ill at ease. While Gerald had apologised for the hostility towards her, it had been unnecessary. What were they expecting to find? Andrea shivered despite the sun. 'We watched you arrive,' Gerald pointed towards the road that led through the small valley, 'I take my hat off to you as you are an intelligent woman. I'm guessing but you must have seen the car coming along the road near the large house where you will hold the fashion show and followed us. When you arrived, you worked out where we were. We had come to mourn where Charlotte died.'

Gerald faltered, 'My background and training took over. I wanted to search for the spot where the murderer had stationed himself while he waited. Edward followed my lead and we climbed the hillside, he's not to blame.'

Andrea glanced at Edward who stood in the centre of the clearing with his hands shoved into his jacket pockets with a scowl of displeasure on his face.

Edward doesn't have an ounce of passion in his boring body. Once again, their engagement seemed a figment of the family's imagination as it would never have worked. Not in a million years.

'I shall have a few private minutes at the place where she died. If I may?' Edward nodded. Gerald moved with an agility that surprised Andrea and started down the slope. Before he departed, he called back over his shoulder 'Edward, help Andrea on the slope, it's steep and slippery in places.'

She glanced down at her inappropriate heeled shoes with a wry smile, 'We will give you time at the bridge on your own. I want to speak with Edward.'

35

Edward moved too close for comfort. 'What do you want to talk about?' He stared at her and sweat beaded his forehead. Rubbing his hands on the side of his trousers, his long thin fingers moving across the fabric as though he wanted to dry them before touching her.

Eyes of watery blue regarded her from shadowed sockets, his eyes slithered across her face and neck, then moved down and paused at her breasts. Every muscle in his face had become tense, it held no warmth but a hard, calculated expression as though assessing his prey like a predatory animal. This creepy man made her shiver.

'Edward!' She shouted as she hoped to break through his lascivious thoughts and the lustful look in his eyes. He jumped but his eyes only slowly slid up to her face. She waited as it gave her time to think. He gave a sickly smile and licked his dry lips and his pale predatory eyes wandered across her face and then began to slide down her body stopping at her breasts again. Andrea sucked in her breath and clenched her fists, her heart beat with a furious intensity as though about to explode.

'Look at me! At my face! You pathetic man! I'm a short phone call away to my husband in which I will tell him I've found you up here.' His eyes leapt away from her breasts and swept across the countryside as though expecting a police officer to appear. The sickly smile disappeared.

'I've been with Charlotte recently but she never mentioned she had a boyfriend and that she would be marrying. Why's that?' Strangely he relaxed at the question and moved away from her and gazed at the road in the valley.

'We weren't officially engaged, but she had agreed to consider my proposal.' But Charlotte had never mentioned it to Andrea. She had to get to the truth as she was desperate to help Martin and heal the rift between them, so she decided to be blunt.

'When did you propose?'

'About three weeks ago, we went away for the weekend to the Lake District. The romantic atmosphere made it an ideal time for a proposal.'

Andrea wondered had she'd made a mistake with Edward as she searched her memory. Charlotte had mentioned visiting the Lakes with a man. Andrea had asked her who, but Charlotte had teased her, 'I'm not telling you but there might be news soon.' So it could be true, what an unlikely partnership.

Edward sat on a tree stump leaned forward, rested his elbows on his knees and put his head in his hands. 'I shall miss her, I loved her.' He gave a few quiet sobs. Andrea sat next to him. 'I'm not good with beautiful women as I make them uneasy.' He took a deep breath. 'You don't like me, I know that.'

Andrea wanted to be kind but couldn't bring herself to speak. Silence fell. He hadn't moved his head from his hands. Andrea heard the gentle desolate sobs and his breathing became ragged as he gave way to his emotions. 'I can only help you and Gerald if you tell me the truth. Will you do that for Charlotte, please Edward?'

Raising his tear-stained face, his lips trembled and his shoulders shook with emotion. There was a long pause while he strove to calm himself. 'Yes, I will.' Andrea sensed sincerity. 'I'm frightened they will arrest me.'

'Why?' Innocence covered his face. Perhaps she could make progress with this odious man. 'The truth Edward, it must be the truth.'

'Yes, I will tell you the truth, but involves Gerald so will you be discreet.'

'Go on.' Would it incriminate Gerald?

'Yesterday evening, Gerald went into the next room to make a call.'

'Why were you at his house?'

'We had finished a game of bridge earlier in the evening.'

'Who did he ring?'

'Charlotte, they had an almighty row, one of the worst.'

'What happened?'

'I could hear Gerald shouting.'

'What did you do?'

'Nothing. They often argued, but last night's had extra venom.'

'Why?'

'The way it ended.'

'What did he say?'

Edward took a deep breath, 'You're no daughter

of mine, I disown you, I don't care if you live or die.' Edward sobbed. A desolate sound as his tears flowed unchecked, his face a mixture of grief and despair. She remained silent allowing his sorrow to fill the air and took deep breaths to calm herself from Edward's words. If they had been the last words Gerald said to his daughter, they would haunt him forever. Edward put his head in his hands. Andrea needed to pacify him. Time was of the essence as she needed to return before Calum missed her.

'The police will not arrest you for listening to Gerald's phone call.'

36

Edward sighed, 'The police will arrest me when they discover my activities later in the evening.'

Urgency filled her, she focused her attention on the sniveling man sat next to her, 'You must tell me, Edward.'

'If I do, you will tell your husband and he will arrest me.' He hadn't looked up, but his taut and venomous voice had turned menacing. Andrea's mouth went dry and her throat constricted. They were alone together on the hillside. She glanced past Edward, to a steep drop, he could say she lost her footing in her high heels. The scenario flew through her mind, but she willed herself to stay focused. A muscle twitched at the corner of his right eye and his mouth set itself into a hard, rigid line. What was he thinking and planning?

She blurted out her question, 'Did you kill Charlotte?'

A sharp intake of breath, followed by a pause. He jerked his head up and glared at her, 'No, I didn't.'

'Then you have nothing to fear as Martin isn't a policeman who stitches people up, he wants justice so would never convict an innocent man.'

'Yes, I'm sure you are right.' The aggression had

gone from his voice.

'Tell me why you think you are the prime suspect.' She stood up and moved away from the precipitous drop as the nightmare scenario still swirled in her mind. He shuffled his position on the fallen tree and turned his face towards her.

'After the call, I left Gerald's house because I wanted to ring Charlotte. She would be upset and I wanted to console her.'

'Did you speak to her?'

'Yes, I told her I'd heard Gerald.'

'What did Charlotte say?'

'Her final words will be ingrained in my memory for ever, Help me Edward, help me? They were her exact words.' Andrea gasped. Poor Charlotte. Before the conversation about the weekend at the lakes and his proposal she would never have believed him. Now she did. 'She suggested meeting.'

Andrea realised Charlotte's dilemma. That would have been difficult for her as she had arranged to meet Luigi. Andrea walked across the clearing, her mind whirling with this last snippet of information. Charlotte had reached out to Edward for comfort and help.

'Did you agree?' Andrea refocused her attention on Edward.

'Yes, but she explained that she couldn't stay long as she had to meet her backing singers for a late night rehearsal ready for tomorrow.'

'Where did you arrange to meet her?'

'She asked me to wait at the Strines pub and she would come as soon as she could.' Charlotte would have driven into this valley expecting to meet Edward within a few minutes. Once again, he became overcome with emotion. He sobbed again. 'At least the last time we spoke she was coming to me.'

Andrea put her hand on his arm, he had solace, but Gerald didn't. She didn't have to ask the next question.

'She never arrived. I waited until closing time and left when the landlord kicked me out.'

'Did you ring her?'

'Yes, many times, but no answer.' He'd regained his composure.

'If you were in the pub, someone will recognise you.'

He shook his head, 'No, when she hadn't turned up, I left the pub and followed a short path and sat on a rock at the edge of the moor. I could see the car park, but I don't know how long I sat there. The landlord said he'd anticipated I'd left when I went for another drink.'

Andrea glanced behind her, a footpath snaked its way through the gorse and heather from the pub. The route by car was longer as it twisted and turned through the valley.

'Edward,' she sat next to him, 'I believe you.'

'Thanks, but you are not the police.'

'Can I ask you a question?'

'Yes, is it about Charlotte?'

'No, have you ever learned to shoot?' His face recognised the significance of the question, his eyes screwed up and colour drained from his face. Andrea could guess the answer even before he started his explanation.

'I fell into trouble at school and joined a local gang. The headmaster and my father gave me two alternatives.' The words tumbled out of him like a torrent, A life of crime or join the army.'

'That wasn't much of an alternative.'

'No, but fair in the circumstances and I wanted my father's admiration, so at seventeen I enlisted.'

'And you learned to shoot?'

'Two bad years as I hated the strict army regime. Totally restrictive, apart from the shooting. I became the best shot in the regiment.' The police would discover Edward's background. 'I'm not as good as Gerald, who is a true marksman, but good enough for whoever pulled the trigger.' Andrea surprised herself as a surge of sympathy for this creepy man swept over her. He might be strange, but he loved Charlotte.

If Charlotte intended marrying Edward why meet Luigi? Aside from her family she had been bubbly and sociable so perhaps the extra sex on the side Charlotte didn't recognise as important. Ideas, thoughts and questions battled for supremacy in Andrea's mind. She checked her watch as she'd been missing from the manor house for a lengthy time. Calum would be searching for her. If he didn't find her, he would alert the nearby police and Martin. She didn't want Martin to find out as he'd be so angry, and she wanted to heal the rift between them not make it worse. Edward's voice interrupted her thoughts of Martin.

'There's something else.'

'Yes?'

'I walked out on the army.'

'Deserted?' Her voice rose in surprise.

'No. I had a dishonourable discharge, for brawling in Aldershot town centre and assaulting a police officer.' Andrea shuddered, the more he revealed the worse it became. The police would arrest Edward as soon as they investigated him, which wouldn't be long. 'After that I went downhill and lived in London. I fell into heavy drinking and petty thieving because I didn't have money and I wouldn't work.' Andrea put her arm around his shoulders. 'Only one good person came into my life in those days, I fell in love with a local girl, Stacey Arthurston, but she kicked me out.'

Determined to keep him talking, 'Where did she live?'

'King's Cross, in London.' Perhaps he had found out about Luigi and possessiveness had overwhelmed him. He had the capability and the opportunity. What would he do if he found his only love had been sleeping with an Italian fashion designer? She jumped at the voice behind her. Andrea dropped her arm from Edward's shoulder in embarrassment.

'Still sitting here.' Gerald scrambled into the clearing.

'Yes, talking about Charlotte.' She hoped Gerald hadn't heard the conversation. Edward looked relieved because he had told someone.

'Will you speak to your husband soon?' Edward mumbled, looking at his feet. Gerald looked confused.

'This evening as I don't disturb him at work.'

Edward squared his shoulders, 'If you are ready, Gerald. Would you like me to drive you home?'

'Yes, that would be kind.' Gerald led the way down the wooded slope. Edward followed offering a helping hand where needed to Andrea. The sweaty hand of earlier had gone and their goodbyes were friendly.

Calum? She glanced at her watch as she'd been away

a long time and would be missed. Her mobile beeped as messages came in as soon as she picked up a signal. No message from Martin, she had become desperate to hear his voice. Andrea's phone bleeped as it received a text message from Pablo. 'Everyone is looking for you!'

37

It wouldn't be long, she pressed the accelerator and willed the car to hurry. As she drove around the bend, she glanced at the long line of parked cars with a group of chauffeurs idly chatting. The show must be on. Andrea's mind raced. Luigi? Patsy? Calum? Martin? A few people walking near their cars waved and doubtless expected models to be late for their shows. A reception and entertainment began the show, so models were not required at the beginning.

The parking space had gone but the large cars had parked well-spaced, so Andrea eased the Mini into a gap and parked it at right angles to the road and halfway up the verge. She wouldn't be able to stroll up the drive for everyone to see. Andrea glanced around as she walked into the tree-lined drive then snatched off her shoes and ducked between the bushes and through the ferns, intending to reach the side of the house without being spotted.

Voices came from the ferns ahead. She recognised the voice and exhaled a sigh of relief as it was Maria, her dresser, also an English man's voice, but not Calum's. What to do? They came closer to her. She dropped to the floor onto a patch of grass. 'Hi, Maria is that you?'

'Andrea.' She yawned and peered up from her seated position as Maria and her young man came through the ferns. 'Everyone is searching for you!'

'The house is noisy, so I came here for some peace and I must have fallen asleep.'

'Are you okay?' asked Maria in her broken English. She must be trying to impress her new young man.

'Yes, I'm fine. Is the show going ahead?'

'Yes. Your outfits are ready, so I've come for a walk before the performance.' She flicked a smile at her young man. Andrea tried to peep above the ferns and bushes.

'I've been asleep and lost my bearings. Which is the quickest way back?'

Maria's young man said, 'Shall I show you?' Maria didn't look pleased.

'Yes, then you can return to Maria.' He walked towards the house expecting Andrea to follow. 'Enjoy yourself Maria.' With a sparkle in her eyes, she nodded. Andrea tried to keep up but bare feet against trainers made the passage through the undergrowth difficult. He glanced back. 'I can see the route, thanks, why don't you return to Maria? She likes you, I could tell.'

'Yes,' he moved past Andrea. Taking a few steps towards a small hole in the privet hedge, she listened. No noise and no voices. She replaced her heels and slipped through the hedge with the intention of nipping into a room through the French Doors. She inched along the house wall, darted around the corner and collided with a man.

Andrea stepped backward and swallowed, 'Chief Constable, I'm sorry I didn't mean to bump into you.' A smile replaced the initial frown.

'Andrea, the person I needed to find.' Calum appeared limping briskly around the far corner of the house. He looked at Andrea, who waved. He did his best to run along the front of the house, but his face showed the pain of moving.

'Go steady,' Andrea shouted to Calum, but he didn't slow.

The Chief Constable said, 'Here she is, Calum.'

'Yes, sir,' he grunted back.

'I've been with Maria, she's my dresser as I wanted private time with another woman. We were just through the hedge.' Andrea guessed the mention of being with another woman would avoid questions.

'Yes, quite,' said the Chief Constable. Calum glared at her.

'Is Martin here?'

'No, I decided the show should proceed. We agreed he would follow up the leads allowing me to come here.' He wouldn't be pleased. Poor Martin, she felt for him.

'Has everyone arrived, Calum?' the Chief Constable rapped out his question.

'Yes, sir,' mumbled Calum.

'Don't frown Calum, this is a high socicty do. You need to fit into these circumstances to obtain results.' The expression on Calum's face suggested he never would but the Chief Constable ignored him.

'Can I help?' asked Andrea.

'Yes, I need you for two matters, I shall take your statement.' Calum glanced at his watch and tried to bite his tongue but changed his mind.

'Sir, it will be a complicated explanation, and Andrea

might not remember crucial details if she is thinking about the show in memory of Charlotte, her friend.'

'Proper advice in normal circumstances.'

He turned to Andrea, 'Also, I need your advice.'

'Do you want me to leave?' asked Calum.

'No, you are part of it.' He faced Andrea, 'I agreed the show could proceed if I could add a few people to the invited list. They will be my eyes and ears throughout the show.'

'Is there a difficulty?'

'Yes, they would benefit from a briefing about the show's organisation.'

'Of course.'

'And that includes you, Calum. This way,' he called over his shoulder, as he strode away.

Calum whispered, 'Deals are off.'

'No, you could be the first to discover my new information.'

'You're bluffing.'

'I could tell the Chief Constable in my interview.' They would soon arrive at the front of the house and he wouldn't be able to continue their conversation.

'You must answer truthfully if he asks.'

'Yes, I will, but he won't ask what I know,' she gave a small conspiratorial smile. They went a few more steps. Andrea continued keeping her advantage, 'Don't forget you lost me again, and in front of the Chief Constable. Black mark!' The door of the house approached. 'It's time for a decision, Calum Brodie,' whispered Andrea, 'deal or no deal?'

'Deal,' he growled, 'but it had better be worth it.'

They walked into the spacious entrance hall with

the Chief Constable three steps ahead. They trouped along a passageway and up the rear stairs. At the top of the stairs a young man, wearing a Motorhead tee shirt and frayed jeans sat in a wing-back chair with his legs over the arm. The Chief Constable nodded, received the slightest of acknowledgements and opened the nearest door. The young man went back to reading his magazine, but whispered to Calum as they went past, 'Lost anyone recently?'

Andrea guessed Calum would be angry as he would become the butt of his colleagues' jokes. She had to support him and through him she could help Martin.

A small room furnished with a large table and chairs had three people present, dressed perfectly for the show. The two men wore black tie suits and the woman a turquoise satin dress, they appeared ready for early evening cocktails.

'No time for introductions, Andrea will brief us on what happens and who goes where.' The circular table had six seats. Calum looked nervous, he must have recognised these people as senior officials. Andrea tried to remember how Martin spoke on the phone. Short, accurate. No extra words.

Police investigations were a different world as she didn't normally have to talk in that style. Andrea settled herself and before starting checked they were ready. 'The audience will start with cocktails and light entertainment in the main dining room, thirty minutes before the show. Everyone will be directed there if they arrive early. Only waiting staff will be present. Shall I describe the long gallery?'

'No,' responded the Chief Constable.

'The show will start between twenty and thirty minutes late. The audience will be ushered into the long gallery ten minutes before the show commences. Many of Luigi's staff and the junior designers, will blend with the audience.'

'Backstage will be our main concern as we don't know what will happen behind the scenes. Is it possible for outsiders to gain access?' asked the woman.

'Yes, easily, it's chaotic, there are people everywhere, many will arrive backstage at the last minute.'

'We've no one in there have we?' said the woman to the Chief Constable.

'No, and that's a problem.'

Andrea felt compelled to take the initiative to help the case. 'You must have people positioned there. Calum knows my dresser so he won't be out of place as she can give him jobs. The others won't take any notice as they will have seen him around.'

'But that's just one.'

'The guy outside will fit as a roadie, and so could a woman constable dressed appropriately.'

The Chief Constable looked at Calum who said, 'WPC Atkins is coming.'

Andrea continued, 'I'll get Maria to find her something suitable to wear.' She looked around at the serious faces. 'Not ideal, but three could blend in. The guy outside can work for Pablo, he is always short of help, he manages the show so is at the heart of everything that happens.'

The Chief Constable turned to Calum, 'Your opinion, Inspector Brodie.'

'I agree sir, with what Andrea has outlined, normal

police would stick out like a sore thumb.'

'Pablo?' questioned the woman.

'I've known him for twelve years as we began together in the fashion world. He is hard working and unusually for this industry, he's a sound family man. He runs the whole show as he is practical and always knows what's going on.'

'Will he ask too many questions if we put police in?' asked the younger man.

'Definitely not, he won't question it, if I ask him to do something.'

'I can verify that, sir,' said Calum as he stared at Andrea.

'That's good enough for me, but I wished we knew more about what happens backstage so we can brief the young officers.'

'That's not a problem, I'll take you backstage and show you the routine and where everyone comes and goes.'

'Won't that cause a disturbance as they are preparing for the show?'

'No, VIPs frequently visit. You will be surprised how much you will be ignored. Shall we go?' She led them through the Long Gallery to the stage. A mixture of people milled around with an air of busy excitement prevailing, some waved to Andrea but carried on with their tasks. 'There are three primary areas. Where the models change, where the clothes are moved, stored and ironed and the third is for the equipment, music, lights. I'll show you each in turn. During the show it's chaos behind the scenes, and a stranger wouldn't be noticed.' She glanced at her party as they stood in the corridor which had a door to the garden. Andrea could see they had noted the means of access.

'First, the room where the models change. Come in.' Andrea opened the door and walked in. 'Most haven't arrived yet. They are not brilliant time-keepers,' she said with a smile, but the joke didn't break the serious faces.

There appeared no one, but a voice said, 'Hi Andrea.'

A topless model came out from behind rails of clothes. 'Hi, Trish, VIP tour.'

'Okay. Hi guys,' said Trish who walked over to Andrea, 'unzip me darling, I can't twist the skirt around.'

Andrea unzipped her, the men had turned away, Trish returned to the clothes rail.

'How many models and support staff are involved?'

'Ten models which means about forty people altogether.' That captured their attention.

'Do you know them?'

'No, I won't know some models. Many dressers will be agency casuals.' The Chief Constable frowned. Andrea shivered, but pointed to a chair inside the door. 'Supposedly for the security staff, but it's to stop gate crashers.'

'Does it work?' said Calum.

Andrea shook her head, 'A police officer could make it work. The models and dressers have a security pass to enter but the models will not wear them during the show.'

'Good thinking,' said the Chief Constable. Andrea moved through the other backstage areas. She remained succinct. After many questions and shaking of heads, the Chief Constable said, 'Thank you, Andrea.'

'Perhaps we can meet in thirty minutes back in our

room.' They agreed and left. The Chief Constable with a serious expression focused his attention on Andrea, 'This way.' He led her through the ground floor of the house into another room where a middle-aged woman waited. She had a computer and another machine that Andrea didn't recognise. 'This effort is precautionary as I don't expect an incident.' But to Andrea the words didn't sound convincing. 'I need to take your statement.'

'Is there time before the show?'

Without waiting for an answer, he waved his hand towards the seated woman. 'This is Hazel. She is a stenographer. Tell her in your own words, a succinct account of the facts from yesterday, she will transcribe it into a statement for you to sign after the show.'

38

'Good work with the Chief Constable, you impressed him,' Calum came from the house and his normal scowl deepened, he scanned in every direction as though expecting an attack.

Andrea walked out of the front door of the manor and breathed a huge sigh of relief at the peaceful completion of the early evening show which had been a fitting tribute to Charlotte. Martin still hadn't rung, and a chill passed through her every time she thought about him.

'What do you think Calum?'

He didn't change his expression, 'It's important the Chief is pleased. I've spoken to that fat bastard Fitzwilliam and he's in the library.'

'Okay,' the moment had arrived to deal with Fitzwilliam.

With less aggression in his voice than normal, 'Do you prefer me to be there? He's a slimy git, I've a good mind to arrest him.'

'What for?'

'When he lies about being a roadie yesterday, I'll nick him.'

‘Yes, he’s not a pleasant man.’ Calum showed no interest. Andrea changed tack, ‘Did you get anywhere with the young singers and his false names?’

‘Nothing yet, investigations take time.’

‘Better to leave him. If something comes through from those enquiries, you’ve an acceptable reason to arrest him.’

‘Yes, maybe you’re right.’

‘I’ll go to the library on my own.’

‘I’m not happy about you and him alone,’ he had sincere concern in his voice.

The meeting with Fitzwilliam would be problematic. ‘I’ll stand in the garden away from the window, so I can see you but will not hear. Stay in view.’

‘Yes, Calum.’ Andrea didn’t hold concerns about being alone with Fitzwilliam, but she must stop the story.

‘At last,’ Fitzwilliam said as she strode into the room through the wide French Doors. After the brightness of outside the room appeared gloomy. The large solemn portraits adorning the wall seemed to be watching. She shook her head in exasperation for allowing her imagination to run riot and focused on the fat balding man who smirked and rubbed his hands together with anticipation. Taking a miniature portable recording machine from his pocket, he fiddled with the controls preparing for the conversation. She had rehearsed about Patsy, Janice and the young singers.

After he’d set the recording machine to his satisfaction, he leered with unashamed insolence, ‘I want background facts about your exploits last night.’ Calum leaned on the sundial in the middle of the rose garden watching. Stalling for time, she fiddled with her hair, hoping for inspiration. 'Your pet poodle gave you the message,' he chuckled at his own joke and stared at Calum through narrowed eyes, 'I don't like him.'

'The feeling is reciprocal.'

Fitzwilliam studied her face as she gathered her thoughts. With a sinking sensation in the pit of her stomach her idea of blackmailing Fitzwilliam about the young girls wouldn't work. When Calum discovers the information about the young singers, he will arrest Fitzwilliam. Or the security guard's statement will be circulated, and Fitzwilliam will be taken to the police station and questioned about his movements as a roadie. If either happen, he will realise he's been duped and will publish the worst version of his story. Andrea's legs went weak, she would have to cooperate. Frustration built up inside her and she wanted to throw a tantrum and stamp her feet.

'Background facts, how did you find the car?'

'You can't publish the facts; it's called perverting the course of justice.'

'Don't give me that crap, I'll write the story then the lawyers can arrange the details with the editor. You've kept me dangling on all day so let's have the information.' He took a step forward and waved his recorder close to her face in an aggressive manner.

'Will you stick with the deal?'

'Get on with it.' Calum stood in the middle of the garden arms crossed. What to do? Andrea stepped aside from Fitzwilliam as he had advanced too close for comfort, 'It's either now or never and I'll publish what I want.'

Andrea stared at him and then at Calum and an idea

struck her which would be worth a try. Towering above Fitzwilliam gave her a sense of power which fuelled her confidence. In a nonchalant tone of voice, 'I'm surprised you are still here.'

'What do you mean?'

'The police…'

'I'm not worried about your poodle,' he jeered with an expression of disdain, 'I've told him to get lost.'

Andrea changed the tone of her voice and willed Fitzwilliam to pick up the alteration. 'You must be the prime suspect, but they haven't taken you in for questioning yet.'

'Don't be so bloody ridiculous, have you gone looney?' He clutched the recorder but allowed it to rest by his side instead of waving it in an intimidating manner. Andrea detected the slightest quiver at the end of the sentence.

A flicker of hope floated into her mind, 'You were here yesterday, pretending to be a roadie.' He forced a weak smile, his pudgy forehead beaded with sweat, 'Did you tell the police?'

She let a silence draw out and moved across to the French Doors. Calum still leant against the sun dial, arms folded staring in her direction. She wandered back toward Fitzwilliam watching the discomfort on his face with pleasure, 'Not yet, it slipped my mind when making my statement, but I could amend it.'

'It doesn't matter, you're not getting out of it that easy.' He had become rattled, his movements became jerky and his frown had deepened into an intense scowl.

'It takes the police time to review statements.'

'What does that mean?'

'The security guard saw you leave a few minutes after your friend the photographer and just before Charlotte drove away.'

'He doesn't know me.' Fitzwilliam stood still in the centre of the room, his pale face set grim like a carved mask.

'The photographer with you earlier yesterday evening, won't be willing to lie to the police on a murder enquiry.'

He gave a sickly grin, and stepped towards her, 'Let's not get heavy about this Andrea as we've known each other for years, I need a few facts, so I can write a good article.' But his smooth well-rehearsed patter didn't fool her.

'You've announced you'll write what you choose so I'm not accepting your word.' Andrea paced back and forth across the carpet, determined to get the better of the big fat creep.

'What are you thinking?' Fitzwilliam still gripped his little black recorder in his pudgy hands though his earlier confidence had drained away.

'One way is to make sure you can't write the story.'

'Not even you can stop the story, I'll guess at what happened then you'll be in a mess with the police for telling me.' She moved closer, looking down on him, 'You can't write if the police have arrested you.'

Fitzwilliam's eyes widened at the suggestion, 'But that will not happen. And I'll write an even worse story when I get out.' A smirk covered his face. Andrea could tell that he enjoyed causing misery by writing malicious articles, perhaps he gets a buzz out of other people's misfortunes.

'When you are released, it will be old news.'

'The story will live for months.'

'But will it live for years?' He stood still eyeing her suspiciously, his jaw clenched, and his bald head shining with sweat, 'You're bluffing.'

Andrea felt a surge of confidence as he no longer controlled the conversation, so she didn't hasten to reply but enjoyed Fitzwilliam's obvious discomfort, 'Patsy told me about Janice. Was young Charlotte one of your conquests?'

'No,' he hesitated, 'I don't know what you mean,' he plonked himself on a nearby chair and swiped a hand across his sweaty forehead.

Andrea gave a meagre smile and spoke with emphasis, 'The police think there is a connection between this murder and the Sheffield armed robbery.' The realisation hit him. 'You are too close, Fitzwilliam. You took advantage of young Charlotte, are friends with the bank robbers and you arrive here in disguise on the day she is murdered. Shall I explain the connections to Calum? The police haven't joined the threads together, but I have.'

Andrea plucked her phone from her pocket and curled her long fingers around it while a smile flickered on her lips. He squirmed and she enjoyed the moment.

'Don't be so ridiculous,' came the abrupt reply, but the confidence and aggression had gone.

Andrea became determined to drive home her advantage over this pesky man, 'You knew Charlotte as a teenager.'

'I didn't.' He avoided eye contact and gazed at the carpet as Andrea stood.

'You must have been one of Charlotte's first men. Did you write that article under the name of Stephens? Perhaps you used a different one in Sheffield.'

'You're making it up,' he snapped, his face as grey as tempered steel and his angry eyes flashing with an evil glint.

Andrea stood her ground and wouldn't be intimidated. 'Who's the one person associated with both the murder of Charlotte and the armed robbery?' Staring at a large portrait on the wall of an imposing military figure, Fitzwilliam walked towards it. Andrea suspected these were delaying tactics while he considered a way to squirm out of her accusations, so she didn't wait for him to turn around but spoke to the back of his head.

'Of course, money must be behind your actions, what will the police find in your finances? I wonder.'

'Why would they choose to do that? he spun round to face her and plastered on a smile. 'Come on Andrea, let's be friendly.' He gave her a long assessing look, 'I'll write a good article about your heroism.'

'Fitzwilliam, if Martin and Calum could concentrate on catching the real killer, then I'm prepared to believe you and give you the benefit of the doubt even though you had the opportunity, the motive and something else to hide.'

He gulped, and his eyes darted towards the garden and the presence of Calum staring stonily at him. Andrea enjoyed the spectacle of Fitzwilliam's agitation and proceeded to drive home her advantage. 'If they catch the real killer, they won't rake up the dirt about you, but they will if I tell Martin and Calum about my thoughts.' He looked stunned, 'No article, Fitzwilliam,' her voice penetrating and cold like an icy north wind blowing across the moors in winter.

'But my editor wants a perfect story,' he spluttered.

Andrea looked out at Calum. 'Fitzwilliam?' He followed Andrea's eyes and focused on the staring policeman. 'How long do you think Wayne Smith would stand up to questioning by Calum?'

'Okay, it's a deal, no story,' he turned and stormed from the room.

39

What had she done? Andrea's enthusiasm at killing the story became short lived as she thought through the ramifications of her conversation with Fitzwilliam. If he's the killer, she could be the next victim. Charlotte could have discovered his background and then he killed her, she went white at the ramifications of the conversation with Fitzwilliam as they hit home. Moving through the French Doors she approached Calum.

'You look pale? Calum's concerned eyes studied her face, 'What did he want?'

'Fitzwilliam always wants a story.'

'Did you give him one, he can be aggressive.'

'I didn't, I'm used to dealing with the press, you aren't!' She walked past him and into the car park as Fitzwilliam's blue Audi pulled away with the wheels spinning on the gravel.

Calum snapped, 'Come here.' His normal scowl had passed, concern registered on his face, so she joined him at the low wall on the edge of the rose garden. Her mind whirled through the conversation with Fitzwilliam. Calum's voice interrupted her thoughts 'We can't go on like this.'

'What do you mean?'

'You're treating this as a game and enjoy trying to lose me,' a deeper frown crossed his face, 'you are trying to solve the case yourself.'

'I'm not,' but she avoided eye contact by studying the nearby roses.

'You mean well but it's too complex for you.'

'How could I solve the case as you are the professionals?' She kept her voice calm although the tension from chatting with Fitzwilliam hadn't left her.

'It's the pattern of your behaviour, you keep losing me, so you can talk to people. Wayne Smith first, then you disappeared again because you wanted to question somebody else.' He paused. 'I don't believe what you're telling me about Fitzwilliam, you were trying to question him.'

Andrea hadn't realised how perceptive Calum could be. 'I'm sorry, my disappearance earlier must have embarrassed you in front of the Chief Constable.'

'I presume you went to see Gerald and Edward.'

'How did you find out?' Her eyes flashed in confusion as she believed he didn't know.

'It's easy when you draw a copper's attention to an old Mark II Jaguar that stops near the murder scene.'

'So you knew,' she burst out in exasperation.

'What if the murderer laid a trap? Even worse, both Gerald and Edward could be involved and wanted to stop you snooping around.' She'd been caught out again like a naughty schoolgirl, so she bowed her head in an expression of shame.

'I found out something useful,' she tried as a peace offering but it fell on stony ground as he scowled in a disgruntled fashion at her. She paused for effect, 'Edward is a marksman.'

'But it's nothing to do with you,' he huffed, his face red with anger and his whole body tensed. Martin would be furious with her. Andrea glanced around the rose garden which had long views to the woods. Could a marksman have encamped there? The policemen below in the bushes wouldn't be much help. Have they checked the woods?

Calum's shoes rustled in the gravel as he walked away from her. 'You are too complicated for me,' he snapped over his shoulder. 'I'm telling Martin and the Chief I can't look after you as you don't want to be protected, it's beyond me.'

'Calum,' but her voice trailed off as he limped away. The older man from the Chief Constable's group walked towards her so she waited for him to cross the garden. Should she run after Calum?

He'd worked out every ploy, she hadn't been clever.

40

The sudden noise made her jump. Several loud cracks accompanied by dull echoes.

Shots echoed around the valley and over the hills. She jumped behind a statue as fear clogged her throat and her heart hammered.

The next noise came from the gravel. Calum crashed into her and drove her to the ground. Andrea yelped as she sprawled face down into the gravel. Stars came into her eyes as her head clipped a stone urn. 'Are you hurt? Are you hurt?'

'No, I don't think so,' Calum gabbled into his radio. Shouting came from several places and a policeman rushed for cover. 'Any casualties?' bellowed Calum into his radio. Andrea lay flat on her front with her face pressed into the sharp gravel. Calum next to her, 'Stay still.'

'My leg hurts.' He remained lying flat but twisted his head to look along the length of Andrea's body and placed his hand down and pulled her dress up. 'It's only grazed, you can see to it later.'

The radio screeched, 'Movement at the edge of the woods.'

Calum said, 'How many?'

'Negative,' came the reply.

Policemen and other people from the show lay flat behind statues and under benches. 'No one move,' shouted Calum both across the terrace and into his radio.

'Shall we engage?' came a strong voice over the radio.

'Negative. Negative,' shouted Calum, 'they could be bloody walkers, there's a public footpath over there. Do not open fire.' There were no further shots. Andrea shivered. Had someone tried to kill her?

'Did you hear any bullets whistle?'

She hadn't, 'No, I don't think so.'

'Then you didn't.' Andrea heard sirens in the distance. Calum's radio crackled into life again with a loud screech.

'This is the Chief Constable. Inspector Brodie will assume immediate command of activities outside the house.' Andrea could see Calum was eager for him to finish talking. Two more sharp cracks interrupted him. Andrea listened but heard no whistling of bullets.

'Report!' shouted Calum.

'Fired from near the woods, sir. Two rifle shots but the targets unclear. Gunmen cannot be seen.'

'Teams two and three, approach the wood. Do not shoot unless in personal danger. Team two, acknowledge.' There was a slight pause and then, 'Team three acknowledge.' 'The remaining firearms officers and Team One and Four, move to a protective shield surrounding the terrace. We will move the civilians back into the house. Team Five join me, I'm with the principal target, by the main statue.'

Andrea didn't see where they came from, but she heard the gravel churning as each of them dived beside her on the ground. Calum issued further orders. While he waited for replies, he turned to her. He put his hand out and gently put his finger on her eyebrow. 'You've cut your eye.' Andrea's face froze. She shivered. 'Nothing serious,' he said with a smile, 'a nick.' He showed her his finger which had a trace of blood. 'Moving principal target to the house. Acknowledge.' Several quick replies came in. Calum counted them.

'Keep low and move as fast as you can. These guys will protect you. Put this on.' Andrea accepted the bullet-proof jacket and slipped it on without raising herself from the floor.

'Go,' shouted Calum. The two policemen raised themselves to crouching and helped Andrea to her feet. All three ran towards the house and a shot echoed in the valley. They bundled her towards the door which opened as they reached it. The force of the two policemen made her trip over the step and she plunged head first along the carpet of the hall. The large oak door slammed with a resounding crash.

'Are you all right, ma'am?' Andrea rolled on to her back and then sat up.

'Yes, I am. A little grazed but I'm okay.' One of them helped her up and escorted her through to a nearby room then led her to a chair away from the windows. He turned his radio volume lower and pulled the thick heavy curtains across the window. Before long movement began in the house and she became engulfed by Luigi and the others from the show. They fussed over her and realising she wouldn't be able to go anywhere for a while, she calmed herself and talked to Luigi and Pablo. The policeman left her with instructions to stay away from the window. Andrea waited. It gave her time to reflect. Martin hadn't rung. She waited and chatted.

After the sound of the sirens had died away, Calum appeared. Luigi and Pablo hurriedly left. No one liked Calum. He closed the door to keep out others. 'Poachers!' Andrea looked perplexed. 'There are deer in the woods. They sell the meat in Sheffield Market.' Calum had been satisfied with the conclusion. 'False alarm, they were not shooting in this direction.'

'We're jittery,' said Andrea.

'Not me,' said Calum without a smile, 'the squad picked them up and they confessed so they will be charged but we do have to make sure.' There's something strange about the shooting. With the last bullet Andrea had heard the whistle but she would annoy Calum by mentioning it as he must have registered the sound. It would be better to stay silent.

'Have you talked to Martin?' she asked.

'No, he's not here so I've spoken to the Chief Constable.'

'Thanks for protecting me out there.'

Calum ignored her. He didn't even turn to face her when he said, 'I left a message for Martin and I've spoken to the Chief Constable to say I can't watch over you anymore.'

'What did the Chief Constable say?'

'I'll put it down to your injuries and that you are not fully recuperated. She does seem to be running rings round you.'

'Sorry,' while she disliked Calum, making him look

incompetent in front of the Chief Constable hadn't been her intention. Helping both Martin and Calum had become difficult.

What are your arrangements now?' said Calum.

Her watch showed eight o'clock, 'Martin won't be home early, and I don't want to be on my own, so I'll travel into Sheffield to meet Patsy.' Calum frowned at the mention of Patsy's name. 'Calum?'

'Yes.' He lifted his bad leg off the ground and rubbed his knee.

'Do you think I'm in danger?'

'You're not helping yourself.'

'That's not what I asked?'

'It takes a couple of days in a murder inquiry to obtain a view of motives and suspects. Until that time, we don't know. Charlotte had a high profile. You have one, so we take prudent precautions.'

'Have you made any progress?'

'Don't know, not my case. I'm on sick leave if you recall.' He rubbed his leg whether because it hurt or for effect she couldn't tell. 'Have you told anyone you will visit Patsy?'

'No,'

Pablo came in, 'Excuse me, Andrea, I have finished here and I'm driving into Sheffield to see Patsy.'

'That's perfect, you can take me too. I'm too drained to drive.'

'I'll drive,' said Calum.

'You said you were giving up on me. You're in pain and need to go home and rest. Pablo will be with me this evening and Martin can pick me up from Patsy's. You can take my car until tomorrow.' He thought through the ramifications. He eyed Pablo up and down.

'The Chief and Martin must determine how to handle you.'

41

Andrea wanted to leave before the Chief Constable changed the arrangements.

Calum said, 'I'll tell the Chief.'

'Come on, Pablo, let's go.' Within minutes they drove past the Strines pub and onto the Snake Pass road then turned towards Sheffield. He didn't speak until they began the long descent to the city.

'Which hotel?'

'The one in the centre by the Winter Gardens, didn't you take her this morning?'

'No, a roadie drove her there and picked her up for the show.'

As they reached the signs to the Rivelin Valley, one grabbed her attention, 'Malin Bridge'.

'Take the next left.'

'That isn't the route to Patsy's hotel.' Pablo swung the car along the Rivelin Valley road. Andrea absorbed in her thoughts didn't reply. They drove the couple of miles along the tree-lined valley and arrived at Malin Bridge.

'Where now?'

'Drive around the corner as I want somewhere near

the tram stop.' After a few hundred yards Pablo pulled into a side road.

'It doesn't look a good area.'

'I will hire a car.' Pablo looked at the building next to the tram stop, Kennedy Vehicle Hire, Limos a Specialty.

'Is this a sensible idea, Andrea, the police have warned you?'

'They are being overprotective,' she flapped her hand in dismissal.

'Do you want me to come?'

'No, wait in the car.' As Andrea strode along the pavement her mind whirled through what she knew about the Kennedy's. They'd been involved in the armed robbery and Fitzwilliam knew them. Had Fitzwilliam persuaded a young Charlotte to have sex with him in exchange for a good write up? He'd looked uneasy when she'd suggested it to him. Wayne Smith used their cars and had been Charlotte's agent. Pushing all these thoughts to the back of her mind Andrea entered the small reception area which had a wooden counter.

She surmised that the door behind the counter led into the office. A mottled collection of chairs were arranged around the edge of the room and music from a local radio station played in the background. The dingy office required a coat of paint. Through a side door, she glimpsed the garage with tightly packed cars.

A thickset, muscular man wearing a well-used suit, as tall as her, entered reception from the office. His rugged face broke into a smile, a second tall man, slightly older joined him. Neither spoke. Trying to control her shaking voice she forced her lips into a smile, 'I want to hire a car.'

'You are a smart lady, so you'll need a nice car.'

'Yes, please. Can I have one immediately?' The man nodded and pushed a pad of forms towards her.

'Fill in a form.'

Andrea took a pen from her bag and completed the form, 'You were recommended by friends.'

'Who?'

'Father Manning and Wayne Smith.'

Andrea heard a movement in the office behind the men, but she couldn't see past them. The second of the men growled, 'I recognise you.' Andrea took a deep breath. She had hoped she could stay anonymous, 'You're that model who is in the newspapers.'

A sharp voice, 'John, Mark, I will deal with this lady.'

'Yes, mother,' they stepped aside and let her come through to the counter. The short wiry woman had no smile, her sharp grey eyes examined her. Andrea gave a flick of a smile but received no change of expression from the woman.

'John recognised you,' said the woman.

'Yes, I'm Andrea Cain.'

'Married to the famous Sheffield detective.' The big men tensed and clenched their fists. One came forward to the counter and crashed his fist down shaking the room. Andrea jumped back from the counter in horror.

'Calm yourself, John, Mrs Cain won't be staying.' The scowl from the old woman only broke to say, 'Do you think we're that stupid we wouldn't recognise you?' Andrea took a deep breath to stop her legs shaking and clutched the counter for support. 'Not a clever plot from the police is it?'

Poor Martin, the focus of so much aggression, he must meet such hostility on a daily basis. How does he cope? She closed her eyes to gather her thoughts, then opened them and fixed the woman, 'Mrs Kennedy, this has nothing to do with my husband, I have lost a dear friend Charlotte Manning to murder and I'm trying to find anything that might help.'

'I can understand you know Wayne, he's a showbiz agent but what about Father Manning?' Before Andrea replied the woman said, 'I didn't know the Father was related to the singer as he had never mentioned her but as they have the same surname, I should have worked it out for myself.'

'They were brother and sister.'

'I still think you're working for the police.' John Kennedy stepped out from behind the counter and came towards her. Andrea shook but didn't move, his smouldering stare bored into her as he closed the gap between them. His face inches from hers, his beery breath and the sweaty smell of him invaded her nostrils.

She held her ground although she wanted to run.

42

A deafening bang reverberated around the cramped reception as the entrance door crashed back on its hinges. Her body shuddered, and she leapt away from John. She spun around towards the noise and gasped with horror. The door frame filled with a police officer wearing a helmet, visor and stab proof jacket. A policeman simultaneously appeared from the garage and rushed into reception. Andrea screamed at the sudden noise and commotion. Why were they here? Had they followed her?

The second Kennedy brother stretched out his hand. Andrea gasped with pain as he clutched a handful of her hair but the officer who came from the garage tackled him from behind and bundled him to the floor. Andrea clutched at the counter to stop herself from tumbling, two officers manhandled him and then handcuffed him. The confinement of his wrists behind his back didn't deter him from kicking and cursing.

John Kennedy jumped over the counter to help his brother, but two officers grappled with him forcing him face down onto the floor. A woman police officer, dressed in riot gear, barged Andrea out of her path on the way to the counter, then grabbed Ruth Kennedy pushing her up against the wall. Andrea sprawled over the counter, her heart hammered, would they arrest her? What would Martin say? Fear clogged her throat making her gasp for breath.

Ruth didn't resist but fury filled her face, her venomous voice pierced the air like a shard of ice. 'You stitched us up!'

'I didn't,' screeched Andrea. Ruth Kennedy yelped in pain as the officer forced her wrists into handcuffs. They weren't needed as she hadn't resisted, the injustice leapt at Andrea, so she reached across the counter and grabbed the officer's arm, 'Stop that.' She tugged as hard as she could and the officer spun around. Andrea screamed from the agony of her hair being pulled as another officer bundled her to the floor. Her head thumped on the wooden boards and she yelped in pain as knees dug into her back. Many hands and feet held her down. In the turmoil her jacket had ridden above her head, so she couldn't see her assailants.

The anonymous officer kneeling on her, wrenched her arms up behind her back. She felt the cold metal of the handcuffs as they tore into her skin. She tried to shout but her face had been forced into the boards and she couldn't breathe from the sudden shock of the attack. Tensing her muscles, she wriggled to free herself as they had no right to treat her and Ma Kennedy in this aggressive fashion.

Then the punches landed. Two sharp blows to the back of her ribs left her gasping for breath. The officer pulled her jacket partly back from her head and she felt a warm breath near her ear. The panting voice said, 'I am arresting you for resisting a police officer. You do not have to say anything, but it may harm your defence if you do not mention when questioned something which you later rely on in court. Anything you say may be given in evidence.'

'Get off me, you bastard,' screeched Andrea and tried to wriggle free. The knees in her back dug in deeper.

'Not until you calm down,' but Andrea continued to fight back. Then, a fist thudded into her ribs once more and she lost her breath.

A loud shout came, 'D.I. Brodie! Let her go!'

'She resisted arrest, sir.'

'Let her bloody go. And undo those handcuffs.'

'Sir.'

Her wrist fell free from the metal and the pressure on her back disappeared, but the throbbing pain made her wince. 'Don't just stand there, help her up,' barked Calum. More hands helped her to stand. She pulled her jacket down and turned to face them.

'Oh, shit!' said the officer who held the handcuffs.

Andrea wanted to shout at everyone there, her body shook with fury, and her ribs ached from the punches. Bleeding from the wrist because of the handcuffs she snarled at the officers. The Kennedy brothers were held and Ruth Kennedy in handcuffs stood by a woman officer.

Calum said, 'Get them out of here.' He turned to Andrea and whispered, 'You're such a bloody pain in the arse.'

She placed her face inches from his face and whispered back, 'Piss off.' The officer moved the Kennedy family towards the door. Andrea didn't pull back from being in Calum's face, she hissed, 'I want to speak to Ruth before you take her.'

'You what? Don't be so bloody daft.' They were face to face.

'These are your friends and colleagues, what story do you want me to tell the Chief Constable? One of your officers beat me up last night.'

'You weren't beaten, anyway you shouldn't have been here.'

'Think what will happen when the police doctor examines the bruises from the three punches to my ribs.'

'No. In answer to your question, you can't speak to her.' His eyes narrowed to thin slits and he glared in angry frustration. Andrea stood her ground as she couldn't shake the growing resentment that bubbled inside her.

'Calum, think about it, I'm bloody furious at the manner I've been treated, not by the Kennedy family but by the dammed police, I can't believe it.' The agony stretched across Calum's face and the police officers probably guessed the conversation without being able to hear it. Would he keep his colleagues out of trouble or do everything by the book and make himself even more unpopular?

'Will you forget about it, if I let you have five minutes?'

'Ruth, could you come over here please,' said Andrea. Calum nodded to the woman officer. 'Take off the handcuffs.' He nodded for the second time.

Andrea said in a quiet voice to Ruth, 'Give me your word you will go with the police officer after we have chatted together.' Calum scowled.

Ruth studied both, there was no smile, but a pair of alert eyes examined Andrea's face. 'Yes,' the single word was spoken in an icy but strong manner.

Andrea went back close to Calum's face, 'You can take the other two, when we've finished our conversation, I'll escort her to the police car outside, now leave us alone.'

'Jim, you wait for Mrs Kennedy.'

'Sir,' came the reply. The room emptied.

'Your last involvement,' hissed Calum.

Andrea felt weak. 'Are you okay?' said Ruth.

'I'm shaky.'

'Rest in the office, I'll make tea.'

The first sip of tea felt perfect. Ruth pulled up a chair next to Andrea, her eyes wary, 'I don't know what you wish to discuss, but I will help you as it's clear the police didn't know you would be here.' Andrea grimaced as she moved, and the pain shot through her ribs. 'You now know what it's like when the police don't like you.'

Andrea ignored the remark, 'I assume they have been arrested over the armed robbery?' Ruth nodded. 'But why you?'

'Mark and John were here during the robbery, I made a statement to that effect, so they will arrest me for perverting the course of justice.'

'Were you with them at the time?'

The simplest of questions, Ruth didn't answer but crossed to the shelf in the corner and brought back the family Bible and placed it on the table. Ruth put her hand on it, 'John and Mark were with me the whole time of the robbery, they were here in this office.'

'Tell me about your four sons.'

'The twins, headstrong and violent, but I don't know why.' Tears brimmed her eyes and her hands shook as she took a sip of tea. 'John and Mark are the contrary.'

'They scared me. They are such big lads.'

'They wouldn't have harmed you. Believe me, they have only ever had jobs as bouncers, so they use their size and weight to intimidate people, but they would have never touched you. They are good boys. If you had been a genuine customer, they would have fetched me as they can't read and write.' Ruth tried to hold back the tears and clutched the cup of tea in her hands. She perched on the chair with sadness engraved on her face.

Andrea wriggled in her chair, she wanted to add words of comfort, but nothing would form in her mind. The few seconds of silence seemed like years, but Ruth regained control of herself, 'I didn't know the twins would commit the robbery otherwise I would have stopped them. They were often out of control, but I could make them listen when it mattered.' Andrea believed her. 'My religion is important, it's my salvation when life depressed me, so I've known Father Manning for many years. But I didn't know your friend Charlotte Manning was his sister. Knowing Father, I don't suppose he wished to own up to his sister as he is a devout and conservative man.'

Andrea struggled to respond, but Ma Kennedy's evident affinity for Father Manning made it problematic. But she couldn't accept his behavior towards Charlotte. It hadn't been the reaction she expected from a man of the cloth. No compassion or forgiveness. No gentle words of comfort, 'He and his sister Margaret had almost disowned her.' Andrea slumped back in the chair and sighed.

Tiredness had come over her. Did she believe Ruth? She agonised. Yes, she did. She couldn't think of any reason why Ruth or her two boys would want to harm Charlotte, so linking the armed robbery to Charlotte's murder through the Kennedy family made no sense.

'If you have finished with me, I'd better contact our solicitor and travel to the police station to my boys.'

'Will the questioning be difficult?'

'No, we are used to it. It happens regularly.' Ruth and Andrea walked outside together. The police officers stepped from their car.

'Ma'am.'

'Mrs Kennedy will go with you.' He nodded and opened the back door of the police car and Ruth Kennedy slid in. Pablo pulled up as the police car drove away. Andrea climbed in. Her mind whirled with questions, ideas and images. She thought about Patsy but said, 'I've had enough, can you drive me home, Pablo?' He didn't question her but headed back up the Rivelin Valley towards the hills. She fell asleep as she laid back in the warm comfortable car. As Pablo turned off the main Castleton road onto the track Andrea woke.

'Nearly home,' said Pablo. As the car bumped up the track, Andrea peered sleepily into the darkness.

'Turn into the house drive after the dead tree.' The black night enveloped them and she shivered despite the heat in the car. As Pablo pulled up to the house security lights came on.

'Do you wish me to come in and check everything is okay?'

'You're a darling Pablo, but no, I shall be fine now.

I'm home. I want Martin so I can forget the horrors of the last couple of days.'

43

Andrea flicked on the light. The noise of Pablo's car leaving over the gravel drive disappeared.

'Martin, why sit in the dark in your anorak?' Rushing towards him, happiness gripped her. It had been a protracted wait to clear up the misunderstanding between them, she would apologise and he'd forgive her. That was how she interpreted the scenario before reaching him, but he dragged himself from the chair and walked away from her.

The action confused her as he invariably greeted her with open arms and a kiss. An empty whiskey glass rested on the arm of the chair and her stomach turned with apprehension. He picked it up and crossed to the half empty bottle on the side table but didn't offer her a drink. His slumped shoulders and the silence stunned her. Had something awful happened at work? Hoping they could resolve the problem, she could then relax in his arms.

He picked up the bottle and turned, 'Martin I'm so overjoyed to be with you at last.' He held the bottle in one hand and the empty glass in the other. As she leaned to kiss him, he moved aside. 'What's the matter, why won't you kiss and hug me?' Confusion swamped her as he slumped into the chair, filled his glass with whiskey, balanced the bottle on the arm of the chair and clutched the replenished glass with two hands. Andrea stared as apprehension increased in her rattled brain. 'What's the matter?' Although sweating, he hadn't removed the thick padded anorak. 'We must talk.'

'Why have you been interviewing people involved in the case?' His monotone voice and impassive face afforded her no clues as to his true thoughts.

Andrea shifted her position and leaned forward, 'Martin,' lifting her voice to emulate a typical conversation, 'I have not been interviewing but chatting to people.'

He clutched the whiskey glass as though trying to crush it, 'I asked you not to become engaged in the case.'

It was as though a stranger sat in front of her, 'Yes, I understand,' her shoulders sagged, 'I'm sorry, darling.'

'You ignored my warnings.'

Clinging to the arm of the sofa, she trembled, 'But I have listened.' Why wouldn't he look at her? His eyes darted as though searching. 'You followed two of the Mannings to a secluded spot.' He didn't look at her but stared down at the glass in his hands. A sheen of sweat covered his pale hardened face.

In desperation, her mind whirled. How could she shake him out of this dark mood? Apologising seemed a good place to start. A sigh caught in her throat. 'Perhaps in retrospect, not the most prudent action but I needed to meet with them.' Although justifying her actions he hadn't listened and carried on as though she hadn't spoken.

'You assume you know if people are guilty.' A note of savage contempt edged his voice.

'No, I don't.' Tears clogged her eyes as this hadn't been the beginning of the evening she had expected.

Martin gulped a slug of whiskey but didn't look at Andrea, 'You're interfering in my case and causing embarrassment.' His words struck home, but she suspected that no matter how hard she argued nothing would change his view.

'I'm not interfering, please believe me,' Andrea couldn't cope any longer, sadness and shock combined to cause tears to roll unchecked down her cheeks. Her chin trembled and her hand went to her mouth to trap the stifled. 'Martin, I'm pleading with you, be normal, return to me.' His face as pale as a ghost and his expression grim and unsmiling gave no sign of yielding. The tension had broken her spirit, her shoulders shook and her breathing became ragged.

44

She lifted her tear-stained face as Martin moved to sit next to her. His green eyes filled with tears and she flung her arms around his neck, 'I'm so sorry Martin, I'm so sorry.' They held each other for several minutes then she kissed him on the cheek. 'After the day you've had you must be exhausted and I haven't helped. With extreme effort she kept her voice soft and calm. 'Take off your coat, let's talk and clear matters between us.'

Martin removed his anorak and jacket as she fetched his whiskey glass from the chair.

'Andrea, you're right, we must talk.' His natural voice had returned. 'This is no common murder.' Andrea eased herself onto the sofa next to him and waited. 'Most murders are domestics and it takes one or two days, sometimes less, to work out what happened and why, so we know who we want.'

Andrea listened to his words, 'That's what Calum said.'

'This murder is premeditated and carefully planned, a rifle shot from the hillside wood killed her. But apart from that, it's a total blank, the case will become extended and complicated.'

Andrea gave his hand a reassuring squeeze. 'I've interfered but I want to help, they are people from my world, they will talk to me.'

He closed his eyes and shook his head, but he didn't withdraw his hands. 'This killer thoroughly plans, leaves no traces and hides the motive.'

'He hid in the trees,' said Andrea.

'Exactly, but to be there he would have had to gain Charlotte's trust, the killer would need to appreciate her movements and her plans and that she would drive along that stretch of road at that time. He must be close to her.' Andrea shivered. Her heart skipped a beat as there were so many unanswered questions. 'The murderer had a perfect plan to ensure no witnesses, but he would have to be patient.'

'But a marksman.'

'A very good shot but people secretly learn so it doesn't necessarily point to the high profile ones who can shoot.' Andrea felt embarrassed at her attempt to help with such a complex case. 'You can't go on interfering Andrea, the killer will gain trust, either with you or your friends.'

'Do you think I'm likely to be a victim?' Asking made her shudder. To be talking about such violence when she was safe at home with Martin seemed far-fetched. She sighed in anticipation of the holiday they would have after the murderer had been caught, picturing blue skies and white sand shimmering in the sunshine.

'What type of person was Charlotte?'

The question caught her by surprise, but she focused, 'Friendly, outgoing, hysterical at times, but she loved people and enjoyed fun.' Charlotte's smiling face appeared but she still struggled to think of her with Edward.

'Exactly. So there's only one reason she would have been killed.'

'She might have had a dark side,' suggested Andrea as she leaned back on the sofa. Martin frowned with concentration.

'No witnesses have suggested she led a double life, so can you think of anything? Drink? Drugs?'

Andrea shook her head, 'So why has she been murdered?'

'Charlotte knew something the murderer couldn't afford to become public knowledge.'

'But you wouldn't murder someone for such a trivial reason?'

'Some people do if they think the information will change their lives, for example, if the information is enough to put them in jail for the rest of their life, then they might murder to prevent arrest and conviction.' Andrea had gone cold and the colour drained from her face. 'If Charlotte knew something, then she might have told her best friend and confidante which everyone believes is you, she had no one else. Charlotte told everyone what a wonderful friend you had become.'

The cold sweat deepened and dread filled her stomach and crept over her like an icy chill, she had to leave the investigation to Martin and stop interfering. His team would sift through the evidence pursuing every small discrepancy until the murderer had been found. Martin put his arm around her shoulder and gave her a gentle squeeze, 'You must think, darling.' She relaxed and rested her head on his shoulder, 'You won't know, a small remark, perhaps something trivial. The problem is, out of context it makes no sense, but when linked it becomes damning.'

'Charlotte had a secret.'

His eyes focused on her face, 'What?'

'Charlotte planned to marry Edward.'

'That's what you said this morning.' Disappointment flickered across his face. Perhaps he'd been hoping for something new, giving a different angle to pursue. 'A suitable match?'

'Unquestionably a surprise. Edward is not her natural choice of men. He's staid and dull whereas she preferred lively and outgoing.' Martin gazed at his whiskey glass, she had told him nothing new. Then Andrea blurted out, 'What did you think of Charlotte?'

He jerked his head up almost spilling his drink, 'What do you mean?'

'After the threats from the audience, she received a string of hate mail, so you met her several times.'

He turned his head on one side and gave her a searching gaze, 'Scatty.' But he had a momentary flicker of something in his expression but with a shake of his head pressed his lips together and didn't enlarge on his thoughts. Martin seemed keen not to follow that line, he glanced away and took a generous slug of whiskey and then fell silent. Andrea made up her mind, she needed to report the conversation with Edward. 'This morning I talked to Edward.'

'Yes?' his voice sounded disinterested and distant as though something else occupied his mind. His lips were curled into a small half smile and he had a faraway look in his eye. Whatever was filling his mind brought enjoyment to his serious face.

Andrea didn't ask what he was thinking but continued to tell him about Edward. 'Edward's youth was problematic, so he went into the army and learned to shoot.' Martin stared at her intently. The smile had gone and an alertness appeared in his narrowed eyes. 'You didn't know?' she said although his surprise became obvious. He shook his head. 'Could it have been one of her lovers?' Andrea said.

Martin shifted in his seat and stared at the drink in his hand. Silence stretched between them. She didn't think he would reply. 'When lovers murder, they are in a rage or temper. Not carefully planned and premeditated.' Martin breathed deeply and he rubbed his forehead allowing his head to flop back on the sofa.

'Bad headache, darling?' she queried studying his pale strained face. 'Another of your stress induced headaches.' Since the shooting at the armed robbery, killing one of the Kennedy twins and badly wounding the other, stress had taken its toll. Andrea had been content that the police doctor had prescribed strong pills to help the blinding headaches.

'Yes, I have one of my headaches starting, it begins slowly but if I don't take something the pain throbs around my entire head. I had pills early this morning, but they haven't helped the stress.' He removed a small tube from his pocket and flicking two tablets into his hand put them in his mouth and washed them down with a gulp of whiskey. 'I hardly remember today, I've been on automatic as it's been so busy.'

45

'What have you done, darling?' The cut on her wrist caught Martin's attention. The jagged wound looked tender and inflamed but she had no intention of mentioning the handcuffs that had been roughly secured around her wrists a few hours earlier.

'It's been bleeding, how did it happen?' Taking a deep breath, she ignored the question.

'When did you come home?'

'I don't know, it must be the stress,' he shook his head and gave a puzzled frown. The anxiety stretched through Andrea as he would receive reports about her visit to the Kennedys.

'Do you know about the arrests of the Kennedy brothers?' She burst out the question before she'd thought through the best way of introducing the event. Realising her mistake but too late the damage had been done. He gave a nod of his head, 'Planned for this evening, but I haven't heard whether they've made the arrests.' Realisation dawned and his expression hardened. 'What do you know?'

Andrea's mind raced and she bowed her head in a gesture of shame. There would be no escape as he waited for an explanation, 'I arrived at the Kennedys when the police showed up to arrest John and Mark.'

'What the hell were you doing there?' he thumped his fist on the arm of the chair. 'Don't answer that! Bloody interfering again!' He pushed her hands to one side.

'Martin let me explain. Please.'

He stood up, went to his anorak and took out his mobile, he snapped, 'Did Calum turn up?'

'Yes.'

He punched the buttons on his phone, 'What's the report on the Kennedys' arrest. Why did you let Andrea go?' Andrea stood, she craved a drink.

'You're keeping something back. Tell me,' he shouted into the phone. Andrea guessed that with Martin's aggression, and Calum's suffering, the whole truth would be revealed. 'That sounds like blackmail, let me get this straight. She interfered in the case and threatened to report our officers.'

Andrea moved to the drinks' cabinet, she had to assemble her thoughts for the inevitable confrontation with Martin. Pouring her drink, she faced the wall. Martin didn't say goodbye, but the click of the disconnection reached her, as did the phone being slammed on the coffee table. She braced herself for the verbal onslaught, 'Turn around,' he snarled. Andrea slowly turned, not wanting this conversation.

'Let me explain, Martin.'

'You had no reason to visit the Kennedys.' His words stung, but she couldn't defend herself.

'No, I didn't and I'm sorry, but I've been desperate to help.' He grabbed her wrist, the gentleness had gone, and he sneered at her with icy contempt as he leaned forward. Andrea yelped. Lifting her wrist, her muscles tensed but his grip held firm. The blue bruises were clear and the dried blood remained, he threw the wrist away but didn't move and ran his hand through his hair with his eyes fixed on her face.

'Martin! I'm so sorry, I won't interfere again.' Shame and embarrassment washed over her, she longed to be able to turn the clock back and behave differently. Admitting her foolishness and trying to justify her actions would be her only option. She looked into his eyes, some green but the black had increased. 'Please let me explain,' her lower lip quivered.

'What did you say to Ruth Kennedy?' he spat the words with ferocity but didn't wait for a reply. 'When the Chief Constable finds out, you will be charged with perverting the course of justice, and he will discipline me.' Grabbing her wrist again and glaring at the dried blood, 'No more than you deserve.'

Andrea couldn't contain herself anymore as the pressure of the day exploded into anger. 'Don't be so stupid, I don't deserve to be beaten up by your thugs,' she screamed. She shook her wrist free and jerked away from him. In one swift movement she pulled her jumper off and threw it on the floor. 'So, it's right for your thugs to punch me when I'm lying on the floor, look what they've done.' Glancing in the nearby mirror large bruises had formed on her ribs and across her back.

He grabbed her by the shoulders and spun her round, with no smile and no sympathy on his face, 'You are ruining my career and you expect me to be concerned.' His words reverberated in her mind while the black eyes glared at her.

He grabbed her wrists again, 'Martin! Martin! Stop! It hurts,' but he didn't let go and the pressure increased as his nails dug into her skin. Andrea began to fight him to become free, she wriggled and pulled, trying to loosen his grip but his strength won. Pain shot through her arm as he twisted it around.

'Stop it! stop it!' she gulped air as she couldn't breathe and gave a choked cry.

46

The black eyes contorted with rage as he closed on her, Martin shouted in her face, 'You've ruined my career,' his raw voice sounded brutal. Releasing her wrist, with astonishing speed he swung his arm back and slammed his fist hard into the side of her face. Her head cracked against the wall and pain seared through her from the impact. She screamed as he punched her a second time. Blood pooled in her mouth as blackness closed in. As she slumped down the wall, his fists pounded her breasts. Wedged between the table and the wall, he punched her with both hands. Pain jolted through her body, nausea swept through her and she crumpled like a rag doll and fell into a heap on the floor.

She regained semi-consciousness as he wrenched her by the shoulders then grabbing a handful of hair forced her to stand. She screamed as pain ripped through her body, but it brought her awareness back and with it came the instinct to fight. Adrenaline surged through her as she pushed him, he lost his grip and staggered under the surprise impact, falling backwards.

'Martin. Martin!' she screamed, hysteria and horror confronted and confused her. The black eyes wore an expression of evil as he stepped forward. Clutching the table for support as her legs failed, her hand caught the whiskey bottle. Survival made her grab it by the neck. 'Martin, don't hit me again,' she screamed and raised the bottle, waving it hysterically in the air as she ranted like a mad woman. 'Get out of this house. Get out and never come back!'

Martin staggered towards her, fists clenched. The black eyes fixed on her face, he tripped and threw punches that missed, he swore and cursed at her, the words vile and venomous. 'Martin, stop it, stop it.' He leapt towards her, she swayed away as his legs buckled and he landed on his knees at her feet.

With his head drooped in front of her, she had the opportunity to bring the bottle down on his head. A mixture of self-preservation and anger swarmed through her and she swung it over her head to deliver the blow, but her nerve failed her, 'I can't hit you, I can't.' Her sobs pierced the air, she threw back her head and let out a blood-curdling scream.

The whiskey mixed with her tears as it gurgled from the bottle and flowed down her body. Her arm flopped in defeat and she allowed the bottle to slide from her sticky fingers to the floor. With no more screams left, she stood before him shivering with cold and fear, her legs wouldn't move. He recovered from the trip and lunged at her again, grabbing her bra. Twisting the material in his hand he yanked.

'No. No, you don't know what you're doing. No more!' she sobbed. Andrea gained a firm grip on the hand that was pulling at her bra and squeezed her nails into the back of his hand. Instead of releasing her his grip tightened. He pushed her away to arm's length and shouted a stream of abuse at her. Once again with his other hand he went into a frenzy and punched her stomach and legs, as though a punch bag. A vicious punch landed in her groin, and she buckled.

Another punch knocked the wind from her and she crumpled down the wall. He ripped her bra away and dragged her across the floor then pinned her to the carpet with his body and grabbed at her trousers. 'No, no. Oh my God what are you doing!' her voice squealed, but he took no notice of her words. She desperately tried to get away from him, but his strength overpowered her as her trousers and knickers slid down her legs. As she writhed on the floor naked, he kneeled astride and the verbal abuse still flowed from his snarling lips. The next punch landed on the side of her head. The pain became too much.

47

'Get off, get off. Leave me alone.' A touch on Andrea's shoulder drew her back to the waking world as she sprawled on the sofa. A man's touch making reality flood back and she screamed for all her worth.

'Calm yourself,' his low voice reverberated through her mind. Horror gripped her, she shrieked again. 'Andrea! Wake up.'

The hand no longer touched but not the voice she'd expected. Opening her eyes, she peered up into a calm face with deep-set eyes and brown hair, 'Calum.'

'Are you okay? It looks like a bomb has hit this room.' His eyes strayed around the chaos taking in the upturned tables, clothes and the empty scotch bottle.

'Keep away from me,' her voice laden with hysteria, rose in volume as she spoke.

'Okay.' Calum stepped backwards and moved away with a face of bewilderment. Andrea must have pulled her coat around her to protect her during the night. Conscious of her nakedness she gripped the garment and yanked it up to her chin. Every bone in her body protested at the hasty movement.

Calum gave her a long appraising stare, not surprising

as she must look a complete wreck. She struggled to force the images of last night's brutality to the back of her mind as she mustn't give Calum any clues about what had taken place. Struggling to appear calm, she blurted out the first idea that sprung to mind, 'I had a nightmare. I must look bad as the bruises from yesterday's incident have come out and you startled me. How did you get in?' Her thoughts whirled around in chaos and she wanted to be left alone with her pain and suffering.

'The front door is wide open, so I shouted but received no reply.'

'So you barged in?' she wriggled on the sofa and checked the coat concealed her. 'What do you want?'

'I've brought your car back.' He ignored her snappiness and maintained a matter-of-fact voice, 'I've left a message on your phone to say I would drop the keys through the letter box, but I couldn't because the door had been left wide open.'

'Thanks,' she glared at him in frustrated fury. Calum held up the car keys. 'Give me the keys and then you can leave.' Although aware of her rudeness she wouldn't apologise as she wanted him to leave.

'Charming,' he muttered as he focused on the far corner where the whiskey bottle lay on the carpet with her bra draped across it. The rest of her clothes were strewn across the room. A large stain from the whiskey bottle had streaked across the pale carpet. A small cabinet had fallen and its contents of glass had broken, giving a trail of jagged splinters across the whiskey stain.

'Come on, give me the keys,' demanded Andrea. Calum focused on the bottle and broken glass. As he took a step forward to hand her the keys, she cringed.

A confused expression crossed his face and he stepped back, 'I'm surprised you had the energy after the day you had yesterday.' He studied the room with exaggerated intensity.

He might make deductions from the chaos, but Andrea guessed he wouldn't come close to the truth which she could barely understand herself, but the pain of movement brought the nightmare into reality. Focusing on his face, she frowned with annoyance, 'Give me the keys and leave.'

This time he walked towards her holding out the keys, she drew her coat more tightly but didn't flinch. She instinctively put her fingers to her eye where the soreness had swollen. 'That's not the mark from yesterday. What happened?'

Calum stared hard at her with a challenging glint in his eye. Her hand jerked away from her face.

'Yes, it is.' Her voice rose as she hugged the coat for comfort. But her own voice had no conviction. Calum leaned forward to give her the keys.

'Shall I examine your eye?'

'No, no!' She half crawled and half scampered to the other end of the couch but couldn't stop a whimper escaping, 'No, no.' Calum threw the keys on the couch as apprehension filled his eyes.

'So you will not tell me.'

'I've a horrendous hangover,' she blurted. A terrible headache made her eyes ache, but it hadn't been caused by a hangover, she hoped he couldn't tell. Her skin crawled as the violence jumped across her mind. 'The death of Charlotte overwhelmed me last night and I hit the bottle. Don't you think I've a good reason to blot out the horror of finding her body?' Calum didn't reply but glanced at the devastation. Her explanation hadn't convinced him. Fixing her gaze on him, 'Now will you piss off, I need time to myself.'

'Why are you so bloody contrary?' Andrea didn't answer as Calum walked towards the door. As he reached the doorway, he hesitated and twisted round to face her, 'Did you see Martin last night?'

Andrea tried to detect a hidden meaning, but he spoke in the usual bored Calum voice. Andrea shivered at the mention of Martin's name and began to sweat as she couldn't believe what had happened. A nightmare, he couldn't have beaten her. The physical pain racked her body as she moved but how could she cope with the mental pain. Would that ever heal? Taking a long slow breath and trying to calm her racing mind Calum stood waiting for an answer. 'Yes, but not for long.' The lie tripped off her tongue, but it didn't sound convincing. Calum waited, his silence unnerved her. She stumbled on with her prefabricated story making it up as she went, 'I drank too much gin, Martin had whiskey. If you must know I became drunk and fell over,' she glanced at the corner with the broken glass.

'But you left the front door open! What a mess you are.' She didn't reply but she could sense the frustration in Calum's voice.

'I get pissed as I did last night, but at least I remember to close the front door.'

'Do you want to give me any other lectures? Calum, just leave,' she tried to say with finality. Andrea didn't want to have a conversation with him as she was afraid he would read between the lines and conclude about a rift between her and Martin.

'Are you going out today?'

'It's none of your business, now will you please go?' she muttered, battling with her annoyance as she wanted to be alone, she stood to encourage him to leave. The room swirled, the blackness crowded in as the cold sweat covered her, she staggered and her knees buckled. Andrea collapsed but didn't reach the floor as strong arms caught her. She went to resist, but before she could react, she lay back on the couch, carried and placed there by Calum who stepped back to give her space. Longing for him to go, tears filled her eyes. He stood silent watching her as she attempted to regain her composure, she didn't want to answer his questions.

At last he broke the silence, 'When did you last eat?' The question took her by surprise.

'I don't know.' With difficulty she moved herself into a sitting position trying not to wince. She kept her coat wrapped around her aching body hugging it close. His eyes were alert and his mouth set into a hard line as he looked around the room. Andrea sighed, he can guess because he must have seen hundreds of domestics. She hated the word, but that's what the police would call it.

Turning away from her, 'You need help.' She went to protest, but he continued, 'You won't let me do anything for you, and you won't tell me what happened.' He turned back to face her. 'Here's the deal.'

'No deal.'

'I will forget I'm a copper and ignore my training,' his hand swept in an arc indicating the devastation in the room.

'No deal,' she repeated.

‘I won’t call in one of our specialist units.’

‘No, definitely not,’ her voice rising in a panic.

‘You look an absolute mess and will convince no one this is normal, so here’s the deal.’ Andrea shook her head but Calum continued, ‘Go upstairs and tart yourself up, put on plenty of make-up and get dressed.’

‘And what if I won’t?’ she challenged.

‘It’s a simple phone call,’ and he let his words hang in the air then dug deep into his pocket, produced his mobile phone and he waved it towards her to emphasise the point. She knew she had no option. ‘While you do that, I’ll cook breakfast as we need to eat. I’ve a bad head from last night’s beer so I can’t imagine your headache. ‘Do you want a hand?’

‘No, I’m okay now.’

‘Tart yourself up and eat, and then I’ll leave you in peace and hopefully our paths will never cross again.’

48

'You're a pain in the arse and a bloody stuck-up bitch but there's something wrong and you won't let me help. So, I'll stick by the deal.' Calum finished washing the last plate and put it on the draining board.

'Thanks, Calum,' Andrea muttered in a quiet voice from the table. The impromptu breakfast had helped. The large fry up surprised Andrea in realising how hungry she had become. She tried her best to smile at Calum but couldn't.

'No one will be fooled. Find someone to help you.' Andrea longed for him to leave.

The front doorbell rang. She shivered. 'Do you want me to get rid of them?'

'I can't face anyone this morning.' Calum left her sitting at the kitchen table. The front door closed, but the voices sounded from the hall. She swallowed deeply. Calum has let them in. I can't face anyone. 'Why did you let them in?' she snapped as he returned.

'It's the Chief Constable and his wife so I've put them in the conservatory, I didn't think the lounge a good idea.' Andrea scowled at him and her head swam at the prospect of holding a conversation. 'I couldn't tell them to piss off, could I?'

Andrea dragged herself to her feet with the help of the table and she stood straight, took a deep breath, 'Come on, let's get this over with.' She took slow and deliberate steps to the conservatory. 'Chief Constable,' Andrea spoke as confidently as she could manage.

'You know my wife, Joan,' who smiled at Andrea and gave a nod of the head in acknowledgement. Calum waited just inside the conservatory in silence. 'I've come to see Martin.' Even his name brought a new shiver. Andrea took another deep breath and tried to talk as normal.

'He's not here. I assume he is at work.'

'Did he come home last night?'

Andrea took a tissue and blew her nose. 'Yes, he arrived home before me.' So far so good, no broken voice and she hadn't cried, 'He had gone when I woke up this morning. Is there a problem?'

'No one has spoken to him since six o'clock last night, but he might be with another officer.' Andrea glanced at Calum but he didn't reveal he had spoken to Martin about the raid at the Kennedys. 'His radio might have failed.' He stared at Andrea as he finished the sentence.

'I don't know when he left this morning.'

The Chief Constable said, 'He's slept and is back out on the job. Good man, no problems if you've seen him.' Andrea turned to look at the garden to hide her tears and used her tissue again. She took a deep breath before she faced them. Joan studied her.

'You don't look well.'

'The stresses and strains of the recent days.' Joan

moved towards her with a smile of sympathy. 'I received a little cut yesterday on my eyebrow, but it makes my eyes look puffy.' Joan smiled and patted her on the arm, she hadn't been convinced.

'These are testing times, my dear.' The kindness in her voice nearly broke through Andrea's thin mantle of control as her eyes welled with tears. She gulped and stared away at the garden.

'Andrea has been a tower of strength. Isn't that right, Inspector?'

'Yes, sir,' Andrea could hear the monotone in Calum's voice. He didn't like her and hadn't forgiven her deceptions yesterday. With embarrassment she realised that she had enjoyed giving him the slip and disappeared frequently during the day. But after the nightmare events of the previous evening she realised how childish and immature her behavior had been.

'We must go,' said the Chief Constable.

'Sir, before you go,' Calum crossed to him. Taking an envelope from his pocket he held it out. 'I know this isn't a good time, but I'm on sick leave so it will not impact operations, I came to tell Andrea the news, but I haven't had the opportunity.' Calum's confident air had vanished. He hovered in front of the Chief Constable.

The Chief Constable opened the envelope and read the single page, 'This is a staff matter, for private discussion.'

'Andrea needs to know and I have no problem with your wife knowing but it would be too impersonal to send it through the post.' Calum sighed as he finished.

The Chief Constable looked at each person in the room, 'This is Inspector Brodie's letter of resignation from the Police Service.'

'Calum.' Andrea stared at his impassive face.

The Chief Constable moved to the far end of the conservatory and looked out across the garden to the fields of Lose Hill. The three others waited for him to speak. 'I'm not supposed to tell you.'

'Sir.'

'Yesterday I had confirmation from the Prime Minister's office, you know what I am talking about, Calum.'

'No, sir, I have no idea,' his face showed he didn't know what the Chief Constable meant.

'The confirmation concerned the firearms' incident during the robbery with the Kennedy brothers.' Calum nodded, but the mention of the family made him uncomfortable. She felt sympathy for him. 'The Prime Minister and Her Majesty have agreed to my recommendation that for your defence of your fellow officers from the Kennedy brothers' fire and focusing the danger to yourself you will be awarded the George Medal.'

'Oh, Calum,' said Andrea as she looked at him with admiration. Joan went to speak but her husband raised his hand, 'It won't be officially announced until the remaining Kennedy brother is sentenced. You are one of the best officers in the constabulary and the reason you have only risen to the rank of Inspector is that you refuse to put yourself forward for promotion.' The Chief Constable paused and added in a more conversational tone, 'I asked the doctor whether you could return to work with immediate effect.' Calum shook his head. 'He said it would be too soon as you are still suffering.'

Andrea didn't like him but hadn't helped, what a callous cow she had been in making his job of looking after her so difficult. She hadn't considered his frame of mind or the pain in his leg. The Chief Constable tore the letter in half and handed it back to Calum with an expression of determination. 'I shall do whatever I can to keep you in the force, you are a brave man and we will provide the support required to return you to full health.'

Calum appeared confused as he stared at the torn letter in his hand. 'On the day you return to work I shall stand in the entrance of Police HQ, with a guard of honour to welcome you.' A genuine look of disbelief replaced Calum's normal scowl. 'Come Joan, time to go.' He walked towards Calum, 'Congratulations, come and see me for a private chat next week when this is settled.' Calum nodded. 'Ladies,' turning to Andrea in particular, 'this conversation is not to go outside this room.'

Andrea nodded. Martin flashed across her mind. Reality had been suspended for a few minutes with the conversation between Calum and the Chief Constable. Within seconds, the harshness and desperation flooded back to her and made her weak, but she couldn't change the happening of the last two days. Martin's attack came to the forefront of her mind. With no answer for his violence it added to the death of Charlotte that still ate away at her. She had a feeling, but only a feeling, that Charlotte's murder and Martin's attack on her were related.

'Are you sure you are okay my dear?' Joan caught Andrea's arm. It brought her back to focus, she couldn't retreat to her own falling apart world.

‘Yes.’

The Chief Constable followed his wife into the hall, but turned to Andrea and Calum, ‘I know I’m placing a tremendous burden on you Andrea, but I believe you hold the key to solving the murder as it is a community you know. Do whatever you can.’ Andrea didn’t have the chance to reply before he added to Calum, ‘I know you’re not at work, but Andrea needs a hard-headed copper to help her out. I can’t spare anyone and you’re best suited. We need a breakthrough, do your best.’

49

'This isn't a good idea.' Calum eased the car through the driving rain and pulled into the small car park dominated by the spire of the medieval church. Andrea's stomach tensed as she peered at the edifice with its limestone blocks blackened by Victorian smoke, its grimness accentuated by the swirling mist and rain. 'The Chief Constable said we should work together.'

'He must have his reasons, but none I can understand.' She had been silent during the journey and had forced last night's attack into disbelief and focused on the death of Charlotte. They'd driven to the church in Hillsborough. Calum had been reluctant but Andrea had insisted, he twisted in his seat to watch her as he turned off the engine. 'Neither of us are up to this, we lack rest and you look dreadful.'

Martin kept flashing through her mind, but she had no right to force Calum through this ordeal. As they had driven into Sheffield, Andrea became convinced of the link between Martin's attack and Charlotte's murder. 'I'm persisting,' she struggled to hide the quiver in her voice.

'Why here?'

'You said it's most likely to be one of the family, so we will eliminate them, one by one.'

Calum wearily rubbed his forehead, 'Keep an open mind.' He made a move to open the car door and get out, but slammed it shut again. 'No!' he thumped the steering wheel in a gesture of annoyance, 'This can never work, you're a complete amateur. I want you to ring the Chief and tell him we have changed our minds and we can't help.'

Andrea shrugged off his words with an impatient huff, 'I'm damn well going to do it so will you plan with me.'

'Plan, plan!' shouted Calum, 'you want to plan to interrogate a priest, you're bonkers!'

'You think it's the family, but I don't, so let's drop them from the list of suspects.' Andrea wouldn't be deflected, but she needed Calum's assistance to make progress. The Chief Constable had asked for their cooperation and for Andrea it had been a lifeline to solve the problem and eradicate Martin's violence from her mind.

'This isn't an American cop film,' his voiced dripped with sarcasm and he fidgeted in his seat adjusting his position and rubbing at his injured leg. He threw her a look of impatience, 'It's dangerous and you could cock-up the whole inquiry.'

'Don't I know it,' growled Andrea back at him, 'that's why you're here.' They spoke at the same moment but neither listening to the other despite their voices becoming louder and more insistent. Calum's phone rang, he pressed the button and shouted, 'Yes!' but uttered no apology. Grunting, he cut the call without saying goodbye, shoved the phone back in his pocket with a deep sigh. Andrea tried to regain the initiative.

'Something I need to know?' If she didn't concentrate, she would fall apart. Indecision washed across his face, but would he tell her?

His voice flat and emotionless, 'Martin telephoned into a conference to discuss progress. He told the duty officer to charge the two older Kennedy brothers Mark and John with armed robbery.'

'But it wasn't them,' Andrea blurted out.

Calum snarled and opened the door into the rain, 'Let's do it and I hope you know what you're doing, because I don't.' Andrea felt sorry for herself as she struggled through the rain into the church porch. The dampness seeped into her making her stiff body ache, but Calum dragged himself even slower than yesterday, his limp had deteriorated and the pain showed on his face. Could they talk to Charlotte's brother in a sensible and coherent manner when in this sorry state?

Andrea pushed open the huge oak door and led the way into the church. Even though a gloomy day she had to wait while her eyes became accustomed to the darkness inside the church. The large ornate windows let in insufficient light as large mature trees enclosed the church. Her heels echoed on the stone floor. Making her way through the chancel with Calum a few yards behind, she stopped at the altar bar and studied the elaborately embroidered altar cloth and ornate candlesticks. The musty damp smell covered her as she stood motionless while the distant drum of the rain on the roof broke the stillness. The gloominess of the surroundings did nothing to lift her spirits and a sense of unease sent a shiver through her.

'He isn't here,' said Calum as he stopped behind her with an exasperated sigh, but she didn't look around.

'The sign outside says it's open for confessions,' Andrea whispered. Both fell silent and neither moved.

Andrea offered her silent thoughts for both Martin and Charlotte as she stared at the picture of Jesus in the stained-glass window above the altar.

50

'Will you pray with me?' the voice echoed around the church. Andrea jumped and shivered. She sensed an uneasy movement from Calum as he hadn't seen or heard the priest. Alexander's dark cassock blended into the grey gloom of the church, he didn't smile and clasped his hands in a pious manner.

'Yes, I will pray.'

'Inspector?'

'No.' Blunt and definite.

Alexander Manning joined her at the altar rail, indicated she should kneel and took the position next to her. She clasped her hands and leant on the rail staring at the picture of Jesus. There were several minutes of silence before the priest said, 'Amen.'

Andrea repeated the word, he made the sign of the cross, blessed her, 'I prayed for the soul of Charlotte.'

Andrea met his look, 'I prayed for the soul of the murderer, Charlotte will go to heaven, but the murderer will go to hell.' Andrea's words echoed, but they were greeted with silence. The priest's dour expression never changed as he offered his hand. Accepting his warm dry hand despite the damp and cold of the church, she rose to her feet with her body throbbing with pain. Pulling her anorak tight in an attempt to stop shivering she peered at the priest. What thoughts travelled through his mind? Had he been saddened by the death of his sister Charlotte? If so, then he concealed it well. Did he reflect on his harsh treatment of her? Had he asked for God's forgiveness?

A light movement of the hand indicated they should follow him. He opened a small door near the church organ and entered. The warmth of the small vestry greeted them and he made a similar hand gesture towards three hard mismatched wooden chairs. Apart from the chairs, one wall had a large dark cupboard presumably for the storage of clerical robes. Gloomy daylight entered the small window where the chairs had been set for a meeting of three. Did he know they were coming?

Calum refused the chair and gazed through a narrow arrow slit stained glass window. Andrea sank onto a chair but didn't wait for platitudes. 'The police have arrested and will charge John and Mark with armed robbery; they believe the four brothers collaborated.' Andrea heard Calum shuffle, a sign of disapproval? Andrea ignored it and focused her attention on Charlotte's brother.

'They are innocent,' said the priest in a quiet voice.

'Yes, I believe the same.' She garnered no reaction from the priest, not a flicker. Alexander sat straight backed on the chair and concentrated on the folded hands in his lap. Andrea fixed her gaze on him, 'But the twins are guilty.' The priest nodded agreement which surprised her.

Andrea became edgy, not with the priest, but with Calum as he stood by the window behind her which meant she couldn't see his face. She persisted and gave the priest a long appraising stare and pressed her lips into a smile. 'Alexander, it's easy to draw the conclusion that the other two brothers were involved. Why not the four of them?'

'The family has a reputation and they are known to be heavies.' He paused, as though choosing his words with care. Then with his mouth flattened into a thin tight line, 'The article by the journalist gave that impression, but it is untrue.' His monotone and flat voice reminded her of a robot which showed no indication to his honest thoughts. Did a priest always tell the truth? Something in Alexander's manner made her doubt him.

Andrea raised her voice, trying to provoke reaction, 'They looked threatening last night.'

Unphased by the change of level in her voice he continued in a bland an emotionless tone, 'They wouldn't have hurt you, if that's what concerns you, Ma can control them.' His passive response annoyed her, but he knew about her visit to the car hire business. Who had told him? It must have been one of the Kennedys as it would not have been the police. A slight movement from Calum made her think he had come to the same conclusion. Andrea shifted her position on the chair so she could see both men, desperation coursed through her. The questioning had stalled. Why had she come? What had she hoped to achieve? The dark thoughts returned and she fought the tears. Although warm in the vestry, even with her anorak, she felt cold and empty. She had to dig deep because the alternative would be home alone.

The determination to help Charlotte and to find the

reason for Martin's attack on her had not dimmed. She feared the worse, but she had to know. If a link existed between Charlotte and Martin, what could it be? Her mind speculated, about Martin, a handsome man and the pretty Charlotte, did they have an affair? Brushing away the thoughts, no, not possible as Martin and her had been the perfect couple, until last night's violence. The emotionless man in front of her waited with his hands relaxed and still on his lap. Somehow, she needed to provoke him and make him shed his shield of apathy, so she started calmly, 'Alexander, your father promised me help from him and his family.'

'Yes, of course.'

Taking a deep breath, she chose her words, as though preparing for battle, 'Then I despise you for being a bloody hypocrite,' she shook her hand at him for emphasis, 'saying one thing and doing the opposite.' Calum became wide eyed and full of concentration.

'Please do not swear in God's house,' the flat monotone voiced riled her and spurred her to action.

'Don't give me that crap,' she stormed hurling the provocative language at him like a venomous serpent fighting for survival. Not her normal language but she'd made the priest uneasy, 'You're not the sole interpreter of what is good. Your sister has been murdered and this brave policeman has been shot trying to prevent carnage. The Kennedy twins were caught stealing, "Thou shalt not steal", Andrea emphasised the quote from the Bible. Allowing her voice to rise in a crescendo of pent up annoyance at this passive indifferent man, shock flitted across his features and he put up a hand and adjusted his clerical collar as he calculated what to say.

Andrea had the upper hand and it gave her the momentum to continue the attack. With a menacing voice determined to make her mark, 'You give me no answers, when will you help?' Raising her hand before he could speak, 'If you refuse then I will return to your father and wash my hands of your family?' How would he respond to the ultimatum? The emotion in his face had changed, the mask of indifference had disappeared. A flush of embarrassment hovered on his cheeks, but his narrowed eyes held a hint of anger, he stood up and crossed himself. 'Well?' Andrea snapped, folding her arms across her chest in a gesture of impatience, she glowered at him.

The slightest of movements from Calum caught her attention, but she didn't want Calum to distract Alexander as she had become hopeful, he might yield crucial information. Calum stood notebook in his hand as he studied the priest. The priest moved away and stood behind the chair he had vacated and rested his hand on the back support. With a deep breath he began in a low whispering voice, 'I lived in Ireland for a long period, initially when I served in the army, but I had a calling and took holy orders.'

Pausing he gathered his thoughts and with a flick of his eyes towards Calum who wrote in his notebook, 'I knew the Kennedy family from my earliest days there.' Another lengthy pause annoyed Andrea, so she barked a question at him, 'How did you meet them?'

'Much the same as you would now, I visited their business to hire a car for a trip to Dublin as I had a long weekend pass from the army barracks.' Once again, he stalled.

Andrea, certain of more story to tell, jumped in with another question, 'Where did the Kennedy family have their car hire?'

'In the centre of Belfast,' he gave her a long thoughtful look and returned to sit on his chair with his former pose, straight backed, with his hands clasped in his lap. Staring directly at Andrea, 'I will truthfully answer your questions, what do you want to ask me?'

Alexander had a calm voice, she'd fall asleep if that was how he delivered his sermons. She exhaled with exaggerated patience, 'Alexander, you know I'm not from the police so I don't have the training or the expertise to elicit information that could help.' The priest glanced up at Calum, who didn't speak, 'Tell me about the family?'

'The husband ran off with another woman leaving Ma with her four boys, the twins were babies at the time. During my time in Belfast my friendship increased with the family.' Andrea mulled over his words while confusion whirled through her like a deluge.

'But an English soldier becoming friendly with a Catholic family, wasn't that dangerous?'

'They ran a business in the city centre and Ma ensured religion stayed out of the business and their lives as she kept her beliefs private.'

'Her neighbours in a Catholic area wouldn't have tolerated any friendship.'

'Yes, but as part of the intelligence section I checked them out. They lived on the premises and not in one of the highly volatile areas. There had been nothing to suggest they were involved in sectarian issues.'

'What happened then?' Andrea prompted him not sure whether he was relating the whole story, but she had an inkling he gave her the edited version, but they had information that could be followed up by Calum.

'Time passed and Ma had crucial decisions to make.'

'What? Why?' snapped Andrea intent on extracting as much information as feasible.

'John had reached his teens and she had three more boys coming through in a Catholic family at the height of the Troubles. The grapevine would target them and Ma wouldn't be able to protect them as they would be expected to join in the fighting if requested.'

'And did they?'

'A couple of men came into the car hire business and talked to Ma about the "cause" which gave the impetus she needed.

'She uprooted her family and moved from Belfast to Dublin to stay out of the limelight.'

'And did your links with them continue?'

'I went to Dublin on leave and became involved in the local church near where they stayed. Army life was no longer for me and I'd been making enquiries about being ordained. The priest at the church I regularly visited indicated he would help Ma and the boys settle in Dublin.' Calum still made notes.

'How did you come back to Sheffield?'

'While I wished to enter into the church in Ireland, I had intended to return to Sheffield. I kept in touch with Ma and the family. The "cause" became interested again in the family after the twins were put into a detention centre. The situation became more difficult for the Kennedys in Dublin so as soon as the boys were released the family came here to join me at my suggestion. I'd already come back and taken up this post.' His eyes focused on Andrea with an intense stare which made her uncomfortable, but she wouldn't flinch. 'And before you ask.' Andrea forced her face to show no reaction, 'the twins were detained for severely beating a man when they were ten-years-old.'

Alexander paused and dipped his head for a few seconds. Andrea couldn't decide if he needed to compose himself or he said of few words of a prayer, then he clenched his hands together until the knuckles were white and looked up, 'Matthew and Luke, the twins, were headstrong. I thought they had learnt their lesson in the detention centre.'

'Short tempered?' asked Andrea.

'Yes, but they controlled themselves after the counselling they received as teenagers.' Silence filled the room forcing Andrea to the conclusion that he had finished his abbreviated story.

'Thank you, Alexander.' Her voice calm but cool, he had given them information but how much had he withheld?

Alexander glanced towards her, 'The article in the newspapers about the Kennedy family has given everyone the wrong impression. The police assume that John and Mark are headstrong because of the twins, Luke and Matthew.'

'The police might think along those lines, I don't,' Andrea replied with a hint of a smile.

What had he hidden from them?

51

'Who do you think murdered Charlotte?'

Alexander didn't hesitate. 'One of her audience. There must be dangerous men that follow singers awaiting the right opportunity.' Andrea waited, he perceived the need to speak again, 'Alternatively...' but he hesitated.

'Yes?'

'It could be a stalker, someone rejected by Charlotte.' Andrea let him talk. 'It must happen if you are famous.' But he held narrow prejudices and misguided views on the world of fashion and entertainment.

'As it's never happened to me, or other models I know, I don't see it's common, but it's a possibility.'

'Yes, I agree,' said the priest too quickly.

'There's only one thing wrong with your idea.'

'What's that?' his expression darkened.

'If she had been attacked or sexually assaulted,' he closed his eyes and crossed himself, 'your ideas would make sense.' Andrea gulped, she found it difficult to continue in such an impersonal manner, but Charlotte would have understood so she gathered her thoughts, wiped the sweat from her hands, shivered with the emptiness and then waited for him to open his eyes again. She needed to see his reaction.

'Alexander, a distant shot from a rifle killed Charlotte.' Calum moved uneasily. The priest didn't speak. Andrea pushed on with determination, 'My father hunted deer and had rifles, so I saw the damage they did to animals when he went shooting.'

'I didn't know,' he whispered as he returned his gaze to his hands which were tightly clenched in his lap.

'Think again about who killed Charlotte. Think about the damage the rifle caused to her.'

His head jerked up and defiance came into his eyes and his mouth tensed, 'It's a police job, not one for a priest.' Alexander's dismissive words annoyed Andrea as Charlotte had been his little sister and she could expect him to do his utmost to help find the killer. As far as she was concerned it wasn't acceptable for him to hide behind his clerical robes and adopt such a narrowminded and indifferent view.

'Not without everyone's help.' She stood up, 'I shall tell my husband he needs to chat with you.' The priest stared at her and squirmed much to Andrea's delight. 'Only to give more help,' she responded with a weak smile.

Within a few minutes Andrea had closed the car door and slumped back into the passenger seat. Calum shuffled to become comfortable but didn't start the engine. Would she receive another lecture, but he pulled out his notebook. Andrea closed her eyes, she wanted this horrible time to end. Weakness washed over her, she couldn't keep up this pretense much longer. She had been attacked by her husband, it couldn't be dismissed and signalled the end of her marriage. Charlotte's death had been the first step in her world falling apart. The police would take their time, but they would capture Charlotte's killer, but what has happened to Martin?

Calum continued to write, so she left him to his scribbling as her mind raced through images. Would she ever be able to forget them? A mix of Charlotte's dead face and Martin's evil stare as he attacked her, they distorted into gargoyles which swam through her mind.

She opened her eyes with a start as though emerging from a nightmare. Calum spoke quietly on the phone as he gave the details from his notebook. 'Let me know if everything checks out.' He closed the call without a goodbye.

'Do you think he murdered his sister?' asked Andrea.

'Not a likely suspect I admit, but Martin will want to keep an open mind until we find a lead.' Andrea gasped at his name, the images flooded back.

Calum noticed her reaction, 'I don't know how to comfort you. Let me get you help, please?' He had unusual warmth and humanity in his voice.

Andrea regained her composure, 'I know you're trying hard for me Calum and I appreciate your concern, and while I'll have moments of weakness I'm determined to do as much as I can.'

'Are we going to see the nurse?'

Andrea touched his hand, 'Thank you, Calum. Yes, let's go, I'll tidy myself on the way.' Before he started the car, 'You're a kind and brave man, Calum Brodie.' He hesitated. 'Please don't stop talking about Martin, I can't go to pieces every time his name is mentioned.' Would he ask questions about last night? No, he'd guessed much of what had happened, Andrea didn't need to confirm the assault. He put the car into gear and pulled away.

'One brave man in the force is enough, so I shall tell the Chief Constable my role has been exaggerated and so I cannot accept the award.'

52

Andrea and Calum sat on two rickety plastic chairs in the hospital corridor. Neither spoke. With little movement or people in the vicinity nothing distracted their thoughts. The operating theatre ante-room opposite had no activity. They could see sinks and gowns but little else. Ten minutes passed and the silence remained between them. Andrea went through Alexander's words, but found it problematic to concentrate, as her mind trawled back to Martin and Charlotte.

The doors from the theatre opened, several doctors and nurses moved from the theatre into the ante-room. Andrea recognised the shape of Margaret among the masked and gowned medical staff. As the others moved away Margaret spotted them but gave no reaction. Blood smeared the front of her gown as she turned and withdrew from view. Five minutes later, Margaret came through the open door wearing a clean nurse's uniform.

'Hello, Andrea.' A polite but not a welcoming greeting and although she nodded at Calum, she barely looked at him. 'It looked bad,' said Andrea nodding towards the operating theatre hoping to put Margaret at ease.

‘A road traffic accident. The surgeon put him back together.’

As Margaret had remained standing Andrea joined her leaving Calum listening from the chair. Andrea needed to encourage Margaret to talk, ‘I didn’t realise you worked in the operating theatre, aren’t you a ward sister?’

Margaret didn’t smile, ‘I’m trained in many aspects of nursing, ward sister is my day job but I’m on call for the theatre.’

‘Which do you prefer?’ She wanted Margaret to relax and talk but it would be hard work because it became obvious from her reception she would say little. Andrea remembered Calum’s words, let them relax and they will talk.

‘I prefer psychiatric nursing, because that is the real challenge, but it’s the poor relation of the health service with no prospects and poor pay increases.’ Margaret glanced at Calum, but then returned her unsmiling gaze to Andrea, ‘You haven’t come to find out about my career, I assume you wish to talk about Charlotte.’ There was a subtle change in her expression at the mention of Charlotte’s name, but it disappeared too quickly for Andrea to label it.

‘Yes, I wish to talk about Charlotte,’ but Andrea doubted she would make progress. Margaret nodded and led them along the corridor and into a cramped office where she pulled herself a chair from the back wall and sat leaving Andrea and Calum to organise their own chairs. Andrea realised that Margaret would only agree to speak with them to comply with her father’s judgement. Otherwise she wouldn’t have given Andrea the time of day. Margaret eyed Calum with obvious and open contempt.

Once they were settled, 'Can you shoot?'

'Yes. At a young age I joined the Rifle Club, under father's tutelage.' Andrea suspected less information would be forthcoming than from her brother. Should she try the same approach? A worried expression came over Margaret's face.

'Margaret?' What's the matter?

Margaret had paled and her eyes widened, 'She must have been shot by a rifle.'

Andrea gave a slight nod of her head, 'By a marksman.'

'The family are marksmen, so you think one of us did it?' Her angry words burst forth in a swift torrent like the rapid fire from a machine gun. 'Why don't the police ask the questions?'

'I'm not here to question anyone,' Andrea kept her voice calm. Would this unfriendly woman relax? 'I'm trying to help your father and, by doing so, I will help my friend Charlotte.'

'Father believes you will support and advise us during the next few weeks.'

'What do you think about my involvement?' Bluntness seemed the best approach. Margaret didn't answer and her hardened expression wasn't reassuring. 'I'm trying to help because I understand Charlotte's world and I am married to a policeman.' Calum moved on his chair.

Andrea ignored him and continued, 'I hoped by linking the two parts of my life together, I could help to relieve the burden on your family.'

'I understand,' but her voice held no hint of emotion and could have been discussing any topic. The murder of her sister should provoke reaction from this hard woman. 'If we could help the police to find the murderer then Charlotte can rest in peace.'

'What do you want from me?' she eyed Andrea and Calum with a stony expression.

'Background information about the family,' suggested Andrea trying to give Margaret a smile of encouragement.

'And?' snapped Margaret with a questioning look, 'I would guess there's something else.'

'You're a perceptive woman, Margaret, so we wish to know about your family's links with the Kennedy family.' Andrea waited and the silence lengthened. Calum's chair creaked.

Would she open up? Margaret's eyes darted between Andrea and Calum, 'I don't mind talking to you,' but her eyes flicked to Calum with a look of disdain. Andrea picked up the hint and attempted to placate Margaret, 'He's resigned from the police force and is acting as a minder for me.' Calum didn't react.

'Get rid of him and I'll talk to you.'

'Okay, I'll go.' Calum stood and took his notebook from his pocket. Margaret's mobile phone rang, so she fished it out of her pocket and checked the screen, 'It's Alexander, I'll tell him I'm busy.'

She answered and turned away from Andrea to whisper into the phone. Andrea guessed it wouldn't have been the first time this morning that Alexander had tried to contact his sister to warn her about the possibility of a visit from them. Andrea jumped as Calum touched her on the shoulder. 'I'll wait outside,' he placed his hand on hers and squeezed, 'Are you okay?' and he pushed a piece of paper into her hand. Calum closed the door behind him as he left. Margaret had her back towards Andrea, so she looked at the paper. One word, inheritance. She crumpled the paper inside her fist as Margaret said goodbye to her brother and turned around.

'Start with that question.'

'What question?'

'I watched his reflection as he wrote.' Embarrassment made Andrea's cheeks flush as she didn't like being caught out and losing the initiative with Margaret.

'Calum wants to know who will inherit if your father dies.'

Margaret scoffed, 'A stupid question from the police, I've no idea as we've never discussed it with father, but I would assume the three of us, but now Alexander and myself. If you want to know ask him.' A silence developed as Andrea thought through how to regain the initiative.

'Will you do me a favour, please Andrea.'

'Yes, if I can, I'm here to help.'

'There is something in my past I'd rather father didn't find out about, but it has nothing to do with Charlotte's death.'

'How do you think I could help?'

'Could you ask your husband and the other police on the case not to mention it to my father?'

'I could try but I can't guarantee.'

'I know you can't but as it's irrelevant, I don't see why anyone needs to touch on it.'

'I assume you will tell me.'

'Yes, I fell in love.'

The surprise registered in Andrea's face, but it didn't deter Margaret, 'You would never get that impression of me, but it happened with a patient I had been treating, we had a quick romance and we married. That's the bit father doesn't know.'

'What happened?'

'The perils of a quick romance, I suppose, he turned against me and said our love had gone sour.'

'I am sorry.'

Margaret fought back her tears, 'I put our break-up due to his failing business which he'd inherited from his father. The pressure became too much for him and he committed suicide,' her voice quivered with emotion.

'That's tragic.' Andrea opened her bag and gave Margaret a tissue, she nodded her thanks and dabbed at her eyes. 'Why did your father never know?'

'We had a spell of several years when father and I didn't speak. During that period, I met James and married him. As he had died before I became reconciled, I kept it from him.'

'Any reason?'

'After I'd had a bad experience, I didn't wish to share it. Alexander helped me become reunited with father and we agreed not to inform him.'

'Thank you for telling me and I shall do my best to keep it a secret.'

53

'Father is an intolerant man.' Margaret gave a shake of her head and pursed her lips, 'Not only am I surprised he has taken to you, but it's astounding he has allowed you into his house.'

'Because I'm a model?'

'He is Victorian in his views, so when Charlotte became well known he had to resign from his CAD group that he had helped form. He agonised as the group had become important to him.' Margaret held a tissue close to her eyes, her face colour deepened and she sobbed. Andrea slid the chair close and put her arm around Margaret's shaking shoulders.

'It's a difficult time but we need the police to find the killer and close this case.' Andrea's words made the crying worse. 'What's the matter?' Andrea found it difficult to have affection for Margaret as she had shown no friendliness.

The sobbing stopped, 'I'm worried that the police will think I killed Charlotte.'

'Why would they think that?'

'Charlotte had been shot by a marksman.' Andrea let a silence develop. 'I stayed at home alone the night she died, but I've had furious arguments with Charlotte many of them in public, and… and... She took a gulp, 'I am a marksman as I won the Ladies Championship at Bisley.'

'Calm yourself, arguments and shooting are different matters.' Margaret gradually settled. Andrea moved her chair away. 'Let's help the police with information that could lead them to the killer.' She smiled encouragement at Margaret who gave a half-hearted smile back.

'Can you explain your links with the Kennedy family?' asked Andrea in a soft and amiable tone.

'Yes, that is easy. The police are wrong about the link between the two cases.' Margaret had returned to her short and abrupt voice.

'The Kennedy family?' Andrea lifted her eyebrows in a questioning manner.

'I met them when I visited Alexander in Ireland. When they came over and moved into his parish, I renewed acquaintances and I now know them well, it's as simple as that.'

'How did Matthew Kennedy come to be on your ward?'

She curled her lip, 'I work on a ward that treats post-operative care, so we take many who are admitted into Accident and Emergency that need operations. I'd arrived for work when a call for emergency theatre staff came through as three serious gunshot casualties were imminent.'

'From the armed robbery?'

'Yes. Luke died in theatre. Matthew had been badly injured.'

'Calum is in pain.'

Margaret scowled, 'He will have no long-term effects, it's not the same for Matthew, his injuries are more serious. The pager on Margaret's belt buzzed, she looked at the screen, 'I need to go, another case is coming into theatre, see yourself out.' She stood and left without a further word.

Andrea left the small office and walked along the corridor towards the noise of Calum hitting the coffee machine. He took a sip and threw it in the bin, 'It's a wonder anyone comes out of here alive.'

Within minutes they had returned to the car and travelled along the road past the Botanical Gardens heading towards Ashford in the Water to visit Gerald.

'Did you ask her why she worked such long hours?

'No, I assumed she's dedicated.'

Calum grunted but didn't ask any other questions.

Andrea made the decision not to tell him about Margaret's brief marriage. Calum listened to her comments about her chat with Margaret and then picked up his mobile phone. He made a short call and ordered the officer at the other end to confirm that Margaret had worked on the day of the robbery. 'Is it suspicious that she wanted you to leave and then broke down into tears as she doesn't strike me as an emotional woman?'

A dismissive grunt came from Calum, 'Even law-abiding people don't like the police as they think we are ham fisted and trawl around stirring up matters that don't concern us and lack sensitivity.'

'Is that true?'

'Yes. The senior people like Martin have the brains, the remainder of the force follow processes, it's how crimes are solved. Amateurs only guess.' Andrea took it as a dig but ignored him. 'We check the details people tell us. If they are true, we believe the other facts a person tells us, but we are not sensitive in our enquiries into people's private lives. Any information on the inheritance?'

'She didn't know.'

Calum nodded, 'Are you going to tell me the information she didn't wish me to know?' Andrea flashed a look of surprise at him.

'She doesn't want her father to know.'

'The police have to decide whether it is relevant or not. What is it?'

Andrea had to tell him. 'She's been married but didn't tell her father.'

'Let's have the details, I'll get it checked.'

'What will you do with the information?'

'Don't know. Give me the information first.' They didn't speak as they went out along the Ecclesall Road and took the route to Bakewell. Andrea thought through the best approach for Gerald.

Andrea's eyes tried to close with tiredness as the afternoon sun warmed her, but she struggled to keep them open as the images of Charlotte and Martin haunted her. Tonight loomed, what would happen if Martin came back again? A tremor of anxiety rattled through her bruised body. If she left home, everyone would become suspicious. As they approached Ashford in the Water, 'Did you know Gerald formed a Victorian style campaign against what he believes is falling moral standards?'

'You didn't say earlier. What did Margaret say?' Before Andrea could reply, 'Try to remember her exact words!'

'Don't snap at me,' she waited for the apology, but it didn't come. 'He had to leave CAD after Charlotte became famous, although he had been disappointed because he helped found it.'

'That's interesting.'

'Why?'

Calum ignored her and put his phone back in the hands-free unit of the car and pressed the number. 'Inspector Brodie, put me through to the Chief Constable.' After a few clicks his voice crackled on the car's speaker, 'Calum have you picked up something for us?'

'Yes sir, Andrea found out from his daughter that Manning is one of the founders of CAD.'

'Where are you now?'

'We are coming into Ashford on our way to see him.'

'Okay, it's worthwhile to pursue, I'll let you do it, but don't become too heavy-handed.'

'No, sir.'

'Can Andrea hear us?'

'Yes, sir.'

'Well done, Andrea, it's a strain for you my dear but please keep going.'

'Yes, I will,' but she sensed her voice lacked commitment.

'Give Andrea the background and let me know what develops.' Calum didn't volunteer any information after the call closed.

'Why are the police interested in his moral campaign?'

'They target individuals or groups and organise disruptions.'

'Are they not entitled to protest?'

'Not when they harass people, some have been jailed for burglary and intimidation.'

'Doesn't sound like Gerald.'

'The front people are young, mainly Bible-bashers who break-into houses and hotel rooms, and they have left threats to murder their victims.'

'And you believe Gerald has been involved.'

'The campaigns were planned with military precision, we caught one group of three, but never the mastermind.'

54

'Get out of the way you scumbags!' Calum shouted out the car window. Andrea frowned in disapproval at his intolerant attitude as they passed a large press corps at the end of the road where Gerald lived. The media machine had taken over the quiet and picturesque village of Ashford in the Water. The reporters scampered onto the pavement and a policeman waved them through. During the car journey Andrea had focused her thoughts on the Manning family. While they presented a hostile attitude to Charlotte and her chosen career, it was another matter to contemplate committing murder.

As they neared the house, she voiced her thoughts to Calum. 'This isn't right, we are treating this family as suspects, a priest, a career nurse and a hero from the Army, they are the pillars of society.'

'We've been through that before, it's what the police do,' growled Calum as he parked the car outside Gerald's house. 'The police investigate everyone, including the family, until we have a clear lead.'

'But I'm not the police.'

'You're trying to act like one, but I'd prefer to take you home and leave the case to the Chief Constable.'

Andrea shivered at the mention of home and noticed that Calum avoided Martin's name. What would she do this evening? Would Martin return for a repeat attack? She brushed the thoughts aside and would decide later.

'We're here now and we'll see Gerald,' Andrea strode up the path to the front door. The oak panels and the soft carpet in the hall didn't make Andrea feel welcome as she followed Gerald through to the lounge.

'I'll do the talking this time,' whispered Calum close to her ear.

'No chance,' hissed Andrea. Gerald indicated the chairs and stood with his back to the fireplace and with his hands behind him in military style. Andrea didn't give Calum a chance to start.

'Gerald, we've been to see Alexander and Margaret for background information about their involvement with the Kennedy family.' Standing stiff, Gerald's face revealed no emotion as he contemplated her words.

'That has been my concern from when your husband first mentioned the links, but I don't know the family and they are no friends of mine. Alexander befriended them when he served in Ireland and has supported them since and so Margaret knows them. Aren't they known as a type of Mafia family?' His voice held an element of contempt reinforced by the sneer which crossed his face.

'Total exaggeration,' interrupted Andrea with a dismissive flap of her hand, the newspapers always embellish by trying to make front page news. The twins, headstrong and violent, were led into the armed robbery, but the remainder of the family are different.'

'Families cannot be assumed to share the same attitudes and view of life, as we are individuals.' The precision of Gerald's words made it sound like a quote he had memorised. Andrea digested his statement. What a pity Gerald hadn't followed his own words. Perhaps he would have treated Charlotte with more respect and tolerance. Calum sat on a chair near the door and riled Andrea with his disinterest. 'Calum, tell Gerald what you think of the Kennedy family,' but she regretted it as soon as the words left her lips.

She intended him to relate the points from the conversations they'd had with Alexander and Margaret and momentarily forgot that Calum had been shot in the robbery attempt.

'Priests and nurses are forced to deal with the dregs of society.'

'Sorry Calum,' she mouthed, but he hadn't looked at her.

Gerald picked up the tone between Andrea and Calum, 'Do you think that as a family we know something linked to Charlotte's murder?'

'No, I don't, which is why the Chief Constable has asked me to talk to your family.' That brought a slight movement from Calum. Andrea ignored it and continued her explanation. 'If the Chief Constable thought your family had any involvement, it would be police officers talking to you.'

Gerald straightened his back, 'Is there anything else you want to ask me?'

'Calum?' He surprised her by shaking his head.

'You are a crack shot, sir?' Andrea kept her eyes focused on his face.

'Yes, we established that yesterday.' Gerald pursed his lips with displeasure at having to reiterate the information he had supplied before. 'The Chief Constable rang me to say none of the rifles, he took away, had been fired for weeks.'

'Yesterday, you went to the site where Charlotte had been killed.'

'Yes,' came the terse reply.

'I found you at the spot from where she had been shot.'

'Yes,' came the same reply.

'Would it have been a difficult shot?'

Gerald frowned and glanced at Calum before replying, 'No. The distance is short and there would be enough light from the car's headlights.'

'Anything else?' asked Andrea.

'One reason which makes it easy is that the position of the driver is unmistakable.' She pursed her lips as she tried to push the image of Charlotte's bloodied face from her mind. Forcing herself back to the present with a large intake of air, 'Would Alexander or Margaret be capable of producing such a shot?' He gulped which was the only sign he gave apart from a slight straightening of his already straight back.

'Yes, they could hit a target at that range under those conditions,' he lifted his head to peer at Andrea, 'are you implying it could be one of them?'

'No, I'm not, but it helps the police to eliminate people if they have the information at the beginning rather than having to dig.'

'Yes', a brief movement of his head indicated his understanding, 'that makes sense.'

Calum showed no interest.

'Would you prefer to sit?'

'No, although I suspect you want to ask me a difficult question.'

55

'Do you still lead CAD?'

Staring with eyes as cold as steel he glowered at Andrea, 'And exactly what is CAD?'

'I've not come here to play games, Colonel, if you will not tell me the truth then I shall leave.'

Gerald closed his mouth, forcing his lips into a thin hard line. Irritation coupled with impatience bubbled up inside Andrea. Didn't he realise that silence wouldn't work when the police came to interview him. Rubbing a hand across her aching forehead she changed the approach of her questions. She wanted the truth.

'Martin knew Charlotte because he interviewed her about threats from puritanical vigilantes.'

Calum's voice broke through Andrea's thoughts, 'On a different case, we arrested and charged three members of the CAD group who were jailed for several years, their actions and the other threats that people received were planned with military precision and up to now we have not known who is responsible.' Calum paused to allow his words to sink in, 'The police will re-interview those in jail with the emphasis on finding the leaders.'

'Why do you think I would have anything to do with this organisation, CAD or whatever you called it?' Gerald's face remained impassive, but his eyes glittered with disapproval.

'Why would Charlotte receive more threats than anyone else unless you were involved?' Andrea posed the question in a low and calm voice.

'You're trying to trick me. You don't know anything, I'll deny it.' He clamped his lips shut and stared towards the window and the garden.

'I'm not playing a game to trick you.'

Andrea stood, squared her shoulders and walked towards him, 'I want the truth. Will you tell me?'

'I wish you to leave my house,' his face flushed red with anger and he barked out his words as a command he expected to be followed, 'I thought you were a friend of Charlotte's who would help me.'

Turning to Calum with a frown of utter contempt, 'Your conduct will be noted for the next time I speak with the Chief Constable.'

Calum stepped forward and stood beside Andrea, Gerald stepped forward so his face moved closer to theirs, 'You are insulting me, please leave my house, I shall report the whole matter to the Chief Constable,' Gerald shouted into their faces.

Andrea stood to her full height so she could peer down on him and in a firm but controlled voice, 'Colonel, you are blustering and bullying and I won't have it. And please do not threaten Calum. I will support him to the Chief Constable.'

Gerald went to speak, but she raised her palm in front of his face, 'And do not continue to be so rude as I dislike being shouted at. You have encroached on my personal space before, now retreat and sit.' Gerald's eyes flared but neither Calum nor Andrea moved, but after a moment's hesitation Gerald stepped back to the fireplace.

'Colonel.' Andrea motioned towards a seat and he moved to the wing-back chair and lowered himself down with slow precision. Andrea sat opposite him on the couch and she indicated for Calum to sit next to her, which he did. 'The Chief Constable will not defend you as the CAD campaign has been nasty and there have been many threats to women.' Andrea didn't wait for either Gerald or Calum to speak, 'If you do not tell us the truth now, I assume Calum will arrest you and you will be taken away in a police car in front of half of the world's media. The headlines within the hour will sensationalise your arrest because they do not have accurate information and will connect you with the murder of your daughter.'

The steely stare from Gerald's eyes had gone, his eyes flicked between Andrea and Calum. 'I will tell you the truth. You're perceptive, Andrea, but I would have told you, only it's difficult with your escort and your husband.' Andrea ignored his comments. His excuses didn't interest her, she wanted the truth.

'Did Charlotte find out you were part of the organisation behind the threats towards her?'

'No, I'm sure she didn't,' he muttered. His bravado had evaporated.

'Are Margaret and Alexander part of CAD?' Andrea kept going with the questioning as she became determined to reveal his involvement.

'No, I didn't invite them to join. Although both have realised I became associated with the group.'

'Why wouldn't Charlotte know?'

'I never had the detailed conversations with her I've had with Margaret and Alexander.

Sweat ran down Gerald's forehead but he didn't move a muscle as he answered her questions. 'What about Edward?' she ventured.

'He knows nothing about the group, it started before he arrived here.' Gerald's military bearing held back his emotions, but the strain showed on his face. 'I left the group when Charlotte became famous.'

'Why?' snapped Andrea.

'The rest of the group made it clear I should publicly disown her,' he gulped and straightened his back again, 'I couldn't do it, but I tried to persuade her in every way possible to quit her unsuitable life style. But like her mother, she could be headstrong and when I couldn't change her, Edward became my only hope.'

Gerald gathered his thoughts and Andrea waited. 'You think Edward is a strange man, but Charlotte liked him, I hadn't seen her eyes light up like that since a young girl. When she came here with Edward, we didn't argue and I had a glimpse of my little daughter again. The atmosphere became tense, but he brokered the peace between us.'

'Would their marriage have had your blessing?'

'Yes, I told them.'

'How did you first meet Edward?' asked Andrea.

'When Charlotte brought him home about six months ago.'

'What do you think of him?'

'A fine man holding an excellent job at the bank.'

'Where is he now?'

'He required time elsewhere and has returned to London to meet old friends, but I believe he informed the police.'

Andrea crossed to the French Doors to stare down the garden, she wouldn't be able to cope much longer. 'Colonel, it is better that Inspector Brodie takes over, as it is a police matter beyond me.' She recognised the sound she heard the morning that Gerald had rung her when he struggled to control his emotions. Calum had stepped towards him.

'Sorry, Inspector, we are hardened men, emotion doesn't sit easy with us. Will you arrest me?'

Andrea wanted to hear 'no' but wouldn't interfere.

56

'Gerald Manning, you admit that you are or were a member of the group known as Campaign against Depravity, CAD.'

Andrea couldn't resist any longer, 'Is this necessary?'

'Calm yourself Andrea, Inspector Brodie has his job to do, I would expect no less of a man in the service of the law, I cannot fault his actions.'

'Sir?' said Calum.

'Yes, Inspector, I founded the Campaign against Depravity.'

'It may harm your defence if you do not mention when questioned, something which you later rely on in court. Anything you do say may be given in evidence.'

'What happens now?' asked Andrea. Calum frowned and ignored her.

'Please consider yourself arrested, sir, however, I have no intention of giving any help or stories to the pack of wolves outside. Therefore, I require you at your earliest convenience to contact the Chief Constable to arrange to make a statement.'

'Thank you, Inspector, you have my word I shall do that.'

'There was something else I want to ask you, Gerald.'

She turned to Calum, 'May I?'

The deep frown on Calum's face remained unchanged. 'You are using Andrea as your adviser and so I have no objection to leaving you alone, so you may discuss matters.'

'That won't be necessary, Inspector, I've made mistakes and it's time to face the consequences of my actions. Please ask, my dear, the Inspector will document my replies, which will be honest.'

'You are entitled to legal representation, sir.'

'I know, please note I have refused such representation at this time.'

He faced Andrea, 'What did you want to ask?'

'The threats to Charlotte stopped a few months ago.'

'Yes, one evening, with Edward present, she explained about the threats and I questioned her, but I guessed their origins. I rang the group and asked them to stop, which they did with reluctance.'

'What happened after that?

'Weeks later, Charlotte tried to convince me she didn't lead a life of sex, drugs and sin,' he took a deep breath, 'we lost our tempers. I made her swear on the Bible.'

'Oh, Gerald!'

'Yes, I shouldn't have, furthermore I decided to prove the type of life Charlotte led so I went behind her back and hired a detective agency to follow her and report back.'

'Which one?' said Calum.

'Burgoynes.' Calum nodded.

'Do you know them?' asked Andrea.

'Yes, they are made up of ex-police and ex-military and are reputable.'

'Did they bring forward any evidence for your views?'

'No.'

'You hesitated.'

'Nothing until the night she was killed.'

'What did they say?'

'They rang me to say they suspected Charlotte was having an affair with a married man and they would investigate further. Edward would have overheard the call.'

Calum said, 'Andrea, given that Colonel Manning has been arrested we should not pursue this any further.'

'Yes, I can understand why.'

Gerald collapsed back into the chair and began to sob uncontrollably.

57

'We're running out of family and it's a pity that Edward is not here as it would have been useful to talk to him again.'

'You must have talked to him at the murder scene, you'll remember, when you deliberately left me.'

'Sorry,'

'What did he say?' Andrea hesitated. 'Come on, I'm not playing your silly games anymore.'

She took a few minutes while they sat in the car outside Gerald's house to give Calum the details of the conversation.

'You've been withholding vital information from the police. It's beyond me why the Chief Constable wants to keep you involved.'

Andrea wouldn't accept the rebuke, 'I believed him, but I intended telling Martin. And then….well...'

'You could have explained to me.'

'The trouble with you Calum Brodie, is you are unapproachable, you don't want to listen, you're hostile and you make it obvious you don't wish to be here.'

He sneered, 'So to summarise, Edward was close to the scene of the murder and admits he had no alibi and can shoot. And….'

'And what?' snapped Andrea.

'And he has a possible motive.'

'I don't see as he loved her.'

'Or so he says.'

'What's the motive then?'

'Manning told us, Edward overheard Gerald's conversation with Burgoynes, the agency, about Charlotte having an affair with a married man. Possessiveness, jealousy or as he perceived it, abject betrayal.'

'When you put it like that, it doesn't sound good for him.'

Calum continued, 'Added to that he is the only one, so far, who knew Charlotte's route.'

'What are you going to do?'

'If we'd known the information you withheld, we would not have agreed he could leave the area.'

'Sorry, but you'll be with me from now, so you'll hear everything first hand.'

'We've finished,' snapped Calum.

'No, we haven't. There's still Wayne Smith and Fitzwilliam to see, you remember, the agent and the reporter, playing at childish games by being the roadies.'

'No, leave them to the police.'

'Let's at least see the agent. Please.' Calum didn't reply and drove off much too fast for Andrea's liking. Andrea waited, but he didn't turn up towards Monsal Head to take her home, so she sat back in her seat.

'This is the last one.' Andrea didn't reply, it seemed a better idea to stay quiet. Calum put the phone into the hands-free so Andrea could hear. He rang the Incident Centre and asked who had given permission for Edward to leave the area. 'There's nothing on the incident card, sir.'

'Find out and ring me back.'

'Yes, sir.'

'Have the brothers been formally charged.'

'No, sir, the Chief Constable is interviewing them.'

'Let me know what happens,' Calum cut the call without waiting for a reply. They travelled in silence until Calum drove into Sheffield along the Abbeydale road, 'Where's his office?'

'On an industrial estate near Tinsley.'

'Hardly the best place to give a reliable impression.' Andrea had to agree. An office near the M1 motorway and an estate of heavy industry would never be termed prestigious. As he drove through the centre of Sheffield, 'Don't cock it up the same as you did with him the last time.'

'Do you want to lead?' snapped Andrea.

'You didn't let me lead with Colonel Manning, you jumped in.'

'You can do it this time.'

'No.'

The next mile they spent in silence. Finally, Calum swung the Jaguar into the car park outside a small industrial unit built with cheap bricks and tiny windows and skidded to a halt in a parking bay surrounded by bushes. Andrea ignored his bad-tempered driving. Aching as she climbed from the car, she knocked on the door which had a dirty sign, Wayne Smith, Theatrical Agent to the Stars.' Graffiti marks covered the door. The security bolt opened with a noisy grind. Calum pushed the door with his foot and walked in. The small outer office had only one desk.

The young blonde receptionist looked up and smiled, 'Are you here to see Mr Smith?'

'Yes.'

She looked at the diary in front of her. 'Is he expecting you as you don't have an appointment.'

Before Andrea could reply, Calum pulled out his warrant card, put it in front of her face. 'He'll see me.' Andrea felt sorry for the young receptionist, but she coped well. After studying the warrant card for a second, 'Under the circumstances I'm sure he will see you, Inspector Brodie,' so she slipped from her seat behind the desk, knocked on the nearby door and went in closing it firmly behind her before Andrea could see inside.

Two men's voices emanated from the office.

58

Glancing out of a small side window, Andrea pointed, 'Calum, it's Fitzwilliam, he's climbing out the window.' Despite his injury Calum moved fast, he threw the door of the office open and rushed in. The receptionist screamed at the door banging back on its hinges and Calum bellowing, 'Come here, you fat bastard.' Fitzwilliam struggled to force his large bulk through the compact window. Calum hauled him back and propelled him into a small chair which broke under the impact dumping Fitzwilliam on the floor. He sprawled across the dirty cracked lino, banged his head on the desk legs then swore. The receptionist screamed again.

'Calm down everyone, please!' shouted Wayne as he came from behind his desk and helped Fitzwilliam to his feet. 'Sit please, Inspector. Get Fitz another chair please, Angie,' he came forward and moved a chair for Andrea. 'Let's sit and talk rationally shall we?'

Fitzwilliam rubbed his forehead and moaned but slumped down onto the chair offered by Angie. Calum waited for Wayne to return to his seat behind the desk and for Fitzwilliam to be seated and then he sat. Andrea had moved her chair away from everyone to the side of the room near the door in case of further action and she perched on the edge of the hard wooden seat.

Calum seethed and his eyes flashed with annoyance, 'Why were you trying to get out of the window?' Andrea thought it a silly question, far too obvious.

'I don't like the police,' growled Fitzwilliam. Andrea nodded to herself. A bland and evasive answer but what reply had he expected? Wayne held up his hand, but no one took any notice of him. Andrea needed to stop the squabbling as they wouldn't be able to make progress.

They needed answers not ridiculous arguments, 'He's not in the police anymore.'

'Why not?' Fitzwilliam sneered looking much more alert and interested in this snippet of information.

'I don't like being shot,' Calum snapped back at him.

Calum produced his notebook and dug around in his pocket finally finding a pencil. Fitzwilliam watched his movements with a smirk on his face, 'You're not the police, so we don't have to answer your questions.' Fitzwilliam and Calum had been so busy annoying each other they'd almost forgotten anyone else.

Andrea's voice cut through their posturing. 'I need to alter my statement to the police, I forgot one crucial observation.' The three men focused on her.

'I forgot to mention I saw the two of you the day of Charlotte's murder badly disguised as roadies.' A brief look of worry flitted across their faces. Wayne moved in his seat and averted eye contact by shuffling papers on his desk, but he didn't offer an explanation.

'Background to a story,' blustered Fitzwilliam, with a dismissive wave of his hand, 'I've done it hundreds of times, you know how I operate.'

'What story?' Calum had his pencil at the ready to record anything relevant.

'It's none of your business.'

Fitzwilliam gave a small superior smile and lifted his chin in a gesture of defiance.

'I can assure you we had an innocent reason,' interrupted Wayne, but his voice didn't have conviction and his eyes flitted nervously towards Calum.

'If it's so innocent why not tell the police?'

Andrea focused on Wayne, 'You told me you were miles away.'

'I became confused, but I see that the police need to know, don't they Fitz, after all, it's only a story.'

'Trying to drag up the dirt on someone,' growled Calum.,

'Fitzwilliam…' but he interrupted her.

'No point in you continuing while he's here,' he poked one of his fat fingers at Calum, 'I'm saying nothing.'

'This sounds dubious,' Calum eyed the fat man with suspicion, 'perhaps this conversation would be better off at the police station.' Andrea frowned as she didn't want that attitude from him. Threatening would mean no progress. Wayne and Fitzwilliam would clam up and they needed to be encouraged to talk.

'You've left the police, remember! Or have you forgotten already?' Fitzwilliam gave a mirthless laugh, 'We don't have to take any notice of you.'

Wayne's hands shook as he sweated. Andrea turned her attention back to Fitzwilliam who acted his usual awkward and arrogant self.

She couldn't allow this to continue any further as

Calum would arrest them.

59

'I've been talking to my friends in the fashion industry about you.'

'We're well known,' boasted Wayne recovering his composure.

'Jack Smedley,' she stared at Fitzwilliam and raised her eyebrows in a questioning manner.

He burst out laughing and his large stomach wobbled as he leaned back in his chair with amusement written over his face. 'You mean my Editor, who hates the fashion industry, he thinks they are overrated and have no talent, I know you will not succeed with him.'

'That's where you're wrong,' she paused and a wry smile hovered across her lips, 'Patsy and I are having dinner with him on Tuesday next week.'

'I don't believe you,' he scratched at his stubbled chin and stared at her through narrowed eyes.

Calum eyed the journalist with disdain, 'Andrea confirmed the call in the car on the way here.' Fitzwilliam still looked dubious. Andrea ignored Calum's interruption as she would prefer him to stay quiet.

'You know him well Fitzwilliam. Don't you? What does he like the most?'

'I don't know,' he said gruffly, he wasn't happy about the direction of the conversation.

Andrea continued, 'First is a good scoop.' Fitzwilliam didn't speak, she fixed a sharp look on his frowning face, 'And second is his campaign supporting British troops abroad.'

'He used to be in the Army,' muttered Fitzwilliam.

'I want to find background information about those close to Charlotte and her murder including you two.' Andrea flicked her eyes between Fitzwilliam and Wayne.

Fitzwilliam's brash voice had gone quiet, 'You're meeting him with Patsy?'

'Patsy and I want to strike a deal with your editor, so I asked him to get me the background on both of you by Tuesday.'

'Believe me, he's not trustworthy,' but Fitzwilliam sounded worried, 'he'd stitch up his own grandmother.'

'I know that, remember the background on you by Tuesday.'

'He won't do it,' Fitzwilliam snapped.

Andrea ignored his skepticism, 'And then if we agree it's good information, he can publish in his paper on Wednesday that Patsy and I will go with Charlotte's friends abroad to entertain the troops.' Andrea sat back in her chair with a sense of satisfaction as Fitzwilliam squirmed. He dropped his head and looked at the floor.

Wayne puffed out his cheeks and wiped a hand across his sweaty brow, 'Fitz, it's no time to be awkward, let's be open and honest with Andrea and Inspector Brodie, we've nothing to hide.' Fitzwilliam had a worried expression.

'What did you want to ask us?' said Wayne without

enthusiasm.

'Gentlemen, shall we start with the truth?' Andrea gave a small smile. 'The only reason you won't tell me is if you are the murderers and you will bump me off before I reach London and find more out about you.'

'Nothing to hide, Andrea,' said Wayne with a false laugh, 'ask away.'

'A close friend of mine since school days works for Harrison Accountants.' Andrea spoke slowly allowing them to absorb the information.

'Fraud specialists,' added Calum.

'Yes, I know,' said Wayne with a tight smile.

'Now, would you be prepared to let them look at Charlotte's accounts in your books?' Wayne took a deep breath and scanned the room with panic in his eyes as sweat rolled down his forehead and he wrung his hands together. Calum gripped his notebook and had his pencil ready.

'Charlotte demanded instant service,' his voice sounded strained and he stared at the desk, 'she always wanted changes to her plans arranged at short notice so I told her they would be expensive. I added extras for the inconvenience.'

'Did she find out?' Calum stopped writing and eyed Wayne with suspicion, 'I don't think so, but I didn't murder her over a few pounds in expenses.' He shuffled in his seat, his face a picture of misery.

'I know the turnover that runs through my agent's books,' she paused, 'and Charlotte topped the music world. That's even more money.' Andrea turned to Calum and in a conversational tone explained, 'I reckon Charlotte's income would have been about three million last year.

Let's say he adds on an extra 10% for inconvenience,' she emphasised the word. With a nod towards the sweating unhappy man, 'that, by my calculations, would make Wayne wealthy.' Andrea folded her arms as the agent squirmed. A modest smile hovered on her lips, but she had no sympathy for the devious toad.

'No, no it's nothing like that,' he blustered under their intense scrutiny.

Calum looked up from writing in his notebook, 'I nicked someone once who worked out of a tatty office, claimed poverty and asked the local council for grants.'

'What happened?' enquired Andrea.

'He drove fifty miles home in a battered old car to a huge country mansion and led the life of luxury.' Calum chuckled.

'Why would I kill her?' Wayne's voice rose alarmingly, 'She became my best client by far. If she had found out, we would have done a deal as she liked me.'

'Friends soon disappear when they are deceived,' said Calum, 'I reckon she found out and told you she wanted a new agent and suggested Harrisons.'

'No, she didn't, she didn't!' he yelled jumping to his feet then realising there was nowhere to flee, slumped back behind his desk and put his head in his hands. Andrea had forced him into this corner. The police would examine the accounts. Calum would suggest it.

Andrea decided on a different tack, 'Where were you on 23 May?'

'What?' Wayne jerked his head up in surprise.

Fitzwilliam gazed at him, 'Where were you on the day of the armed robbery?' Terror crossed Wayne's face.

'Your website biography shows you used to be a rally

driver,' added Calum with an air of nonchalance. Wayne's ashen face stared in terror at the policeman. 'Witnesses reported the getaway driver in the armed robbery had good driving skills.' Calum smirked as Wayne fidgeted with worry.

'Don't say anything more,' Fitzwilliam thumped the desk with his fist, 'they are winding you up. At least you can't think I'm part of the armed robbery. Even the dumbest witness could have reported my shape.' The conversation had turned in the wrong direction for Andrea and had become aggressive, caused by Calum's rough questioning. A low key approach would have produced better results so she would make one last attempt to get helpful answers.

'Fitzwilliam,' she said in a quiet voice, 'why do you write under so many names?' It drew the focus of the conversation away from Calum and Wayne. Andrea continued, 'You're a famous journalist, why not do more under your own name?'

'Fame doesn't pay the rent,' Fitzwilliam muttered. He looked around the faces, and decided to continue, 'It started when a mate of mine didn't have long to live and became too tired to write, so I ghosted work for him. He had a column, but it didn't carry his name, so I continued for his wife and kids after he died.'

Fitzwilliam continued, 'I had bills of my own to pay so I extended the idea, it's only freelancing without my editor finding out, and keeping it away from him is the way I'd like it to stay.'

'Last question.' Andrea smiled with encouragement. Wayne sighed with relief. Calum didn't look happy but Andrea couldn't be bothered with him. 'The story about the Kennedys.'

'I don't know why everyone keeps raking that up, it's straightforward.'

'You need to explain, it isn't straightforward,' moaned Calum.

Fitzwilliam ignored him and gave his answer to Andrea, 'I came to Sheffield looking for a story but made no progress then I bumped into Wayne and explained I needed a hire car.'

'I took him over to the Kennedy's,' Wayne added.

Fitzwilliam continued with the story, 'Ma likes to chat so I had a cup of tea with her and she told me business had gone downhill. Later her sons came in. You know they're heavies, you wouldn't want to meet them on a dark night.'

'So?' barked Calum.

'I came up with the idea for the story, Irish gangland and I spoke to Ma and it took off from there. It made national news and then there was plenty of follow up and it got my editor off my back.'

'How much investigating did you do?' Andrea queried.

Fitzwilliam leaned back in his chair which creaked alarmingly, 'You asked for the truth. Well here it is. None. I sat with Ma and we made it up.'

'But.' Andrea shook her head in confusion.

Fitzwilliam was in full swing and would not be interrupted, 'Another truth about stories. Gangland stories can be invented.'

'How? I don't see,' Andrea gave him a long encouraging look. She wanted to keep him talking.

'No one will admit it, everyone including the police

deny gangland feuds exist. The story leaves the doubts but with the pictures of the brothers to reinforce it the public believe the story.'

A stillness came over the room. She wanted more information. 'What happens then?' Andrea queried.

'It runs and runs.' Fitzwilliam smiled and rubbed his finger and thumb together indicating that it made money and sold newspapers. 'The police deny it but do nothing about it,' he turned to Calum, 'You didn't think it worth investigating did you?' Calum remained silent and shook his head. 'The only ones who took it seriously were Ma's rivals, so we accomplished our mission and I received a good bonus and Ma got her business back on its feet.' He gave a smug smile of satisfaction at a job well done.

There was silence while the four of them digested Fitzwilliam's story. Andrea broke the silence, 'They've arrested, and will charge, the two elder brothers with armed robbery.'

'They've got it wrong as usual,' Fitzwilliam snapped, 'You can't trust the police to be right.' He stood up, 'And now, unless you arrest me, I'm leaving.'

Calum's phone rang, he answered. The others remained quiet, then he cut the short call with a curt, 'Thank you.'

Three pairs of eyes waited, 'The Kennedys were released by the Chief Constable.' Andrea mulled over this snippet of information. That's strange as they had been told they would be charged.

'The two big brothers will be roaming Sheffield to find the person who stitched them up.'

60

'I'm hungry,' said Andrea as they went towards the car.

Calum gave her a withering look but his eyes focused across the other side of the industrial estate, 'It's a hotdog stall, that will do.' It wouldn't have been Andrea's choice. 'We'll leave the car here, it'll be quicker,' and he set off. Calum's limp had become worse, but he moved faster as her high heels wobbled as she crossed the cracked and pitted tarmac. Her body ached as it didn't want to move. Why did she dislike him? The gap between them increased and he arrived at the hot dog stall before her.

Crying, she slowed her walk, 'I can't go on.' No one heard her words. Concentrating on what Calum thought of her, would distract her from thinking about Charlotte and Martin. It's not only his lack of manners but he never asks my opinion. Everyone apart from Calum pays me attention and gives into me, but not him, he doesn't respond. I make him dig his heels in and become even more stubborn and bad tempered. Andrea couldn't stop crying as she reached the van. Calum had ordered two hot dogs, so she nodded when asked whether she wanted onions. She took the hot dog from him and took the first mouthful, it didn't taste good, but her stomach rumbled.

The owner spotted her.

'You're that famous model, Andrea Cain.' She smiled, her tears still flowed but the men would think it rain on her face. 'Can I take your picture?' he said taking out his mobile phone.

'Piss off,' said Calum.

'No, it's okay,' she smiled and he took the snap.

'Will you sign this?' he held out a serviette.

Andrea signed, 'Nice hot dog, Andrea Cain.'

'My wife will never believe it; I'll frame the picture and the serviette.' They moved a short distance away from the van and munched their hot dogs in silence while the rain continued to fall. Andrea ate as her mind worried through other issues. Calum ignored her. What should she do now? They threw their rubbish in the bin, Calum marched away from her across the car park. She called out, but he barely waited for her to catch up, 'You took a bloody dangerous line in that interview. You're a liability. If one of them is the murderer…' But he never completed the sentence. Andrea let the silence fall. 'It will suit the headline writers,' growled Calum.

She gave him a confused look, 'What will?'

'Model murdered, it's an alliteration,' but he had no smile. Calum marched away and shouted back over his shoulder, 'These are low life, I extract the first part of the truth from them and I will have the full story when I take them to the police station.'

'They told you what you wanted to hear and it didn't do them any harm to admit what they did. Fraud would be near impossible to prove.'

'I don't give a damn,' shouted Calum waving his arm in the air, 'I'm out of the police and I'm out of here.

Give me a lift back to my car and I'll be out of your life.'

'No, we're in this together despite you being a rude and obnoxious man.' Calum increased the pace but Andrea stayed with him. It rained harder, her thin jacket dripped. He tripped and fell with a cry of pain. Andrea reached to help him up, but he pushed her away, staggered to his feet and carried on across the car park. He climbed into the car whining with pain and slammed the door. 'I'll drive back into Sheffield and I'll get out at Wicker. After that you are on your own.'

Andrea stared at him in astonishment. 'I want to talk to you about progress and find out what's happening about Edward.'

'Nothing is happening absolutely nothing!' he shouted. Andrea sat in silence taken aback by the ferocity of his words as she hadn't anticipated his outburst. Her thoughts twisted and large tears rolled down her cheeks as he reversed out the car park and turned towards Sheffield. He drove fast along the wide road.

The traffic lights turned red, he stamped on the accelerator.

61

The siren from the police car waiting to cross the junction screeched as the blue light flashed, they turned after the Jaguar. Calum went to grab his radio from his pocket, 'Damn, where's my radio,' he cursed as the car increased speed. Andrea gripped the sides of the car seat.

What had happened to him? The car lurched and lost power. By now the police car had reached them with its siren blaring and blue lights flashing.

'Red lights on the dashboard,' said Calum ignoring the police car, 'power has gone,' so he drifted the car into the side of the road in front of the massive darkened walls of the steelworks.

Andrea glanced back at the policeman who approached the car and guessed he wouldn't be impressed that Calum didn't stop as soon as he could. The constable knocked on the window. Calum lowered it and showed him his warrant car, 'Sorry sir, but you've jumped a red light and you are in an unmarked car.' Calum looked like he would explode as his face went red and he gripped the steering wheel with unnecessary force.

Andrea went to intervene, but the constable's radio cackled, 'All units, we have lost radio and mobile contact with Inspector Brodie and he is urgently required by the Chief Constable who is concerned he may be in danger.' Calum felt to his pocket again, 'I've must have dropped my radio and phone when I fell. Damn it.'

The young constable stood and stared with wide anxious eyes. Andrea leaned over, 'Constable, would you give Inspector Brodie your radio please?' He appreciated the solution to dealing with an irritable senior officer and detached it from its holder and handed it through the window.

Calum snatched it, 'Brodie here.'

'There is a message from the Chief Constable, sir.'

'Can you patch me through?'

'No, sir. He said he wouldn't be able to take your call.'

'What's the message?'

'Could you come as quickly as possible to HQ, he wants to see you in person.'

'Did he say to bring Mrs Cain with me?'

'Message reads, Calum, please come urgently to HQ to see me. Make all necessary arrangements for the safe keeping of Andrea. End of message.'

'What does that mean?' Andrea said.

'I'm not sure what's happened but if the Chief doesn't want you there it must be serious.'

'But you will go, won't you?' He hesitated. 'Please go, don't give up on me and the Chief Constable yet.'

Calum put the radio back to his mouth, 'I'll come, but I'll need another squad car.'

'Yes, sir, it will arrive in four minutes.'

'You!' he snapped at the constable.

'Yes, sir.'

'Look after Mrs Cain. Get this car to a breakdown garage and ensure she is taken home safely. Is that clear?'

'Yes, sir.' Andrea went to protest but decided it would be better to stay quiet. If the Chief Constable wanted Calum urgently, then something had happened. He had to go. The sound of a distant siren came closer and a few minutes later another police car pulled up alongside the Jaguar. The Sergeant in the car called across, 'HQ, sir.'

Calum hesitated. 'Go, these officers will protect me.' Calum climbed in the back of the police Range Rover and it sped away.

'Would you like to join us in our car Mrs Cain, we can call the breakdown business from there.' It rained hard and the towering works made it dark and gloomy, she only felt safe because the police were with her. She climbed out of the Jaguar and into the back of the police car, 'We need to look after Mrs Cain and arrange for the car to be picked up by breakdown,' the young policeman explained to the driver.

'It could be difficult as there's a major crash on the motorway and the breakdown garages are in full use, but I'll try.'

'Thank you, officer.' The night loomed and the risk at home from Martin would be best avoided. 'I'll make calls while you try to get a breakdown garage.' She picked out the number on her phone, 'Hi, Patsy, it's Andrea. Can I crash with you tonight? That's great I will see you soon.'

Andrea pressed the second number. 'Pablo, will you do me a big favour? Can you round me up day clothes?' She listened. 'Yes, everything. You're a star.' Andrea laughed, 'Yes, I know how many favours I owe you. How soon could you manage it? Later on this evening will be brilliant. I'm staying with Patsy. Thanks Pablo.'

'Is there anything we can do, ma'am?' asked the constable's warm and friendly voice, a contrast to the gruffness of Calum. Why had Calum been called to police headquarters?

'No, thanks.' Andrea smiled at him.

'The breakdown lorry will be some time.'

Their presence gave her reassurance.

62

'A man is walking towards us, do you recognise him?'

Andrea leaned between the two front seats so she could see. 'Yes, it's Wayne Smith, we've been to see him. I'll speak with him.'

'Do you need an escort?'

'No, that won't be necessary.' Andrea climbed out of the back seat into the rain, 'Wayne.'

'Hi, what's the matter?'

'The car has broken down.' She didn't know whether to mention the meeting with Calum, but decided she couldn't avoid it, 'I'm sorry about...'

'Not now, I don't like your friend, but there again I don't suppose many people do, he's obnoxious.'

'I've a long wait for the breakdown as there's an accident on the M1.'

'I'll get the Kennedys to fetch it if you like, they can be here in ten minutes.' He extracted his mobile phone. Andrea looked alarmed at the thought. Wayne could see it in her face even though the overcast day had become dark. 'There is nothing to cause alarm. Look at you, you're soaking wet,' he took off his coat and put it around her shoulders.

'Thanks.' The kind gesture almost reduced her to tears.

'You're distraught about Charlotte.' He patted her on the shoulder, 'You shouldn't be doing the police's job for them. Leave it to your husband. You've gone pale and I can see you're shivering, you need to go home.'

'I'm staying in town tonight.'

'Wherever, it's better than standing here in the rain.'

One of the police called out, 'It could be an hour, sorry ma'am, but we'll keep trying.'

Wayne studied her, then a slow smile worked its way across his face and into his eyes. 'I've come up with the perfect solution, I'll stay with your car until the Kennedys reach here so you need not go to them. They've their own breakdown truck, they can transport your car to their garage and you can have it picked up in the morning, I'll explain everything to Ma,' he smiled and then added, 'she likes you.'

Andrea wasn't sure why but she shivered at the remark. Weariness came over her fast and her head ached. The cold racked her body. Wayne's idea seemed an acceptable option as she wouldn't have to visit the Kennedys and could keep her intended location a secret. She wanted no one except the police to know in which hotel she would stay. After calling an officer over to join their conversation, she explained the arrangements and the police offered to drive her to the hotel.

Andrea tapped on the door of the penthouse suite in the city centre hotel. In a few seconds, the door was flung open and an exaggerated, 'Darling,' came from Patsy who stepped forward and hugged her.

Andrea pecked her on the cheeks, ‘It’s lovely to see you again, Patsy.’

‘Come in, it’ll be like old times when we used to share when we were on tour.’ Andrea sighed, everything seemed to have moved on so much since those days, but they were good memories. As Andrea went into the small entrance hall of the suite, Patsy stopped and turned, ‘And I’ve a wonderful surprise for you, come into the lounge.’ Andrea followed Patsy but stopped in the doorway.

63

'Martin!' She froze and grabbed the doorframe for support as her legs threatened to buckle. He came towards her; Andrea gasped and couldn't move. Her eyes locked onto his face.

'Could you leave us please, Patsy, so I can talk to Andrea,' Martin smiled.

'Sure, babe,' but puzzlement crossed her face.

'Don't go, Patsy, please stay,' Andrea's voice rose as hysteria gripped her. She couldn't be alone with Martin, her aching body couldn't take more abuse.

'Hey, what is going on between you two, you're not like this,' as she glanced between the pair of them and hesitated.

'Please leave us,' his authoritative police voice shook Andrea to her core. He took another step towards her. Patsy shot a look at Andrea who shook her head. She willed Patsy to stay. Panic welled up inside her.

'Don't go,' Andrea attempted a severe tone though it sounded more like a strangled cry, 'Martin is leaving.'

'Oh, God, you guys have split up, I don't think I can cope.' Patsy's eyes were wide with astonishment.

'Just stay,' pleaded Andrea with a small sob.

Martin stood with his hands on his hips and faced Patsy with the smile plastered on his face.

'I think I'm entitled to at least a few minutes in private with Andrea,' his smooth tone sounded persuasive. But Andrea shook her head, she wanted to scream, but no sound emerged from her open mouth. She could see the tears running down Martin's face, but they evoked no sympathy in her. 'Please I beg of you. Please forgive me. Please talk to me.'

Patsy stood in the middle of the room open-mouthed and switching her gaze from one to the other as though watching a fast game of tennis. 'No Martin, I can't. I can't forgive you,' her voice quivered, tears filled her eyes, 'Get out!'

'Is there anything I can do to help?' Patsy whispered.

'Yes, stay there,' Andrea gave her a desperate glance.

'Please, please forgive me,' Martin pleaded, he still had the false smile on his face. The eyes gave him away. Too much blackness and no green. 'I'll get help, whatever I need, but I can't live without you,' he took a small step forward and held out his arms towards her as though suggesting a cuddle.

'Martin, please believe me, I can't forgive you,' she still clung onto the doorframe. 'I can't.' Martin took another small step forward. 'Keep away from me,' she sobbed cowering backwards like a frightened animal. Martin ignored her distress and closed in on her. 'I need to comfort you and ask for forgiveness.' The smile remained ingrained on his face like the painted mouth of a circus clown.

'Keep away from me,' Andrea backed away, but he came close and stood in front of her breathing hard. She could smell the whiskey on his breath. Andrea brought her hands in front of her face, filled her lungs with air and screamed, 'Keep away.' His hand touched her on the shoulder. She peered between her fingers and the deep black eyes in front of her, with no hint of green.

Panic gripped her and she lashed out with clenched fists towards his face, but her attempts had no effect, he pushed her arms away with contempt written across his face. Then he grabbed the front of her jumper, holding her at arm's length and raised his arm. She cowered and pulled her arms across her face and waited for the blow to land as her mind flashed back to the previous night. She screamed with terror at what would come next.

The blow never came, instead she heard a huge groan so with trepidation she raised her head. Martin lay crumpled on the floor holding his groin which still had Patsy's shoe embedded in it. He writhed in agony on the floor, moaning and swearing. With open mouthed amazement Patsy withdrew her foot, took another swing, this time hitting him in the chest. Patsy screamed at him shrill and loud 'Get out, you bastard, get out of here before I bloody kill you,' Andrea scrambled away as the next kick landed on Martin's head. 'Get out!' shrieked Patsy. Martin half crawled and half staggered away from the next blow and towards the door. Andrea rushed forward to make sure he didn't get up and attack Patsy. The point of Patsy's stiletto dug hard into his thigh and ripped his trousers.

As he opened the door into the corridor, he turned and shouted, 'If you won't be mine, then I shall kill you.' Patsy landed another kick which sent him sprawling on the corridor floor. She slammed and locked the door, leaned against it and slid to the floor. Andrea rushed forward and crouched next to her, 'Pats, are you OK, did he hurt you?' She opened her eyes and hugged Andrea. They lay on the floor in each other's arms, both trembling and gasping for air.

'Yes, darling, I'm fine, I need a stiff drink but, my God, did you see his eyes, he looked as though he would kill you.'

'Thanks, Pats,' Andrea cuddled into her friend and worried how close Patsy had come to the truth. A cold icy shiver travelled through her body.

'No one will hurt my friend,' Patsy hugged Andrea.

64

A knock on the bedroom door turned Andrea's body rigid with fear. The bright morning light streamed through the window. Patsy snored next to her on the bed. Andrea put her hand to her head and remembered the combination of Patsy and gin until the early hours. The knock came again. Tension gripped her and her heart raced as she strove for calmness, 'Who is it?' She pulled the sheet around her.

'The housekeeper,' she entered the room.

'What do you want? It's six o'clock?' Andrea's indignant voice made the housekeeper's face go pale.

'There is a man outside who says it is most urgent he speaks to you.'

'Who is the man?' Andrea found it hard to talk as her throat had constricted and her whole body moved in pain.

'The Chief Constable, he has a card but isn't wearing a uniform.' The housekeeper crossed the room and passed the card to Andrea, who read it. Andrea sat up still clutching the sheet.

Patsy stirred, 'What's the matter?'

'I don't know yet.'

Patsy sat up and blinked her eyes until they opened fully, 'God, that's bright.'

'Describe the man, please.'

'Short, round and bald.'

'Strange time to call,' Patsy pulled the sheet back over her head, the housekeeper nodded agreement but didn't comment.

'Tell him I'll be with him in a minute.' Andrea picked up a dressing gown from the trunk that Pablo had delivered last night and flicked at her hair in the mirror as she went past, 'You look bloody awful.' She opened the door to the entrance hall, 'Come in, Chief Constable.'

'I can't stay long, but I needed to tell you personally.' Andrea could see he studied her face as she perched on an armchair. The Chief Constable remained standing 'Do you need to sit?' his expression serious.

Andrea hesitated too afraid to ask, 'What's happened?'

'It's Martin, I'm afraid.'

'Tell me, has he been injured?'

'Not that I know, but I must talk to you about him.' The Chief Constable moved from one foot to another. Watching him made Andrea more anxious.

'I have information for you about Martin.' She would have to reveal the attack to the Chief Constable.

'After we spoke yesterday morning Martin turned up to work as normal, however...' the Chief Constable took a deep breath, 'his behaviour became more erratic as the day progressed. The final straw came when I interviewed and then released the Kennedy brothers.' Her body tensed but she attempted to keep her face calm. He rubbed a hand across his forehead, 'Just after the release he attacked a young woman officer hitting her because she gave him the wrong file, then he stormed out of the building. We've been searching for him. That's why I urgently called Calum in to help.'

'I'm afraid he was here earlier last night and he would have attacked me again, except for my friend Patsy's intervention, he then ran off. He attacked me the previous evening.' She couldn't stop the shiver which sped through her body as scenes from the nightmare flashed through her mind.

The Chief Constable paused as though assessing this information, 'My wife became concerned during our visit to your house, but we had not contemplated such a cause, you are having to bear a great deal. It is better we find him as soon as possible, but what help can I organise for you? I will do whatever is necessary.'

'I am upset and shaken but apart from bruises I am uninjured. Please use your resources to find Martin before anything more serious happens.'

The Chief Constable prepared to leave, 'I'm sorry to have to bring such bad news but I must go. Please be assured I will do everything in my power to find him.'

'What about Calum?' Andrea asked with concern.

'After he coordinated the search for Martin, he told me he meant his resignation and he'd had enough as he couldn't do any more.'

'So, he will not help?'

'It was all I could do to persuade him to meet me in a month when he is fully fit.' The Chief Constable departed.

After showering, Andrea inspected herself in the mirror,

purple welts and dark bruises adorned her body and stood out in stark comparison to the pallor of her skin. She had been lucky to have avoided broken bones.

Patsy came into the bathroom, 'My God, did he do that?'

'Yes, the night before.'

'What are you going to do?'

'Charlotte has been shot and my husband has turned into a maniac, I will find out why.' Andrea found the loosest dress that didn't touch the bruises. Her mobile rang, she looked at it suspiciously but couldn't keep hiding, she didn't recognise the number.

'Hello,' she clutched the phone.

'It's Wayne,' came the deep voice.

'At this time in the morning?'

'I assumed your phone would be switched off and I wanted to leave you a message about your car.'

'What's happened?' her voice rose expecting bad news.

'Nothing as far as I know. I spoke to Ma last night and she arranged for it to remain in the garage until the morning, do you want a lift?'

Andrea had to think. 'Will they be open?'

'Yes, Ma's always there early.' Facing the outside world would present a challenge. She wanted to run away and hide but had to remain strong and resolute. In order to find Charlotte's murderer, she had to talk to people.

65

'Hello, look who we have here. It's the policeman's wife.' John Kennedy swaggered into the garage. Wayne pushed open the large door that led from the forecourt. Andrea followed. Her Jaguar had been parked in the middle of the floor.

'Where's Ma?' asked Wayne looking round in alarm at the sound of his voice. Mark then sauntered into the garage from the office. The two brothers stood side by side radiating patent resentment. The sneer across their faces sent an icy chill chasing up her spine.

'This is interesting,' Mark's eyes narrowed as he walked along the side of the garage and slammed the main door shut. The sound of rattling metal echoed around Andrea as she stared with trepidation at the closed door. 'The lady we've been wanting to meet.'

John moved across to join his brother blocking off the only exit. The huge pair once again stood shoulder to shoulder. 'She set us up, Mark,' hissed John.

Growling he jabbed his finger towards Andrea who shuddered at the aggression in his voice. 'Yes, she did John.' Andrea took a step back as they came towards them. Andrea swallowed and clutched the sleeve of

Wayne's jacket.

Wayne stood his ground, 'Come on guys, where's Ma?' Andrea could hear the attempted lightness as he spoke the words. 'She's gone to church,' Mark gave a small satisfied smile. 'So there's us and the lady who had us arrested.' He rubbed his hands together and took another step towards them. Andrea released her grip on Wayne and shuffled closer towards the car. Would she have a chance to yank the door open, get inside and lock it again before they reached her. No. They came closer with each deliberate step.

Wayne hissed, 'Don't threaten.'

Mark grabbed Wayne by the jacket lifting him off the ground, 'Now, you shut up and don't say a word now or ever.' He released him with a violent shove which sent him sprawling to the ground, he groaned as he hit the hard concrete floor.

Andrea filled her lungs ready to scream when a shrill voice filled the garage, 'John, Mark, what do you think you are doing?' Andrea breathed a sigh of relief at the sound of Ma's voice.

'Dealing with this copper's wife,' Mark stood in front of Andrea with hands clenched and menace written over his face.

'Out of my way,' came the clipped tone of Ma Kennedy as she barged between her two sons, she patted Andrea on the arm.

'Please come this way, my dear,' she guided Andrea past them with her hand on her shoulder. Wayne struggled back to his feet and scampered after them with a furtive glance at the two brothers. Over her shoulder Ma shouted, 'John, Mark, get outside and wash the cars, they should have been done by now.' They didn't move. 'Now!' her loud voice rang with authority. Without a word they yanked the large doors open with a resounding rattle.

Andrea and Wayne followed her into the office, 'Sorry about them, I didn't expect you so early. The police hassled them,' she paused and added with emphasis, 'your husband.'

Andrea gulped at the thought of Martin, 'I am sorry.' Her breath caught and she exhaled in a series of short breaths before she could continue, 'I believed you when we chatted together at the time of the arrest and the Chief Constable released them but I can imagine that the interviews were not a pleasant ordeal.'

A tall heavily built man that Andrea had not met before came into the office, wearing a blue overall splattered with black oil marks. Ma said, 'Donald, this lady's Jaguar came in last night. Can you check and find out what's wrong?'

'Red warning lights came on and it ran out of power,' Andrea added to be helpful.

Donald nodded while wiping his hand on a greasy rag, 'Come through, I'll have a look now.' As they followed him into the garage, he wandered towards the car, then stopped and knelt near one wheel and inspected a greasy patch which covered the ground. The patch had a pale yellowish tinge which he prodded with his finger then wiped it clean with his oily rag.

He crossed to the ramp controls, pressed a large green button and accompanied by the loud sound of grinding metal the car moved upwards. Switching on an inspection light the intense bright beam lit up the garage.

No words were spoken as he moved around under the car shining the light near to the wheels. 'Come here,' he beckoned them with a solemn expression on his face. They went under the raised car. Ma and Wayne appeared to move with confidence, but Andrea reluctantly joined them.

66

'The brake pipes have been cut. It's a straight cut so it is deliberate.'

A shock of weakness went through Andrea as she looked at him awaiting an explanation. Unease flowed through her like a chilled dark wave and a fine sheen of sweat formed on her forehead. The realisation hit her like a thump in the stomach. Someone had tried to kill her.

Andrea's legs went weak and an icy chill of fear swept through her making her tremble. Wayne and Ma looked at her with open mouthed astonishment on their faces. John and Mark stood by the open garage door and stared at her in silence. Andrea felt too weak to speak, she opened her mouth, but no sound emerged from her dry constricted throat.

'This is a job for the police, the pipes were cut deliberately.'

There was a stunned silence until Mark growled, 'No police.'

'Is this your car and were you driving it yesterday?' Donald looked at Andrea for confirmation to his questions. She nodded as though in a trance but couldn't bring herself to speak.

Receiving no reply or explanation from her, he twisted round, 'What's going on Ma, someone tried to kill this lady yesterday, you must call the police.'

'No police,' John's voice was a low growl, deep and rugged. Donald searched each face. He shrugged. 'What's going to happen?' he focused on Ma Kennedy.

She mirrored Donald's action and searched each face leaving Andrea until last. The two women's eyes met. Neither of them broke the stare. No one else in the garage moved or spoke. The silence hung like a dark impenetrable cloud. A tear rolled down Andrea's cheek. If the plan had worked Calum would also be dead. She wanted to curl up, close her eyes and wait for the horror to disappear. Her life had spiralled out of control. Up to now she hadn't seen why anyone would want her dead and had brushed away the warnings with a flippancy that now deserted her. But someone had tried, but who?

Neither woman flinched. Andrea searched the faces of each person. Apart from Donald any of them could have done it. Mark and John had a chip on their shoulder about the police and they blamed Andrea for their arrest. What would have happened this morning if they hadn't been interrupted by the return of Ma Kennedy? Their eyes glittered with hatred as they stood shoulder to shoulder fists clenched as though ready for action, she looked away from them. Wayne stood in the far corner of the garage looking pale and frightened. Was he a good actor? Had he cut the brake pipes while they went to get their hot dogs from the other side of the car park? Perhaps she had asked him one question too many and he had something to hide. What about Ma? Would she kill to protect her sons?

Andrea let out a deep breath and caught Ma's eye again. Without doubt she would be the person to decide the way forward. A strange sensation came over her. A sudden realisation swept through her that she needed someone to turn to. Calum sprang to mind, she didn't miss his grumpiness, but she missed his thinking and decisiveness. She couldn't put it into clear thoughts but Calum's presence would ease her anxieties. She had complete faith in his ability to deal with the problem.

Without breaking eye contact with Ma, her head reeled through the possibilities. Time seemed frozen. All eyes were on Ma as they waited for her to speak. The word murder kept repeating itself like an echo reverberating around her head bouncing out of control. This is the third incident. The first, Charlotte's murder and the second Martin's attack which would end in murder if he ever cornered her again. The evil in his eyes reinforced the idea. This is the third problem to solve. Attempted murder, she quaked as a tremor engulfed her. But they are linked.

With a rush her senses awoke, the time for action had come. In an instant she had a plan, 'Ma.' The single word sounded loud and echoed in the silence of the garage. All eyes focused on her. She pulled back her shoulders and drew herself up to her full height. 'I will not call the police,' she paused, 'but I must do something. The cut brake pipes cannot be ignored.'

Ma nodded, 'Thank you for thinking of my family.'

Donald said, 'But...'

Andrea held up her hand, 'I need Calum's advice, I know he's a policeman and you don't like him, but I need his support. Ma, we need to trust each other.'

'Yes, we do.' Andrea moved towards the garage doors. She stopped and scanned the car, 'Will you promise that no one will touch the car while I go for help? You must trust me.'

Donald stared at the car still up on the ramp, 'This is attempted murder.'

'Donald will stay here on guard in the garage on his own until you return,' Ma's voice firm but calm. Andrea studied Donald. A big man, easily as broad as John and Mark and probably heavier so he wouldn't be intimidated.

'I will not be long,' she pulled her jacket around her as Ma organising the other adults, 'Come, John, Mark and Wayne, we will wait in the office.'

Andrea walked towards the main door and Donald accompanied her. 'You mentioned Calum.'

'Yes.'

'Is that Calum Brodie? I know him well. He's a fine policeman.

'Yes.'

'But I now recognise you, Andrea Cain, why not go to your husband? Why Calum? I don't like what's happening.'

'Please trust me, Donald. Will you guard the car?'

'I'm reluctant but you only have an hour and then I shall ring the police myself.'

67

'Piss off.' Calum's low growl came from behind his unopened front door.

A neighbour came out of the next flat, in an angry whisper, 'There's a baby in here struggling to sleep, stop banging on that door.'

'Sorry.' Andrea bent and opened the letter box, 'Calum Brodie I want to speak to you and not through a front door. You are disturbing your neighbours.' No reply or movement came from inside. 'Calum, at least hear me out, if the answer from you is no, you will never see me again. I promise.'

'Wait a minute.'

'Open the door.'

She heard the door latch click. Nothing happened, so Andrea turned the handle and it opened. Calum sat in his underpants on a chair in the hall with his head in his hands.

'You look bad.' Andrea walked into the scruffy untidy lounge, Calum followed.

'Listen first, because I've come for your help, but after that the choice is yours.' Calum looked at her and sneered. 'Before you walk away, you must listen.'

'Why?'

'Someone cut the brake pipes on the Jaguar yesterday in an attempt to kill us.'

'Where's the car now?'

'It's at the Kennedys.'

'What the hell is it...' He stopped, crashed his fist on the coffee table, 'I'm not getting involved. Call the police. How do you know it's genuine, the Kennedys could have done it themselves?' Andrea continued with determination.

One way or another she needed to persuade him to help, 'I'm not arguing with you Calum, I want you to come.'

'No. They will have hidden any incriminating evidence by now.'

'I left the mechanic who works for them guarding it.'

'He's in the pay of the family, you stupid woman!'

'He knows you,' Calum's bleary eyes fixed her the best they could as he stood in front of her. She could see the full damage to his leg by the bullet.

'Who?' he shouted.

'Big Donald, he said you'd know him.'

'Yes.' The change of expression meant he recognised the name, 'Good man,' he muttered. Calum remained silent studying the carpet. Andrea hoped he would think through the implications. He lifted his head and glared at her, 'Call the bloody Chief Constable, he'll arrest the lot while he thinks through what action to take. That's it, I've listened to you, now get out!' Calum remained intent on rejecting her.

'There is something else?' Andrea snarled.

'No.'

'Well I'm damn well going to tell you!' she shouted. 'You were right?'

'What about?' Calum snorted.

'When you found me in my lounge, you would call it a domestic.'

'Nothing to do with me, find proper help, as I expect you realise that tea and sympathy are not my line.'

Andrea wouldn't be deterred by his bad mood and dismissive manner, 'I don't want your bloody sympathy, I want a damn police officer who knows what he's doing.'

He took a step closer, the anger showed on his face, 'I'm never put on domestics, you can guess why, now get out.'

'You will listen before you walk away from me,' she shouted at Calum.

He shouted back, 'I don't want to know.'

'Then I will bloody show you.'

Andrea threw off her jacket and grabbed the hem of the long dress and pulled it off over her head and threw it onto the couch.

'What are you doing?' he shouted at her as he went to turn away.

She grabbed his arm, 'Bloody look at me!' she wrenched him back around. 'Look at me, I can't wear a bra because of the bruises. Look at my thighs, he punched me in the groin,' she lost her breath so she gulped air and shouted, 'Look, look at the bruises!' Then she dissolved into tears. They stood in their knickers staring at each other's legs. Andrea didn't move.

'Oh, my God, Martin?'

'Yes.'

'Cover yourself up, I can't stand to look at it,' he shook his head and turned away.

68

'Anne, I need a big favour, can you meet me at Kennedy's car hire in ten minutes.' He listened then added, 'Don't ask, you won't want the answer, that's why it's a big favour.'

A woman talked to Donald as Andrea and Calum walked into the workshop. Calum nodded to her and she smiled back. Donald shook Calum enthusiastically by the hand, 'Great to see you again.' Andrea guessed the woman must be Anne. She wore civilian clothes, her long dark hair tied back showed a pretty face. The sound of voices brought Ma and her sons into the garage. Mark and John clenched their fists. Ma looked worried.

'It's only him, no one else,' Andrea attempted to sound reassuring, 'he's the one we need, trust me. Where's Wayne Smith?'

'He left after you for an urgent appointment in London.' Calum grunted.

Mark went to speak, but Ma said, 'Hush the pair of you,' they stood menacingly, but remained silent.

Anne and Donald together examined underneath the car and spoke in whispers. Calum leant against the open garage doors, 'She's the best car forensics person we have on the force. We were lucky she's not working today.'

Donald peered under the car with a spotlight and then stopped his examination, tapped Anne on the shoulder and pointed. A look of amazement crossed Anne's face.

'What is it?' Andrea moved towards the Jaguar. Donald put his fingers to his lips and shook his head. He and Anne communicated by hand signals and remained silent. Donald lowered the ramp and climbed inside the car. In a few minutes Andrea could see he'd found an item and he indicated to them to go outside. They followed, and he led them round the back of the garage away from the road and the buildings. He stopped at the far end of a yard surrounded by a large factory wall with the distant drone of machines.

'It should be safe here.'

'What is it?' said Calum.

'The car is bugged, it's a sophisticated device, a professional job and it's been well hidden.'

'How long has it been there?' Andrea enquired.

'It has road dirt on the outside, so I would say at least several days.'

Andrea looked around the group and even Mark and John looked surprised at the news. 'Are they listening now?' asked Andrea.

'What is its range?' said Calum.

'That's the clever part, it will store the conversation until back in range and then download it. If they are near, they could be listening, it's a good distance transmitter.'

The distant ringing of the telephone in the office caught the attention of Ma. She nodded to Mark and John who followed her back across the yard. Ma appeared so small and dainty beside the massive builds of her two sons.

Calum asked, 'Is it the same people who cut the brake pipes?'

Anne smiled, 'I'm forensics, you're the detective, you tell me.'

'What about the cut pipes?'

'It is nowhere near as sophisticated, if it's the same person they know about bugging but not cars, it's clumsy in comparison.'

'Why?' asked Andrea.

'Modern cars have a shut-down mechanism, often called "limp home". The normal power disappears but the car will be drivable at slow speeds. So, it would be difficult to kill someone by cutting the brake pipes, because as soon as the fluid leaked to any extent it would shut down, which is what happened yesterday?'

'But it's still attempted murder,' Donald said.

Anne responded, 'Yes it is, they didn't know it wouldn't work that way, she hesitated unless of course.' But she stopped.

'What were you going to say Anne?' Andrea needed every scrap of information if they were to solve the murder, Martin's assault and the attempted murder of her. She still hesitated.

'Let's hear your thoughts,' Calum encouraged, 'this is nothing like a normal investigation, you might as well share your opinions.'

She fixed them both with a penetrating gaze, 'It's so crude I wonder whether it's a warning.'

Calum responded to the suggestion. 'If the

Kennedys were responsible, they would have refused breakdown help? And why wouldn't they have removed the bugging device? They didn't plant the device.'

Andrea added, 'So whoever it is could have heard our conversations in the car over the past few days?'

'Yes,' smiled Anne, 'I hope you didn't swear too much Calum.'

Ma and the two boys reappeared into the yard. Donald reiterated, 'Attempted murder. That's the important issue. The bugging device is secondary. A minor irritation.'

Calum listened to his words and nodded in agreement. 'You're right. I will ring the Chief Constable.'

The two brothers stepped towards him in unison as though joined at the shoulder. Aggression emanated from every pore of their body, 'Ma, we've got to stop him, he's the police they'll stitch us up. They don't listen to us even when we tell the truth.' Their faces had become red and their hands were balled into fists. Would Ma be able to keep control of them if their anger boiled over? 'They shot our brothers, Ma.'

'Boys, boys, please listen to me. This situation cannot be solved with aggression.' She walked forwards and grabbed their hands, 'You are two wonderful boys who are loyal to your brothers, and I'm proud of you. But you must try to understand that the twins started shooting in a public place with innocent people near them. No matter how much it grieves me, I can't see the police had any alternative.'

Muffled sobs filled the air and Ma's shoulders heaved with emotion, 'John, Mark, please don't do anything.'

In a deadpan voice Calum said, 'You agreed the

car could be delivered here and had time to hide the evidence if you had sabotaged it, so I conclude you had no involvement.'

Andrea said in a quiet voice, 'Thank you, Calum.'

Andrea put her arm round the woman as she wept, hoping to give her reassurance. The brothers stood in bewildered silence.

Ma recovered herself in a few minutes, she swiped away the residue of her tears and let out a deep shuddering breath. With a quiver in her voice, 'There's nothing to do boys, we have to trust Andrea.' Anne and Donald meandered back to the Jaguar to disable the transmitter. Anne explained she would arrange it so that the listener thought that it had developed a fault.

While they waited Andrea and Calum sat on a low wall outside the garage, but they didn't speak. Andrea's thoughts shifted to Martin. What had happened to him? She didn't have the answer, but he would be injured from Patsy's attack, but the thought gave her little satisfaction. Calum sat with his head bowed staring at the ground. What would be passing through his mind? She didn't ask in case he decided to return home and leave her to sort out her own problems.

69

Having been assured Anne and Donald would produce a full report, Andrea and Calum climbed into the Mercedes they had been loaned, Andrea touched his arm, 'We need to go to London to eliminate or include Wayne and Fitzwilliam then we should attempt to find Edward.'

Calum settled himself in the passenger's seat, and with an audible sigh, 'And leave the Mannings? The Met could pick up Edward and bring him back.'

'He'd be defensive whereas we want him relaxed. If we find him in London, he will talk to me.' Andrea gripped the steering wheel and concentrated on driving through the streets of Sheffield.

Calum took time before he answered, 'Okay, it's a good idea.'

Andrea glanced across at him as she waited for the traffic lights to change, 'Please stop the police going to the Kennedy's garage. You realise what could happen. Even at the mention of the word police the two sons would become aggressive and belligerent again.'

'Yes, but the Chief Constable will have to give his agreement.'

‘Tell him the minimum possible.’ Andrea put her mobile in the hands free and Calum leaned across and dialled the Chief Constable’s private number.

‘Hello,’ his crackly voice filled the car.

Calum raised his voice above the sound of the car engine ‘Chief Constable, it’s Andrea and Calum.’

‘Thank you, Calum.’ He gave the Chief Constable a summary of the cut brake pipes.

‘Who has examined the car?’

‘Big Donald who works there part-time and I called in Anne from her holidays.’

‘Good people, I’ll be happy with their report.’ Calum continued and explained about finding the bugging device.

‘Desperately difficult, Andrea are you okay?’

‘Yes, Calum has been a great help.’

‘How do you want to proceed, Inspector? I would like your recommendations. This is far from normal.’

Calum glanced at Andrea and touched her on the arm before asking, ‘Any news on Martin?’

‘No, I’m afraid not. I must make it formal if we don’t find him in the next few hours.’

Calum drew in his breath, looked at Andrea, ‘The tampering with the car incident should be kept low key. Anne will look after the evidence. I’m wary of raising the whole issue in the Incident Room as it might be counterproductive and put Andrea at more risk.’

‘Yes, I agree. I’m asking West Yorkshire for a senior officer to take charge, but they are hard pushed themselves.’

Andrea had kept quiet up to that point but wanted to put forward her ideas, ‘We could go to London to obtain background information from those in the entertainment business and to find Edward, Charlotte's fiancé, for a chat.'

'Your view, Inspector?'

'A good idea as it will remove Andrea from Sheffield and we might pick up useful information.'

'Will you go with her?'

'Yes, I will.'

'Good, I will make sure you are not followed at the railway station, you know the routine.'

'Yes, sir.'

'Please be careful. Martin is not rational, so we cannot predict his behaviour. I'm sorry to say this Andrea, but he has had a breakdown. Also, we have a killer on the loose and we are no closer to finding him.'

'We'll take every precaution and I shall follow Calum's advice.' She heard Calum's soft huh and smiled to herself, but he had agreed to help her although she didn't deserve his support after the way she had treated him.

'Calum use my private number to keep me informed, but if there is any threat then use the full emergency code. I will instruct the Incident Room if you ring on that number it is a full alert.'

70

Bins and air conditioning units outlined the small door in the mews. A pile of plastic bags lay in a messy heap. Many had split and spilled their assorted contents across the cobbles.

'What's here?' asked Calum.

'Our primary source of information about Fitzwilliam and Wayne.' Andrea paid the taxi which had stopped in a mews behind Bond Street and entered, marched up to an internal scruffy door, with peeling paint, and went straight in. Her heeled shoes clicked on the wooden floor. Calum gave a grunt of disapproval.

An old man in a thick green jumper sat in a small glass fronted office where the paintwork had turned brown through age. 'Is this the right place?'

'Yes, fashion behind the scenes is shabby.'

'I've come to see Maggie, 'she announced. He shrugged and pointed a grubby finger towards the stairs.

'What's that supposed to mean?' said Calum.

'Go through, come on.'

They climbed steep narrow wooden stairs using the rickety handrail for support and then wrenched open a door. Calum's face registered surprise as they stepped into an elegant and spacious Georgian hall with its gold foil embossing. Everything gleamed. Calum touched her arm as he stopped in surprise. 'They embellish it with the flash décor to give it a hint of elegance but it's not one of the good fashion houses.' Andrea couldn't decide which door to open until she heard giggling.

'This way,' she marched in with a confident air. A tall young woman, about twenty years old, stood in her bra and knickers. 'Where's Maggie?' asked Andrea. 'Straight through,' the woman smiled and pointed. Calum hesitated.

'Come on, don't be shy,' chuckled Andrea at the embarrassed look on Calum's face, 'they won't take any notice.'

With Andrea in the lead they wended their way through a room crowded with both men and women trying on an assortment of flamboyant and colourful clothes. 'It's a fitting room,' explained Andrea to Calum over her shoulder. A woman with vivid red curly hair with fingernails and lipstick to match sat at a desk in a glass fronted office. 'Maggie?'

'Come in,' she grunted. A look of displeasure replaced the initial smile and her frown deepened as they stood in front of her desk.

It hadn't been the welcome Andrea expected, 'I don't want to talk to you,' said Maggie as she leaned back in her chair and folded her arms across her ample bust. Her eyes travelled across their faces and her expression hardened. Calum shuffled his feet and let out a resigned and weary sigh. Andrea put her hand on his arm.

'Why not?' she asked with a hint of surprise.

'You're Andrea Cain,' she jabbed a finger in her

direction, 'but you're married to a policeman.' She spat out the word policeman.

'So!'

'He's a policeman,' she pointed her a long scarlet nail at Calum, 'plain as a pikestaff.'

'He's my minder.' Maggie scowled at Calum who frowned back. A plan formed in Andrea's mind, she hoped Calum would play his part. In a belligerent tone of voice Andrea continued, 'I've had to have him since Charlotte was shot.' Maggie eyed them both with suspicion. 'The police have told me I might be next.' Andrea pouted and rolled her eyes, 'I need help.'

'Why turn to me when you've got the police.'

'Who can I trust?' Andrea sat on a nearby chair and Calum followed suit, 'I can't keep him in tow, can I?' He acted the role he had been given and gave her a sullen look and shrugged.

'I didn't like Charlotte Manning,' announced Maggie with an air of defiance.

'Why not?'

'She messed with one of the good guys. Taking liberties.'

'Who?' asked Andrea.

Maggie's eyes narrowed and she fixed her stare on Andrea. 'Because you believe you're a superstar, don't think I'm daft. Don't try to act the innocent with me, her and Luigi were having a fling.' The slightest shift on his chair told Andrea that Calum had become interested in the conversation.

'Luigi is a wonderful guy, you are right,' Andrea nodded in agreement, 'I get on well with him.'

'Yes, I know you do, he thinks the light shines...'

Andrea interrupted her, 'Will you help me?'

She jabbed her scarlet fingernail at Calum again, 'It smacks of the police and he's not bright and not subtle.' He didn't rise to the bait and waited for the end of the examination by Maggie's eyes. 'I wouldn't normally, but everyone I speak to says you're a good person and you've helped my friends, Sammy is relying on you this afternoon.'

Andrea swallowed in horror as she remembered her commitment. With everything that had happened recently it had slipped her mind, but she couldn't let him down. She plastered a smile across her face and looked hopefully at the red-haired woman across the desk who scowled back at her.

'What information do you want?'

'I want background information on two people.'

'My official job is a publicist, but I only deal in rumours and speculation, although I do a little journalism as I like to keep true to my roots.'

'I always read your two columns.'

A slight smile crossed her lips, 'I'll answer your questions and give you the information you want,' she paused, 'I'm now a police informer.' She huffed, 'Whatever next!'

'Wayne Smith and Fitzwilliam,' said Andrea.

'Thick as thieves, springs to mind.'

'Have they been linked together long? Or did the article on ganglands make them friends?'

'They are at the centre of ghost writing, backhanders, second-rate models and even worse singers. They give praise where none is due. And to answer your question, they have been working together for years.'

'Fitzwilliam first?' Maggie turned to her computer, clicked a few times and the printer issued three pages. Spreading them out on the desk, Andrea and Calum leaned forward to look at them, 'Very attentive for a bodyguard,' Maggie muttered.

'They are practically the same words,' said Calum.

'They appeared in three different newspapers about different singers.' She took the papers back, 'As I'm sure you noticed, three different parts of the country and under different names.' Pointing at a list on the screen, 'These are the names he writes under, it amazes me how such a fat slob can keep on top of them.'

'You don't like him?' said Andrea.

'As a person he is a complete shit…'

'But...' said Andrea.

'It was once expected that he would be a top flight journalist, he had plenty of talent when young, probably still could do it if he decided to, but most of the time he's too lazy to move his fat arse.'

'Why use so many names?'

'He syndicates work through news agencies until sub-editors recognise his name, then he goes direct.'

'What about references?'

'At best a busy sub-editor of a local paper will check the NUJ records but Fitz set them all up with forgery, so it passes through. Subs don't worry that much as they only pay the basic rate.'

'Is it that simple?'

'Yes, Fitz plays on the weaknesses, local papers struggle with fashion and music, they can get any trainee to do the local deaths and gold watches, but fashion and music are different. That's why Fitz does it.'

'Fitzwilliam must earn a good bit from these sidelines plus he has a full-time job at the tabloid...'

Maggie smiled, 'But he has a weakness.'

'Yes,' Andrea's eyes widened with interest.

'There are never any articles in February.'

'Why not?'

'He takes his holidays.'

'Where?'

'Monte Carlo or Las Vegas.'

'Gambling,' Andrea nodded thoughtfully.

'Yes, and it answers your question about where the money goes, he likes the lifestyle and rubbing shoulders with the rich and famous.'

'Thanks Maggie, that answers many issues. What would happen if he thought anyone would expose him, both with the ghost articles and the gambling?'

'That's difficult to say.' Maggie fiddled with the papers on her desk, 'He has a nasty temper and likes revenge, particularly against editors that have rejected him.'

'Is he a good shot?'

Maggie raised her eyebrows at the question, 'Not that I know, he's too fat to do anything well these days, but in his youth at Cambridge he had a talent in athletics.'

'It's hard to imagine,' Andrea chuckled.

'Cambridge has a popular shooting club doesn't it?' A narrow grin twitched at her lips.

'Thanks, and the second one is Wayne Smith.'

Maggie leaned back in her chair and took her time before speaking, 'Wayne is a good agent, takes extra when people aren't looking but nothing serious.'

'Does he have a weakness?'

'Yes, he likes them young and thin.'

'Revolting,' Andrea visibly shivered, 'how old?'

'Most of his are sixteen or seventeen. Grooming is a word you hear today, but he checks they are sixteen.'

Andrea shifted in her chair, 'Preying on young women is despicable.'

'Don't be too harsh on him, I agree it's a nasty habit, but he's not a complete bastard.'

'Are you sure?'

'For an agent he is good at spotting talent and although he takes liberties, he sets them up well in the industry by handing them on to other agents.'

'Was Charlotte one of his protégés?'

'I don't know.' Andrea frowned at her wondering whether she knew more. 'I'm being genuine, it would have been before he came on my radar.'

Calum moved in his chair. Maggie looked at him with disdain, 'At long last, Andrea, your policeman wants to ask a question.'

'These are serious accusations, why aren't you threatened?'

'I took a beating, but survived.'

'But you still do it?' queried Andrea.

'Rich people have bank accounts throughout the world, I have something similar, my information is stored in many countries. The links are with my solicitor and I have instructed him to give it to the police should I be killed.' She smiled, 'If I am murdered there will be exposure, court cases and ruined careers. So I have guardian angels who want me to live to a ripe old age because most don't know what secrets I hold about them.'

Andrea wondered what information Maggie had

about her but it wasn't the time to dwell. 'Thanks, Maggie, it's useful information.' Calum nodded.

'Now, I've kept my side of the bargain, now you keep yours and give Sammy the best you possibly can, he's relying on you.' The tension of thinking about Sammy gripped her stomach, it would be difficult to miss, but she didn't want to do it.

She smiled at Calum as he would try to stop her.

71

'I forgot about Sammy's launch show.'

'Please tell me you aren't even considering going on a catwalk.'

'It's a small low-key show.'

'When is it?'

Andrea checked the diary on her phone, 'In about two hours.'

'You can't do it.'

They stood on the cobbles next to the pile of rubbish, 'Please don't say that, Calum, it's so important for Sammy as it's his comeback. He's had a hard time, with many disasters in his life and everyone deserted him, it nearly killed him, but this is his first step back.'

'Why the loyalty to him?'

'He was a top designer when I started and gave me my first big chance, so I must repay him.' Andrea tried to divert his attention away from Sammy by saying, 'Useful information from Maggie?'

'Yes.' They walked along the mews, but he wouldn't let the show drop, 'I suppose the whole world knows you will perform at this show.'

'No, I'm the surprise guest and it's by invitation

only, I'm not listed on the programme. I said I would listen to you Calum, but please don't say no on this one.'

'I'll look at the set-up first, is that fair, but I'm not happy.'

'Yes. Let's go, it's nearby.'

'How can you model with the bruises?'

'It'll be okay, it's a winter collection so I'll let the others do the party clothes.' They had a short walk to a side road off Carnaby Street and Andrea led them in the rear door. Calum lagged behind and spoke on his phone.

Sammy rushed across the room shouting, 'Andrea! Andrea.' He didn't draw breath or let Andrea speak, 'My god, my god, I prayed you would come, but my mind kept telling me that the world's top model wouldn't come to my poor little show.'

'It is by invitation only, isn't it?' Calum would be listening.

'Yes, but you came, you are my star, it will be such a surprise.' The tall lanky man bounced with excitement and a broad smile covered his face. The buzz went up around the room.

'Andrea, are you in this show?' said one of the nearby models. Andrea nodded. 'Wow, on the same catwalk as Andrea Cain, that's so brill.'

'I've an important friend who needs a ticket, the end of the front row would be good.'

'No problem, I'll arrange it,' said Sammy.

'Can I have a copy of the invitation list?'

'I'll fetch it.'

He shot away and returned flapping a piece of paper which Andrea scanned and handed it to Calum. 'Fitzwilliam and Wayne are on it.'

‘Is that normal?’

‘Yes.’

Calum’s phone rang again and he left to take the call.

Andrea checked her running order.

After about ten minutes she heard, ‘Have you seen Andrea?’

She pushed her head out between the clothes rail. ‘In here. Come in, I’m changing in this corner so the others cannot see the bruises.’

‘Before Martin left yesterday, he checked out two handguns and ammunition?’

‘How could that happen?’

‘He’d drawn them earlier in the day and no one thought twice about him being armed.’

He paused. ‘And…’

‘Yes, Calum?’

‘It’s difficult to tell you.’

‘Go on. I’m ready for bad news.’

‘There has been a warrant issued for the arrest of Martin under the Mental Health Act.’

‘Oh, that makes sense as he’s in desperate need of professional help.’ Calum looked more relaxed now he’d given her the news. She dropped her dress to the floor and put on a long evening gown with a shawl covering her bare skin.

‘There are two detective constables in the audience and one will keep an eye on Wayne and Fitzwilliam.’

‘Thanks, I’m sure it will go well.’

‘Ladies and Gentlemen,’ said the announcer as the music died away, ‘we have a unique surprise for you today, Sammy's Collection, and it is led by.... and wait for this, ladies and gentlemen, it is led by the world's top supermodel, Andrea Cain.'

Andrea stepped from behind the curtain to the centre of the stage as rapturous applause greeted the pose she held. The walk up and down the catwalk had become automatic as she had completed it so many times. She couldn't see the audience because of the bright lights but could hear the success for Sammy.

Making a few quick changes she dived into the regular swing of the show which required her entire concentration to show off the clothes. As she walked back along the catwalk, she looked towards Calum who had a real smile. A crack sounded as a spotlight blew near her head. She jumped but took no notice as it had happened to her many times on the catwalk.

But the piercing scream above the music caused her to turn. Calum shouted, 'Get down!' Taking two strides, Andrea felt the full force of the rugby tackle. She landed on the wooden floor with a yelp as Calum sprawled on top of her. He pressed her head to the catwalk as the lights went out. People screamed and shouted. Chairs scraped as the audience headed for the exit and safety.

'Were you hit?'

'A spotlight blew,' her tone dismissive.

72

'A bullet hit the light,' said Calum close to her ear, 'stay here.'

Within a few seconds, a megaphone voice above the noise and screams of the audience, 'Armed police! All lie on the floor and do not move your arms.' The lights came back and Andrea could see several police officers. Calum didn't let her move as more police piled in through the doors.

'Over here,' shouted Calum.

'Yes, sir, it's clear for you and Mrs Cain to come through.' Calum helped Andrea to her feet and shepherded her through to an office at the back of the stage. Andrea could hear sirens and see the reflections of the blue flashing lights in the windows.

As she walked into the office, the realisation hit her that someone had attempted to kill her and it could be Martin, 'It's too much,' she said in a hushed voice as the room began to spin and she crumpled to the floor. When she opened her eyes the green uniform of a paramedic greeted her, Calum had left the office but she hoped he wouldn't be away for long.

'You're okay, you fainted,' the paramedic's voice was

soft and reassuring. He helped her to a chair and gave her a glass of water.

'That's better, what a shock, it happened so quickly.' Calum's rugby tackle had been impressive, he'd moved with speed. He'd been sitting in the audience one minute and had flattened her the next. A few more bruises to add to the others were the least of her problems. Someone wanted her dead. An icy chill swept over her.

The door opened making Andrea jump and she clung on to the blanket that the paramedic had wrapped around her. For a split second, terror gripped her, but she relaxed as a small plump woman in a police officer's uniform stood in the doorway. The police constables left and the paramedic, patted her on the hand, picked up his bag and closed the door on his way out.

Andrea looked at the uniform, and recognised the crown on the epaulette, her eyes widened with surprise, why had such a senior officer come? With a great effort Andrea concentrated on making her voice sound normal, 'Good afternoon, Commander, I'm sorry to have caused you so much trouble.'

Andrea guessed from her body language that this wouldn't be an officer who would beat about the bush, her intelligent eyes scanned the room including Andrea in one quick sweep. Her manner brisk, Andrea guessed a woman used to making decisions. 'Can you answer questions before leaving for hospital?'

The woman settled herself on a nearby chair with her eyes fixed on Andrea's face. 'I do not need medical attention.' Andrea gave her a slight smile to reinforce her words, 'It's been a shock, but I'm not hurt, so yes, please ask questions.'

'I've spoken to the Chief Constable and he has given me the background details,' her voice authoritative yet reassuring.

'Has he told you about Martin, my husband?' Andrea found it challenging to say his name, but she wouldn't hide from the difficult task.

'Yes, first your friend was shot and then your husband has had a breakdown and now someone has attempted to shoot you.'

'I cannot understand what is happening,' Andrea blurted out. 'I know nothing...'

The Commander held up her hand to stop Andrea's words, 'Let's not speculate, it's hospital for you.'

'I'm not hurt and do not need a hospital.'

'But shock ...'

'The shock came when my husband beat me up, but I will not give in. I will keep doing whatever I can, where's Calum.'

'He's helping with the statements.'

'Did you catch anyone?'

'No, in the chaos the gunman escaped. If this is related to the death of Charlotte,' the Commander paused and pursed her lips, 'then you both knew something in common. Somebody doesn't want you to tell anyone and they are attempting to silence you.' Andrea pulled the blanket around her shoulders trying to find warmth and comfort. The Commander's words had a chilling effect on her mind and body.

'I've tried hard, but I cannot think of anything,' she stuttered. As she spoke, her mind raced back over her encounters with Charlotte. One possibility jumped into her mind, the secret she shared was Charlotte's affair with Luigi. Had Luigi told the truth?

73

The Chief Constable entered, nodded to the Commander and stood inside the closed door, his arrival came as a surprise to Andrea, his face stern and anxious. 'I'm so glad you are uninjured Andrea, but I blame it on myself.'

'Certainly not, it was my decision and my decision alone, Calum advised against it.'

'I need to explain the current situation to the Commander.'

She looked directly at Andrea, but the Chief Constable said, 'There's nothing she can't hear.' The worry covered his face as he began, 'My force has mishandled two major crimes, the armed robbery and the murder of Charlotte Manning.' He took a deep breath. 'Added to them has been the mental breakdown of my most senior officer and this poor woman's husband.' Andrea could see the strain in his drawn face. 'I shall resign in due course. I flew to London to inform the Home Secretary but will stay in post to assist Scotland Yard.'

'I am sorry to hear about your resignation, your leadership of the Sheffield and Peak constabulary is without equal.'

A brief nod of acknowledgement came from the

Chief Constable, 'As the senior officer on the case I have been asked to formally hand the entire investigation to you Commander.'

'Can we review progress so far?'

'Unfortunately, as a force we have made none, our main information has come from Andrea.'

'And Inspector Brodie,' Andrea added as she wanted to ensure that Calum received his share of praise. Without his assistance she would have achieved nothing. The Commander used her mobile to ask Calum to join them. The Chief Constable explained that Calum had been on sick leave since the robbery, he arrived, looked at the Chief Constable and then hard at the Commander and took a seat. It took twenty minutes to bring the Commander up to date with the relevant information.

Andrea let Calum do the talking as he was better at summarising in a police manner, so she sat back in her chair and attempted to concentrate on the conversation. The word murder echoed in her head.

The Chief Constable said, 'There are two additional pieces of information from this morning.' He glanced at Andrea, 'Unfortunately they are about your friends. The airport police arrested Luigi as he tried to board a flight to Italy.' Andrea sighed, he hadn't listened to her advice. 'He's admitted an affair with Charlotte.'

'Will he be charged with perverting the course of justice?' The Chief Constable nodded. 'It's such a pity, I did my best to persuade him to tell you the truth.'

'Unfortunately, information from the Italian Police suggests he has campaigned to become Mayor of his town based on family values, so he had a good reason for the affair not to become public knowledge.'

‘Two pieces of information?’

‘The second concerns, Pablo.’

‘Yes.’ Andrea gave an incredulous stare with wide eyes. ‘We know of no motive why he would want to kill Charlotte, but the Italian police tell us he comes from a notorious family and has a cousin in jail for a contract killing.’ Sadness gripped her as two friends had been implicated. ‘Both men have been ordered to remain in Sheffield and report daily.’

The Commander continued in her brisk matter-of-fact manner, ‘This will be difficult. With the shooting today it will become world-wide news. I have briefed Scotland Yard’s press office and they asked if I expected an early arrest, but I had to say no. It is always a difficult case when conducted on the front pages of the world’s press.’

Andrea became aware of the need to marshall her thoughts and keep her emotions in check. Time to be positive. ‘I’m shaken, but I want to help as I know from Martin how difficult it is when an investigation is split over two forces and the links between three crimes are unclear.’

‘Your wish to help is appreciated but….’ Andrea wouldn’t be dismissed; she drew her shoulders back and fixed her gaze on the senior officer.

74

'Commander, it's not an idle wish to help as I believe I can make a difference, I don't doubt that sustained police work from you will bring results, but it will not happen quickly.' She glanced across at Calum, his presence spurred her on and with more assurance in her voice, 'Let me help.'

'We would prefer you to be in a safe environment and give us insights into the people involved.' Andrea detected a brief hesitation as the Commander had been speaking.

'Andrea is a brave and astute woman who has been a considerable help so far, but I will leave the decision to you, Commander, it's your case.' The Chief Constable's words gave Andrea a flicker of hope.

'Inspector, your view please,' said the Commander.

'Yes, ma'am,' Calum smiled. 'Andrea understands the people involved and gains their confidence. She has knocked several days off leads on Fitzwilliam and Wayne Smith because she knows the right people to approach for information. We will get there, I've no doubt about that, but it will be faster with Andrea helping.' A sense of satisfaction passed through her as she listened to Calum's positive words about her involvement and help.

'I'm not sure,' said the Commander but Andrea could again detect a slight hesitation in her voice, 'I admit the music and fashion industry are difficult for the police to penetrate as they don't volunteer information.'

Calum nodded, 'But they will talk to Andrea.' She could see the Commander had wavered, so to reinforce her involvement, she added, 'I promise no more shows and I'll concentrate on researching background information. Calum will be with me so I would suggest visits to check out information that we have collected so far.'

'I must admit that make sense,' said the Chief Constable.

'Very well,' conceded the Commander with a brief smile, 'you must remain with the Inspector at all times and I shall give you escorts wherever you go.' Andrea nodded and looked at Calum who had his usual deadpan face. At least he didn't object, though she did wonder whether he would be pleased or not as she had aggravated him too many times.

The Commander brought in her staff and issued orders. The cramped office became overcrowded and Andrea was no longer the centre of attention. She turned on her mobile phone and glanced down the lengthy list of missed calls. Luigi, Alexander, Margaret Manning, Fitzwilliam, Wayne, Pablo. She stopped, her breath stalled and her throat went dry as one of these could be the murderer. We need to catch the person, but let's hope it's not a friend. With a growing sense of unease, she continued to flick through and listen to her messages. There were newspapers and television channels trying to contact her. No matter how many times she changed her number they would still obtain it.

The next message made her go cold, she recognised the voice from the first words, 'Please forgive me.'

'Are you okay Andrea, you've gone white?' Calum's voice showed concern.

'Yes. There is a short message from Martin, it came as a shock. But I'm okay.' Before the Commander could speak, 'Please take my phone, you will wish to trace the details.'

75

'Will this be a wild goose chase?' asked Andrea as her and Calum sat in the rear seat of a police car negotiating its way through the London traffic.

'It may be, but we are waiting for the arrangements of the more significant meetings we requested and King's Cross isn't far.'

'Do you want us to drop you at the house?' asked the police car driver.

'No, please keep out of sight.'

'Yes, sir.'

'I assume we're not going to mention that we are from the police,' said Andrea. Calum nodded.

'The third block of flats around the corner is the one you require.' They left the car turned the corner and strode down the road in silence. Calum scowled as his eyes roved over the rundown shops and buildings. After climbing the dingy concrete stairs on to the balcony they passed several front doors and knocked on the final one. They heard the chain being fitted into place, it opened slightly. A small boy's face appeared then a woman's face half hidden, 'You the Old Bill?'

'No,' said Andrea.

'He looks like one,' mumbled the woman.

'Look how tall I am, I'm hardly going to date a midget.'

'What do you want?'

'Are you Stacey Arthurston?'

'Are you from Benefits?'

'No, we're not from anywhere like that, I'm trying to find an old friend.' The boy's face disappeared, bored with the conversation.

'How did you find me?'

'Telephone directory.'

'We are ex-directory.'

'Not in the one I used, you can't rely on these phone companies,' added Andrea with a smile, 'can we come in?'

Stacey eyed them up and down, then released the security chain. They sidled past the pram into a cramped lounge which only had a television and a couple of chairs. The boy glanced up at them as he charged around after a grubby tennis ball, but his mother ignored him and plonked herself down on one of the chairs, Andrea took the other leaving Calum to stand. He moved across the room and leant against the window sill.

'What do you want?' her tone held a note of suspicion.

Andrea kept her voice light and friendly, 'Edward Stonehouse came to London, and I must find him, but his phone isn't on.'

'Never heard of him, why ask me?'

'He intended looking up some friends from his youth.' Andrea tried to settle herself in the uncomfortable chair placing her large handbag on the floor. 'I happen to remember your name from conversations with him about London, so I thought I'd give you a quick try as I've come into King's Cross.' It didn't sound plausible, so Andrea gave her a reassuring smile and expected they would be found out. Stacey didn't reply.

Andrea could only think of one more ploy, she stood up from the uncomfortable chair and moved across the room to Calum. 'Christ, you're tall,' Stacey blurted out, 'Hang on, aren't you that model.'

'Yes, but I'm not working, look at my eye.'

'Oh yeah.'

'Drunk Ex came around and beat me up.' As the words left Andrea's mouth, she realised her lie had a ring of truth.

'All men are bastards,' Stacey eyed Calum suspiciously.

'You're pretty,' Andrea hoped the comment would sweeten the woman, so she would give them information about Edward.

'Thanks,' she flushed slightly, 'but I'm not tall enough to be a model.'

'So, you've never heard of Edward Stonehouse.'

'No.'

Andrea allowed a pause to develop, 'He mentioned you as his girlfriend.'

'How long ago?' she stared at Andrea, 'must be great being a model, wearing those fabulous clothes and visiting posh places.' She gave a loud envious sigh, 'Why not do a public appeal on the tele or the radio?'

'Believe me you'd get a right bunch of weirdos replying.' Andrea chuckled trying to keep the mood light and the conversation going.

'Yeah, stupid me. Of course, you would.' The boy produced a toy car from his pocket and proceeded to crawl around the floor crashing it into anything he could find with accompanying loud noises. Stacey started to eye them up again and shifted around in her chair. She's not convinced. Before she could come up with another question, a baby started crying.

'You woke him up,' she snapped accusingly at her visitors.

'Sorry,' said Andrea as she glanced down at the boy who'd been making the noise.

A second baby started as well. Three young children in such a cramped flat, how does she manage?

'It's both, I'll have to get them.' She stepped into the hall, but within listening distance so Andrea couldn't speak with Calum, then returned with a baby in each arm.

'Here you are, she'll go to sleep in your arms.' Andrea took the tiny bundle. The crying soon stopped to be replaced by a few gurgles, 'They are pretty babies, are they girls?'

'Jade and Keira,' said Stacey with a smile. Andrea gently rocked the baby in her arms and used her head to indicate to Calum to play with the little boy as it might help Stacey believe them. Calum frowned but followed her prompt and tapped the tennis ball with his foot towards the boy whose face lit up when he realised he had someone to play with him.

It wouldn't be Calum's idea of how an interview should be conducted.

76

'I had a few boyfriends in my time but never an Edward.' Stacey smiled down at the baby in her arms and had relaxed with the extra help with the children. This encouraged Andrea to persevere.

'He dated you.'

'No, not me.' Her forehead creased with concentration. 'Never with an Edward, I would remember.'

'How old are you, Stacey?'

'I'm thirty.'

'You are a year younger than Edward. About ten years ago.' Once again, she shook her head. Andrea paused and rocked the baby. Calum continued to play with the boy. She racked her brains to think of a different approach to prompt Stacey into remembering. Perhaps instead of repeating his name she could try telling Stacey some background. In a casual tone, 'He did admit he lost you because of his drunkenness and committing petty crimes.' Stacey's eyes sharpened, so she continued, 'He told me you were the prettiest girl he'd ever met.' Andrea paused allowing Stacey time to absorb the information, 'It maybe twelve or thirteen years ago.'

A narrow smile appeared on Stacey's face and her eyes glazed as memories came back, 'Your description reminds me of one boyfriend. I lived with him after I left home, he got into drink and drugs, but he wasn't called Edward he was Tony Montague.' Andrea heard Calum shuffle, his interest aroused by her words. The same man but a different name?

Andrea tried to keep the excitement from her voice, 'What happened?'

'I liked him at first, smart and well-dressed but he changed and became a pain when he began to drink.'

'What made him start drinking?'

'A crisis with his parents, I never understood the details, but his father had just left the army.' Her eyes had a dreamy faraway look and a smile tweaked the corners of her mouth. The memories invoked by this man gave her pleasure.

'Did you just drift apart or was it more acrimonious?' asked Andrea.

'One day we went to the pub together. He never liked me talking to other men. When we arrived home, he accused me of making eyes at a man, we argued, he lost his temper and hit me.'

The words jolted Andrea back to Martin, but she shoved the memory aside and focused on Stacey. 'Oh dear, were you badly hurt?'

'I had surprise on my side, so I whacked him in the eye and kicked him in the crotch. I aimed well clouting and kicking as hard as I could.' She gave a smug smile at the memory, 'The wimp ran away and I never saw him again.'

'Do you have a picture of him?'

'Might have, hang on,'

She nipped out and returned with a shoebox. Placing the sleeping baby in the chair, she tipped the contents of the box onto the floor. Kneeling down, she pushed the photos around, 'Here he is,' she waved it with a flourish of triumph and gave Andrea the photo.

Andrea studied the photograph then shook her head, 'No, that's not Edward.' Calum looked over her shoulder and shook his head.

'What a shame, we're sorry to have bothered you,' Andrea smiled at Stacey and set down the sleeping baby.

'It's okay, it's lonely with the kids while he's at work and it's been nice to meet an actual model. Before you go...'

'Yes,' said Andrea with a smile.

'There is a picture of you in today's paper, will you autograph it?'

'Sure,' said Andrea and she scribbled, 'Stacey, with best wishes and many thanks, Andrea Cain.'

'You must wear smart clothes all the time.'

'Yes, I do.'

'I love that bag, it's an original Luigi, isn't it?'

'Yes, you know your fashion as there's no name on the outside.' Tracey looked pleased with herself.

Andrea smiled, opened it, and removed the few contents putting them in her pocket. 'Here you are Stacey, a present for being so helpful.'

'Wow!' she clutched the bag to her chest and her eyes danced with excitement. Calum stood by the door ready to leave.

Once they were far enough away from Stacey's

door, Andrea voiced her thoughts, 'Definitely Edward.'

'Yes, I agree. A good interview, she would have clammed with the police. You did well to remember Stacey's name.'

'Thanks.' Andrea's spirits soared, the praise from Calum meant a great deal to her.

'Wasn't that bag worth hundreds of pounds?'

'Yes.'

'And you gave it away.'

She gave a dismissive wave of her hand, 'Luigi will give me another.'

'I don't understand your world.' Andrea smiled. They reached the bottom of the concrete stairs when four young men in tracksuits with their hoods up sauntered out of the alleyway opposite, their sneering voices were loud and arrogant.

'Looks like something interesting here.'

'Very rich I'd say,' said one of the others.

Calum in an equally loud and arrogant voice said, 'Don't even think about it, lads.' His hand went to the radio in his pocket. 'A mugging in broad daylight.' The four boys stopped in front of them. The smile on their faces showed that they were not deterred by his bravado. Andrea and Calum stopped.

Calum's radio crackled into life, 'Inspector Brodie, come in please.'

'He's a copper,' one shouted but the others were already running as the police car came around the corner.

Andrea breathed a sigh of relief as she slid into the rear seat of the car. The past days had been so different from her normal life.

Would she be able to cope long enough to see the

culprit caught and Martin safely placed into medical care?

77

The police car sped away from King's Cross and despite the heavy London traffic Andrea and Calum entered a nursing agency on Gower Street only a few minutes later. A trim woman with short grey hair waited for them in reception. She had been observing them since they had stepped from the police car, 'Please come through.' Waiting until they were seated in a tidy office, 'I'm Agnes Pritchard. The police officer I spoke to on the phone said you wanted to ask me questions.'

'I'm Inspector Brodie,' he flashed his warrant card in her direction.

'I'm Andrea Cain.' She gave no sign of recognition to her name.

'Now what can I do for you?'

'It's about Margaret Manning who has been a nurse on your agency's book for many years.'

'Oh dear, I didn't realise you wanted to talk about one of the staff as I could have saved you the trouble as I will not discuss individuals as their information is confidential, so you have had a wasted journey,' she pressed her lips together and shook her head for further emphasis.

'We don't want confidential information,' Andrea used her most charming voice.

The woman wouldn't be swayed and her firm expression didn't alter, 'The answer is still no,' she frowned, 'please allow me to see your warrant cards again.'

Calum handed his to her, she studied it and gave it back, she looked at Andrea expecting her warrant card, 'I am not a police officer.' Agnes scowled at this last piece of information. She picked up a pen from her desk and twiddled it in her fingers, confusion swirled across her face as her eyes narrowed and she tilted her head to one side.

'May I speak with the managing director?' Calum asked in a quiet and steady voice.

She eyed him with disapproval, 'I am the owner and managing director.'

Andrea had to pacify her as they needed information about Margaret's background and Agnes had seemed the ideal person. 'I am not with the police and can understand your position, but we need help.'

'I will not give information about the people on my books.' Calum would soon point out that the police would raise a warrant and take whatever they wanted. The woman watched Andrea with antagonism. She needed a different approach. In a chatty voice, 'A few days ago a singer was murdered.'

'Yes, the report was on the television news, I didn't follow her music, but she appeared a lively and pretty woman. It's a pity that there are so many guns and drugs in the entertainment industry,' she tutted with disapproval.

Taking a deep breath Andrea announced, 'The singer who died was Charlotte Manning, Margaret's sister.'

'Oh dear, I'm very sorry,' her tone of voice was flat, it sounded a mechanical reply, but her disapproving stare remained.

Andrea pressed on, 'We are working in the background to help prevent another murder. Following Charlotte's death, the family asked me to assist them and the police in any way possible. I am most willing to do that for the sake of Charlotte as she had become a close friend. Her murder came as a great shock.' This brought a smile of acknowledgement from Agnes. Andrea continued, 'Does your computer link to the Internet?'

'Yes, why?' but Andrea detected a hint of irritation in her voice.

'Could you bring up the most recent news.' It only took a few seconds before a picture of Andrea appeared with the headlines, 'Shooting at Fashion Show.'

The woman stared with a frown, then glanced at Andrea before returning her attention to the screen. 'That's you,' she pointed in astonishment.

'Yes, a frightening experience.' Anxiety ran through Andrea's body, she gripped her chair to stop the shudder.

'You should be resting under medical supervision as you could be traumatised and you shouldn't be here.'

Andrea brushed the concerns aside, 'I want to help and the police are at full stretch.' An uneasy silence followed, with the only sound, a continuous rumbling of the London traffic.

Calum cleared his throat, 'I'm on sick leave, but agreed to help Andrea. I've been in hospital because I was shot during an armed robbery.'

'Oh dear,' Agnes stared at him, 'you are a brave man.'

Calum pulled a face at the compliment, 'My recuperation has been in a ward with Margaret as the ward sister. She is an accomplished nurse.'

'Yes,' Agnes responded in a clipped voice and shifted uncomfortably on her chair but her wide eyes suggested unease with the direction of the conversation, 'Margaret is an excellent nurse, one of the best.'

'We wish to find information about a possible vendetta against the Manning family and we hope that Margaret will not be the next target. Agnes clenched her thin bony hands together on the desk and took a long look at them. They waited in silence as turmoil came in Agnes's expression. With a grimace, 'Nothing confidential though, it's reasonable to assume under the circumstances that Margaret would expect me to help you. I couldn't have it on my conscience if something happened to her and I might have prevented it by talking to you.' Agnes moved to the filing cabinet where she extracted a buff coloured folder and placed it on her desk. Opening it she examined a few of the pages.

With a long deep breath, she lifted her eyes and stated, 'Margaret worked for me for many years, a model nurse for the whole period, dedicated to the job and skilled in many aspects of her vocation.'

'Were there any complaints or problems?' queried Andrea trying to prompt Agnes into explaining about Margaret. Agnes frowned. 'Did someone take a dislike to her, perhaps for the wrong reason.'

'I see what you mean,' said Agnes, 'I received no

complaints, the hospitals where she worked, always wanted her to return.'

'Did she move between hospitals?'

'Yes, after a spell at one hospital she would move on. The hospital always wanted to keep her, but she insisted on a change. It's the exact opposite of most agency nurses who prefer to stay in one place as they become used to the routines expected of them.' Once again Agnes paused to give the impression that she wouldn't elaborate further. So far nothing Agnes had told them had thrown any light on Margaret Manning.

'What about her family?' suggested Andrea.

'She is devoted to her brother, but never mentioned a sister. When she went to see her brother for a long period, she would change hospitals. 'Do you know her brother?' asked Agnes, 'as I've never met him and know little about him.'

'Yes, Alexander, he is a priest in Sheffield, but took holy orders in Ireland.'

Agnes nodded, 'That explains why Margaret went to Ireland on several occasions.'

'Margaret is settled in Sheffield now and often sees her brother.'

'That's good because she is close to him.' Agnes gave a narrow smile and reorganised the papers on her desk. Calum had been quiet allowing Andrea to lead the conversation, but asked, 'Did she have any long periods of time off, excluding the family visits?'

'No, she often worked seven days a week.' She checked the papers on her desk before continuing. 'The only prolonged period occurred when her marriage broke down, although she never did tell me the details.' Once again, Agnes checked the file on her desk, 'It's unusual, but she never changed her next of kin from her brother, so I have no details of her husband.' She stopped and scanned their faces with a worried expression, 'I hope I'm not saying more than Margaret would wish.'

Andrea gave her a reassuring smile, 'Margaret told us yesterday of her full agreement to whatever we were trying to do.' On impulse she added, 'I can't think why it would be any use but could we have a copy of her work record from you?'

She smiled bleakly but shook her head, 'I can't agree.'

'We don't know whether it is important, but we do need to examine it.' Andrea contemplated the woman who had closed the file on her desk with a gesture of finality.

Calum said, 'Many people find it distressing for the police to raise a warrant and examine files.' The shock of this statement registered on Agnes's face.

'Very well,' she muttered, 'I'm sure in the circumstances it will be okay,' she reopened the file, selected a single sheet of paper and rose from her chair, 'I will copy it for you.' She handed over the photocopy and her face showed relief as Andrea and Calum departed.

A police Range Rover, parked outside, waited for them and they climbed into the back and flopped onto the seat, 'I'm tired,' said Andrea.

'That's the last in London so we're going back to Sheffield,' Calum announced as the police car pulled out into the busy traffic.

'Are you dropping us at the station?'

'No ma'am, we have instructions to drive you to

Sheffield, as you have two meetings arranged for this evening and a safe house later.'

Andrea's heart sank. More meetings sounded daunting, she sighed, 'I shall need clothes.'

'It's arranged, ma'am, they are being picked up from the hotel and taken to the safe house.' As she sat back in the seat, coldness ran through her and she rubbed her forehead with her fingers. As she closed her eyes, visions of Charlotte, Martin and the shooting this afternoon merged into one and she abruptly opened them to blot out the images.

Calum hadn't spoken since they had been in the office with Agnes. She looked at him, slumped on the seat with his head back and his eyes closed. She squeezed his arm. With alarm in her voice, 'You're shaking.'

'I'm weak,' he mumbled not opening his eyes.

'Do you need the hospital?'

'No, let's go back to Sheffield, I'm too exhausted to be on a major case,' his voice was flat and full of weariness and his eyes remained closed. 'And how you are surviving is beyond me.' The thudding and insistent ache inside her head forced her to close her eyes. 'We need the rest,' said Calum.

'No,' said Andrea, 'we're not giving up.'

Calum grimaced, 'We'll see it to the end for Martin.'

78

'Your Grace, Inspector Brodie and Mrs Cain.' A priest showed them to seats in front of the broad imposing, ornate desk, its polished surface free of clutter, apart from a single unopened folder and a green desk lamp. The Bishop wearing a purple clerical shirt sat behind the desk in a high-backed leather chair with his hands resting on the arms. A large gold ring adorned with a central amethyst glistened from the light cast by the lamp. The Bishop nodded in greeting and his intelligent grey eyes rested on each of them before he spoke.

'The Chief Constable has contacted me and explained the background, so how may I help?'

Andrea had agreed with Calum she would ask the first few questions. Pushing her weariness aside she hoped a wide smile would make her task easier. With no preamble she came straight to the point, 'Is there any past event in the Manning's family background that could lead to a vendetta against them.'

The bishop returned her smile and didn't appear fazed by the bluntness of her approach.

He spoke with a smooth and deep voice, 'May I assume you wish to talk about Alexander?' Andrea nodded. 'He is a good hardworking priest and has made significant advances since he has been in his parish.'

The answer she expected but too superficial and bland to reveal anything of interest.

Andrea had to dig deeper, 'Were you aware he had a sister, Charlotte?'

He leaned back in his chair but kept the full focus of his attention on Andrea's face, 'Not until yesterday, I've met his other sister, Margaret, but he has never mentioned Charlotte before.'

Andrea shifted uncomfortably in her chair not sure how to proceed as she needed to be diplomatic and choose her words with care. With a long drawn out sigh, 'This is difficult, your Grace.'

'Please take your time, I prefer difficult topics and questions out in the open, it is my style, then we all know where we are. With the grace of God, we will work through any difficulties together.' He raised his hands palm upwards in a placatory gesture. His calm manner gave Andrea a modicum of reassurance.

'Thank you. One reason for Charlotte being killed could be that she had crucial information, but we do not understand what that might be.'

The Bishop didn't hurry with his answer and he mulled over her statement about Charlotte. 'I am naïve, thankfully, in such matters as murder,' his warm gaze fixed on her face. 'Do you mean the person would then have a reason to kill her to stop her speaking about it to someone else?'

'Yes, that's right and the difficulty is whether she would have said anything to Alexander before she was killed, but that perhaps he cannot divulge.'

The Bishop nodded gently, his expression solemn, 'Yes, I do see... priests must be led by God as to the best course of action.'

'Yes, but if the murderer suspects that Alexander knows.' She left the end of the sentence hanging in the air. The Bishop didn't require the implication to be spelled out.

'Yes, I do see,' his forehead creased and his jaw tightened, 'I am due to see him tomorrow. Would you like me to raise the matter with him?'

'Yes, that would be helpful.' She gave him a small smile but had made no progress in this tricky discussion and gave a quick glance at Calum who had been so quiet, he sat staring at his hands in his lap, his face expressionless.

The Bishop added, 'Yesterday when I met him, he appeared strained, but the death of a sister affects everyone differently.'

'He didn't have a good relationship with Charlotte, neither did Margaret nor their father Gerald.' Andrea pursed her lips and shook her head in a bemused fashion, 'They disliked her chosen profession as a singer.' The Bishop nodded but offered no comment. 'Can I ask if you know the Kennedy family?'

'Yes, Alexander has done his best for them for years and became upset when the twins were shot. He said that one had died and he had given the other the last rites.'

Calum stood, 'Will you excuse me,' he muttered, 'I'm in need of air.'

79

‘He looks under a great strain,’ the Bishop’s voice intoned seriousness.

‘Yes, he is the police officer who was shot by one of the twins during the armed robbery.’

‘Oh dear, most insensitive of me, but I didn’t know. Let me talk with him in private.’ The Bishop rose from his chair and walked across the room closing the door behind him.

Left alone Andrea tried to marshal her thoughts. A great weariness came over her, but she pushed it aside. The conversation with the Bishop needed revitalizing, so the gap gave her thinking time, she must be missing something as they were no closer to identifying suspects. Despite her attempts to remain focused, her mind drifted. Had they found Martin yet? If so, would they tell her? His mental breakdown explained his violent behavior, but their marriage would be over. The violence had been unforgettable and unforgivable.

The Bishop and Calum returned breaking into her thoughts and she gave a last shiver. A glance at Calum’s grey face jolted her back to reality as his forehead beaded with sweat. Tiredness seemed ingrained into every crease on his face.

'Do you want to leave, Calum?' she asked with a worried voice.

'No, carry on please.' Calum sat and flashed her a small reassuring smile.

The Bishop settled himself back in his chair, his expression benevolent and his voice gentle, 'The Bishop's House is a peaceful place and one that the real world touches little, but it has now arrived on my door step as you have armed police guarding you.'

'It is a difficult time for everyone, my world has been turned upside down,' Andrea's voice faltered and her eyes glazed with tears but she blinked them away.

'Bless you my child, God will give you the strength you need.' His lilting voice intoned a sense of calm to Andrea's racing mind and she refocused all her energies on the questioning as they needed to make a breakthrough.

Trying a different angle to the conversation. 'I believe Alexander took holy orders in Ireland?'

'Yes, he did.'

'Do you know the seminary personally?'

'No, Alexander wrote to me and I subsequently interviewed him as he wished to become a priest in this diocese. One of the Cathedral priests dealt with the paperwork.'

'Is there anything unusual about his tenure?'

'No, he worked in the Cathedral for a few months. Because of his commitment we offered him a minor parish of his own, however, he turned it down and requested to move to the Malin parish in Sheffield.'

Andrea recognised the name as where the Kennedy

family lived and where they had their car hire business.

'Did it have a vacancy?'

'No, only an elderly priest, the incumbent for three decades. He needed help, but rejected most of the young priests I offered to him, but he took to Alexander. So it seemed opportune and enabled me to solve two problems at the same time.'

'Is the older priest still there?' Andrea hadn't remembered seeing or hearing anything about him when they had visited Alexander.

'No, not long after Alexander took up his post, the old priest fell down the steps in the church yard and died later in hospital without regaining consciousness.' The Bishop crossed himself and raised his eyes towards the ceiling, 'We had told him not to walk in the church yard after dark, but he didn't take our advice. Such a pity. A wonderful priest, the heart of the community, a great loss.'

'Did Alexander take over?'

'Yes, he took to his new position with great vigour and his efforts in restoration and raising money for charity have been outstanding.'

'Thank you, your Grace.' The bishop had answered her questions with clarity and calmness although making no progress they had tried.

'I'm sorry I couldn't help,' apologised the Bishop, 'but I will speak to Alexander tomorrow.' She glanced worryingly at Calum's ashen face and grim expression as the Bishop led them through the door into the outer office. Alexander Manning entered the office and stopped in his tracks, his eyes narrowed.

His expression hardened, 'Andrea? Inspector

Brodie? he snapped, 'may I ask why you are here?' his voice rose almost to a shout. The sudden outburst made Andrea lost for words, his hostility shocked her and her heart hammered as he stared at them with contempt.

The Bishop's calm voice cut through the tension, 'Alexander, please be more temperate with my guests.'

'I apologise,' spluttered Alexander looking away. Andrea felt the words held no sincerity.

The Bishop continued as they stood awkwardly in the outer office. 'They wished to seek information from me about the Kennedy family who are involved in a crime that has taken place.'

Alexander's disapproval was evident, 'But...'

The Bishop held up his hand and said, 'Alexander they are collecting information, there is no implication of guilt. Now please go into my office and I will join you.'

Andrea and Calum escorted by a priest left through the front door of the Bishop's House to blue flashing lights and two armed police officers. The Range Rover had been flanked by two police cars and four police motor cyclists, with blue lights flashing.

'This way ma'am,' indicated one of the armed officers, 'as quickly as possible, please.' Andrea rushed to the open door of the Range Rover with Calum close behind her.

'A new driver?' asked Andrea as she organised her seat belt and made herself comfortable.

'Yes, ma'am,' said a female police officer behind the wheel, 'I'm Julie, ma'am.'

'I'm Andrea, no need for the formalities.'

Julie gave a small chuckle, 'With a Chief Constable,

Commander and a Bishop involved I shall stick to "ma'am".'

'Have we somewhere else to go, Julie?'

'Yes, ma'am.'

'Where is it?'

'Could you call this number?' Her colleague in the front seat passed back a piece of paper as the police convoy set off at high speed. She took the paper as Calum already had his eyes closed although she could tell he hadn't fallen asleep, but his pale complexion worried her. He needed rest.

'An unusual number,' mumbled Andrea as she dialled it.

'It is a restricted number for the army, ma'am.' Andrea waited as the phone rang a few times. A powerful man's voice answered, 'General Turner.'

'General, I was given this number, I'm Andrea Cain.'

'Yes, come straight round, we are expecting you. We'll see you soon. Good evening.'

'Where are we headed, Julie?' asked Andrea as the call finished.

'Ministry of Defence barracks at Totley, ma'am.

80

The barrier lifted and the guards saluted. The police escorts pulled to the side and the Range Rover passed through the gates, slowed and then fell into convoy behind two armoured Land Rovers. A further Land Rover joined their tail to escort them across the barracks.

They passed various army buildings and soldiers' houses before the convoy sped into a large courtyard of a former country house with converted stables to the side. As they came to a stop, the front door was opened by the General in his uniform and next to him a woman in a tailored suit. Andrea shook Calum awake. Fully armed soldiers leapt from the convoy vehicles and took guarding positions across the courtyard.

The General shook hands as Andrea reached him, 'General we have met before, at the fashion show at the Strines.' Andrea recognised him from the group she had briefed for the Chief Constable.

'Yes, I had been approaching you after the show that evening to introduce myself when the shooting started. This is my wife Martha.'

'General, it is kind of you to give me such a welcome, but I am embarrassed by this attention.'

'The first objective of the Armed Forces is to protect Her Majesty's subjects and we do that with pride.' He gave her a warm smile and offered his hand to Calum, 'Inspector Brodie. Welcome. Excellent work when the shooting started at the show. Deploying different police units to specific areas around the house and ensuring that the prime target was kept safe, you'd make a good army man.'

'Thank you, sir.'

Martha interrupted them, her voice firm, 'George, I insist no business yet, as this poor woman looks tired and so does the Inspector. They have had a difficult day.'

George nodded in agreement, 'Yes, come through,' they followed him into a large lounge. A range of table lamps lit the room where the curtains had been pulled, giving the room a cosy feel despite its size. Sandwiches, tea, coffee and cakes spread the length of the oak sideboard. Andrea eyed the feast and her stomach rumbled as she couldn't remember the last time she'd eaten.

Martha insisted that Andrea sit on the broad and sumptuous settee and brought her a selection of food and drink. Andrea ate hungrily and Calum devoured food at an alarming rate. She relaxed among people who would protect her. Martha having satisfied herself that both Calum and Andrea had food on their plates announced with a firmness that allowed no argument, 'Andrea and Calum will stay here tonight, it's by far the best solution as they are exhausted, they can't possibly travel further today.'

Andrea welcomed the invitation as she relaxed on the sofa, 'We don't want to be any trouble, I believe the police have organised a safe house.'

The General dismissed her comment with a wave of his hand, 'Of course, Martha, you are correct.' He crossed to the marble fireplace and pressed a bell.

Within seconds a Captain opened the door, 'Sir?'

'Arrange for Mrs Cain's clothes and the wardrobe for Inspector Brodie to be brought here. Please inform the Chief Constable that they will be staying with us.'

'Sir.' The door closed behind the Captain. Andrea felt too tired to protest further.

Martha, having been satisfied that they had eaten and had drinks available said, 'Not too long now, George, keep the meeting as brief as possible.' She left the room.

'This is difficult, sir,' Andrea glanced at the tall imposing man standing by the empty fireplace.

'No formalities necessary, it's George.'

'I asked the Chief Constable to find me someone who had been in the army with Gerald Manning.'

He nodded his understanding, 'Arthur rang me. We've been friends for years and I've known Gerald for a long time and I am only too willing to help.'

'Did you know Charlotte?'

'Yes, a long time ago, when she would be about thirteen, I remember a pretty girl in a pink dress.'

Andrea had no doubt having seen Charlotte's room at Gerald's house he gave an accurate description. Everything had been pink. 'I didn't associate the little Charlotte as the same person who had been shot until Martha pointed it out, it came as a surprise that she had become a successful singer. I never heard her sing, not my style of music,' he gave a small apologetic smile.

'Do you know Gerald well?'

‘Yes, he served under my command for many years, we came through the same regiment. He paused, his eyes glazed with a faraway look, recalling those times. It’s the regiment that is based here, my current role is across the whole army, but I’ve chosen to be located here. Sheffield is my home town and I know a great many people locally. Gerald and I became good friends for several years.’

‘That makes it more difficult.’ Andrea’s shoulders slumped with a mixture of anxiety and exhaustion. She stared at the General who despite his air of authority had a friendly open face.

‘Let me change that,’ he sat straight in a large armchair and fixed them with his blue eyes. ‘The army stands for courage, truth and justice, we have bad’uns but over the years I have learned to keep an open mind, but hear me loud and clear, the truth must out, so the sooner you receive answers to your questions the earlier we will arrive at the truth.’

‘Thank you.’ The General’s blue eyes now focused on Calum, ‘If I understand police methods, you would wish to eliminate members of the family from the investigation, as most murders are committed by people close to the victim.’

‘Yes, sir, that is correct,’ Calum’s face remained pale but his eyes were alert and focused, ‘We will always complete a thorough check on all members of the family.’

‘Have you found out information about Gerald that you wish to discuss? Let’s not beat about the bush, I’m under instructions from Martha to keep the meeting brief.’

Andrea said, ‘Gerald is an expert shot.’

‘Yes, as far as I remember as a young trooper, he

became a sniper and never lost the skill. He is such a disciplined man, he practiced regularly and still holds a senior post for the Rifle Society.' He drew his lips together and focused on Andrea, 'If the real question is, "could Gerald have made the shot that killed his daughter" then undoubtedly the answer is "yes". Although he left the army many years ago, I would assume he is still a first-rate shot.' He paused and then added, 'but you have more concerns than that? I can tell by the expressions on your faces.'

She nodded at his perceptiveness, 'We have found out that he has been a forceful campaigner against what he sees as a decline in moral standards, particularly in the entertainment industry.'

'He has always been a highly principled and inflexible man when it comes to standards.'

Calum shifted in his chair and rubbed his injured leg, 'Have you heard of a group called CAD, Campaign against Depravity.'

'Yes,' he gave a brief smile, 'a militant Mary Whitehouse group.'

'He has admitted to being the organiser.' Andrea wondered how George would respond to this information.

'Yes, that would fit the man,' his immediate acceptance gave Andrea a surprise. 'Definitely,' he nodded to himself and pressed his lips into a tight line. 'I advised him on several occasions to be relaxed and forgiving but he felt strongly about such issues. If I remember correctly, people from the group were arrested. That would pose a dilemma and stress for Gerald as he would never step back from rigid adherence to moral standards, but he would also never break the law.'

'Gerald argued with Charlotte about her career as a singer as he wanted her to give it up. He didn't recognise her talent but regarded it as flaunting herself which he disapproved of wholeheartedly.' George stood up from his chair and moved to stand in front of the unlit fireplace.

He adopted a stand easy pose then rubbed his chin with his hand, 'That would be an even greater dilemma for him. Gerald sees the world in simple terms, so when his beloved daughter went against his moral standards it would cause him great anguish.'

Andrea fumbled for the right words, 'I have known Gerald for a short time, but I have seen the anguish and the suffering he is undergoing.'

'You've been helping the family, I believe.'

'Yes,' but she struggled to phrase the next question.

'You look troubled Andrea. There is something you are concerned about asking me, please don't be,' his voice smooth and professional.

Andrea marshalled her thoughts and took a deep breath forcing herself to continue, 'Calum believes I'm being used by the family as I'm gullible and could easily be fooled. If Gerald killed Charlotte is he ruthless enough to use me as a smokescreen?'

The General didn't hesitate, 'Yes, without doubt. If he has killed his daughter, he would definitely be that ruthless.' Andrea couldn't hide her surprise and she fixed her wide-eyed gaze onto his face. She opened her mouth intending to comment but closed it again the words unspoken, he raised his hand, 'But I do not believe he would kill Charlotte. He would be unforgiving of her but it's hard to imagine how he could survive the agony of the murder of his own daughter.' As he finished speaking a momentary flicker of something passed across his face. Before she could attempt to identify its cause, it had disappeared.

Andrea studied the General's face, searching for clues.

81

'There is something troubling you,' ventured Andrea after a short silence.

'Yes,' his blue eyes focused on her face, 'I cannot make a judgement for you or for the police so I must give you his background so you can make the judgement for yourself.' He paused, searching for the right words.

Andrea waited and her heart raced in anticipation.

The General gave a tight smile, 'He became a ruthless soldier and drove himself to extremes.' He shook his head as he said in a quiet voice, 'deeply disturbing. Deeply disturbing. You know he was awarded the George Cross.'

'Yes.'

'An extreme act of bravery in the defusing of bombs, he went into an area which had been booby trapped and single-handedly defused several devices, it was the first GC for the regiment in the 20th century. He joined the army a few years behind me in officer training and was destined for far greater things. Everyone, including me, expected him to rise to the highest ranks in the Army.'

'And why didn't he?' asked Calum.

'A few doubts over his temper, also reports of being

too rough with young troopers in his command.' Andrea and Calum waited as more revelations would come. He needed time to compose his thoughts. Andrea believed they had reached a defining moment, she let out a long silent breath and tried to still the racing of her pulse.

Emotions of sadness and determination wrestled for dominance on his frowning face. With a deep breath he began to speak, 'He led his troops in a January expedition across the mountains in Norway. There were hellish temperatures and winds as you can imagine.' Having decided to tell the story the General relaxed and returned to his chair. 'The weather, already bad, turned worse but he wouldn't give in.' His voice was low and ponderous as he retold the tale, 'When they reached the camp site several men were injured but he still wouldn't call in support.'

Andrea could see the strain this recount had on him. 'One of his subordinates, a Major, arrested him, and relieved him of his command and then called for help. Thirty-six men suffered from hypothermia.' The General went silent. Sadness flowed across his face, his eyes lost their focus and his mouth formed a thin tight line.

'Relieving a senior officer of command must be a grave matter,' said Calum.

This comment prompted him to carry on. 'On return to England Gerald formally requested that the Major be court-martialled.'

'Was he?'

'In the end, no, as the senior officers couldn't decide the best outcome. Looking back, it became a shambles. Gerald had made bad decisions and the Major tried every avenue first before resorting to his action. I don't think the army made the right decision, but they offered Gerald a desk job, which he refused and left the army.'

'What about the Major?'

'The army had a dilemma. What to do with him? The Major took the initiative himself and asked to be transferred to United Nations duties.'

'Is that what happened?'

'Yes, he would remain part of the regiment but went abroad as an adviser to African armies. But I spoke to him before he went to Africa and he said he would never return because Gerald had broken his spirit.'

'What happened to the Major?'

'Two years later, I was commanding officer of a United Nations force monitoring a civil war ceasefire in Africa and off-shore on the Ark Royal.' He wiped his brow. 'A small UN peace keeping group from other African countries had been brought under fire by rebels who were massacring a village. The rebels intended killing the UN troops. The senior officer, the Major, radioed to my command room.'

'What happened sir?' said Calum.

'I scrambled fighters, helicopter gunships and Marines.' Andrea could see how difficult it had become for the General. His forehead covered with beads of sweat as his face had paled, he took a long intake of breath before continuing. 'For his actions the Major became the second member of the regiment to be awarded the George Cross. He returned to this country, refused to accept the medal, left the army and died an alcoholic a year later.' A stillness came as the shock of the story whirled through their minds.

‘Two brave men, legends of the regiment but never reconciled.’

Andrea recovered her composure with an effort, ‘Thank you for such honesty.’ As she finished the sentence, she allowed her eyelids to close and fell asleep in the warmth and comfort of the armchair.

82

'I'll fetch you a dressing gown, my dear, otherwise the men will not be able to concentrate.' Andrea yawned as she wandered into the dining room for breakfast. The General and another officer she did not recognise were at the table with Calum and Martha. Andrea looked at the short tee-shirt she had slept in and smiled gently as she helped herself to coffee from the sideboard.

Martha wrapped the gown round her shoulders and Andrea sat at the table with a quiet, 'Good morning.' The men talked, but she didn't listen as she hadn't fully woken. Her sleep had been deep and restful as the images and terror hadn't returned during the night. She only vaguely remembered Martha helping her to bed. What would today bring? Her mind struggled to concentrate. There was a question from last night she wanted to ask but it remained elusive like a cloud flitting across the sky. Then it came back to her, but it's not relevant and she shook her head in annoyance.

Andrea drank more coffee and watched the others at the breakfast table as though through a thick mist, she wanted to understand the jumble of ideas that swirled endlessly around her mind. But there was this nagging doubt about the question and the answer, should she ask? If she didn't ask, she would never know. This assumption was so obvious it made her smile. The conversation paused.

Before she changed her mind, she blurted out, 'General, when you spoke last night you never did say the name of the Major.'

'Didn't I? I thought I did, but it was Major John Montague.' Suddenly her eyes opened wide. She'd heard the name Montague recently. Could there be a connection? Calum caught her eye and they both turned and looked at the General.

'What have I said? Do you recognise the name?'

'Did he have a son?'

'Yes, but he became a tearaway. When I went to visit his wife, after John had died, she said John's death had affected the lad and that he'd left home and had fallen into drink and drugs.'

Andrea leaned forward her heart racing, with difficulty she kept her voice calm, 'Would the son be about the same age as Charlotte?'

'Yes, within a year.'

'Do you know if the mother still keeps in contact with him?'

'Unfortunately, John's death affected her and she died a year later. Such a tragic tale of misery.'

'Can we call the Chief Constable, sir,' Calum asked as he pushed his chair back. 'This could be the breakthrough.' Andrea could hear a frisson of excitement in his voice as he smiled across the table at her.

'Yes,' replied the General.

'Would you mind joining the call, sir, as you know

the background of the Montagues.'

The General addressed the other officer at the table, 'Please join us, we'll use the briefing room. Colonel Jennings is the local commanding officer for the regiment; we might need his assistance.' They followed the General to the stable block. Inside they passed along a corridor until reaching a spacious room where the General indicated to Calum the phone in the middle of the table. As soon as they were seated, silence filled the room as Calum dialed the number. Andrea held her breath until the chief Constable answered on the third ring.

Calum gave the Chief Constable a summary of their visit to Stacey's flat the previous afternoon including the information about Tony Montague who now called himself Edward Stonehouse and added the General's account of Major Montague.

At the end of Calum's explanation the Chief Constable said, 'I will inform the Commander, but I will request a warrant for the search of Edward's house which will take less than an hour to acquire.' They could hear him issuing orders to the others who had joined the call, he paused, 'General, given the shortage of time may I request your assistance?'

'Gerald Manning and John Montague are the pride of the army. I will mobilise the whole regiment if necessary and they will be proud to do it.'

83

'You look very weak my dear,' said Martha, 'your face is pale and no amount of makeup has managed to hide the dark circles under your eyes.'

'Yes,' Andrea's chin trembled, 'but I will not give in.'

'I know you won't,' she patted her arm in encouragement, 'they are waiting outside for you.' Andrea stepped out into the extensive courtyard.

The General addressed a soldier standing nearby, 'Take Mrs Cain for personal armour.'

The reply was deafening, 'Yes, sir.' Andrea jumped, 'This way ma'am, please,' again delivered loudly.

'The full military machine in action, Andrea,' said the General with a proud wave of his arm to indicate the assembled soldiers all of which were armed.

'Yes,' she gave a cautious smile and followed the soldier.

Andrea wearing a protective vest which she found bulky huddled in the back of a heavily protected army Land Rover. The tight strap from her helmet dug into her chin, it was an uncomfortable and bumpy journey as it sped across the barracks. Andrea peered out through the darkened windows. Army vehicles were joining them from every direction. The scene was unreal as though she was a part of a film set. Anxiety gripped her making her pulse race, she sweated with the weight of the protective vest. It became part of a convoy, headed by the police escort as it left the gates onto the main road.

The General and Calum were in the leading vehicle. Andrea had the company of three unarmed soldiers. They were equipped with body armour and helmets, their eyes were alert and their faces grim with concentration. She stared at them while she hung on to a nearby handle for support as the Land Rover sped through the streets of Sheffield the blue lights of the convoy flashing to clear the route. 'I don't want to be any bother,' she said. Fear prickled her. The harsh reality had hit her. Although she had the company of three soldiers to protect her, a sense of loneliness wrapped its tendrils around her squeezing the breath from her body.

'No trouble at all, ma'am.'

Andrea needed to talk to calm herself. Silence had become too terrifying. 'Are you just escorting me there?'

'No, ma'am, we are your personal protection.'

'What does that mean?'

'We will be with you at all times and look out for danger and take whatever action is necessary to protect you.'

'Thank you,' she said, but she knew the weakness came across in her voice, 'you are not armed.'

'No ma'am, we are not allowed to carry arms in civilian areas except for ceremonial occasions or at the request of the Home Secretary. Armed protection will be provided by police officers when we arrive.'

Fear engulfed her making her whole body drained and exhausted. Outwardly she appeared calm, but that was the complete opposite of her body's reaction. A cold trickle of sweat ran down her spine despite the weight and heat of the armour she wore.

'We are nearly there. ma'am, could you lower the visor on your helmet?' Andrea did as requested. She turned her attention to the events outside. The blue lights continued to flash but their vehicle was too far away for her to ascertain what was happening. She continued to stare unable to take her eyes away from the window in case she missed something vital.

'The raid is commencing now ma'am, we will arrive at the scene in three minutes and will wait until called forward.' Andrea checked her watch. The unerring precision of the swoop scared her. People often referred to military precision, but she was now experiencing it at first hand. Would Edward still be there? She guessed not. If guilty, he would have disappeared. But what would they find?

Andrea didn't know whether they would tell her, so she sat quietly enclosed in the body armour, in the heavily defended Land Rover and shivered with cold although she sweated. Despite the protection she realised the vulnerability of her position. They arrived at the end of the street in Stoney Middleton after passing through the roadblocks where police cars straddled the road. The street, full of policemen, standing outside houses prevented people leaving. Somewhere in the distance a car door slammed. Several armed police were outside the house at the end, she sat and waited, with images of Edward swirling in her mind.

A radio message relayed no inhabitant in the house. She sat with her personal guards in silence as the images of Edward intermingled with those of Martin. Her life had changed forever but when would the horror and evilness end?

Finally the Chief Constable and Calum emerged from the house. They beckoned towards her vehicle. 'If you're ready, ma'am?' she climbed out of the Land Rover and walked with speed towards the Chief Constable and Calum.

Her army escort remained next to her. In front of her and behind were armed police officers.

84

'He's not there,' said the Chief Constable, 'but there is enough to give us concern. Forensic will go in shortly.'

'May I go in?'

'No,' said the Chief Constable and Calum simultaneously.

'Can I ask why?' She crammed her clenched fists into her trouser pockets and eyed the two men through narrowed eyes.

'There are several offensive objects.' The Chief Constable's voice was firm.

'I'm not easily shocked and I believe it could help if I could see.'

'No, definitely not.'

'Is the offensive material about Charlotte?'

'Partly,' said the Chief Constable.

'Then it's about me as well.' Her voice rose with irritation and they both went silent. 'It is, isn't it?'

'Yes,' said the Chief Constable, 'you have been under considerable pressure, Andrea, and I have no intention of adding to it.'

'Please do not make the judgement for me, I have been warned but allow me to make the decision. If I find it repugnant, then I will leave straight away. Please do not decide for me,' she spoke with the most emphatic voice she could manage. Andrea stared at the house as officers left. 'That is a woman officer.'

Andrea called, 'Sergeant, could you spare me a minute?' Andrea moved away from the men, 'In private.' She briefly spoke to the Sergeant who looked surprised at first but answered her questions. Andrea walked back to the Chief Constable and Calum. 'I want to go in.'

'Very well, but you will leave if...'

'Yes,' said Andrea as she set off to the house. The two men followed. Andrea walked through the ground floor with its poor quality furniture and bad decoration resembling an unloved home.

'Upstairs?' They nodded. She glanced in the two standard bedrooms, with drab faded furnishings but nothing of interest so she stepped into the long thin room where a single bed under the window and a chest of drawers comprised the only furniture. Each long wall had a pin board its entire length, one full the other empty.

About sixty pictures of semi-naked Charlotte and Andrea covered the board. She examined them one by one in a slow methodical manner. Both men watched her as two female officers entered the room.

'Are you okay?' asked the Chief Constable.

'Yes, I'm fine, you are ridiculous trying to keep me from these, I am not naïve and know men will have semi-naked pictures of me on the wall. Most of them are poor quality, they have come from web sites. Many were taken with long range lenses by the paparazzi.' She stood back and looked along the length of them and pointed, 'That one comes from the Maldives, I recognise the hotel in the background.'

She stopped at one, completely naked as she had begun to dress, 'This is an old one, someone planted a camera in the changing rooms which remained there for a long time before discovery.' She moved on, 'Changing rooms are now always checked for cameras. Looking at Charlotte's, I would assume they come from a similar source, except the ones she did for a calendar.' One photo caught her attention as it was the only one of Charlotte fully dressed, taken on top of a hill on a cold day. She had pulled her anorak around her. Charlotte in the Lake District? With Edward? She couldn't be sure. The pattern of the pictures captured her thoughts.

All of Charlotte's pictures were neatly laid out across the board with each one attached with four drawing pins. All of hers had one drawing pin, with most of them stuck in the gaps between Charlotte's. The board on the other side of the room was empty although the pin marks suggested a systematic layout. She guessed it had been the original location of her pictures, but why had they been moved? She crossed to the blank board on the wall above the chest of drawers which she peered behind. 'A photo has dropped, can I see it?'

The Chief Constable spoke to the forensic officer in the white overalls. He lifted it out from behind the chest and popped it into a plastic bag, then handed it to Andrea. A picture of Alexander and Margaret with two other men and a sign in the background indicating last summer's church fete. 'Do you recognise these two?' she said to Calum.

He took a quick glance, 'It's the Kennedy twins.'

Andrea didn't reply, but searched the picture for other people, but only recognised Gerald.

'What do you think?' she said to Calum as they went to leave the house, but she didn't expect a meaningful reply.

'Your helmet and visor, please ma'am.' Andrea put them back on and walked with Calum to join the Chief Constable and the General.

One of the soldiers came racing up. 'What is it man?'

'Sir, an unidentified man on the ridge.'

'Probably a walker…'

There was a loud shout from the back of one of the army vehicles, 'Gun spotted, gun spotted. Take cover.'

Andrea heard the whistle of the bullet as she was swept off her feet to behind the Land Rover. The bullet tore into a police car not far from where she had been standing. She didn't have a chance to regain her footing as the back door of the Land Rover opened and she was thrown in and caught by people inside. Her two guards dived in, 'Are you hit ma'am?'

'No, frightened but not hurt.' She felt weak but sat on the floor of the Land Rover listening to the sirens. The radio cackled, 'Helicopter on its way.'

The resonating thud of an explosion filled the air, but it hadn't occurred close to the convoy. 'Explosion on Eyam Ridge,' came across the radio.

Suddenly nearby sirens started simultaneously and the Land Rover took off without warning at high speed throwing Andrea across the floor.

'Where are we going?' she stuttered.

'Back to the army base ma'am. Senior officers have decided it is the safest place for you.'

'Thank you,' but Andrea didn't speak for the rest of the journey. The swaying motion of the car added to the tension gripping her stomach. She crouched as tears rolled down her cheeks.

Someone had again tried to kill her.

85

The security of the army barracks didn't comfort Andrea as the convoy swept pass the security guards and crossed the base to an immense square building where, supported by armed guards, they proceeded to a briefing room. A semi-circle of chairs faced a large board which contained a map of the local area on which several small flags had been added at specific points and Andrea recognised one as being her home. Shifting her body weight from one foot to the other while trying to calm herself, she studied the location of the flags as it gave her something to occupy her mind and distract her thoughts from the trauma of the past few days.

Within a few minutes, the Chief Constable and Calum had joined her. The Chief Constable's grim expression had deepened, 'Either the person shooting is Edward Stonehouse, or we have a breach in security.'

Calum in a low and serious voice, 'Andrea, the concern is that Martin still hasn't been traced and he has a police radio. If the murderer has captured Martin, he may have the access to the radio and be able to listen to police messages.'

Andrea could detect the reluctance to take the

conclusion to its next step, so she added it for them, 'Or if he has killed Martin...' she said in a shaking voice.

The police radio broke the silence, 'The Commander will be landing in a police helicopter shortly.'

'What happened back there?' asked Andrea, mustering the strength and forcing herself to concentrate on the current issues.

'The shot came from the ridge,' the Chief Constable pointed to the precise location on the wall map, 'then in the same location an explosion occurred.' The helicopter arrived on the scene within minutes and observed a black car drive away at speed, which it tracked until it disappeared into a wooded area. Afterwards smoke came from the trees.'

The arrival of the Commander interrupted the conversation. With no preamble, 'We need to make rapid progress, and mobilise available officers.'

'Leave has been cancelled and we are trying to contact officers to come into work,' said the Chief Constable.

'Thank you.'

The Commander said, 'Myself and my officers have been through the information available so far, and this is our conclusion.' Andrea slumped on a nearby chair and listened with apprehension, 'We have the murder of Charlotte Manning and two attempted murders of Andrea. We propose treating these incidents as one case.' Andrea went to speak but decided it wouldn't be appreciated by the Commander as the meeting would not be an exchange of views. She forced herself to be quiet and focused on her words, 'I will set up a team to investigate the armed robbery which I intend treating as a separate case until any irrefutable link is established.' Andrea didn't agree but remained quiet. 'Calum you are suffering from your injuries but any help you can give the robbery team would be appreciated.' He grunted acceptance.

Andrea could see compassion in the Commander's eyes, she caught her hand, 'My husband is a police officer, it is a dangerous world in which we operate and we fear more for our loved ones, than we fear for ourselves, I shall leave the tragic absence of Martin to the Chief Constable.'

The Commander rubbed the back of Andrea's hand, 'I do not believe his absence is linked to these cases and as Arthur and Calum know Martin well, they are best equipped to find him.'

'Can I help?' asked Andrea with a tremble in her voice.

'No, you have done well, but this is a full police operation led by Scotland Yard and I would like you to stay in this safe environment until further notice.'

The smile she gave Andrea was full of warmth and understanding, 'Yes, I will.'

The Commander's radio burst into jabbering. Andrea listened but the crackle of the interference and the jargon made the information undecipherable, but Pablo's name came across loud and clear.

86

'Pablo has been arrested at Manchester Airport.'

'Why?'

'His photo along with the others in this case is at the airports and he arrived in a hurry and looked agitated.'

'So?'

'The team tried to detain him, but he drew a gun.'

'Pablo?' said Andrea in disbelief.

'Then grabbing a member of the public, he attempted to use them as protection to board a plane.'

'Pablo? Have they shot him?'

'No, but it came close. The officers couldn't shoot because of the public in the vicinity but after they had cleared the area, they gave him a last chance which he accepted.'

'It's hard to believe,' said Andrea, trying to stop herself shaking, she found it painful to equate this view of Pablo with her helpful friend. 'Pablo on the ridge?' she muttered.

The Commander's voice was firm, 'We don't know, but he is a link between you and Charlotte.'

Andrea's next question made her nerves flutter, 'Does he have the capability?'

The Commander pressed her lips together and gave a slight shake of her head indicating that she would not answer the question. The Chief Constable said, 'Please tell her.'

'Very well, we have further information from the Italian police, his family are the masterminds behind the organised crime in southern Italy and they are experts in using guns and explosives.'

'Oh dear.' The words sounded inadequate. Would this nightmare ever end?

The Commander continued, 'The motive isn't clear, but he will be interviewed,' she caught Andrea's hand and guided her to the door. 'Take heart my dear, I'm sure the Chief Constable will find Martin now that the Met has added extra manpower.'

87

Despite her weariness, 'Can we talk, Calum?' They left the room together as he was not needed by the Commander.

His shoulders slumped and he gave an audible sigh, 'Yes.'

'In private,' Andrea glanced around, they were alone but not an ideal location as the hall wouldn't stay empty for long. Calum's weary eyes searched her face. Andrea rested her hand on his arm, 'You must say what you are thinking Calum, even if it's painful for us.'

'I will.'

'My room will be best.'

'The lounge is empty,' he pointed towards the open door indicating the empty room.

'No, Calum, I don't want us to be interrupted, my room, come on,' she helped him up the stairs.

As she closed the door of her room, he walked past her to the window. 'We can't keep avoiding it,' she let out a slow controlled breath and stared at the back of his head.

'No, we can't,' he muttered.

She crossed the room to stand behind him, 'Calum, please turn to look at me.' She reached catching his hand but felt him hesitate. Finally, he twisted around but avoided eye contact and studied the carpet with his jaw clenched.

'Calum,' her voice soft, 'please look at me.' Worry etched his face, and with reluctance he raised his eyes, the normal bright sharp eyes had dulled.

She caught hold of his hands, 'You're finding it difficult to understand Martin's behaviour.' He nodded but didn't speak. 'How long have you known him?'

'Since he joined the force,' his voice low and strained, 'I started off as a beat copper and rose through the ranks, but he joined the force as a high-flying graduate. I'd been promoted to Detective Sergeant and after his formal training he was assigned to me.' Andrea could feel his hands relax as he spoke.

'Did you resent that?'

'No, part of the job is to train the know-it-all graduates, but Martin showed he would be different as he listened, took advice and then used his intellect, so I knew he would reach the top.'

'He overtook you in promotion.'

'Martin is a better detective, it's more sensible I work for him.'

'What do you think has happened to him?' her voice wobbled and she swallowed to regain control.

Calum shut his eyes and tensed his hands. 'I don't know. Why did he attack you, as he idolised you? What he did is what he hated, mindless violence. He had two desires in his life, you and the Police Force, I can't believe the past few days.' She gripped his hands as he continued, 'I'm supposed to be a hardened police officer but I'm struggling to cope with his actions to you and the Force.'

'Do you think he is still alive?'

Tears streamed down her face, but she wouldn't let go of his hands.

'I don't know.'

'Tell me what you think, please.'

He raised his head, with tears in his eyes, 'I don't know what's happened to him, whether a breakdown, but…'

'I must know what you think.'

He didn't respond straight away as confusion flitted across his weary face. When he spoke his voice was low, 'My concern is that he will realise what he has done and cannot live with his actions.' Andrea flung her arms round his broad shoulders and hugged him.

'I'm frightened.'

'You've been so brave,' he hugged her, several minutes passed and then he stepped back. 'You must be brave a little longer, now the Met is here we can concentrate on finding Martin.'

'Weakness and tiredness seem to be my constant companions as my world has been turned upside down, Martin needs my help now, but I don't know what to do.' She brought her hand up and wiped the tears away.

As he walked away, Calum stumbled.

Andrea steadied him, 'Lay on the bed and rest your leg.' As she fetched two glasses of water, she caught her face in the mirror, pale, hollow eyes and old make-up had smeared down her face.

'We must be systematic,' he said as she perched on the edge of the bed. Calum took out his pills and within a few minutes he said, 'They have numbed the pain in my leg, I'll sit up now.' Something elusive nagged at the back of her mind just beyond reach.

'Give me a few minutes,' she plodded into the bathroom, washed her face, brushed her hair and put light makeup on to hide the hollowness of her eyes.

When she came out, he had moved from the bed and had settled at a table next to the window. He pointed to the pile of papers on the table, 'I've picked up relevant files and up-to-date information from the incident room downstairs.'

'Do you think Martin's disappearance is linked to the murder of Charlotte?'.

Calum sighed, 'I think it's linked, there are too many coincidences.'

'Let's recap everything,' said Andrea.

'Yes, I agree. I've collected the latest briefing reports, and the background info we requested.'

Andrea settled in a chair and tried to focus, shaking the nightmare thoughts away, 'Anything further on Pablo?' she asked on impulse.

'No.' Calum opened the next briefing report. He read one page then pushed it away and turned as though looking out the window. Andrea knew instinctively that the document had upset him.

'What is it?'

She leaned forward and touched his hand which rested on the table, 'You must tell me.'

He let out a long slow breath, 'Just don't jump to conclusions.'

Sensing the information would be unpleasant, 'Okay.'

'The gun used to shoot at you yesterday in London

is the one in Martin's possession, a police weapon.' Andrea's thoughts swirled out of control and her hands gripped the edge of the table.

Calum's words bounced around inside her head, 'No, not Martin,' her voice rose to a shriek, 'someone must have stolen it.'

'You seem so sure.'

She gave him a long assessing look, 'Yes, both times he attacked me, he talked normally at the beginning, but then the attacks came as he lost his temper. The shooting at the show had been planned so it wouldn't be Martin.'

'Let me find out the circumstances when he attacked the woman officer.'

'The Chief Constable told me the officer had made a mistake,' said Andrea.

'So the pattern fits,' Calum continued looking through the papers.

'Why would someone want to kill me?' she moaned rubbing the back of her neck to ease the tension.

'I don't know, but it's not random,' he fixed her with a sharp gaze, 'it's planned.'

Andrea shivered as his words hit home, somebody wanted her dead, would they keep trying until successful? Slumping back in her chair, she tried to control the trembling that had gripped her body, 'The killer must realise I have told the police all I know?'

'Yes, so there must be something else.'

'Either it is personal and a vendetta against you and Charlotte, or they are gambling it's something you haven't realised you know.'

'Such as?'

'That's the problem, I don't know.' Andrea stood

up and paced across the room thinking through her conversations with Charlotte certain that the clue lay in their friendship. With an edge of desperation in her voice 'I keep trying to think what it could be.'

Sensing her agitation, he suggested, 'Let's leave it and look at other details, shall we?' He spread out several papers, 'These are the background checks from Ireland about Alexander.'

'Is there anything obvious?' She slumped onto the chair, placed her elbows on the table then rested her head on her hands. Calum appeared focused.

'No, Alexander's information seems to stack up. He moved papers aside and picked up a different sheet. The army records office confirms the same. And the records match what he related about the Kennedys and their movements.'

'What's this?' She picked up another file with confidential in large letters at the top of the page and passed it over to Calum as he could sift through the jargon. He scanned through it.

'Briefly it's a report about Ma Kennedy's sister and niece who were both killed in the Troubles.'

'Nobody has mentioned that to us. How were they killed?'

'Security forces.' Calum continued to read through the remainder of the report and added, 'There was another niece, she was shot but survived.'

'What's her name?'

'Mary O'Donnell.' She scanned back through her memory of the various conversations with Ma Kennedy but became certain that she had mentioned no one called Mary.

'Do you think it might be important?'

'No, I don't think so,' she moaned, 'I'm clutching at straws.'

'Do you want to check the reports about finding Charlotte?'

'Yes, let's be systematic.' They each picked up a report and began reading. Suddenly Andrea dropped the report and put her head in her hands.

'Andrea, what is it? Is this too much, shall we give up, we're not progressing?'

'No, no,' she jerked her head up, 'I've realised something.'

'What? Is it about Martin?'

'Where's that report about the audience threats towards Charlotte?' He passed her a sheet of paper. She wiped the tears away and caught the hand that rested on her shoulder and looked up at Calum.

88

'Martin had an affair with Charlotte,' saying the words gave her pain.

Shock registered on his face and he moved away, she remained silent. Finally, he came back and plonked himself down on the chair opposite her again. 'How have you reached that conclusion from reading a report?'

'The report indicates only one threat to Charlotte and a Sergeant dealt with it. Martin only briefly attended the interview. However, he told me there had been numerous threats and he had interviewed her many times.'

Calum flapped his hand in a dismissive gesture, 'Don't build evidence on missing reports, in every investigation there are reports that disappear for one reason or another, they have been filed elsewhere,' his voice smooth and comforting.

Andrea would have liked to believe his explanation, but Martin and Charlotte had been lovers.

'No, there's much more, it's clear now.'

'Go on.' He leaned back in his chair and folded his arms preparing himself for her explanation.

'In the Porsche, Charlotte's multi-coloured anorak

was on the seat, it's distinctive as the swirling pattern is bright and garish.'

'Yes, it is, there was a picture of it at Edward's house when she had been standing on top of a hill.'

'I couldn't think why the colour and pattern kept coming back into my mind. Do you remember my visit to the hospital?'

'Yes.'

'I looked out the window.'

'You thought you saw Martin, but you said two lovers.'

'Martin had been to see you.'

'Yes, and you had returned unexpectedly from London.'

Andrea nodded, 'The photo shoot had been cancelled and I returned to Sheffield a day earlier than anticipated. I didn't text Martin as I wanted to surprise him.' They stared at each other.

'Charlotte was in the car park, they were the two lovers,' her chin trembled. Andrea didn't want to accept it, but the proof stared her in the face.

'Is there anything else?'

'Yes,' she gave the merest nod, 'before the fashion show at the Strines Manor, Martin brought you in and his face dropped as he saw me talking to Charlotte.'

Calum shook his head, 'He must have known about Charlotte from you?'

'I never talked about my work and I never mentioned the friends I'd met through the fashion business.'

He gave a deep frown and his forehead puckered, 'But Martin adored you.'

'I'm convinced, Charlotte was pretty and…'

'Don't torture yourself.'

'No, but she admitted to me that she enjoyed seducing married men as she enjoyed being a mistress with no ties.' Calum took a deep breath and shook his head. 'What are you thinking?' asked Andrea.

'Don't think about it anymore.'

'I must.'

'You're guessing.'

'What if Charlotte decided she wanted Martin and it wouldn't be an affair?'

'Stop it. Stop it!'

'It would have ruined his career and our marriage if it had come out. His breakdown could result from…'

'No, no, I can't believe Martin shot Charlotte, I can't.' He stood in the middle of the room staring in wide eyed astonishment.

'We have no other explanation for his breakdown,' she swiped a hand across her face to brush away the tears.

89

'Ahhhh, that hurts,' she put her hand to her groin, the pain shocked through her body as she stretched to pick up another file. The pain shot through her again and she gasped.

'What's the matter.'

'A pain but it's easing now,' she took a sip of water.

'Is it where you were bruised?'

'Yes, I think so.' Andrea moved and the pain came again, 'Ouch.'

'Lie on the bed, you've gone white.' But Andrea stayed in the chair and bent forward as it seemed more comfortable.

'You need to go to hospital.' Calum moved across the room.

'No wait, there is a doctor at the Thornbury Hospital I know from charity work, I shall ring him?' Andrea grimaced again.

'I'll arrange transport and protection,' said Calum, 'you need a doctor, I'll leave my painkillers, if it worsens take one.'

She telephoned the doctor and explained the background and told him it hurt. He agreed to see her that afternoon.

'Also, when I come to see you, can I ask your advice about another matter?'

He sounded doubtful but said he would make the necessary arrangement when she came. Andrea lay there thinking, it was only an outside chance, but it would be worth doing, so she eased herself from the bed and went to the table and picked up one file. She took her phone and dialled a number.

Closing the call ten minutes later she gave a small satisfied smile. It began to make sense.

90

Andrea trembled as she looked at the press conference lights through the glass door of the building near the main gate of the barracks. The trip to the hospital had taken less than two hours, she had no permanent damage and tablets would take care of the pain. After speaking with two doctors her mind now raced with the knowledge they had provided. She would wait until Calum came free from his duties, but nerves ate away at her.

Normally at ease with the press, this time it would be different as she appealed for her husband. She read through the conference plan. It would be difficult not to become emotional, but the message had to be delivered.

'I think we are ready,' said the Chief Constable, coming into the room from outside.

'Will Fitzwilliam be there?'

'No, he's being interviewed by one of the Commander's team.' Andrea nodded with a smirk despite her tension.

The police press officer came into the back room, 'Chief Constable, Mrs Cain, we are ready to go,' so they accompanied him into the main room. The spotlights came on. Neither the Chief Constable nor Andrea flinched. He took the central seat and Andrea sat to one side.

'Ladies and gentlemen, shall we start?' He waited for silence, 'We have called this conference to ask for your help in locating Chief Superintendent Cain.' A small murmur passed around the room. The Chief Constable waited for silence. 'Chief Superintendent Cain went missing at eight p.m. the day before yesterday. There is every reason to believe he is unwell and in need of medical attention, so it is imperative we find him as soon as possible.' A louder murmur resonated as the press realised this would be big news.

'Chief Superintendent Cain is at the centre of a murder enquiry.' Andrea braced herself as she had been forewarned what would come next, 'It is possible he has been abducted.' A flood of excited voices in the room followed by a flurry of raised hands.

He lifted his hands until quiet had been restored, 'Unfortunately, because of the murder enquiry I cannot offer more information or answer questions, but I wish to appeal to anyone who has seen Chief Superintendent Cain since eight o'clock on the day before yesterday to contact the police. We believe it is imperative we find him.'

A few hands shot into the air, the Chief Constable snapped, 'No questions.'

He waited for silence, 'Mrs Cain, will say a few words.'

'I have never sat in front of the world's press and been so frightened,' her voice wavered, she swallowed to control her anxiety. 'Please can I beg of you to inform the public we are looking for my husband? Please circulate his picture as I want him back safe and well. Martin is unwell and in need of medical attention. It is possible he may hear or see this appeal on radio and television, if you are out there, Martin, please contact me.'

Cameras flashed continually.

The noise level rose, the Chief Constable went to call for silence, but Andrea touched him on the arm. Andrea put her hand up and silence fell, 'I fear Martin has been kidnapped. Please help me get my husband back.'

The Chief Constable put his arm around Andrea's shoulders as the tears flooded unchecked down her cheeks and led her into the back room. 'Good, my dear, you can't do more.'

91

The door being flung open made her raise her head.

Calum rushed into the room, 'Sir.'

'Yes, what is it?' He glanced at Andrea who realised he would think about the words to use. 'We believe we have found Edward Stonehouse. A body has been found in a limestone cave in Wolfscote Dale not far from the old ruins of Beresford Hall. The police officer called to the scene recognised him from the picture circulated before the raid on his house this morning.'

'Another tragedy. That poor family have had more than their fair share of misfortune. First the Major, then his wife and now their son.'

'The Commander has been making arrangements with the General while you have been involved in the press conference and she wishes to leave for the scene as soon as the permissions are granted.'

'May I be included?'

'You are not up to it, you should rest.'

'I cannot rest until this is resolved. I could confirm it is him.'

'No, certainly not,' interrupted the Chief Constable. 'Gerald can make the formal identification.'

The Commander came into the room in her usual brisk and authoritative manner followed by the General.

Andrea said, 'Please may I come with you?' but she could tell from the Commander's look the answer would be no, she continued, 'You have found a body, I cannot rest I must make sure it's not Martin.'

'But I can't spare the police manpower to protect you.'

The General said, 'Given the authority we are seeking for a joint operation, the Army will protect Mrs Cain.'

'Very well,' agreed the Commander. Andrea hadn't had a chance to speak to Calum, but it needed to be a private conversation so would have to wait. Many army vehicles were assembling. Platoons of soldiers climbed into lorries. She peered along the road where police cars waited inside the entrance to the barracks with more in the road outside.

A Major knocked and entered, stood to attention and saluted the General.

'Yes, Major.'

'Vehicles and personnel assembled, sir. The control centre is briefing them via radio.'

The General nodded and turned to the Commander, 'Ready and waiting.'

'Thank you, General. Now we must wait.' Silence fell across the room.

The Commander's radio came on, 'Force Control to Commander.'

'Go ahead.'

'I have the Home Secretary on a scrambled line. Clearance sought to patch through.'

‘Patch through.’

‘Good afternoon, Commander.’

‘Good afternoon, Home Secretary.’

‘I have your request here. Is this necessary?’

‘Yes, sir, a body has been found in a remote valley. It has high limestone slopes with rough terrain and we cannot assemble enough trained police firearms officers to comb this difficult area.’

‘Do the soldiers need to be armed?’

‘Yes, sir, we encountered an armed ambush this morning, they have been given the rules of engagement.’

‘Who is leading the soldiers?’

‘General Turner, sir.’

‘Personally?’

‘Yes, sir,’ said the General.

‘Do you agree with the assessment of the terrain?’

‘Yes, sir, without sufficient armed manpower it could take several days but we can complete the task in a matter of hours.’

‘Very well, General, will you please secure the area requested under the terms of engagement?’

‘Yes, sir.’ The General stepped outside, ‘Colonel!’

‘Yes, sir.’

‘Commence deployment.’

‘Yes, sir.’ The Colonel stepped into the leading vehicle and it pulled away. As it went through the gates, it fell in behind police motorcycle outriders with blue lights flashing and sirens wailing.

92

'Calum and Andrea, you can come with me,' said the General. After the main convoy left a smaller one drew up with an armoured Land Rover at its centre. 'The regiment will secure the surrounding hills and check for booby traps and bombs before we are allowed close as it could be a trap the same as this morning.'

Andrea's conversation with Calum would have to wait. As they reached within a mile of the scene, they were waved through the first road block. Police at a further checkpoint along the road saluted as they passed through. Finally, they slowed and stopped near another group of police and army vehicles. As they drew to a halt a mixture of police and army formed the guard around the Land Rover. Calum dozed. Andrea sat in silence.

Finally, the General received the all clear. 'We can walk across the field to the nearest point they will allow us, beyond that it is forensics only.'

Andrea, stiff and aching, climbed from the back door of the Land Rover. The sharp pain had gone but her body ached. She raised her eyes to look at the countryside. The limestone hills were covered with armed soldiers, a terrifying sight.

Andrea met the Chief Constable on the other side of the footbridge over the river. His voice solemn, 'There is no doubt it is Edward Stonehouse.'

'Thank you, Chief Constable, I had to come.'

'That is understandable.'

The Chief Constable said, 'The body had been hidden far beyond where the public would go. It could have lain undetected for months or even years. We contacted the local caving society who said it went nowhere, about twenty metres back into the hill.'

'How did the discovery take place?'

'Fortunately for us, a local farmer had been rounding up his sheep for shearing. His dog had been sent into the cave to check for sheep but when he came out, he turned and lay down facing the cave. He wouldn't move. The farmer fetched a torch and followed the dog to make the discovery. The first officer on the scene recognised the body and then we started the whole operation.'

'Have the soldiers found anything?'

'No, everywhere is clear. The pathologist has finished and they will bring the body out soon.' Andrea and Calum went back across the field to their vehicle. As they arrived, a car pulled up. Gerald, Alexander and Margaret stepped out.

Gerald said, 'Andrea, my poor woman, I have seen the news. I hope Martin will be found safe and well.'

'Thank you.' Margaret didn't speak, she stood to one side and looked across the field.

Alexander came up to her, 'May God's blessing be upon you,' and then stood with his sister.

Gerald said, 'The Chief Constable asked me to make myself available to identify Edward until his next of kin can be found. Is it Edward?'

'Yes.' A long procession of men in white coveralls crossed the field carrying a stretcher.

The Chief Constable led the way and said to Gerald, 'Identification won't be necessary, there is no doubt.' Gerald stood to attention as the body of Edward Stonehouse passed him. Alexander made the sign of the cross. Margaret bowed her head.

Andrea turned to Gerald, 'Were Alexander and Margaret with you when you took the call from the Chief Constable?'

'No, I met them as they had stopped up the road and they joined me in my car.' The General returned from the field and issued orders for the soldiers to stand down and return to base.

A radio operator with a headset in a nearby police car waved his arm to attract attention. 'Excuse me, sir, an urgent message.'

The Chief Constable strode to the car and spent several minutes in a hushed conversation, then putting on headphones turned his back while he listened.

Relinquishing the headset, he spun and grim faced strode straight to Andrea.

93

'We have received a short message from Martin.'

'What? How?' She covered her mouth with her hand, eyes wide as hope bubbled up inside her. He must still be alive. Can I listen to the message?' Andrea waited impatiently while the radio operator twiddled knobs and pressed buttons.

Suddenly a voice crackled from the speaker, loud, garbled and short, 'Davison, Davison, alone as usual.'

'Yes,' her voice trembled, 'that's Martin, it's his voice.'

'Davison, Davison, alone as usual' she repeated the short message almost to herself.

'What does that mean?' asked the Chief Constable scanning Andrea's face with a puzzled expression.

'I don't know,' she murmured as her thoughts whirled, 'but he is alive.'

'He's rambling, it makes no sense,' said the Chief Constable.

Alexander's mobile rang, no one took any notice, but he went up to Gerald, 'Father, there is an emergency at the church, it's one of my parishioners and I need to return.' Everyone agreed that a return to base had become essential.

As they arrived back at the barracks, the Chief Constable said to Andrea, 'Please wait in the house, the team are doing everything possible to find him, there is not a police officer in the constabulary who hasn't come into work to help.'

'Please help,' she clutched at the sleeve of Calum's jacket, 'I'll wait in the house for any news.'

'Are you sure?'

'Yes, it is better you help in the incident room, you understand him so well. Can I ask one question, Chief Constable?'

'Yes?'

'Where did Martin's call come from?'

'From a mobile phone in Malin Bridge.'

'Thank you.'

Fatigue and tiredness vanished replaced by determination for the ordeal ahead. Concealing her inner thoughts she yawned and looked away.

The Chief constable patted her on the shoulder in encouragement, 'We are swarming the area and will visit the Kennedys.' Andrea nodded absentmindedly as her thoughts raced. Then she turned away and disappeared inside the house.

A woman soldier came from the kitchen. 'I wanted to speak with Martha,' said Andrea.

'I'm afraid she has been feeling unwell today and has gone to bed to rest, with instructions not to disturb her.'

'Thanks,' she murmured, trying to suppress the smile that hovered on her lips.

'I'm finishing duty, but I can prepare any request you may have.'

Andrea shook her head and looked away attempting to appear disinterested, but she waited until the soldier had closed the front door then checked her watch. Seven-thirty. 'I've an hour, I'd better not delay in case anything goes wrong.' It would be dangerous but she had to do it.

Martha's malaise was a stroke of good fortune as she would have hindered the plan that had formed in Andrea's head. She hoped luck would be on her side and crept through to the kitchen and sneaked out to the garage which contained Martha's car, then she returned to the house and after a short search found what she wanted. She listened for noises in the house, but only distant sounds came from the briefing room in the stable block. One last item would complete her planning and she located it in a cupboard.

94

Andrea put on Martha's wide-brimmed summer hat and her jacket, took the keys from behind the cupboard door and calmly walked to the garage.

Jumping into the car and with shaking fingers she inserted the key into the ignition. Holding her breath, she twisted the key and the engine spluttered into life. With a surreptitious glance around she put the car into gear and drove across the barracks. She gripped the steering wheel with fierce determination willing herself to remain calm and focused.

The gatehouse could be a problem, she held her breath, but the barrier rose and she drove out unchallenged. The guard outside gave a friendly wave. She turned towards Owler Bar along the busy road. Martin's voice and the word Davison echoed in her mind. Overcast skies turned everything dreary and cold but she sweated and pressed on with grim determination towards her destination. When would they miss her? She kept glancing in the mirror but there was no sign of police or army vehicles.

Every muscle in her body was rigid with tension as she drove towards Monsal Head, not her destination but she wanted to check if she had been followed. A police car came the opposite way and she pulled the hat down a little to shield her face but they showed no interest in her. When she arrived at Monsal Head, she stopped the car. She rubbed her damp palms down her jeans and momentarily leaned back in the seat to organise her thoughts.

Her mind raced, the sequence of events made sense, but she needed a final confirmation. An idea struck her and she flipped open her mobile and rang the Bishop. The call lasted less than a minute and told her all she wanted to know. She took a deep breath and with trembling fingers pushed Calum's number.

'Yes, I'm tied up with the Commander, can it wait?'

Andrea gripped the phone knowing he would be angry, 'I'm not in the barracks.'

'What! Where the bloody hell are you?'

Andrea snapped, 'Listen, please.'

'The message did make sense, didn't it? His enraged voice bellowed down the phone. 'You've gone to meet him.'

Andrea interrupted his tirade, 'Calum! Please listen.' The short silence at the other end gave her the chance. She attempted to calm her agitated voice, 'I will meet Martin, but I need your help.'

'What is it?' he snapped with undisguised fury.

'I want you to arrest Alexander and Margaret,' her voice rose, full of confidence as she spoke the words.

'Why! I must have a reason.'

She didn't take any notice of the interruption, 'For the murder of Charlotte, the murder of Edward and the kidnapping of Martin. Also, they committed the armed robbery with the Kennedy twins.'

Before Calum could speak, Andrea pressed the button to end the call. Flopping back in the seat she trusted that Calum would follow her instructions. Excited but scared, she hoped and prayed she could reach Martin, 'He must talk to me and he must listen to me,' she said out loud.

Placing the car into gear, she drove towards the meeting place but after checking her watch for what seemed like the hundredth time, she calculated she would arrive too early. Should she go home and wait there? It would remove the car from the road and would anybody guess she would leave the barracks to return to her house? Her mind shivered at her thought of her home as it held the bad memories of Martin's attack. She couldn't face it. No, she would arrive early and hide the car from view.

What reaction would the investigating team have? They would all have advised against being alone with him, but it held her only chance. Martin was a clever man and experienced at setting traps to catch people. They know I have left the barracks, but they won't be able to find me. Calum realised the message from Martin had made sense. But he won't be able to interpret it. Davison only meant something to her and Martin.

She drove past the track that led to her house, anxiety made her stomach lurch, but she needed to remain calm and focused. Gripping the steering wheel with determination she drove on. The tourists caused the drive through Castleton to be slow, but she turned towards Market Square and then took the empty Pindale road, sped up through the woods and drove past the place where Martin wanted to meet.

She had met him there so many times when they were dating, a bench in memory of someone from the Davison family, their meeting had always been at eight-thirty. She drove up a track on the right and parked the car out of sight. No one else would know they would meet there so she wouldn't wait in the car in case he arrived early. She walked back down the road to the meeting place and sat on the bench which overlooked Castleton and the Hope Valley. A wave of nostalgia flowed through her as she remembered the times she'd sat there with Martin. The valley stretched out before her and the sweeping distant hills painted an idyllic picture.

It would be easy to spot blue flashing lights, but only normal traffic flowed along the road through the valley. She wrung her hands together, another twenty minutes to wait. Tension gripped her like an icy claw making her shiver. To distract herself, she focused on the light from the setting sun over Mam Tor as it lit the valley, painting the sky in swirling shades of pink and lilac. She looked towards her house on the track near Losehill Hall, she yearned to go home and shut this terrifying world away.

Glancing at her watch, fifteen minutes until the crucial meeting. A distant rumbling of machinery came from the quarry, but the countryside near her was quiet. The noise of a siren filled the air making her jump, but it came from the quarry buildings. They often sounded a siren to clear an area. The noise lasted for a few minutes, she breathed a sigh of relief and sat back on the bench. She sweated and her stomach turned. Please come Martin, please come, she repeated the words like a mantra.

95

An explosion reverberated around the valley, but it hadn't come from the quarry. A blinding flash, then thick dark smoke billowed into the sky, swirling outwards, her hands flew to her mouth as a silent scream emerged. 'My God, our house has exploded! Did they think I might be there?' Panic gripped her. She moved to the edge of the grass for a better view. A high-pitched whine then the bench split apart, she screamed and dived flat on the floor.

Someone had tried to shoot her. Adrenaline heightened her senses. She lay still, hardly daring to breathe, straining to hear. Listening for the slightest indication that her attacker closed in. There were no footsteps. No rustling through the nearby bushes. Not Martin, surely not Martin. Oh my God, he's the only one who knows she would be coming here. He's trying to kill me. She moved to gain a view of her surroundings, but another whine came and the bullet hit a rock near her head.

She scrambled through the long grass in between rocks but couldn't escape as there was insufficient cover to shield her. Her whole body trembled, why would Martin want to kill her? She could see through the grass to a car approaching across the moor road. Andrea moved to behind the rocks. Another bullet whined and hit the rocks. She tried to flatten but a near impossible task, then another shot came but no whine and no impact.

A car pulled up about fifty metres away. Calum. She shouted for all her worth. 'Get down, rifle fire. Get down.'

He heard and skipped behind his car, 'I'm coming to you,' he shouted. Andrea lost sight of him as he disappeared behind the bushes on the other side of the road. 'Keep down, I can't see them,' he yelled. There was a short delay, 'I'm coming over.' With that he rushed from behind the bush, took two large steps and dived for cover behind the rocks. He yelped in pain as he landed on the side of his injured leg.

The whine of the bullet came and smashed into a fence post near Calum. Andrea couldn't see him. 'Are you hit?'

'No,' he said, as he slid through the long grass and came alongside her.

'Is it Martin? ' he whispered.

'I don't know.'

One further shot came, but no whine and no impact. 'What do we do now?' pleaded Andrea.

'The rest are on their way, fortunately someone in the incident room made the link and I left straightaway. We'll stay here until they arrive. Don't move.'

Andrea went cold, as icy fear coursed its way through her whole body, she whispered, 'I can hear footsteps.'

'Yes, he has come to finish us off.'

Andrea swallowed. 'Leave Martin to me.'

'No way, you talk, I'll rush him.'

A voice near to them shattered the silence, much closer than she thought. 'You can stand, the shooting has finished.' The voice flat and expressionless. 'That's not Martin's voice, it's Gerald's,' said Andrea.

'I'll rush him,' said Calum.

Andrea's mind raced and rapidly came to a conclusion reached out and grabbed his arm, 'No, don't.' She raised her head, Gerald sat on a rock nearby, his grey face stared at her. He seemed to have aged at least ten years since she'd last seen him earlier in the day, a rifle lay on the ground at his side and his officer's pistol rested in its holster.

'No further shooting,' he repeated in a flat monotone voice.

Andrea went to stand.

Calum grabbed her arm, 'No, no! What are you doing?'

She moved away from him, 'You can stand up Calum, there is no danger from Gerald.' The man looked ashen.

'Sir, give me the guns please.'

'Calum, it's not Gerald, he is no danger to us.'

'What do you mean, he's fully armed, the shots?'

Andrea looked around for Martin, but she couldn't see him.

'You are safe, Inspector,' said Gerald.

'Be careful, Andrea,' said Calum.

'We are safe aren't we, Gerald?'

'Yes, they are both dead, they were traitors, so it had to be done,' his eyes filled with tears.

'Who's dead?' said Calum.

'One in the tall pine trees and the other behind the large limestone boulders,' said Gerald pointing. Andrea realised the valley had become a mass of sound. Police, ambulance and fire service sirens. The blue flashing lights merged with the red setting sun.

96

A noise came from the woods as Martin rushed towards them carrying a gun.

'Martin, Martin, darling.' Her delight at seeing him vanished as she looked at his eyes, they were black. 'Martin, you must listen.' He stopped and his eyes narrowed, his grey unshaven face full of hostility. He stared at her with contempt. 'It's the drugs, let me help you. Please, my darling let me help you.'

He opened his mouth and a full-throated scream ripped through the air like a wounded animal. She reached out her hand, but he stepped back and raised the gun towards her with a jerk. His hand shook and his knuckles turned white as he clenched the handgun. 'I said only you, only you,' his voice rose to a shriek as his expression hardened.

'Martin,' she stuttered, trying to find a smile, 'no one here will hurt you, everyone wants to help.'

'I said only you,' he shouted at the top of his voice

'Let me help you,' she put out a hand towards him. Terror filled his face. He moved in agitation shifting his weight from one foot to the other. He raised the gun, pointing it at her head.

'I will be hanged, they will hang me!' screamed Martin. His coal-black eyes fixed on her face while sweat beaded his forehead. Andrea didn't know how close the police marksmen would be. Martin still pointed the gun at her. 'I killed Charlotte, they will hang me.'

'Martin listen, you didn't kill Charlotte.'

'They will hang me.' His voice became quieter. She hoped to persuade him before the marksmen settled into place and received orders to shoot but the black eyes made it difficult. When they were like this, he wouldn't listen to reason, but she needed a way into his mind. Gerald stood at her side. Calum behind her and to one side. Gerald moved, Martin waved the gun at them. 'I killed Charlotte,' he wailed.

'Martin, it wasn't you, Alexander killed Charlotte. You have been his prisoner. Margaret has been giving you drugs.'

'You are evil, you are lying, God has told me,' he shouted again.

'Let me help you, you trust your wife, don't you?'

'You are evil,' shrieked Martin back to her. The black eyes glittered.

'I will help you, but you must give me the gun.' Calum moved a little. Martin waved the gun. She took one step forward, 'Give me the gun darling.'

His finger moved on the trigger, 'No, Martin!' The gun flashed and a searing pain shot through her. She looked at the blood as it poured down her front. She lurched to one side from the impact as he fired again.

Calum grabbed his leg and gasped, 'Martin.'

The gun was pointed at her, his finger moved again but it disappeared as Gerald's body came across and pushed her to the ground. As she collapsed she heard two shots. Martin fell to the floor. And Gerald slumped on top of her. A policeman's face came through Andrea's haze, 'Help Martin,' she whispered and then it went black.

97

The Bishop stood in silence, eyes closed as the sunshine sparkled on his ceremonial robes and the sweat dribbled down his forehead on the hot August day. The horses shuffling their hooves on the gravel broke the silence of the cemetery where the mourners and the crowds remained silent. The Chief Constable and General flanked the Bishop, who opened his eyes and made the sign of the cross. His eyes moved around the mourners crowded in front of him and he allowed his tongue to moisten his dry lips.

The Bishop's eyes stopped on one mourner, his smooth voice uttered, 'Mrs Cain,' then closed his eyes with a prayer. Andrea became the focus of attention and stood to her full height, with the satin of her black trousers rippling in the summer breeze. A rigid sling on her bandaged shoulder dominated the white sleeveless blouse. Glancing at the Bishop from under her black, wide-brimmed straw hat she squeezed Calum's hand who sat in a wheelchair next to her.

The Chief Constable offered his arm, but with a shake of her head, she took small wary steps forward. Silence filled the air as she scooped a handful of soil, stepped to the centre of the graveside, and closed her eyes to say her favourite childhood prayer. She went to speak, but the tears welled up and her throat gagged with emotion. She took a deep breath, in a low shaking voice, 'Martin, you poor man, you never knew the truth, I can only remember our wonderful life together before the evil people wrenched you away from me. Goodbye my love.' The soil slipped through her fingers on to the coffin.

Andrea scooped more soil and moved to the next grave, she looked skyward and closed her eyes to control her emotions. Andrea eyes scanned down to the grave where two coffins lay. 'Charlotte, my dear friend, you lost your life too early to mindless violence and evil, I will never forget you.' With downcast eyes she dropped soil across Charlotte's coffin and moved around the grave to the second coffin.

She picked up a third handful of soil, 'Gerald, you were such a brave man, the pain you must have suffered when you realised what had happened. You wished to be united with Charlotte, Andrea hung her head, her voice trembled, 'Gerald, my hero, you will both be blessed and united in heaven.'

She dropped the soil onto the regimental flag that draped his coffin then stood in silence staring across the churchyard. The warm breeze wafted across her. After a deep breath, she straightened her shoulders and, with her head held high she returned to her position next to Calum.

The crunch of heavy boots on the gravel broke through the silence. The graveside mourners stood on three sides of the graves, the fourth side remained vacant. Other graves and then grass stretched up the hill in the cemetery. The marching footsteps passed behind the mourners.

A woman police constable became the first to march into the gap, she was followed by four other constables, a sergeant and an inspector in full police uniform. Andrea smiled at the young policewoman. The bruise on her face, where Martin had assaulted her, remained visible. When she had learned of Martin's death and its cause, she volunteered to be in the police Guard of Honour.

The seven police officers filed along the side of Martin's grave. They turned and came to attention with their backs towards the hillside. Andrea's eyes were drawn up the cemetery to seven soldiers in blue ceremonial uniforms. A Regimental Sergeant stood apart from them. He saluted. Andrea heard no commands, but the soldiers raised rifles to their shoulders.

The police Guard of Honour, the Chief Constable and the General saluted. Following the order, three volleys of seven rifle shots echoed across the silent cemetery. The soldiers shouldered arms. The heavy marching of two soldiers filled the breeze as they passed the mourners and faced the graves.

A soldier brought a bugle to his lips. Andrea closed her eyes and bowed her head as the distinctive mournful notes of "The Last Post" reverberated across the churchyard. As the melancholy sound drifted away silence fell. The bugler stood to attention, the Regimental Pipe Major played the "Flowers of the Forest" lament. The sound of the bagpipes flowed over her as salty tears gushed onto her cheeks. As the last notes floated away, she stood collecting her thoughts and composing herself.

Andrea opened her eyes, gazing across the hillside with a faraway expression. Martin had achieved peace.

The Bishop intoned the closing prayer. He let the silence fall, nobody moved. The Bishop lifted his bowed head, 'Mrs Cain, at the General and the Chief Constable's request will you lead the mourners.'

'Be at peace my darling,' she said on leaving Martin's grave. With the Chief Constable on one side and the General on the other she passed through the Police Guard of Honour lining the cemetery path. The officers saluted their most senior officer as he walked at Andrea's side. Andrea choked with emotion at this last show of respect from Martin's colleagues. The Regimental Sergeant Major issued his orders to the soldiers lining the last part of the route from the cemetery. The soldiers saluted their General.

Life without Martin would be onerous but she brushed the thoughts away as he would expect her to do her duty to those that had supported her. She looked up the Rivelin Valley at the soldiers and police officers who had formed the funeral procession, they had been joined by those coming from the cemetery. Andrea said to the General and Chief Constable, 'Gentlemen, I do not wish to interfere with your formalities but I wish to thank the soldiers and police officers.'

'Regimental Sergeant Major, Chief Inspector,' said the General with a nod from the Chief Constable. They marched over and saluted, 'Mrs Cain would like to thank members of the regiment and constabulary.'

'Do you wish them to stand easy, ma'am?'

'Yes, please, Sergeant Major.' The orders were issued and Andrea walked through the ranks and talked to the soldiers and police. Approaching the young policewoman with the black eye, 'Thank you so much for your loyalty to Martin.'

'An honour, ma'am, for a brave police officer killed performing his duty.' She returned to the main group, and stooped down to talk to Calum, 'Are you okay,' her voice was soft and full of concern, 'Do not inflict more pain on yourself by staying here.'

A warm smile twitched at his lips and he touched her hand, 'I have every intention of seeing it to the end.' Andrea squeezed his shoulder in appreciation and lifted her head to look down the road towards Malin Bridge. The pavements were lined with a mass of flowers. The number of personal and public tributes could not fit into the cemetery. Beyond the flowers were the crowds. They had lined the cortège route and were still there. A few policemen lined the route. The service had been relayed into the centre of Malin Bridge. The crowd remained quiet as would be expected but showed no sign of leaving.

Calum rubbed his chin and gave her a fixed stare, 'You are going to speak to people in the crowd, aren't you?'

'Yes.'

The Chief Constable overheard, 'Are you feeling well enough? You mustn't overstrain yourself.'

'Many people in the crowd didn't know Martin, Charlotte or Gerald but they have turned out to recognise their bravery. I cannot thank them all, but I can speak with many. Some will be Charlotte's fans and former members of both the police and regiment who knew Gerald and Martin.'

'I can see you are resolved on the matter,' Calum

said.

'Andrea is right,' said the General. 'May we join you?'

'Of course, you may,' and she turned to Calum, 'I'd like it if you could make it too.' He bit his lip. He didn't want to do it. 'Please Calum,' she implored.

He gave a defeated sigh, 'Yes, okay.'

Andrea walked past the flowers, stopping and examining them. Some of the press shouted to her but she took her time. Her legs felt weak and her shoulder hurt, but she had a duty. Martin would have expected it. The press were behind barriers further along the road. They shouted questions to her and the others with her.

'Hey guys, slow down, I'm not feeling too good.' With the General at her side, she walked to them. Calum had reached the end of the flowers.

'May we speak to Inspector Brodie?'

Andrea called to Calum, 'They want to talk to you.' Andrea gave herself a short smile. Astonishment came across his face as the young woman police officer guided his wheelchair to the front of the press corps. The look of disbelief increased as the press gave him a round of applause.

'Thank you.'

The police had issued a press release about the death of Martin and Gerald. Calum's role in attempting to save Andrea had been stated.

'How are your injuries, sir?'

'I've been lucky there is no permanent damage.'

'How does it feel to be a national hero?' Andrea guessed that question would come so she put her hand on his shoulder to reassure him. He took a deep breath.

‘There are only two heroes. They are Martin Cain and Gerald Manning, I acted as any officer would.’

One of the photographers asked, ‘Can I get over the barrier for a picture of Inspector Brodie?’ The Chief Constable nodded and the photographers took the picture of Calum in his wheelchair with Andrea, the Chief Constable and the General behind him. Andrea wondered what Calum’s reaction would be when he found himself on the front of the national daily newspapers.

Andrea then went to the crowd standing along the tree lined road. The large beech trees formed a tunnel where their branches met overhead. The afternoon sunshine filtered through making shifting patterns of light and dark. She heard a retired police officer talking about Martin to the Chief Constable, and an ex-soldier chatting to the General about serving under Gerald. She felt hot and her shoulder had become uncomfortable. The big crowd had spilled around the corner towards Hillsborough and stretched past the Kennedy Car Hire business, which had closed.

Andrea remained determined to perform the duty Martin would have expected.

98

Someone screamed. Out of the corner of her eye a policeman moved suddenly. Two men had barged their way through the crowd and blocked her path.

Two guns pointed at her. More women screamed as the crowd saw the guns. Andrea glanced at the young special constable who had been knocked to the ground, he appeared ready to rush the gunmen.

'Stay there,' shouted Andrea, 'nobody move.' Weakness washed over her, she struggled to keep focused as her head spun. The two men waved their guns.

A megaphone voice boomed, 'Armed Police. Lay down your guns.' An uneasy silence hung in the air as though the assembled crowds were holding their breaths.

Andrea shouted in as strong a voice as she could manage despite the fear that clogged her throat, 'Please no shootings,' she begged, 'let me speak to them.' The young special constable remained sitting on the ground, his eyes wide, he sat motionless. Even without moving her head she could see three armed officers with guns aimed towards the two gunmen. Andrea weakened. Fear prickled her scalp. In a slow and precise movement, she removed her large brimmed black straw hat and let it fall to the ground as the two men needed to see her face.

Andrea staggered on her high heels but regained her balance and her senses. The Chief Constable, a few metres behind, with a deep and resonant voice, 'Let me come and support her, can't you see she is weak. I am not armed,' he held out his hands palms facing towards them.

'Please,' she directed her plea at the main gunman who acknowledged the request with an imperceptible nod. He hissed through clenched teeth as he gestured with a slight flick of his gun, 'Slowly.' Andrea heard movement behind her as the Chief Constable edged forward and caught her arm. The reassurance of the powerful support helped to steady her both physically and mentally. The crowd shuffled. Some were creeping away while others remained rooted to the spot watching the alarming scene unfold. She blocked out distractions and stared at the gunman.

The megaphone voice boomed again, 'Armed police, lay down your guns.'

Without moving her eyes away from the main gunman's face, she implored, 'Please tell them not to shoot, Chief Constable.'

His shout pierced the thick edgy silence, 'Hold your fire, let Andrea speak to them first.' Tension sent an icy chill through her body, but she willed herself to remain calm as her eyes flicked across the two angry faces.

'John, Mark. Listen to me.'

Their expressions hardened, 'Ma's in jail and it's all your fault,' growled John.

She searched for the right words to diffuse the situation, 'Neither of you have done anything wrong,' her voice cracked with emotion as she spoke.

'Our twin brothers are both dead,' Mark snarled back as the gun shook alarmingly in his hand. Andrea hadn't realised the other twin had died from his injuries. Mark raged, 'Father Manning always helped us, but he's dead. That's your fault.' Both pairs of eyes locked onto her face. The brothers' agitation and anger bubbled visibly, their faces red, nostrils flaring they narrowed their eyes. They moved from foot to foot waving their guns. Andrea stared searchingly at the two men. The police marksmen wouldn't wait much longer. A voice inside her head muttered, keep talking.

'Lay down your guns, we want no one hurt,' implored the Chief Constable. The crowd were gradually being edged away from the danger zone. Keep talking the voice in her head repeated.

'John, listen to me.'

He looked around as though becoming aware of movement and he waved his gun, 'Keep still everyone or I'll shoot.' Everyone froze. The thick silence hovered over them.

'John look at me. I'm not an evil woman, let me help you, I help people.' The words spilled out of her in a desperate bid to keep talking. He waved the gun, someone in the crowd screamed. 'Look at me,' she commanded with a ferocity she didn't know she had. He jerked his head towards her. She'd captured his attention, so hope remained, 'John, you are now the head of the Kennedy family. The family will look to you for decisions, advice and leadership.' Then she repeated, 'You are the head of the family, that means you must look after them.' A flicker of recognition crossed his face, he blinked and gave her a challenging stare.

Picking up the direction of Andrea's words, the Chief Constable asked, 'Have you a big family to look after John?'

'Think of your cousins.' He waved the gun as he screwed up his face with a mixture of confusion and pride. The gun in his hand drooped as his grip relaxed. 'Let me help you, John.'

'Stand still,' he shouted as he tightened his grip on the gun once more and his eyes flashed with aggression. The two guns still pointed at her and the tension made her stomach clench. The voice in her head shrieked, keep talking, stay calm.

'John, I spoke to your cousin Mary, I had a long chat with her not long ago, she told me about your family, you must remember her. Mary O'Donnell, you do remember her, don't you?' Mark looked at his brother as though waiting to see his reaction.

'She went away,' John's voice stayed flat. Both guns remained trained on her.

'I know she did, she went to Australia.' The shadowy trees moved in the breeze. Sunlight flickered. The armed officers would be in a position for a clear shot. Andrea willed herself to remain focused. 'She went to Australia, do you remember her?' she gulped in a breath and leaned more heavily on the Chief Constable.

'Do you remember cousin Mary, Mark?' He nodded. Somewhere in the distance a car door slammed. 'I spoke to Mary last week.' John waved his gun. And his brother copied him.

'Bullshit!' he snarled 'You are lying. You don't know Mary.' He pointed the gun straight at her as an arrogant sneer crept over his face. She froze with terror as her gaze focused on the gun, and she held her breath, while her insides rolled and salty tears escaped from her eyes. Her pent up breath escaped in a long silent sigh.

When she spoke, her voice quivered with tension. 'Mary told me about her sister, Caitlin.' John kept the gun pointing directly at her, his cold eyes stared but a flicker of recognition came from the dark depths. 'Do you remember Father Manning when he was a soldier before becoming a priest.' He didn't respond and his face hardened and his jaw clenched. She took a deep breath, 'Caitlin was Father Manning's girlfriend when he was a soldier. Wasn't he? Mary told me that.'

His eyes widened, 'Ma said that's a secret,' he looked at his gun as confusion washed across his sweaty face and he staggered.

The Chief Constable pleaded, 'Let Andrea help you, she talked to Mary.' John had wavered, Andrea could tell.

'I spoke to her and she said she wanted to speak to Johnnie, no one else calls you Johnnie, do they?' She waited for the information to sink in. The gun wobbled alarmingly. Sweat beaded his forehead glistening in the sunlight which filtered through the trees. Gradually the recognition came across his face and his bewildered gaze searched Andrea's face, his mouth opened as though he wanted to speak but no words emerged.

A faint hope arose that talking about Mary would be a way through this nightmare. With a deep breath and a calm voice she pressed on. 'Mary wants to speak to you, John, it would be good to talk to her again wouldn't it? You liked her, didn't you John?' she told me about the fun you had when you were kids.

He nodded as his Adam's apple bobbed in his throat as he gulped. 'Let me help you, I will give you Mary's telephone number.' The hand holding the gun trembled and he glanced at his brother.

'You are the head of the family, you must look after Mary,' her words hung in the silent air. Nothing moved, the crowds had melted away. 'You want to look after Mary and the rest of the family, don't you John?' He nodded. She stared at the gun still pointing towards her head as he shifted from one foot to the other. 'Give me the gun then, let's make the call to Mary.'

Andrea with a slow movement held out her hand, 'Give me the gun, John, you're the head of the family. Make the right decision.' He walked toward her with the gun still pointed at her head. Andrea heard the police marksman ready their weapons which brought a flash of recognition in John's eyes. He stopped and she held her breath, but he took another step towards her. Her insides screwed into knots as his narrowed eyes bored into her. The silence stretched as his gaze wandered across her face. Tears blurred her vision.

With a deep shuddering breath, he lowered the gun until it hung limply at his side. With a look of weariness, he placed the gun into her outstretched hand. The weapon glinted in the afternoon sunlight, her fingers closed over the warm metal. Andrea felt the Chief Constable tense on her arm, she handed the gun to him.

John stood motionless, head bowed, shoulders rounded, staring at the ground. The silence lengthened. Mark took a few hesitant steps forward. His gun still pointing towards her. Once again, she held out her hand, 'Give me your gun, Mark,'

'I'm not sure,' his eyes narrowed with disdain and he sneered at her, 'she put Ma in jail. Father Manning died because of her interference.'

Andrea glanced towards John, 'You are the head of the family. You must decide.'

John swung round to face his brother, 'Give me the gun, hand it over Mark. I'm the head of the family, I decide.' There was a long moment of silence as uncertainty moved across Mark's face and his grip on the gun tightened. Andrea closed her eyes. Please, please no more bloodshed.

'Give me the gun,' John demanded as he stretched out his hand towards his younger brother. As though moving in slow motion Mark allowed his arm to relax downwards and he handed the gun to his brother. Mark sank to his knees and put his head in his hands. With an empty stare John handed the gun to Andrea. As soon as it was in her hand, she wrapped her fingers around it and snatched it away. Bewilderment swept across his face. With slumped shoulders he stared at his younger brother still crouched on the ground.

As though from nowhere they were overwhelmed by police.

99

'The soldiers appreciated you taking time to drop into the regimental wake and for the kind words you said about Gerald and the regiment.'

Martha took Andrea by the arm, 'Please sit, the funeral would have been difficult to bear but after the confrontation with the gunmen, you must be exhausted.'

Andrea looked back over her shoulder at Calum being pushed along in his wheelchair, 'I'm more concerned for Calum, his injury is much worse. How are you coping?' she asked as she stood at the side of his wheelchair with her hand resting on his shoulder.

'Like you, I'm tired but today has been important.' The General followed his guests and stood in front of the empty fireplace. While he waited for his guests to settle a thoughtful frown covered his face drawing his eyebrows together. 'I'm still unclear on the role of John Montague's son and why he changed his name to Edward Stonehouse.' His voice was laced with confusion.

He looked at the Chief Constable who with raised eyebrows and the slightest shake of his head said, 'I'm not clear about some aspects but we've been following through Andrea's information.'

'Any success?' said Andrea. Martha interrupted the conversation by ushering them towards seats and fussed over Andrea ensuring she was comfortable on the large sofa and placed herself next to her. Andrea found her presence calming and comforting.

The Chief Constable picked up the thread of the conversation once everyone had settled, 'The success of the investigation has moved forward and even at this early stage your suggestions have been proven.'

'One day I wish to understand the events,' the General said.

He glanced questioningly at Calum, who responded with a small smirk and wide eyes, 'Please don't look at me, the only one who knows is Andrea, I take my hat off to her, we both looked at the same evidence and she worked it out, I didn't.' He gave an exaggerated sigh and looked up at the ceiling, 'I still don't know how it fits together.'

Andrea smiled to herself at the compliment from Calum and made herself comfortable on the couch. 'The cup of tea has revived me and I'm relaxed and happy to explain.'

'Excellent,' the General changed his position to a chair and sat upright, with an alert expression on his face, 'How does someone who is a good soldier and then a priest turn out to be a killer?'

Andrea looked around the assembled group before beginning. All eyes were fixed on her awaiting her explanation.

100

'The important relationship is the one between Ma Kennedy and Alexander Manning, they were friends, but she exerted a strong and manipulative influence over him. For a small diminutive woman, she possessed amazing powers to achieve what she wanted. When I first spoke to her at the garage I was fooled by her friendly manner. Her control set off a chain of events which were stoked to higher and higher levels of determination and violence.'

Andrea pursed her lips and ran her fingers through her hair, her shoulder ached although the sling gave it support. 'All that Alexander told us about Ireland turned out to be true, but he withheld the crucial bits.'

The General leaned forward, arms resting on his knees and his hands clasped together. 'Cousin Mary? You mentioned her name to influence John and Mark to surrender their weapons, didn't you?'

Andrea paused mulling over the details that needed to be explained. 'It's confusing, let's go back to the beginning, some bits I'm guessing but they could be confirmed without difficulty. Picture the scene in Belfast. Ma owns a car hire business and has four sons but no husband and a sister who has two daughters, Caitlin and Mary. They lived as one big family, the two women and the six children together behind the business,' she gave a small laugh, 'must have been a lively household.'

The General asked, 'Do you think Ma Kennedy was part of the republican movement at the time?'

She nodded, 'It would be worth checking whether her husband did leave her or…'she hesitated.

'Or what?' interrupted Calum. Andrea ignored his eagerness, she would continue the explanation at her own pace taking time to divulge her information.

'As the Chief Constable has now found out Ma Kennedy was a quarter-master responsible for buying and supplying arms. Did something happen to her husband in one of the far-flung places like Colombia when trying to obtain guns for the cause? I'm sure there's a story there somewhere as nobody ever mentions him.'

'I'll check,' said the Chief Constable. All eyes focused on her waiting for the next part of the story.

'So, along came a soldier called Alexander Manning to hire a car and he took a fancy to Caitlin and dated her. Ma and her sister must have allowed this to happen. The question has to be why?'

'Against army practice,' said the General.

'Alexander as an intelligence officer in Belfast would know about suspicions concerning the family.'

The Chief Constable shifted in his chair, 'Do you think he altered or disposed of any information as soldiers weren't encouraged to go out with locals?'

'It's difficult to know,' she rubbed the back of her neck and gave a doubtful shake of her head. 'Once he fell in love with Caitlin, then she became his sole motivation and the Army took second place in his life while previously he had been committed to a life as a soldier. It appears he planned to leave the army and marry her but until that time Ma had a spy in the British Army. Given her position in the Republican movement she would have wanted to use that association to her advantage.'

'He wouldn't have told her anything, would he?'

Andrea paused, her eyes looked away as she thought through the most appropriate response to the question. 'I met Ma, she appears genuine and plausible, but she is also clever.' The image of the short wiry woman with determined grey eyes filled her mind. 'She appeared a friendly woman who loves a cup of tea and a chat and would have made a fuss of Alexander as he dated her niece.'

'You have spoken to Mary, haven't you?' Calum gave her an incredulous stare.

'The background information about the family in Ireland came from her.'

'So you weren't bluffing when you told John.'

Andrea smiled at his surprise. 'If you remember Calum, we sat and looked through the confirmation report of Alexander's time in Ireland.' He nodded. 'In the details I came across Mary's name and it set me thinking. Caitlin died at the hands of the security forces, Mary survived.'

'But you didn't have time to track her down,' he slapped the flat of his hand on the arm of the wheelchair in frustration.

She laughed at his exasperation, 'You're right I didn't have time to do it, but my agent's office helped as they have ways of finding information about celebrities that are not public knowledge. It didn't take them long to trace a normal individual like Mary who hadn't tried to hide away. They rang me while I attended the hospital with her number and I spoke to her from there.'

'She lives in Australia,' interrupted Calum, 'so is she relevant to this case?'

'Very relevant.'

'I'm losing it,' moaned Calum with a smile at the corners of his mouth and a twinkle in his eyes.

She laughed at his confusion, 'Caitlin, Mary and their mother were shot in an incident in Belfast between troops and the Republicans. They weren't involved, apart from being in the wrong place at the wrong time, Caitlin and her mother died and Mary was badly wounded.' She looked around at the faces and found it hard to believe she had deduced the link between the events and others hadn't.

'Mary became one key link back to the Kennedys and to Alexander and the life they lived in Belfast and only Mary knew the passion and the anguish caused by the death of Caitlin.' She smiled at the thought of the next part of the story. 'In true romantic fiction, the pretty patient marries the young surgeon who saved her life and that's exactly what happened many years ago in an Irish hospital.'

'In this case an Australian junior doctor travelling the world treated Mary after she had been shot, they fell in love and so Mary, wanting no more of the violence of Northern Ireland, went to Australia where she married him.'

Andrea took a deep breath. 'Are you all right?' asked Martha, 'you've turned pale.'

'Yes,' Andrea gulped and her chin trembled, 'the next part involves an incredible coincidence that led to Charlotte's murder,' her anguished eyes filled with compassion.

Calum winced as he wriggled around in his wheelchair trying to get comfortable.

Andrea waited until he was settled using the time to regain her composure, 'Just before Luigi's show at the Strines Manor, Charlotte had been in Perth, Australia, where Mary and her husband live. Charlotte performed at a charity dinner with invited guests only. Mary and her husband, now the Head of Surgery in Perth, were in the audience.'

'And they met?' the surprise in Calum's voice was evident.

'A huge coincidence,' Andrea gave a warm smile, 'charity dinners are not large and whoever is on the stage will circulate and talk to the guests at the tables. It's routine for those events and I've done it many times. When they met Charlotte, Mary asked about her surname. As you know, people just shake their head because there is no link, but in this case the connection soon became apparent, Charlotte's brother was Alexander.

If Caitlin had married Alexander, then Mary would have been his sister-in-law. Charlotte went back to their house that evening and they talked until the early hours.' Mary must have explained about Alexander's life in Belfast. There was silence while they all digested this last piece of information. All eyes were downcast. Andrea waited. One by one they resumed eye contact.

But before she had a chance to continue Calum asked, 'Did you know about the meeting before the investigation into Charlotte's murder?'

'Yes, Charlotte told me about her tour and the meeting with a relation of the Kennedy family. She'd been very excited about it although unfortunately she hadn't revealed any of the details about life in Belfast but I made no connection that it would be the crucial piece of information we needed.'

The General rubbed his chin in a contemplative gesture, 'Surely such a meeting was no threat to Alexander, and not enough to warrant murder.' Did it matter that Charlotte knew about his relationship with Caitlin and her subsequent death? I would have thought it would have helped their relationship as brother and sister.'

101

'To understand we need to examine the wider picture. We have to look how things had developed since the Northern Ireland days, in the lives of Ma Kennedy and Alexander.'

'Okay, but a man turned from the cloth to become a calculating and sadistic killer is difficult to believe,' the General sat back in his chair and gave a visible sigh.

'I believe part of the problem was the underlying attitude of the Manning family. They had high standards for themselves and for everybody they met. General, you mentioned Gerald set the highest standards which everyone usually failed to reach.'

'Yes.'

'Alexander had that same trait, but it showed itself differently. The killing of Caitlin is crucial. It became the turning point in this tragic tale that set subsequent actions spiraling out of control. Now remember the army didn't know he dated Caitlin, so Alexander mixed with the same soldiers who'd shot the love of his life. The woman he had wanted to marry.'

'Ah, I see,' said the General, 'Alexander could have encouraged them to talk as he was desperate for more information on the tragedy. In his grief stricken state he intended discovering who had pulled the trigger.' He paused, assessing the information, 'Did Alexander meet a soldier who didn't care about the killing?'

'Exactly,' Andrea rubbed a hand across her eyes and grimaced, 'or perhaps one admitted that it wasn't necessary to kill them but he made sure, as they must have been Republicans, we will never know for sure.'

The General said, 'I will investigate the circumstances.'

Andrea nodded her agreement, 'Alexander left the army and became distraught about losing his Caitlin. In his mind, she'd been murdered by a callous and indifferent soldier. A soldier who now had a name. His despair must have been enormous because Mary mentioned they feared he might kill himself. When people suffer pain and adversity, coupled with injustice, they will seek solace and many turn to religion. Alexander followed that route when he took holy orders, however, he inherited traits from his father and could never forget the injustice of Caitlin's death. Revenge gnawed away at him.'

'When he left the army, that couldn't have suited Ma Kennedy,' commented the Chief Constable. He'd been quiet for some time, but every time Andrea had glanced in his direction she could tell he was hanging on every word.

'No, she would have preferred him to stay in the army, but his disillusionment meant that he became ripe for enlistment into the Republican cause. And with Ma's persuasion I'm certain that's what happened.'

'What about Margaret Manning?' asked Calum, 'so far you haven't mentioned her.'

'A little sister devoted to her older brother, Alexander. She would have seen the pain he suffered and she would have been the only one who would hear the full truth. Although not in Ireland permanently she visited him on numerous occasions. She would have met Ma who would have befriended and manipulated her.'

'Did Ma draw them both deeper and deeper into the Republican cause?' asked the Chief Constable.

'Yes, Ma built on their sense of injustice as a way of leading them to her way of thinking. I suspect they were putty in her hands.'

Calum pursed his lips and his penetrating gaze studied her face, 'Margaret's marriage?'

Andrea nodded, 'I would guess it's linked to Northern Ireland but it will need the Chief Constable and the General to unearth the information.'

'What are we going to check?' queried the General.

'Which soldier killed Caitlin.'

The General nodded. 'No problem. That should be easy.'

Andrea gave a whisk of a smile, 'Then we could check the man's name that Margaret married. I'm guessing they will be the same person.'

'That seems ridiculous,' interrupted Calum, 'it makes no sense. Why would she marry someone who had killed her brother's fiancée?'

'That's where Ma Kennedy's influence comes in, I would guess she would have stoked the fires of injustice with them and made it her business to find the man as I'm certain that Alexander would have told Ma his name. No doubt she had other informants who could supply her with details of this soldier. I can see her saying it, "Look at the man who killed our Caitlin, he goes on to a good life and inherits a fortune with his own business and we are poor." As a result, Alexander and Margaret became part of Ma's cause. They'd been seduced by injustice.'

'Do you think Margaret killed her husband?' Calum queried with a searching look.

'I don't know, perhaps the original intention would only be financial, to take his money. When she explained about her marriage, she mentioned he'd committed suicide. Whether she was involved, we may never know.' Andrea shoulders dropped at the unhappiness that had been inflicted.

'I will ensure the whole matter is investigated,' said the Chief Constable in a firm voice.

Andrea forced herself away from the past and back to the present, 'Ma would have concocted a story of injustice around her twins and used that as a reason to leave Belfast. She would be encouraging Alexander and Margaret, by twisting and distorting the information to suit her own ends.'

'The ceasefire must have taken place?' added the General.

'Yes, but Ma didn't want it, she wanted to keep fighting, but she had no alternative and had to accept it. She became intent on forming a new breed of Irish Republicans and around that time she left Belfast and settled in Sheffield, Alexander's home town. She wanted her new group to be separate from the old Republicans but to build an arms stash she would need money, and Alexander and Margaret could be a great help.'

Calum arched a questioning eyebrow in her direction, 'Did Ma tell them the whole truth?'

A ghost of a smile crossed her lips as she contemplated his question 'No. She's a woman who manipulated the truth for her own ends and would have said the money was to launch a political young people's party, not for guns, but to solve the injustice in Ireland.'

'It explains one thing at least,' the Chief Constable grinned and let his eyes wander around the assembled group.

'What's that?'

'You asked for a report for the hospitals where Margaret worked.'

Andrea raised her eyebrows questioningly, 'What did it say?'

'Margaret's employment list was given to a bright spark in the computer pattern matching section at Scotland Yard, I never knew any police force even had one but he found a pattern of credit card frauds while people were in hospital. They were all elderly or suffering mental health problems, but the total amount was above £100,000. The thefts occurred sometime around the time Margaret left the hospital and they told me that such a coincidence would be impossible.' A stunned silence filled the room. Outside the marching of soldiers broke the silence.

Andrea broke into their thoughts, 'I don't know the reason for the urgency, but Ma told them they needed money quickly.'

'Told who?' challenged Calum with widening eyes. Andrea grinned to herself as she enjoyed being one step ahead of Calum.

'It would have been Alexander, Margaret and the twins, Matthew and Luke. You've met John and Mark, they cannot cope, but the twins were bright, lively and intelligent.'

Calum interrupted, 'I still don't understand. How could this woman have such control?' he shook his head in bewilderment.

'She manipulated everyone around her and so the four took desperate steps to obtain substantial amounts of money.'

'Alexander, Margaret and the twins carried out the armed robbery,' Andrea added and let out a long deep breath. Tiredness gripped her, but she had to stay focused and tell the end of the story.

'Incredible!' exclaimed the General.

'It has been confirmed,' added the Chief Constable, 'we have enough evidence from the photos and witness statements. When you match the descriptions they fit, but we also found bank bags and ties for the notes in Alexander's church vault.'

Calum rubbed his chin in puzzlement, 'But why take such a risk?'

'I guess a large cache of arms became available. She had to obtain the money quickly.'

Calum interrupted before she continued, 'But she couldn't tell them that.'

Andrea nodded her agreement, 'Ma's version to them would be something like this. The Irish government is likely to fail over the course of the next year and it will be the usual opposition who gets in. We need to rid Ireland of this two party politics and launch a young people's party that will remove the many injustices from the Irish people.'

'Yes, I see,' he nodded. There was a grave expression

on his face and his wheelchair creaked as he leant back and half closed his eyes.

'For Alexander, Margaret and the twins she left out the bit about arming her new young party.' Andrea with a quick glance at Calum added, 'the shooting of Luke and Matthew added to their sense of injustice. I think by that time they had a compulsive and blinkered view.'

'Their next step must have been to kill their sister?' the gravity of the Chief Constable's words cut through the air. An agonised silence descended on the assembled group.

102

With a stutter of emotion in her voice Andrea spoke first, 'Yes, they came to see Charlotte before the show and I think it was then she explained about meeting Mary in Australia. Naturally she expected Alexander to be pleased, but Margaret slapped her and they stormed away.'

'Did they speak to Ma?'

'Yes, she told them the whole cause would be broken, the monies lost and the robbery would be discovered. I'm sure she told them to do whatever was necessary, but she impressed upon them that Charlotte must not speak about the connections with Northern Ireland, and must be silenced.'

'So Alexander took it upon himself,' said the General.

'Yes,' Andrea's eyes narrowed, 'although I think he would have agreed it with Margaret.'

'I'm getting the full picture now,' said the Chief Constable, 'but they couldn't go on forever.'

A sorrowful sigh escaped Andrea's lips, 'They had a plan which is why I spoke to the Bishop a second time.' Calum's head jerked up.

'A second time,' he queried. 'When was that? How does he come into it?'

She responded to his questions with a small satisfied smile. 'After I left the barracks to meet with Martin, I rang the Bishop for confirmation of my thoughts before I called you. After the robbery Alexander went to see the Bishop to ask him if he could leave the parish and go abroad on missionary work. His sister would accompany him, it would be their insurance. And after the robbery it appeared they were not suspects.'

'Never even thought about them,' muttered the Chief Constable.

Andrea continued, 'But then they killed Charlotte and had to wait for the case to subside before they could go. After all, they couldn't leave early as it had been their sister who had been murdered. And so, they had to do the best they could to monitor the investigation and disrupt the case as much as possible, and as soon as the police enquiry became routine they could slip away. They wanted to find out about any progress as it would help their timing.'

'How did they do that?' queried the Chief Constable with a puzzled expression, 'the public can't find out the details of a police investigation.'

She pressed her lips together and hesitated before she spoke, 'They knew I would be involved and so they put a bug on my car, they would at least receive information after Calum joined me. Alexander's would be familiar with bugging devices from his military intelligence background.'

'Yes, he would,' agreed the General. Andrea took a deep breath. A cold shiver ran through her. All eyes focused on her.

'I'm okay,' her voice trembled, 'but I'm coming to Martin's involvement.' She scanned their anxious faces and gave a slight smile of reassurance, 'Shall I continue?'

'Yes,' answered Calum, 'if you're sure you can.' Concern flickered in his eyes and with a smile she waved a finger in his direction.

'You made me realise what had happened to Martin.' A look of disbelief crossed his face and his brow furrowed, but he didn't speak. 'When you were in a lot of pain, you lay on the bed,' Andrea reminded him.

'Yes,' he groaned at the memory, 'and I took the tablets.'

'Yes, in your case it eased the pain.' Andrea hesitated and glanced at the gold band on her finger her heart stuttered. 'It took me back to the night Martin attacked me.'

'Oh dear,' Martha patted her on the arm, 'you poor thing, this is so upsetting.'

Andrea blinked away the tears and lifted her chin in determination. Her voice faltered as she spoke, 'We were stressed and argued at the beginning of the evening, but then we calmed and talked. Martin's eyes held the key to his behaviour that evening. When we talked they were green, but he complained of a headache and took his pills. It wasn't long after that, he attacked me. When his behavior changed his eyes turned from green to black. When his eyes were black, he wouldn't listen to reason,' she shivered.

'Who would be able to change his pills,' queried Calum, he flapped his hand as annoyance filled his face, 'No don't answer that, It's so obvious now. Margaret.'

Sadness rolled inside her as she thought about poor Martin.

'Yes, if the man investigating the armed robbery became unwell he wouldn't think straight, so one time at the hospital she substituted pills of her own to ensure his mind became disorientated.'

'Good grief,' Calum puffed out his cheeks and gave a long slow whistle, 'I remember it. He came to visit me. Martin asked her for a tablet. Margaret told him off as he wasn't a patient. But a few minutes later gave him a small bottle of tablets.'

'Unfortunately for Martin, after the murder of Charlotte, she did the same and increased the strength of the tablets. I suspect that each time he went back to the hospital, either to visit Calum or to check on the injured twin she gave him more pills. When I went to the hospital to be checked, for my stomach pains, I spoke to a psychiatrist who confirmed that the symptoms I described in Martin could be drug induced.' She rubbed her forehead gently, 'As more things happened that they couldn't control, they had to take increasingly drastic actions and therefore more risks.'

'Had Edward become the next problem?' suggested Calum.

'Yes, although his actions are unclear. I suspect that one time when Edward talked to Alexander he explained about the precise details of money transfers at the bank. After all, he was a senior bank employee and liked to boast about his job. Anyway, telling a priest didn't matter, he wouldn't rob a bank.' She raised her eyebrows in amusement.

'But he did,' added Calum with a large grin.

Andrea glanced at the Chief Constable, 'When we were at Gerald's on the morning after Charlotte died Martin asked the questions. Edward became uncomfortable when Martin pointed out he worked at the bank where the robbery had taken place. My guess is that It must have registered with Edward about the details he had explained to Alexander.'

A thoughtful expression appeared on Calum's face. 'He must have spoken to Alexander afterwards. Following on from that conversation Alexander and Margaret decided Edward had to be silenced. Also, they couldn't be sure that Charlotte hadn't told him about meeting Mary in Australia.'

'Exactly,' agreed Andrea with an enthusiastic nod, 'but I think Edward tried to do his own bit of detective work.'

'Why do you think that?'

She gave him a challenging stare, 'Do you remember the back bedroom in his house there were two walls with pin boards?'

'Yes.'

'Most of Charlotte's pictures were old. An odd new one but most were three to six months old whereas mine were more recent. They were after I met Charlotte,' she hesitated and gnawed at her lower lip while images of Charlotte whizzed around inside her head.

Calum noticed her agitation, 'Stop if this gives you any discomfort Andrea.'

'No, it doesn't, I'm sorry.' Her mind drifted, I didn't like Edward he made me uncomfortable. But he moved my pictures from one board to the other because he had other photos to pin up. Of the new ones only one remained and it had fallen behind the cabinet. Alexander and Margaret missed that one when they cleared away his detective work.'

Calum leant back in his chair and fixed his gaze towards the elegant chandelier. He paused then inhaled 'I can't remember what was on it,' his voice held a hint of irritation.

'The picture showed the four armed robbers together at the Church fete. I assume the pictures on the second board would have been the Manning family. He pinned them up, made the connection and asked Alexander about the twins thinking the priest had been duped himself.'

The General leaned forward in his chair, 'Montague's son, Edward as he was now called, why did he come and find the Manning family?'

'That I don't know. But it's too much of a coincidence to have met the family by accident. So my guess would be revenge. There seems a big gap from when he walked out on Stacey in King's Cross to the present time. During that period, he had changed his name and obtained a job in the bank. I think he came with revenge of some type on his mind against Colonel Manning's behavior towards his father. I suspect he blamed him for the deaths of both his parents. However, it didn't go as planned because he met Charlotte and fell in love with her.'

'He seemed a weak man so perhaps he couldn't go through with his planned retaliation. He found himself with a family that liked him and a millionaire girlfriend, so it would easily be enough for him to forget about revenge.'

Calum said, 'Only one other matter to explain.'

‘What’s that,’ responded Andrea with a smile. The comfortable settee, the food and drink had made her sleepy.

‘Gerald’s involvement?’ questioned Calum, ‘it’s not clear in my mind.’

Andrea paused and regarded the alertness of Calum’s eyes while he waited for her response, ‘Gerald lied when he said anyone could make the shot. It required a marksman. He then asked me to help, but he followed his previous pattern of activities himself behind the scenes.’

‘What did he do?’

‘I think he found out from his friends in CAD that they had not been threatening Charlotte since he’d asked them to stop, and from the private detective agency that there was no sign of any madman around the music scene that would have shot Charlotte.’

‘Do you think he suspected Alexander and Margaret?’

‘No, but when Edward was killed, it became a different matter. As we know he expected everything to be clear and in its right place. He had to make sure they weren’t involved. I suspect that their friendliness with the Kennedy family made him uneasy.’

‘So, what did he do?’

‘I think he investigated himself to put his mind at ease. He wouldn’t take anybody else’s word but didn’t expect events to move as fast as they did.’

‘So, it was his intention to prove them innocent,’ added Calum.

‘I believe he intended a different approach and would find Charlotte’s murderer himself. As it would be high risk to confront a killer, his guns went with him when we all went to Wolfscote Dale to identify the body in the cave.'

Calum added, 'Alexander and Margaret were nearby and he picked them up.'

'Yes, that was a surprise, at the time he couldn't work out why they were there and dismissed it as unimportant just like the rest of us, but later I think he noticed their reaction when Martin's voice was played on the recorded message about Davison. Martin had been their prisoner in the church. They were wary of killing a police officer, but the breakdown strategy had worked.'

'Yes,' said the Chief Constable, 'they held him in one room above the church hall. He appeared to be sedated, without doubt, Margaret's work.' Andrea grimaced at his words.

'Gerald didn't want to believe Alexander and Margaret had killed Charlotte but being an intense man he couldn't dismiss it. So he followed them. His suspicions must have grown because they didn't go back to the church but followed me because they guessed that Martin must have escaped. They were nearby when Martin's message came through but they had already decided what they would do with me.' This statement produced a look of surprise on everyone's face.

'Your house?' asked Calum.

'Yes,' said Andrea, 'they would assume I would return there. They were desperate as I had been asking questions and they couldn't be sure how much I had deduced so they had to stop me. I assume it was Alexander's work.'

The Chief Constable nodded, 'Our forensic team

said it was an elaborate bomb set as a booby trap. A sheep had triggered it by entering the garden.'

'Margaret and Alexander could see I recognised the message. The psychiatrist explained it would be possible to get people back to their normal state enough to help them. That's what I intended trying with Martin. I proposed talking about deep seated times from our early days together.'

'But they followed you?'

'Yes, I checked behind me for police cars and army vehicles, but I didn't look for other cars. I then sat there in full view whilst they set up their rifles. Gerald had followed them and could see what they intended. I guess he found a position where he could see both. He couldn't have done anything until they acted and he became sure. He waited for them to fire and then killed them. Andrea lay back further and yawned.

'That's enough,' said Martha.

'Martin will now be with me forever.'

Andrea's eyes closed.

'My poor dear?' said Martha.

Andrea made one last effort to open them, 'When I went to the hospital for my injuries they told me I'm pregnant.' She looked around at their smiling faces and knew she was among friends. 'And I have chosen Calum to be his Godfather.' With a huge relaxing sigh, she closed her eyes and went to sleep. But not before she heard the groan followed by a snort of laughter from Calum.

THE END

Enjoy this book?

Thank you for reading my book. If you have time I would appreciate a rating or review. They are a great help to me in developing and writing my books.

You can find more information about my books on my website:

T M Goble's Website

www.tmgoble.com

Action Thrillers

Detective Murder Mysteries

Standalone Murder Mysteries

Historical Fiction

Contemporary Fiction

History of Peak District Literature

Seasonal Recipes

I occasionally send newsletters with details on new releases, special offers and other bits of news relating to my books.

Printed in Great Britain
by Amazon

22770950R00280